"Someone just tried to kill you," Emmett said.

"I'm not leaving until I check out your apartment," he added on the stoop of her building.

Belle sighed. "I'm also law enforcement, Marshal Gage. I can take care of myself."

"Still," he said, his blue eyes intent.

Relenting, she led the way to her apartment. She opened the door and stepped inside, almost stumbling on a yellow envelope.

His gaze moved from the envelope to Belle. "Were you expecting mail?"

"Not shoved underneath my door, no."

Emmett picked up the envelope with a tissue and Belle found latex gloves so she could open it.

The handwritten scribbles said it all.

I intend to finish what I started. You ruined my life. I intend to ruin yours. Maybe I'll find one of your sisters next.

New York Times Bestselling Author

Lenora Worth

and

Terri Reed

Hidden Enemies

Previously published as *Deadly Connection* and *Explosive Situation*

LOVE INSPIRED
INSPIRATIONAL ROMANCE

LOVE INSPIRED®
INSPIRATIONAL ROMANCE

Recycling programs
for this product may
not exist in your area.

ISBN-13: 978-1-335-42458-7

Hidden Enemies

Copyright © 2021 by Harlequin Books S.A.

Deadly Connection
First published in 2020. This edition published in 2021.
Copyright © 2020 by Harlequin Books S.A.

Explosive Situation
First published in 2020. This edition published in 2021.
Copyright © 2020 by Harlequin Books S.A.

Special thanks and acknowledgment are given to Lenora Worth and Terri Reed for their contribution to the True Blue K-9 Unit: Brooklyn miniseries.

This edition published by arrangement with Harlequin Books S.A.

For questions and comments about the quality of this book, please contact us at CustomerService@Harlequin.com.

Love Inspired
22 Adelaide St. West, 40th Floor
Toronto, Ontario M5H 4E3, Canada
www.Harlequin.com

Printed in U.S.A.

CONTENTS

With over seventy books published and millions in print, **Lenora Worth** writes award-winning romance and romantic suspense. Three of her books finaled in the ACFW Carol Awards, and her Love Inspired Suspense novel *Body of Evidence* became a *New York Times* bestseller. Her novella in *Mistletoe Kisses* made her a *USA TODAY* bestselling author. Lenora goes on adventures with her retired husband, Don, and enjoys reading, baking and shopping…especially shoe shopping.

DEADLY CONNECTION

Lenora Worth

Have not I commanded thee?
Be strong and of a good courage; be not afraid,
neither be thou dismayed: for the Lord thy God
is with thee whithersoever thou goest.
—*Joshua* 1:9

To Brooklyn, New York. Thanks for letting me visit in my imagination. Thanks also to the NYPD for working to keep one of my favorite cities safe.

ONE

Brooklyn K-9 Unit Officer Belle Montera glanced back on the shortcut through Cadman Plaza Park, her K-9 partner, Justice, a sleek German shepherd, moving ahead of her as she held tightly to his leash. She had a weird sense she was being followed, but it had to be nothing. Checking her watch, she noted it was almost 5:00 p.m. Still plenty of summer light left, but the skies were darkening with the threat of an afternoon thunderstorm. Brooklyn in the summer—always full of surprises. Rain showers could be one of those.

Belle was used to the ever-changing weather and she was used to keeping her radar on full speed. She always felt safe in her city, but she never let her guard down, either.

Justice lifted his black nose and sniffed the humid air, then gave a soft woof. He might have seen a squirrel frolicking in the tall oaks, or he could have sensed Belle's agitation. Still on duty, she kept a keen eye on her surroundings. Justice could always use the exercise, and she loved having him with her all the time, but this was official business.

"No time to go after innocent squirrels," she told Justice. "We're working, remember?"

Her faithful companion gave her a dark-eyed stare, his black K-9 unit protective vest cinched around his firm belly.

They were both on high alert.

Her service weapon sat nestled in its holster around her duty belt, her NYPD badge shone on her black uniform shirt and her partner was highly trained in protection.

The entire department had been a little antsy lately, so no wonder she had a trace of the jitters.

This meeting could provide the lead the Brooklyn K-9 Unit had been waiting for. A recent double homicide had been eerily similar to one that had taken place twenty years ago in Bay Ridge. Thanks to new technology, evidence in the cold case—an old leather watchband— had finally provided DNA on the killer. If this meeting panned out, Belle could help the unit get closer to finding that killer. *And* if he'd struck again two months ago.

Sergeant Gavin Sutherland, the head of their unit, had warned her to be careful. He'd explained to the entire team that their suspect perp could be watching and waiting. Two members of their K-9 unit, brother and sister Bradley and Penelope McGregor, lost their parents in that twenty-year-old cold case, and either the killer had returned or they had a copycat on their hands. The team needed to stay alert.

Belle intended to do just that.

"It's okay, boy," she said, giving Justice's shiny black-and-tan coat a soft rub. "Just my overactive imagination getting the best of me."

She had a meeting with a man who could have information regarding the McGregor murders. The DNA match from that case had indicated that US Marshal Emmett Gage could be related to the killer.

The team had done a thorough background check on the marshal to eliminate him as a suspect, then Belle had been assigned to meet with him.

Justice lifted his head and sniffed again, his nose in the air. The big dog glanced back. Belle checked over her shoulder.

No one there.

After a few years as a beat cop and now one year into working as an Emergency Services officer, Belle had cross-trained to be tough and unemotional no matter the situation. But added to the grueling training, sometimes her anxieties kicked in and turned things up a notch. Since she did have good instincts in spite of those anxieties, she slowed and listened to hear if any footsteps hit the strip of pavement curving through the path toward the federal courthouse near the park.

But the only sounds were the birds chirping in the rustling trees and the swish of a hot summer breeze moving over her skin. The never-ending traffic noise echoed out over the trees and distant laughter followed but, for the most part, she was alone on this path. Rain clouds formed overhead while humidity covered her clothes and moistened the short ponytail at the nape of her neck.

Slowing her pace, Belle listened. She heard through the trees what sounded like a motorcycle revving, then nothing but the birds chirping. Minutes passed and then she heard a noise on the path, the crackle of a twig breaking, the slight shift of shoes hitting asphalt, a whiff of stale body odor wafting through the air. The hair on the back of her neck stood up and Belle knew then.

Someone is following me.

Justice let out an aggressive growl and Belle turned around, ready to draw her hidden Sig Sauer pistol. Nothing there. No one behind her. Maybe a jogger who'd left the path?

This time, she heard footfalls in the thick underbrush just off the trail. No doubt someone moved close behind. But were they after her or just taking a different route?

A swoosh of air hissed by. A silencer?

Belle waited for the impact of a bullet but instead she heard Justice let out a soft whine. Then her beautiful, brave partner fell over on his side, a tranquilizer dart sticking out of his right shoulder. He lifted his head and whimpered, his eyes beseeching. Then he passed out, his head dropping.

"No," Belle screamed. "No, Justice, no. Get up, boy."

Belle knelt next to Justice and scanned the woods and paths. Before she could get a fix on who had shot the tranquilizer, big hands grabbed her from behind and squeezed at her midsection, knocking the air out of her lungs. A sweaty man pulled her up against his chest, his hand moist and rancid-smelling over her mouth, his big signet ring digging against her skin. "Now you'll pay for what you did."

Using all of her might, Belle grunted and tried to trip her captor, but he slapped at her and then flipped her around to face him. He wore a black baseball-style hat and dark shades. She fought to get free while she studied his face, but he held her back and then shoved his hands around her neck.

Choking, Belle tried to grab at his hands but the pressure of his splayed fingers digging into her neck and cutting off her air supply caused her head to swim. Stars pricked at her eyes. Fighting against him, Belle knew she'd faint soon, and he'd finish the job. She tried again to save herself, kicking at him, but he shifted back. She grasped his sweaty shirt and raked her fingernails down the thin dark material, hoping to save some DNA. That gave her an opportunity to smash her heavy black boot against his left foot, bearing down enough that he screamed in pain. With all her might, she tried to free her arms so she could get to her weapon.

But he didn't let go. Instead, the angry brute applied more pressure as he shoved her down to the hard asphalt and held her throat, his grunts matching each increase of force against her neck and windpipe.

She blinked, kicked, wished Justice would wake up and attack. Prayed she'd be able to use what strength she had left to get this brute's hands off her neck. But the stars bursting against her skull like a sci-fi war began to explode with pain now.

She wasn't going to make it. This man was going to get the best of her if she didn't find one last measure of force. With a grunt that took every bit of her strength, she shifted her body and dropped both her hands to her side, causing him to think he'd finally done her in. When he released the pressure, Belle reached for her weapon. The man pushed at her arm, making her unable to shoot. She slammed the weapon hard against his head.

He yelled and blinked, rage turning his olive skin red. Knocking her gun loose, he sent it flying onto the grass. "You just made your last mistake." His hands renewed their assault and this time, Belle had no energy left to fight.

But somewhere through the ringing in her ears, Belle heard a shout. "US Marshal! Let go of the woman and show me your hands."

The man stopped, his nasty clammy fingers lifting away from her neck, his grunt of frustration loud. He looked down at Belle, rage pouring off him along with sweat. Belle blinked and started coughing.

The man who'd shouted at her attacker inched his way closer and repeated, "I said get away from the officer. Now."

Her attacker crouched near and gave her one last hostile glare, then shot up and spun away. Still disoriented, she heard a grunt and then realized he had pulled out a gun. As a last resort if choking her wasn't going to work?

Belle tried to get to where he'd tossed her weapon but shots rang out, causing her to throw herself over Justice. The man took off running into the nearby woods, shooting backward toward her and her rescuer before he scrambled into the heavy thicket.

Then she heard the sound again. A motor revving. The same motorcycle she'd heard earlier?

"You all right?" the marshal asked as he ran toward her.

"Sí," she managed to croak out. "Yes," she repeated, her shocked brain registering her lapse into Spanish. This man had to be her contact. "Go. Find him."

He took off, but Belle knew the perpetrator was probably long gone. She crawled toward her weapon, then hurried back to Justice.

Belle clung to the dog, more concerned about her partner right now than the man getting away. She thought she had a good description of her attacker and she'd remember that chunky ring jabbing against her skin. How would she ever get his angry expression and the feel of his beefy hands out of her system?

"Justice." She knew he'd have to sleep this off, but she prayed it wasn't worse. Her partner had to wake up. They'd been together since day one. She trusted this loyal shepherd with her life and today she'd let him down by not being as diligent as she should have been.

Her hands shaking, she reached for her cell to call for backup.

Before she could get her bearings, the man who'd gone after her attacker came crashing through the underbrush and then kneeled down beside her, his phone to his ear. "US Marshal Emmett Gage. Need backup and an ambulance at Cadman Plaza Park. Assault on a police officer, shots fired. Suspect headed west into wooded area north of Tillary."

"Motorcycle," she whispered. "I heard one."

Emmett repeated to the dispatcher what she'd told him.

"Justice needs help," Belle gasped, her throat raw with pain while she pointed to the big shepherd. "Ask for veterinary help. Tell them I'm Brooklyn K-9 Unit Officer Belle Montera, Emergency Services, and that my partner, Justice, was hit with a tranquilizer dart."

The man beside her gave her a surprised stare but reported her words to the dispatcher. Then he put the phone on speaker while he checked her over, his steel-blue eyes burning her like a laser, his frown set in place and his demeanor nothing but professional. "Victim has ligature marks around her neck and bruises to her face and hands. Eyes somewhat bloodshot. Hurry."

Belle took in deep breaths while she studied US Marshal Emmett Gage. His official photo didn't do him justice. Once they'd found him as a match to the DNA, she'd immediately vetted the man. Tall with stormy blue eyes and hair the color of dry wheat. Stoic, stand-offish and serious—that's how people described the man. But one of the best in doing his job. He'd helped hunt down and bring in dangerous fugitives from all over the country.

He looked tough and no-nonsense and she immediately felt better. No, she felt safe. Up until this moment, Belle had always taken care of herself. But right now, she allowed this man to comfort her. Shock. She had to be in shock from the attack.

Trying to focus while the marshal at her side stayed on the phone, Belle went over the case to calm her frantic mind.

Penelope and Bradley McGregor, her colleagues— Penny the front desk clerk and Bradley a K-9 detective, deserved justice for their parents' murders, which had gone unsolved for so long. As did little Lucy Emery, whose parents were killed with the same MO on the twentieth anniversary of the McGregor murders. Like toddler Lucy, Penny, then four, had been spared by the killer, disguised in a clown mask and blue wig. Lucy was an only child, but Penny's brother, Bradley, had been sleeping over at a friend's house the night of the homicides, and the fourteen-year-old had been unfairly deemed a suspect for too long. The recent murders had brought up all kinds of questions and, so far, very few answers.

Tonight, despite almost being killed herself, Belle still planned to interrogate Emmett Gage.

Now, she could vouch for how the people she'd questioned had described Emmett. His calm radiated a commanding respect, but he seemed as tightly coiled as a giant snake and ready to strike. Yet he managed to hold all that power in check while he tried to keep her calm and watch his own back at the same time.

His voice went low and husky when his gaze softened on her as if she were the only person in the world. "Backup's on the way."

He checked Justice, rubbing the still animal's stomach. "His pulse is weak, but I'm guessing the tranquilizer won't keep him down long." Lifting his chin toward the dart, he added, "Your lab can analyze this to see what they used. The dispatcher said they'd get in touch with the unit's official vet."

Touched that he'd been concerned, Belle nodded and tried to speak. Then she pushed with her bruised, burning hands on the gritty walkway and tried to stand. But she promptly plopped back down into a sitting position, the dizziness swirling inside her head making her nauseous.

"Don't," he said, steadying her. "You'll be hoarse for a while and your shoulders and neck will hurt and be sore. A lot. You might have fuzzy memories and nightmares for a brief time, too. Strangulation is nothing to take lightly."

She swallowed, wishing she had some cold water. "You've been choked before?" she asked on a whisper.

He let out what might have been a chopped-up chuckle. "One or two times when I've wrestled with junkies full of drugs and adrenaline."

Pushing at her lopsided ponytail, she croaked, "He got the jump on me."

His eyes softened. "Don't like that, huh?"

She shook her head, mortified that she hadn't managed to shake her attacker. "I'm usually more prepared."

With a curt nod, he stood and searched around for any evidence of who might have attacked her. Then he sank down beside her as sirens shrilled in the distance. "You were headed to meet me, right?"

She nodded. "I need—"

"We'll discuss that later," he responded, getting up to wave to the EMTs and the patrol officer running toward them. "Right now, let's get you and your partner some help."

Belle could only keep nodding as *her* adrenaline rush slowly began to sink down while the shakes took over. She wouldn't let anyone see her falling apart but she did feel an overwhelming gratitude toward Emmett Gage.

The man she'd come here to interrogate had just saved her life.

Emmett kept a close eye on the woman impatiently waiting for the paramedics to return from giving Gavin a report so she could sign off on no further treatment. She tapped her hands against the ambulance door and strained her neck to see what was holding them up.

To keep her calm, he started talking. "I live in Dumbo, but I got home late. If I'd left a few minutes earlier—"

"He might have shot you," she said on a raw whisper. Then she looked up at him with eyes the color of dark rich wood. "Thank you for helping me with Justice. I need to make sure he'll be all right."

Emmett glanced to where the dog had been moved off the path. "He should be fine. Might be off his game for a few days, though."

"I think we'll both need to debrief," she replied, checking on the still-unconscious K-9 again.

When she moved to get up, Emmett held her back. "He's sleeping. You need to sit here for a minute."

"I'm not good at sitting," she admitted. Giving him a questioning glance, she asked, "So you know why I wanted to talk to you, right?"

Emmett nodded. "I wasn't late in an attempt to put off talking to you. I got held up with some red tape regarding a case we just closed."

"But you had good timing, anyway," she said on a husky whisper, each word forced through pain.

"Thankful for that," he replied, taking his time in studying her. Her dark hair shimmered in the waning sunshine, but her eyes went dark each time she glanced at the still canine beside her.

Belle fidgeted and glanced around again. "Why are the paramedics still talking to Sarge? I told them when they examined me earlier, I'm fine."

"You should go to the hospital."

"No. I can't leave Justice." She stood and leaned on the back of the ambulance, clearly not happy. "I can sign off. I don't need anything. Is our veterinarian on her way?"

"I heard your sergeant say she is," Emmett told Belle, thinking the officer was single-minded about her partner. A good trait, but he wished he could reassure her about the canine. "Bringing her van and a special wheeled cot to get Justice back to her office in the K-9 training center. He'll have his own dog-sized gurney."

He offered Belle some water and she took a tentative sip, then said, "I want to go straight there."

Emmett didn't argue with her, but he figured the K-9 would sleep most of the night. "Then I'll make sure you get there." When he glanced up and saw an auburn-haired female wearing silver glasses approaching with a small rolling cot, Emmett touched Belle's arm. "I think your vet is here."

Belle's head shot up as she hurried toward the veterinarian, her anxious eyes showing fatigue and concern.

While Belle talked to the doctor, Emmett thought back over the meeting they hadn't had yet.

Worry gnawed at his gut while he wondered about her. According to the request that had come into his office, she needed to verify the hit the NYPD had received that revealed *his* DNA matched the sample found on a watchband that had been collected as evidence at the cold-case murder site. Emmett could probably answer her question without a doubt. The DNA might be a match for his, but twenty years ago, he'd been twelve years old, living in South Brooklyn with his parents and grandparents, all of whom were dead now.

The Brooklyn K-9 Unit needed information on the unknown relative he'd matched and since he only had one living relative who could have possibly been in the area, he was pretty sure he knew who they were looking for.

Randall Gage. But he couldn't picture his dad's cousin Randall as a murderer. Always in trouble and always with one foot in the fire, yes. But capable of murder? What if Randall was? How would Emmett handle that?

Emmett wanted to get to the bottom of this and fast.

But first he needed to convince Belle Montera that she should go home and rest. Or go somewhere close. His place wasn't far from here. Taking her there, however, might turn out to be more difficult than tracking the fugitive he'd been chasing over the last two days. She'd balk at that suggestion.

From the way Belle was questioning the calm, patient veterinarian, he had a feeling she'd rather be with her partner right now than find out any facts from Emmett. The woman had been almost choked to death and her partner had been tranquilized. She was still in shock and worried about her K-9.

"Let me help, Dr. Mazelli," he said when the tiny woman tried to lift the dog. Justice had to weigh at least eighty pounds.

"Thank you," Dr. Mazelli said. "Belle should go home. Based on whatever was in that dart, Justice should wake up in an hour or so but he'll be too groggy to notice anything, so it's best if he has some quiet time. He should be fine tomorrow, but we'll keep him off duty for a couple of days to be sure."

"You might want to convince Officer Montera of

that," Emmett replied. "She's insisting she wants to stay the night with him."

After they'd lifted Justice up onto the cart, the doctor went over to where Belle stood talking to Sergeant Sutherland.

The vet touched the officer's arm and told her in a gentle tone that the best thing she could do was get some rest. "Justice will be fine with me. I won't leave him alone, Belle, I promise. You need to take care of yourself."

"Do as she suggests," Gavin told Belle as Emmett came hurrying up to them. "That's an order."

"But, sir—"

"Rest, Belle," Gavin added.

"I'll get her home," Emmett said, daring anyone to argue with him. He and Gavin had been officially introduced earlier so he hoped he wasn't overstepping.

The tough-looking sergeant stared him down, then said in a gruff voice, "Good idea. You two have some unfinished business, anyway. And when you're done, I'd like a full report."

Sutherland didn't give Belle time to argue. He marched off to talk to the other K-9 officers moving across the park. When her unit had heard the call coming through, they'd all come to assist. Dedicated and tenacious.

Both she and Emmett had given their statements, but Emmett had noticed Sergeant Sutherland sizing him up earlier. Impressed that her commander hadn't taken over the task he'd sent her to do, Emmett decided Gavin Sutherland was tough but fair. He'd want answers, but he'd let Belle do her job to get them.

Belle turned to the dog sleeping on the cart. "I'll

walk with you back to your van," she said to Dr. Mazelli before glancing over at Emmett. "I don't like this but an order's an order."

"I'll come with you," Emmett offered. "After you see Justice off, we can go somewhere and have our talk if you feel up to it."

Once they had the dog settled in the back of the big van, Belle rubbed Justice's fur and patted him on his head, her eyes misty. "I'll check on you soon, Justice. I promise."

"I'll call in about an hour or so," the doc said. "I'll give you a full report."

"Gracias," Belle replied, reminding Emmett of her Hispanic heritage. Then she turned back to Emmett. "I live in Fort Greene, but I can take a train home."

The rain came then, fat cold drops that would soon turn into a downpour. They took cover under the trees.

"My place is close by," he said, glancing at the dark sky. "We can talk in private there and… I can keep an eye on you. I'll give you a ride home later."

"I don't think so," she said on a huff of breath, exhaustion tugging at her. "But the sooner we get this over with, the sooner I can go and see Justice. If your place will get me out of this rain, I'll go. But you don't have to worry about taking me home. I'll spend the night at the station so I can be near my partner."

Emmett decided not to argue with Belle Montera.

But he was curious about more than the DNA match the K-9 team had discovered.

Now, he also wanted to know more about this woman and why someone would want to strangle her to death.

TWO

Why had she allowed Emmett to bring her to his apartment? Belle didn't know this man, but she did believe she could trust him. He had a stellar reputation as a high-ranking deputy marshal who served in SOG— the Special Operations Group, a tactical unit, which pretty much gave him carte blanche to do what needed to be done in any situation. He'd certainly done just that tonight. All of that aside, she'd rather be sitting with Justice. But Sarge had reminded her they needed information regarding the DNA match.

"I'll make sure you get back to the station to check on Justice," Emmett said after giving her a towel to dry off. The drizzle outside hadn't soaked them too much. "This was the closest place to talk in private."

He moved around the sparse kitchen, banging some pots and pans before he came over to hand her a glass of sparkling water and two pain pills. "Take these. I'm warming up some soup."

"I don't need soup," she said, exhaustion overtaking her. "I need information."

"Okay, then." Grabbing a soda from the refrigerator, he came back into the den of the well-appointed apartment he'd told her he shared with a lawyer and a doctor. He'd explained on the quick walk over that he and his roommates never saw each other much so they wouldn't be interrupted here.

"Before I answer *your* questions, do you know why anyone would want to kill you?"

Shaking her head, Belle took a breath, swallowed the pills and drank the water. "No. I mean I've collared a lot of people, but other than shouting at me on the way to the slammer, no one has ever threatened me before. This guy said I'd pay for what I've done." Shrugging, she pushed at her falling hair and tried to readjust her ponytail. "That could be anyone that I've helped put away."

The man sitting across from her studied her for a moment. "So you didn't recognize your attacker?"

"No," she said, a shiver moving down her spine. "He had on dark glasses and a big black hat. His face was full and puffy and he was heavyset. Like a weight lifter, maybe. But he wore a chunky ring—a signet ring. Gold. I remember the gold flashing in my face. Gold etched in black."

Emmett moved closer. "Maybe you can describe both the face and the ring to your forensic artist and then you can run the sketch through the system."

"I'll do that first thing tomorrow," she said, her throat protesting with every word. "Right now, I need to verify the DNA evidence found from a cold-case murder site twenty-years ago when Eddie and Anna McGregor were murdered. You're a match to that DNA evidence, as you know. Can you tell me anything more? Are you familiar with this case?"

Emmett's eyebrows went up. "No, I wasn't familiar with the case, but I did look it up once I was informed that I was a match for the DNA. Am I a suspect?"

"No. We did a thorough background check on you. You were a preteen when the first murder happened, and you lived in another neighborhood. You were the closest match we could find on the public genealogy search site when we reopened the cold case recently. We pulled up this case when we had a similar case a couple of months ago. Double homicide and a child at home at the time. The assailant wore a clown mask with blue hair and gave the child a stuffed toy in a bag."

Filling him in on how twenty years ago Eddie and Anna McGregor were murdered in Bay Ridge, Brooklyn, she said, "Now, we have Alex and Debra Emery shot to death in their home two months ago. Same MO but different neighborhood than the first killings."

"And a child left at the scene?"

"Yes, unharmed but given a stuffed animal in a bag."

Emmett's eyebrows lifted. "And now I'm older and I live close by? So I *could* be considered a suspect in these new murders?"

"Relax, you've been cleared. You were out chasing criminals in the Village on the night of the current murders. We have the exact time and location of your whereabouts."

He let out a sigh of relief. "Of course you would. But someone who's related to me might be involved in both?"

She took a sip of the sparkling water Emmett had

given her, the fizz soothing on her throat. "Yes, according to the worn leather watchband found at the cold-case crime scene. It's been tested for a match over the years but no hits. Until now. A relative of yours."

"What happened to the child in the first case?"

"The McGregors had two children, Penelope and Bradley, who were adopted by the lead detective on the case and his wife. Penelope was found at the scene, but outside of the house. She was holding a stuffed animal. A monkey covered in plastic that she said the *bad man* gave her."

Emmett shut his eyes for a moment. Like her, he'd seen the worst of humanity.

"Incidentally, both siblings work in our department now—Penelope, who goes by Penny, is a front-desk receptionist. Bradley is a K-9 detective and works with me in Emergency Services. However, Bradley was a teen when his parents were murdered and also a suspect because of some altercations that took place between his parents and him, but he was cleared. That stigma has stayed with him, though. So this new case—with either the same killer or a possible copycat—hits close to home for our unit."

"I don't remember the original case," he admitted. "And I've been too tied up recently in this undercover sting to even watch the news. But this does sound suspicious on the part of the second murder, especially since you work with the siblings involved in the first case. So you're trying to find a connection?"

"We're trying to find out who was at the scene of the first murder and then we'll see if it ties to the current case, though we have even less evidence to go on from the Emery site."

Emmett rubbed a hand down his face, fatigue coloring his expression. "I can see why this would be a priority for your unit."

"It's been hard on Bradley and Penny. Being at the front desk, she hears everything. It's traumatizing for her."

"I guess it would be terrible for both of them to relive that kind of trauma," Emmett said. "My gut's telling me this can't be good for whoever this relative is, but I will tell the truth if I can pinpoint anyone for you."

"Tell me about your relatives," she said.

He glanced out the wide windows. The bright lights of the surrounding buildings gave them a great view of the skyline and the Brooklyn Bridge off in the distance. Belle searched his face, thinking he looked honest, but then, people could hide a lot behind a calm demeanor and a handsome face. She knew that firsthand. But she wasn't here to accuse him of withholding information— yet. She had to find out about his family tree so he needed to be honest with her.

Finally, he turned back to her, his stormy eyes pinning her to the comfortable chair by the window. "I only have one close living relative who could be nearby, my father's cousin who's in his sixties now. His grandfather and my mine were brothers. He grew up in Brooklyn, but I have no idea where he is now. Most of our distant relatives are scattered all over the country. That leaves him. But Randall couldn't be a killer."

She let that declaration slide because he'd inadvertently given her a name. "Are you two on good terms?"

"Not really. My dad knew him better since they were closer in age. I saw him every now and then at family gatherings. I think I remember him at the funeral when his grandfather died ten years ago. He's a lot older than me and he stays in and out of trouble and can't seem to get a break in life. I tried to keep up with him, but Randall is a loner."

"Do you have his last known address?"

"No. Last I heard he was living in Pennsylvania in a rural area. He's a recluse and likes living off the grid. He doesn't trust the law or the government, according to what my dad told me."

Shaking his head, he looked at Belle. "Kind of ironic that you got a hit since Randall would balk at being on a family tree. My mom loved genealogy stuff, though. She found most of her side of the family and had just started on my dad's side but…she suffered a fatal stroke and never recovered. She only lasted a week before she died."

Belle lowered her head and lifted her eyes to him. "I'm so sorry, Emmett. How long ago was that?"

"Couple of years," he said, his tone flat. "My dad passed away five years ago from a heart attack. He'd only been retired a year or so."

"That's tough," Belle said. "Tell me more about your mom's research, if you feel okay about doing that right now. It might help us."

He gave her a slight smile. "She'd be willing to help, I know. She tried to load in every relative she could find—just their names since the site is public. But some of them wanted to send in their information and DNA, too. She was big into that kind of stuff—a hobby of sorts after she retired from working in a Brooklyn retail store for over twenty years." Nodding toward another room, he said, "I have all her findings in a file somewhere in my closet. I wanted to pick up where she left off but can't seem to find the time."

Belle believed him. "So your DNA is in the database because of her efforts?"

He nodded. "My mom had joined up with some of our long-lost relatives to fill in the family tree. I don't know how far she got but I can search her handwritten notes and her computer files. Like I said, most of our living relatives are scattered all over the country."

"Let's get back to the name you mentioned," Belle said, trying to stay focused. But her heart went out to Emmett. He must be all alone now. "Randall, you said?"

Rubbing the back of his neck, Emmett stared at his drink, "Honestly, I haven't seen him in years. He tends to shy away from the law and since my dad was with the NYPD, Randall sure didn't want to hang out with him." After a long pause, he looked over at Belle. "Randall had a hard life, from what my mom told me. His daddy was a mean man who drank himself to death. Randall's mother left when he was a little boy. I don't think he ever got over that. Dad told me once that Randall was always searching for his mom. Breaks my heart, since I had a set of solid, loving parents."

Belle saw the veil of sadness coloring his eyes. "I'm sorry about your parents and I'm sorry your father's cousin had to suffer that way."

"Yeah, me, too." He stood and took her water glass. "I stay busy these days, but my folks are never far from my thoughts. They both had such a strong faith. I wish

I could feel the same but doubt seems to follow me around these days."

Belle thought of her own family and was thankful that her parents were still alive and that she had siblings close by, too. They all lived near each other in one of her father's inherited properties in Fort Greene. They fought and argued but they also stuck together, no matter what. Their faith was a big part of their lives. She'd expect no less from Emmett, but if his cousin turned out to be the person of interest in the case, she hoped Emmett would do the right thing.

"That's tough," she said, wanting to know more about Emmett. "It's nice that you wanted to finish things for your mom, though. So you don't keep in touch with Randall?"

"Not much," Emmett refilled her water glass and then came back with the tomato soup he'd made and handed her the mug along with the fresh water. "He moves around a lot. I know he's been in trouble with the law. My dad tried to watch out for him through the years, but Randall's as stubborn as they come. Likes to do things his way."

"Well, since we can't identify who in your family might be connected, he obviously didn't offer your mother much help. We found the match through a DNA sequencing firm after getting a warrant to do a search. We used a sleuthing geneticist to help us fill in the gaps. But we hit a wall."

"Which means you want me to lead you to Randall, right?"

"Right. We could really use your help in finding him. We need to ask him some questions."

"Sure you do. So, what could be my cousin's DNA was found on this old watchband tagged at the murder scene. That's pretty amazing, but a match is a match."

"It's a fresh lead," she replied, wondering if he'd hedge or try to stall them. Or he could alert his cousin so they'd never be able to question the man. "I can show you the watchband. You might recognize it."

"I could try but remember Randall would have been forty-one years old then. I wasn't exactly into hanging out with him even when we were kids since he's older than me. Barely saw the man except when he'd come by to ask my dad for help or money. The few times I was around him, my father was always present. I don't think he trusted Randall a whole lot."

"He's not in the system, obviously, or we wouldn't be coming to you for answers. Now that I have his name, I'll do a thorough search. Maybe juvie has something."

"That's a possibility. I can search through my dad's old personal records, too. He would have tried to protect Randall, but he would have also followed the law."

Belle thought about that. "If Randall is involved, he did a good job of hiding all the evidence. The watchband is broken so someone must have lost it at the scene."

"So you think he was at the scene of the original murders and that he might have something to do with this latest double homicide?"

She nodded. "But there's no record of him being a suspect because there were no definitive prints found at the scene. The DNA on the watchband is relevant only to the first murders but if we find a connection, he could be questioned regarding the Emerys, too."

"If he killed the McGregors *and* the Emerys, that

would mean he's back in the area. Or was," Emmett said. She could see the wheels turning. After all, he was a US marshal. He knew the drill. "I wonder if my dad knew of the cold case. He had to have heard about it but if Randall was never indicated as a suspect, it could have been off Dad's radar."

Or his well-meaning father could have hidden some evidence? She didn't want to believe that, but it did happen at times. Maybe his father had been at the scene as a police officer? She'd have to check into that.

"So Randall lived in Brooklyn twenty years ago?" she asked to verify before taking a sip of the creamy lukewarm tomato soup. Her throat burned with a hot-pepper fire.

Emmett's eyes went wide while he stood as if debating. "Yes, he did." Giving her a direct stare, he added, "He lived in an apartment above a deli in Bay Ridge."

Belle dropped her pen. "Where the first murders took place."

Emmett sank back against the plaid couch and stared across at her. "This is beginning to sound bad for Randall."

"Do you have any photos of him?" she asked, trying to keep her head while her heart seemed to open a crack or two for this man. He looked so devastated. Emmett might not be close to Randall, but he cared about the family connection. That much was obvious.

"I might. I have my mom's favorite old photo album around here somewhere along with her genealogy files." He got up and went to what must be his bedroom and came back with a thick battered floral album. "My mom kept all kinds of family photos, and I know I saw one in here. One of the few things I saved when I sold my parents' house."

After searching through it, he tugged an old snapshot out of its protective plastic shield. "Here. This was Randall about six years ago at one of our last family get-togethers before both of our fathers passed away."

Belle took the photo and studied the tall wiry man. Randall Gage looked nothing like the man sitting here with her. Where Emmett was all muscle and broad-chested, Randall was skinny but fairly muscular, his face shadowed in a world-weary darkness and his thick hair full of gray streaks.

"Thanks," she said. "We can do a facial recognition on this, I hope."

"Sure. You can scan it on my printer if you want and send it in from here."

Deciding she'd have to trust Emmett, she said, "I need to call this in to Sergeant Sutherland, too."

Emmett nodded and got up to stare out the window.

Could she trust him? He'd mentioned his father keeping notes. Would a good officer have tried to hide evidence to protect a relative?

Belle moved to the kitchen and made the call. But she had to wonder if Emmett would immediately get in touch with his cousin the minute she left.

Stop that, she told herself. Just because she'd had a bad breakup with a security guard who wanted to be a super cop and had told her how to do her job, didn't mean she couldn't trust any other man ever.

Besides, this tall drink of water was off-limits. She'd found Emmett Gage to question him about a murder, not go all gaga over him.

But…

"Belle, are you there?"

"Yes, sir," she replied to Gavin's pointed question. Then she told him what she'd found out. "I'll scan the photo and send it to you and the lab right away. Maybe we'll get a hit on his last known address. Maybe the deputy marshal can help with that, too."

"If he's willing to cooperate, use him. The man is good at his job." Then Gavin added, "When you come by to check on Justice, which I know you will, bring Marshal Gage with you. Now that you've made contact and found a possible lead, I'd like to talk to him."

"Yes, sir." Belle ended the call and went back across the room. "I could use that scanner. Sarge wants to get on this right away and…he wants to speak to you again, too."

Emmett agreed to that. Then he said, "Hey, you mentioned stuffed animals. I found another picture of Randall here. He's very young in this one, but my mom wrote his name and the date on the back of the picture."

Belle stared down at the grainy black-and-white photo. Randall Gage held on tightly to a stuffed animal—a fluffy dog about the size of the two animals found with both of the children in these cases.

"Interesting," she said. But when she saw how crushed Emmett looked when he turned away, she added, "But it doesn't mean anything. We all have stuffed animals and favorite toys as children."

"Randall collected toys and such." Emmett turned around, concern shadowing his face. "I sure hope he'll be cleared. He's got some issues, but murdering someone? A couple with their child close by? I don't know. I can't see it."

"Sometimes, we don't want to see what's right in front of our eyes."

"Spoken like the voice of experience."

Belle followed him into a small office filled with all sorts of electronic equipment. "I'm a pretty positive person and I like to believe the best about people. But I'm also realistic because I've seen the worst in people."

Emmett quickly scanned the photo. "So, you've been disappointed?"

After giving him her phone number so he could message it to her, she said, "Yes. I guess it brings out the bitterness in me."

He put his hand on the black office chair. "Here. You can send it once you receive it."

After emailing the scan to her unit and the lab, she stood and gave Emmett a bold stare. "What's your story, anyway?"

He chuckled, his discomfort evident in the way he rubbed the back of his neck and moved back into the larger room. "I don't have much of a story. Always wanted to follow in my father's footsteps. Got hooked on being a US marshal after watching *The Fugitive* over and over. Worked hard to get a degree and found a place to land."

"And you landed here in New York? Or are you native like me?"

"I grew up right here in Brooklyn," he said. "This is home. But I travel a lot. Work—that's what I do. I work."

"I should go and check on Justice," she said, thinking they didn't have much left to discuss. He'd been more than willing to cooperate, but he had to be as tired as she was. Emmett Gage seemed like the loner he'd been reputed to be. A self-confirmed bachelor?

"I'm going, too, remember. I mean—I've been summoned. Could wait till morning but your sergeant strikes me as the kind who doesn't like waiting."

Surprised, Belle felt little sensations of awareness dancing up her spine. Little foreign sensations that made a beeline right to her heart. *Don't go there*, she warned.

"I can make it to headquarters by myself but, yes, you might as well talk to him while this is fresh on your mind."

"And I plan on getting you where you need to be in one piece," he told her in a firm tone. "You were injured just a few hours ago and the man who did it got away. I'm escorting you back to the precinct and then home safely, Officer Montera. Got it?"

"Are you always this bossy?"

"When I need to be."

"You do realize that I can be bossy, too."

"Wouldn't want it any other way."

Her cell buzzed, saving her from setting him straight. "It's Dr. Mazelli." After reading the text, she turned back to Emmett. "Justice is awake. I need to go and see him."

"I'll give you a ride," Emmett said. "My truck is down in the parking garage."

"I'd rather take the subway," Belle said. "I'm staying with Justice tonight so no point in you bringing your truck out. I said I'd be okay."

"I can get you there in about half an hour."

Belle mulled that over. She didn't want to depend on

him, but she did want to get to her partner. "Okay. This time we don't have much choice."

Emmett gave her a tight smile. "I have a feeling there'll be more than just this time, Officer Montera."

There they went again. Those warm and fuzzy sensations dancing up and down her spine reminded her that this was such a bad idea, but... Emmett made her feel safe in a way that being confident had never covered. Belle bristled. She *was* confident but this attack had shaken her. Or maybe it was just the pain pills and soup making her all warm and fuzzy.

Which only aggravated her even more because up until tonight she'd always been capable out on her own with Justice.

How could she be a good K-9 officer if she didn't feel confident anymore?

Rubbing her sore neck, Belle knew she'd have to work double time to get her groove back.

And this big, tall, fascinating man could not get in the way of that. She appreciated Emmett's help and his honesty, and while he'd been cleared of being a suspect in this case, she still wondered how far he'd go to protect Randall Gage.

THREE

After Emmett parked across the street from the Brooklyn K-9 Unit building in the only available slot, he followed Belle and took in the precinct building. The limestone building near Owl's Head Park was three stories and had a unique arched facade that made it stand out. The vet's office was right next door in the K-9 training center. Belle had told him he could wait in Sergeant Sutherland's office in the main building. She'd quickly shown him the way to the office and then left in a fast trot to check on her furry partner.

Too antsy to sit, Emmett stood and looked at several pictures of Sergeant Sutherland and his team. Then he noticed a picture of Gavin in a suit with a woman wearing a wedding gown. Obviously, his wife now. The happy couple smiled and held each other while two K-9s stood with what looked like happy grins on their faces.

"That's Stella and Tommy with Officer Brianna Hayes—now Sutherland—and me at our wedding last year," Gavin said from the doorway. "Those two are inseparable unless they're working. Stella's a yellow Lab and she's my wife's partner in bomb detection. They work back in my old precinct in Queens. And Tommy's right here with me—a springer spaniel and also trained in bomb detection."

Emmett turned to face Gavin, noting the man's no-nonsense demeanor had softened when he mentioned his wife and his K-9 partner. Emmett had a feeling this man was inseparable from his wife unless they were working, too. He'd heard how they'd taken down a bomber last July.

"Sounds like a great life."

"I can't complain."

Gavin shook Emmett's hand and offered him a seat. The sergeant's partner, Tommy, gave Emmett a curious look, but Emmett knew not to interact with the dog. Gavin ordered Tommy to stay and the dog settled down beside the big desk.

"So," Gavin began, shuffling files as he went, "Justice is going to be okay. Just groggy. He's off duty for the next couple of days."

"Officer Montera sure is close to her partner," Emmett pointed out. "She wanted to stay here tonight."

Gavin put down the files. "I saw Belle and assured her that she needs to go home tonight." Then he chuckled. "No, I had to make that an order. But yes, we're all close to our partners. They put their lives on the line every day and do it so they can have playtime."

"I need to try that formula for playtime on myself," Emmett admitted. "I understand you have questions for me?"

Gavin nodded. "Belle filled me in. So Randall Gage is your dad's cousin."

"Yes." Emmett repeated the information he'd given

Belle earlier. "Since he seems the only likely suspect, I'd like to be involved in tracking him down, if you don't mind."

"Why?" Gavin asked. "You're not planning to tip him off, are you?"

That question riled Emmett, but he knew it had to be asked. "I'm planning on doing my job. If Randall's your man, I want to be there when you take him in. I don't want him to do anything stupid and get himself killed."

"Fair enough," Gavin replied, his dark eyes as blank as an empty pistol. "You might keep an eye on Officer Montera, too."

"Excuse me?"

"Someone tried to kill one of my officers tonight. You were there. You want in on this investigation, then you watch my officer's back, got it? Because Belle will be front and center on this case."

Emmett lifted his head. "Got it. Watch and stay out of the way unless needed. I can observe and offer my assistance but not overstep, right?"

Gavin gave him an appreciative stare. "Exactly."

They talked a bit more, Emmett giving Gavin as much information on his cousin as he could remember. "If he's back in the area, I'll find him and bring him in myself," he assured Gavin.

A knock at the open door caused both of them to glance around. "Nate?" Gavin motioned the muscular blond-haired man in. "Marshal Emmett Gage, meet K-9 Officer Nate Slater. He's a detective and his partner, Murphy, is cross-trained to deal with anything."

Emmett stood and shook the officer's hand, prepared

to leave. "I'm cross-trained myself. Give Murphy my best."

Nate's blue eyes widened. "I'll do that. Actually, I need to ask you a question, Marshal Gage."

"Sure," Emmett said, his gut telling him this had to be about the McGregor case.

"Does your cousin Randall happen to have a deep baritone voice?"

Emmett thought about the last time he'd talked to Randall. He had to tell the truth. "He does but it's grainy now from years of smoking. But yes, I'd say his voice is deep."

"Thanks," Nate said, his expression turning grim. "That may be of help with the most recent case."

"Is he a suspect in the second murders?" Emmett asked, his gut now burning.

"We don't know yet," Nate admitted. "Too early to tell." He thanked Emmett and left. Meaning, he didn't want to reveal too much too soon.

"Okay, we have enough for now," Gavin finally said. "I'd advise you let us work on this as much as possible while you do your job, but I'll keep you informed and you can ride along with Belle as needed. If push comes to shove, you can move in with us."

"Deal." Emmett liked Gavin's straight talk.

Gavin stood. "I'll show you the way to the vet's office."

"I'll escort Officer Montera home," Emmett said, making it clear he wouldn't back down.

"Thank you." Gavin pointed to the hallway and then turned to leave. "And thanks for your cooperation."

Emmett nodded and then Gavin led him to the vet's office.

He found Belle sitting by a table where Justice lay sleeping, her hand holding the big dog's paw. Studying her from the door, Emmett took in her straight dark brown hair and her olive skin. She was a beautiful woman and a tough one at that. From here, he could see the bruises and marks on her slender neck.

His blood boiled. He not only planned to help her find his cousin. He planned to help her track down the person who'd done this to her, too. Emmett knew the kind. If this guy had a vendetta, he'd keep coming. Sure, she was trained in one of the toughest jobs in the city but…still…she was in danger and she'd have to watch her back.

But Emmett would have her six, whether she wanted him to or not. That's just the way things had to be right now since the attacker could come back for both of them.

And meantime, he'd work with Belle and the Brooklyn K-9 Unit to find Randall. He only hoped his cousin wouldn't be given a guilty charge before he had a chance to be exonerated. Maybe Randall had an alibi or maybe he could explain why his watchband had become evidence toward a double homicide.

Emmett had to know the truth, either way. He'd start by searching his father's old files.

Belle glanced up and saw him at the door. Taking a last look at Justice, she leaned down and whispered in the big dog's ear, her hand brushing his silky coat.

Emmett's heart did a funny little twist after seeing the sweet gesture. There was something about this strong, tough woman that made him appreciate her and also want to protect her. He knew she'd balk at the protection. She had been trained in all things tactical, so she didn't need a hero to come to her rescue. He'd just watch over her without making a big deal of it.

He had to. He was all in now.

Belle glanced back at Justice one more time. She really didn't like leaving him. "We're rarely apart," she said to Emmett as he led her out of the building. "I should stay in case he wakes up."

"Your sergeant told me he ordered you to go home and rest and to stay home tomorrow, too. You need to take it easy. You'll be sore in the morning."

She didn't answer but she didn't bolt, either. It figured that Gavin would alert Emmett that he'd ordered her to go home. They'd ganged up on her along with Gina Mazelli and a couple of her coworkers.

Once the word was out about what had happened, several members of their unit had come by the precinct to check on both Belle and Justice. Her friend Vivienne Armstrong and her K-9 partner, Hank, a border collie, happened to be running through some training sets when they'd brought Justice in. Vivienne had sat with Belle while she'd talked to Justice and lulled him back to sleep.

"He'll be fine, Belle. I know it's scary to see him so still and out of it, but the doc knows her stuff."

Vivienne's reassurances had helped but this day seemed to be dragging on and on. And now, she had a big US marshal shadowing her. She should have been appreciative but instead she felt defeated.

"I'm too tired to make a big deal out of this," she admitted as they headed toward Emmett's truck. "But you don't have to take me home. I can take the subway."

She stepped out ahead of him and checked the street. In the next instant, a motorcycle roared to life and came screeching toward Belle. She looked up, the bike's bright headlight blinding her and freezing her to the asphalt.

Then she felt strong hands wrapping around her waist and lifting her into the air. Emmett grabbed her and pulled her back, both of them toppling over onto the sidewalk in the split second just before the biker flew by. Emmett managed to take the brunt of the fall but Belle landed across his chest, her eyes crashing with his as they stared at each other.

Her heart beat in triple time and she thought she might pass out again but Belle felt the pull of his gaze.

"Are you all right?" he asked as he quickly sat up and helped her do the same. Belle noticed the spicy scent of his aftershave and reminded herself that she was tired and someone had tried to do her in twice tonight. Her mind was playing tricks on her in too many ways to analyze right now.

"Yes," she said, out of breath. "Did that guy try to run me down?"

"I think so," Emmett replied, the sound of the bike roaring off in the distance. "I didn't have time to get a good look. All I saw was a blur of man and machine."

"I didn't see anything," Belle said, wondering if she truly would be out of commission for a few days since her mind didn't seem to be functioning. "You saved my life again, Emmett. I'm pretty sure that's the same man who attacked me in the park. Remember, I heard a bike cranking before I was attacked and then right after he ran away."

"Yeah, well, I'm just glad I was here to help and witness this. Makes sense it's the same person. We need to report this to Sergeant Sutherland."

Belle shook her head. "I'll call him from your truck. The guy on that bike is long gone, I'm beat and every muscle in my body aches. I can't bring myself to file another report tonight. I want to go home but I don't know what I'll do without Justice. He's always by my side. Now I have to worry about him getting hurt."

"Hey, you're still tough and so is Justice," Emmett said. "You'll both be fine soon enough. But you shouldn't be alone. Too dangerous."

"I live in a building that my parents own," she explained. "My grandparents bought up apartment buildings in Fort Greene way back in the seventies and my dad took over when they moved to a retirement home. He now owns several rentals. We all live in one building. I have a younger brother and two younger sisters who pound on my apartment door day and night. I'm never alone, trust me."

"All right." Emmett checked her over, his piercing glances giving her an up close and personal opportunity to look him over, too. Again, a heated awareness covered her. His winded whisper only added to that. "Are you sure you don't need a doctor? Maybe you should talk to Gavin?"

Suddenly feeling smothered and all too aware that someone wanted to do her harm, she shook her head. "I want to get out of here. Now."

Emmett gave her a concerned stare. "Okay."

She was close to a crash and burn, and she didn't want it to happen in front of her team or her sergeant. Maybe Emmett had figured that out.

"Let's go," he said, guiding her to his truck. Once he had her inside, he leaned against the passenger-side door and said, "You know, you're kind of exciting to be around, Officer Montera."

"Yeah, I'm just a barrel of laughs," she retorted on a shaky voice. "Except someone doesn't think I'm much fun."

"*I* think you can be," he said, "when you're not being chased by someone out to do you in."

Once she'd called Gavin to give him the latest, Belle didn't say much on the drive to Fort Greene. Instead, she stared out at the buildings along the Brooklyn–Queens Expressway just before they passed Sunset Park. She could barely hold her eyes open, but she managed to direct Emmett to her apartment off Lafayette Avenue. Emmett pulled up to the curb in front of the multi-level brick building with white trim and white wrought iron mini-balconies. The foursquare looked like a big row house, but right now it looked like home. Belle was ready to go to sleep in the safety of that home.

"I'm on the bottom floor because of Justice needing a dog run," she said, pointing to a corner apartment of the three-story apartment building. "We have a nice little yard out back with a sturdy fence."

"I'm walking you to your door."

He didn't let her say no. Now she'd have to explain to her parents. Maybe they could sneak by the main entryway to the stairs without any family drama. Her family worried that she hadn't dated since her last fiasco of a boyfriend. Hard to explain that her line of work didn't allow for any fun late nights or online dating sites.

But if her sisters got a glance of Emmett Gage, they'd get the wrong impression. Then she'd have to give her family the real reason for his being there.

"I can make it from here," she said when they entered the stoop and she keyed in the door code.

Emmett kept standing there. "I'd like to come inside."

"You're annoying."

"I hear that a lot."

"I'm fine, really," she said as they went through the vestibule. A long central hallway ran the length of the bottom floor. The apartments on the other side of hers were used for family members passing through and storage. The rest of the building was her family's two-story home, where she hung out a lot. Her siblings slept on the third floor.

Emmett filled the hallway with his presence. "I'm right behind you, really."

She made it to her door and tried to get the key in the lock. Emmett took it and managed to unlock the door, adding to her humility.

But when he opened it, he stumbled on a yellow mailing envelope, his gaze moving from that to Belle.

"Were you expecting mail?"

"Not shoved underneath my door, no." Glancing around, she added, "How did someone get in here?"

"We can figure that out later. Right now we need to find out what this is," he said. "Don't touch it yet."

Belle shifted around the letter-sized envelope. Emmett picked it up with a tissue he'd found in the box on the counter and Belle found latex gloves so she could open it.

The handwritten scribbles said it all.

I intend to finish what I started. You ruined my life. I intend to ruin yours. Maybe I'll find one of your sisters next.

Belle's heart accelerated as her gaze met Emmett's. Then her mind went wild with speculations. Was this just an idle threat or was her attacker going to come after her family, too?

FOUR

"That's a *definite* threat," Emmett said, his eyes scanning the dark street and the trees around the building. "It had to have come from your attacker but when did he leave it here? We'll brush for prints and you should alert your sergeant."

"I'll report it now and talk to Gavin tomorrow," she said. "I'm thinking we won't find any prints since he slipped it through the door. First, I want to check on my family."

She stopped in the hallway. "I don't want to alarm them but I do need to beef up security and alert them on what's going on. This man is dangerous. I feared that they'd be targeted because of me and now it's happening."

"Okay. *I'll* call it in and report we're together and things are under control," Emmett replied. "You're right. Your family needs to be aware."

Belle searched the bottom floor but found nothing unusual while he made the call. Quick and efficient and in charge, Emmett handled everything with a strength she wished she had.

Thankful that he was with her, she motioned toward the entryway stairs. "My parents and my brother and sisters live up here. My dad converted these two floors into one unit."

Emmett followed her up the stairs. "The door looks solid. No sign of a break-in."

"I have a key. We need to check on my family." Belle silently unlocked the door. Darkness greeted them. "They should all be in bed by now. Wait here."

Emmett took in the apartment. Average in size but clean and neat with a long narrow hallway toward the back with stairs up to the next floor. Her family had obviously taken over this whole foursquare and turned it into a big family unit.

After she'd done a room check, Belle tiptoed back. They were almost out the door when Emmett heard footsteps.

"Belle?"

"Cara, what are you doing up?"

From what he could tell in the muted darkness, the girl was in her teens and looked like a petite version of Belle but her dark hair was longer. "I heard a noise."

"Just now, you mean?" Belle asked, urgency in her question. "Did you hear anyone coming in earlier?"

"*Sí.* I was reading and I heard you open the door." The girl's eyes widened when she noticed Emmett. "But Joaquin came home about an hour ago. Is something wrong? Your voice sounds funny."

Giving Emmett a warning glance, Belle replied, "I strained my throat earlier when we got into a scuffle with a perp. I'll be fine. Sorry I woke you up. I was just checking since I had to work late." Then she glanced around. "Was our brother okay?"

Cara bobbed her head. "Snarly, as usual, and sneaking in. I didn't rat him out, though."

Belle didn't comment. Emmett wondered if their brother had seen someone or had even taken the envelope from someone in front of the building and left it under her door.

The girl motioned to the kitchen. "We have leftover chicken spaghetti in the fridge."

"I'm not hungry," Belle said on a low note. "You should go back to bed."

Cara rubbed her eyes and crossed her arms over her big nightshirt before sending Emmett a direct stare. "Who is he?"

Emmett had to smile at that blunt question. "I'm Emmett, a friend of your sister's."

Cara's eyes widened as she came fully awake. "A friend? Belle, you didn't tell us you were dating again."

"I'm not," Belle said on a slightly agitated sigh. "We're not. It's not that way. We had a business meeting."

Her sister's eye roll was classic. "Right. Nice to meet you, Emmett. I'm going back to bed now."

Belle waited until her sister was back in her room. "Sorry about that."

"She's something, huh?"

"You could say that. Her twin is not quite as forthcoming. Anita is quiet and loves to read. Cara is more of a girlie girl with an attitude. Sweet sixteen and going on thirty."

They moved back down to her apartment. Emmett

could tell she was embarrassed by the way she refused to look at him and then started explaining. "I was in a serious relationship for a couple of years, but it ended badly. Now they all hold their breaths hoping I'll find someone new."

Emmett followed her inside the apartment and let that tidbit settle over him. "Have you been dating again?"

Giving him a stern stare, she said, "Is that really any of your business?"

"Nope. Just curious."

He had to watch himself around this one. She was pretty and smart and tough. No flirting. No anything but finding out the truth about his cousin possibly being a murderer and trying to protect Belle. Moving with her around the combined kitchen and dining area that flowed into a tiny den, he waited when she turned on the lights and checked the bedroom and bath, all the while reminding himself that he had rules about dating any woman in law enforcement and apparently she had her own set of rules.

"All clear," she said. "Normally, Justice makes the rounds with me. I miss him."

Safe subject. "How did you and Justice become partners?"

She smiled and pushed at her messy bun. "I joined Emergency Services a little over a year ago, after being on another K-9 team with the NYPD for two years. My K-9 partner, Rocket, stayed with that unit after a trainer moved up the ranks. Justice had finished his initial training when he became my partner. We trained in Emergency Services together and he's been by my side almost every day since training."

"You two obviously make a good team," Emmett said. Then he looked her over. "How you feeling?"

"I'll feel better after a hot shower and more pain pills. And sleep."

"That's my cue to leave." He pointed to the dead bolt and the chain locks. "Lock up tight and fill in your sergeant a little more tomorrow."

"I will. I'll take this straight to the lab to be analyzed and then I'm going to search mug shots and old case files."

Emmett knew she'd do it, too. "I'll check with you tomorrow and report anything else I can find on Randall."

"Thanks." She looked down at the floor and then back up to him. "It was nice to meet you, Emmett." Then she let out a nervous little laugh. "Really nice, considering."

He smiled at that. "We dodged a bullet, literally. That guy's aim was seriously off."

"Which means at least he's not a professional."

"Nowhere near." He studied her for a moment. "I'm thinking he's someone you put away and now he's back and out for revenge. Report the motorcycle incident, too. Like you mentioned, he must have used that to get away at the park earlier."

"I don't know how he got access to this building," she said, thinking of how she'd always gone to a lot of trouble to make sure her family's home was secure.

"He might have slipped in when someone from your family opened the main door. Or it could have been a person your family knows and trusts."

"I'll go over my cases and I'll talk to my parents,"

she said. "I certainly never expected this when I made plans to meet with you."

"Me, either."

"Good night," she said. "I'll talk to you soon."

Emmett left but he checked around the building before he got back in his truck. That man tonight had been serious. He would have killed Belle if Emmett hadn't come along in the park, and he'd come to the police station and waited for her to exit. Now her attacker had made a bold move by coming to her home to leave a threat.

Emmett would urge Gavin to put a watch on this place in case the intruder returned.

Emmett said a prayer of thanks and drove back to his apartment. Unable to sleep, he pulled out his mother's genealogy files and tried to decipher the many ways to find a family member and narrow down the odds of a match. Any one of the several distant relatives he had on his father's side could also be a match, but none of them lived in the state of New York.

He'd need to find Randall and try to get some fresh DNA to back up the K-9 Unit's claims. But in his gut, he figured Randall looked pretty good for the cold-case murder.

Randall, who'd been abandoned by his mother and abused by his father, ultimately had suffered a lot of setbacks in life. What would have motivated him to kill the couple, though? Had he known them? And had he also killed little Lucy Emery's parents or was that the work of a copycat?

Just a few of the many questions he'd have to ask Randall if he ever found him.

* * *

The next morning, Belle looked up from the laptop on her desk. She'd been going through mug shots for what seemed like hours, but now she saw Emmett walking toward her with two cups from her favorite coffee shop.

"Here," he said, greeting her with a weary smile. He also offered her a small white paper bag, then pulled out a bagel and held it. "I brought you an apple Danish, too. Softer on your throat than a bagel."

"Thanks, that was thoughtful." Ignoring all the warning bells in her head, she took a long sip of the coffee and grimaced when it hit her sore throat.

"Still tender?" he asked, examining the red welts over her collar.

"Yes. Sore and bruised and uncomfortable, but I told my family I might have a stalker. I also asked Sarge to put a patrol on our apartment building and then came here and updated him and the team on everything that happened after we left the park. I talked him into letting me come in today to go through mug shots."

"Wore him down?"

"Something like that." Tapping her fingers on the desk, she said, "My parents are concerned, of course. But my Papá has a whole system of people who watch out for our neighborhood. Not vigilantes but a strong watch, all the same. *Familia* is very important to him."

Her parents didn't like her line of work, so the stalker talk had not gone over well, but she'd assured them she was okay and as long as they were careful, they should be safe. Papá said he'd inform the neighbors. He'd put citizen watchers on every corner.

"As long as you don't take the law into your own hands," she'd warned. Her father respected the NYPD, so he knew the rules.

"How's Justice?" Emmett asked now while he tore into the giant bagel.

"I saw him first thing," she said, keeping her voice low because it hurt to try to talk on an even keel. "He's much better. We had some playtime, but Doc suggested I pamper him for a couple of days. Since Sarge told me to take it easy, Justice and I will hang out in the training arena later and do some low-key practice runs. I should be able to take him home tonight."

"That sounds like a good plan."

"But first, I'd like to see if I can ID the man from last night."

Belle broke off a piece of the fluffy Danish and chewed it. Then she took a swallow of the herbal tea with honey and lemon her friend and coworker Lani Jameson had made for her. "I need a caffeine boost so I'll drink the coffee, too," she told Emmett since he'd gone out of his way to bring it to her.

After explaining that she was drinking the tea to soothe her throat, she went on to tell him about the female K-9 officer who'd taken Belle under her wing when Belle had first started here.

"Lani likes to nurture everyone. She's married to Noah Jameson, the chief at the NYC K-9 Command Unit in Queens. Her partner is Snapper, the German shepherd that worked with Chief Jordan Jameson. Sadly, he was murdered last year and Snapper went missing for a while."

Emmett rubbed a finger on his chin. "I remember that—a big shake-up and such a senseless murder."

"Yes. I worked in another unit but…it shook up the whole NYPD."

"Glad they found the killer." Emmett finished his bagel. "So what's the status on *your* attacker?"

She pointed to the screen. "I've met with the forensic artist and based on the sketch and the man's build, I'm trying to narrow things down while the lab works on getting a facial match."

"Any luck yet?"

"No, but the techs are going over the epidermis scrapings and hair follicles they found on my clothes so we should get something one way or another. The artist sketched the ring, too. Our techie, Esme Chang, offered to do some research on that, but it might be nothing." Shaking her head, she added, "I have nothing to go on for the bike. But Sarge has people looking for any motorcycles in this area. A long shot."

He sat next to her and ran a hand down his jawline, giving her a chance to see him in the light of day. Handsome but looking kind of world-weary. But those eyes. Stormy gray and so serious. He was a nice-looking man. Today, he wore a navy polo shirt with a Justice Department emblem on the top left side and khaki pants, his badge on a black lanyard around his neck.

"Did you get any sleep?" she asked to take her mind off the way he seemed to stare right through her.

"Not much." He took a sip of his coffee. "How 'bout you?"

She shook her head. "Too much information jarring

my tired brain and too many images of that man with his meaty hands around my throat."

"It'll take time to get over that, but you're tough." He glanced at her neck. "I'll do my best to track Randall down, online, finding his last known address and work records, and through my local sources in this area, and I'll continue to stay on the alert regarding your attacker, but… I can only do so much."

Surprised, Belle frowned at him. "Hey, I can fight my own battles, but thanks. Besides, we both need to locate your cousin."

Emmett nodded in greeting to some officers moving around. They probably all knew who he was since Belle had given a thorough report in this morning's briefing, her voice still hoarse. He seemed to take the scrutiny with ease. Nothing seemed to ruffle this man.

Glancing back at her, he said, "I went through some of my mom's files and found out I have several cousins all over the state of New York but they're only listed on her tree so their information could be private and the rules on how law enforcement can obtain information seem to change frequently. But we could get more warrants. This might turn out to be someone besides Randall."

"But still someone you're related to."

He shot her a wry smile. "Yep. I guess we can't all be in law enforcement."

Belle could see he was worried. "I'm sorry we had to drag you into this, Emmett. If you don't want to be part of the search, I'd understand."

"I do want in on the search," he replied. "If Randall is guilty, I'll be the first to handcuff him. But I'd like to keep him alive and I'd like to obtain DNA from him to verify our suspicions."

"We'll do our best. That's why we need to find him."

Emmett eyed the half of her Danish she hadn't eaten.

"Are you still hungry?" she asked through a grin.

"I guess I am," he replied. "I usually cook bacon and eggs but left in a hurry to get here."

She stopped her search long enough to offer him the rest of the half-eaten Danish. "I guess I wasn't too hungry but thanks."

Emmett gave her a grateful smile.

Then she turned back to the screen. "Hey, wait." Putting down her food, she pointed to a mug shot. "I think this is him, Emmett."

Emmett studied the photo and the information, then read it out loud. "Lance Johnson. Twenty-eight years old. Repeat offender." He read off the rap sheet and then halted. "Domestic abuse." He looked at Belle. "Well now, that makes sense."

"I remember him now," she said, ignoring the shiver that slipped down her spine. "Big and hefty and a bully. I caught him attacking a woman over a year ago in the very park we were in last night. One of my first collars and Justice was there to help take him down."

"That would explain why he tranquilized your partner."

Belle studied the mug shot. "He's changed some. More beefed up. He must have worked out in prison."

"I got a good look at him but couldn't make out his face. I do remember he was hefty." Emmett sat up and scanned the photo. "Are you sure he's your assailant?"

"Oh, yeah. The woman he attacked that night was his

ex-girlfriend. He'd beaten her before, and she'd left him but he tracked her down. She called 911 and I was in the area and first on the scene. She testified against him, and the prosecution also brought out that his ex-wife had filed abuse charges against him and then dropped them."

Shrugging, she said, "But the judge ruled that as inadmissible since the ex-wife had dropped the charges. That incident happened before the new state law allowing prosecutors to go forward on those types of charges even if the victim didn't press charges."

She hit print on the file and then whirled her chair around. "It was ruled as a misdemeanor, and he did go to prison but the sentencing was not long enough in my opinion. Domestic abuse cases can swing both ways, depending on probable cause and the strength of the evidence and testimonies. Only a year in jail, a fine and then probation. Which I'm thinking he's probably already broken."

"We need to check with his probation officer."

"On it," Belle replied to Emmett's suggestion. "Let me go and talk to Sarge so he'll reconsider making me stay by my desk. If we can get this suspect off my back, I'll have more time to help you search for your cousin."

Emmett wouldn't mind spending more time with her, but their duties had to come first. He needed to remember that and keep his head in the game.

FIVE

Two hours later, Belle and Emmett walked into a small office inside the Kings County courthouse. They needed to talk to Johnson's probation officer, a man named Sam Blain.

After they explained why they were there, Sam Blain sank back in a rickety office chair, his face dour and his eyes bloodshot.

Rubbing his bald head, he grunted. "Lance Johnson hasn't checked in the last two weeks and I couldn't find him at his last known address. I've alerted the proper authorities and filed a violation with the court. Since no one can locate the man, I had no choice."

"Can we have his last known address?" Belle asked, her mind on getting this done. "I really need to question him."

"Humph. You and me both, lady." Sam grunted again and pulled out Lance Johnson's file. "He's one angry man. Didn't like jail and keeps saying he was framed. Started griping the first week he reported to me and now it's three weeks in and he's a no-show. I wouldn't put it past him to go after everyone involved in this case.

If he did attack you, he might try to find all of his exes, too. Could get ugly."

"We'll alert them," Emmett replied, giving Belle a knowing glance. "Has he made any threat toward anyone that you're aware of?"

"That boy makes threats toward anybody who looks at him sideways. I see jail again in his future regardless. Hotheaded and desperate, not willing to follow the program."

They left and headed to the address he'd jotted down on a sticky note. It was located in Canarsie, on the fourth floor of a rundown apartment building over a dry-cleaning business.

Once they cleared the crumbling stairs up, the heat inside the dank, narrow hallways made the air stifling, the smell of this morning's bacon still lingering in the air. Belle twisted the collar of her uniform, her raw skin burning once they'd climbed to the fourth floor. "This should be the place."

She knocked loudly on the flimsy door.

No answer.

But a couple of dogs down the way started barking in response to the knocks.

Emmett knocked this time and called out, "Lance Johnson."

Other doors creaked open as people peeked out to see what the ruckus was and after seeing uniforms, slammed their doors shut.

"I have a feeling our man's not at home," Emmett said on a whisper.

"Let's go to the lobby and see if we can find the super or a manager."

They trekked back down to the shoebox lobby that held mailboxes and a small office.

Belle walked into the office. "NYPD," she announced. "Anyone here?"

They heard shuffling and a bald-headed man wearing a faded green shirt and paint-splattered black pants came out of a back room carrying a Chinese takeout box.

Giving them a worried stare, the man put down the container. "Sorry, I'm on break."

"This won't take long," Belle said, flashing her credentials. After introducing herself and Emmett, she asked, "What's your name?"

The man's brow furrowed up. "Albert Stein." Eying his lunch, he shifted on his feet. "What do you need, Officer?"

She pulled out her phone and showed Albert Johnson's mug shot. "We're looking for Lance Johnson, fourth floor, apartment 410."

The grumpy man eyed the photo and moved some papers around before he dropped his lunch on the counter, his expression going blank. "Yeah, I know him. Ain't seen him in a week or so and he owes me rent. He won't be living here much longer if he doesn't pay up."

Belle noted the man's downcast eyes. What was he hiding? "He's late on the rent?"

"Yep, he's been here a month now and next month's rent has been due for a week." He waved his hand up. "Not the best tenant I've ever had."

Belle saw a flash of gold on the man's hand.

He wore a gold signet ring rimmed in black.

Giving Emmett a warning stare, she went on. "So you don't have any idea where we can find Mr. Johnson?"

"Nope. Like I said, he owes me money. But good riddance. The man is always fighting with somebody about something, you know what I mean?"

"Yeah, we know," Emmett replied on a droll note. "We might be back with a search warrant. He could be in a whole lot of trouble."

Albert plopped down on a rickety chair. "I'm the landlord and maintenance man here and I'm telling you, I got nothing. No information on that troublemaker."

Belle motioned to his left hand. "That's an interesting ring you got there. Where did you get it?"

The man dropped his food and stood up. "Look, I answered your questions about Johnson. Where I shop is none of your business. Now can I please eat my General Tso's chicken before it congeals?"

"Sure, you enjoy your lunch," Emmett said. "If you spot Johnson, give my friend here a call, okay?"

Belle handed him a card. "It's important."

"It always is," Albert said, his chopsticks ready. "If he's in trouble with the law, he's outta here."

After they were headed back to her SUV, Belle glanced over at Emmett. "That's the ring my attacker wore. I know it is. Gold with an onyx rim. Like a crest."

Surprised, he asked, "Do you think Albert is your man?"

"No. I matched the attacker to the mug shot we found. It's Lance Johnson. But I think Albert knows more than he's letting on."

Checking traffic, she peeled out of the parking space they'd found down the street. "I'll keep an eye on Albert while I try to find out more about that ring. Why would he and my attacker both be wearing the same kind of unique ring, anyway?"

Emmett ended his phone call and turned back to watch Belle go through some paces with Justice in the indoor training arena. He'd had to get special permission from the chief US marshal of the East New York district to help Belle find his cousin. He couldn't shirk his own duties too long. Due to his Special Operations status, he could get called to travel and he'd have to leave at a minute's notice.

All the more reason to get this done and soon. Emmett tended to get antsy when he was out chasing bad guys. Watching Belle now, he decided this woman made him antsy, too. It had been a while since he'd even tried to date anyone. He needed to remember his rules and stick to his standards. Dating was tough enough without adding in law enforcement on both sides. Watching his mother fret and worry when he was growing up, he'd told himself time and again he didn't want to put anyone through that and most of the women he'd dated didn't appreciate him being absent on a regular basis.

This woman lived and breathed the danger. She got what his job entailed. He couldn't deny she'd gotten to him, but he had to stick to the job of finding bad guys.

"That's a good boy," Belle told Justice as the big dog jumped over a hurdle and climbed up a ladder. Belle had explained how Justice only got one meal a day—at dinner, and he rarely got treats. Instead, these dogs were rewarded with playtime. Emmett was learning more and more about the Brooklyn K-9 Unit as he moved through the corridors of the main building and the training areas.

Dedicated and hardworking. Determined, too, from the way Belle and Justice both tried to bounce back from their ordeal. These officers and their K-9 partners were together almost 24/7. He felt like a third-wheel.

Meantime, he'd put out some feelers regarding his wayward cousin. Nothing on that yet, but he held out hope that Randall would turn up in the old stomping grounds around Brooklyn.

After he left here, he'd try to find his dad's files. He'd have to go to the storage unit he'd rented to hold some of the things he'd kept from his parents' house.

"What are you looking so serious about?" Belle asked after she and Justice were done.

"My old home," he admitted. "I sold it a year after my mom passed. Since I travel a lot, I needed something smaller and with less maintenance. The roommate situation came up and I jumped on the apartment in Dumbo. But I did save a few things. I rented a storage unit not far from where we used to live. I'm going there later on to see if I can find any of my dad's files and notebooks."

"So there might be information on Randall there?"

"I don't know. My dad would have followed the law, but like me, he would have tried to do his best by Randall, too. I know he kept some personal files at home, and he took meticulous notes on all of his cases."

"I could go with you and help," she offered. "Justice is clear to go, and he can stand guard. An easy assignment."

Emmett laughed when Justice's ears perked up. "I

think he likes that idea but as long as you don't overdo it. I'll buy dinner."

"I'm starving," she said. "Let me get cleaned up."

They started walking toward the locker room.

"Hey, what did you find on our friend Albert Stein?"

"Nothing yet," she said. "Looks like he has a clean record but... I got the impression he could be shifty. You know how you get a certain vibe?"

"Yep, part of the job. Instincts kick in. I felt the same way."

"I'll be back in a few," she said. "C'mon, Justice. You get to go home with me tonight."

Justice woofed and danced around. The canine seemed to be on the mend.

Emmett settled into a chair in an anteroom and watched as officers and their partners returned for the shift change.

A tall officer with auburn brown hair walked by, a sleek Malinois at his side. The man glanced at Emmett and kept walking but then he turned and came back.

"Hey," Emmett said when the officer stepped into the room. Noticing the name on the officer badge, he added, "Officer McGregor."

"Bradley. And this is my partner, King."

"Long day?" Emmett said, knowing why Bradley McGregor had come back around.

"You could say that. You know who I am, right?"

"Yep, and I'm guessing you know who I am?"

"Right." Bradley stood there with his hands by his sides. "I not sure what to say to you."

"Say what's on your mind," Emmett suggested. "Or I can say it for you. My cousin might have murdered your parents twenty years ago." He saw a flash of pain in Bradley's eyes. "I'm truly sorry for what you and your sister have been through."

Bradley sank down on the chair across from him and told his K-9 partner, King, to stay. The dog got comfortable by his boots.

"Yeah," Bradley said. "I'm not judging, and I won't jump to conclusions. I hope we can both get some answers."

"That's why I'm hanging around," Emmett said. "I've already told Officer Montera I'll be the first to bring Randall in for questioning. That's part of my job, same as yours. But I want this to be handled in a fair way, too. He's innocent until proven guilty."

"I agree," Bradley said. "I know how it feels to be accused of something you didn't do."

Emmet could understand that. He knew that Bradley McGregor, as a teenager who hadn't gotten along with his parents, had been the prime suspect in their murders until he'd finally been cleared. But the suspicion had lingered in public perception. Emmett had heard enough of those kinds of stories from his dad. "I'll find my cousin and we'll get to the truth so you and your sister can find some closure, okay?"

Bradley stood and offered Emmett his hand. "Okay. Thanks."

"You got it." Emmett watched Bradley and King head toward the locker room. He needed to keep digging. These people wanted answers and so did he.

Belle finished her salad and glanced over at Emmett. "You've been kind of quiet. Is all of this catching up with you?"

Emmett pushed his plate back, his hamburger steak

finished. Belle had recommended a diner near the precinct and they'd scooted in for a bite before they headed for the storage unit. Justice sat at her feet. He'd had his dinner earlier after they'd finished their workout and he'd had playtime with his favorite hamburger-shaped squeaky toy.

"I talked to Bradley McGregor while I was waiting for you earlier," he said, his tone quiet. "He saw me and stopped in. I think he wanted to check me out and see if he could trust me."

Belle gave him a sympathetic stare. "The whole team is on this case and…it's not easy. We knew bringing you in would be awkward, but you have every right as an officer of the law to want to find your cousin."

"But it could be considered a conflict of interest. I don't want anyone to resent me being involved."

Belle couldn't help it. She liked this man. He was the real deal and he put the law above everything else, just as they all did. She wasn't ready to drop her guard yet. "Look, people will talk, but Sarge vouched for you and I've reassured people that you want to find Randall and question him. That's the first step. We'll worry about who we offend later. We don't know much now. We need Randall's DNA to know if he's a match for the particle found on that broken watchband."

Her cell buzzed and she held up a finger. "It's our tech guru, Eden Chang.

"Hey, Eden. Do you have news on the DNA lifted from my clothes and fingernails?"

"Yep," Eden said. "I'm reporting for the crime scene techs since we compared notes. DNA matches Lance Johnson. Same with the envelope he left under your door. No prints on the envelope but one or two prints on the actual paper. He's your man. We got facial recognition from the sketch to back it up. Sarge put out a BOLO on him. So be aware."

Breathing a sigh of relief, Belle asked, "What about the ring?"

Eden told her that the ring Belle had described could be a knockoff of an expensive gold signet ring.

"I'm guessing he either stole it or he bought it on the cheap from a costume jewelry store," Eden said. "If he'd stolen it, why would he wear it? He'd hock it right away. Until we have the ring, we can't really say. But we can rule out it being any type of insignia for an organization or club. I didn't find any matches on that and didn't find anything on that type of ring missing or stolen recently."

"Thank you," Belle said. Then she ended the call and reported back to Emmett. "So…now we need to locate Lance Johnson *and* your cousin."

"Let's get to the storage unit," Emmett suggested after he tossed two twenties on the table. "We'll start there, and I can run some more detailed checks when I get home, too. The sooner we find Randall, the sooner we can end this one way or another."

"Meantime, I've asked for the NYPD's assistance guarding my apartment building," Belle said. "I don't need Johnson snooping around there and messing with my family." Or worse, hurting one of them.

SIX

Belle watched while Emmett went through heavy plastic storage bins and cardboard boxes marked to show their content. Some of the containers came with the storage closet and some he'd obviously brought here himself. But this wasn't much stuff and certainly didn't give her a clue as to who he really was.

But then, like most law enforcement people, he lived for his work and probably liked to keep to himself. No time for sit-down dinners or taking a day to goof off. She knew that feeling.

Which made her stop thinking about the man beside her so she could get back to the reason they'd come here in the first place. She'd only agreed to come with him since she hadn't wanted to go home without getting in a little productive work. Even if this was off the clock and even if her heart was leading more than her head.

The building in a border area of Bay Ridge looked like an old industrial type that had changed hands. Rows and rows of orange-colored doors lined up on long wide hallways with concrete floors. Emmett's unit was on the first floor above the parking garage and near an open catwalk that offered a feeble wisp of air now and then, thankfully.

"They close up at seven," he said as he shuffled pots and pans and boxes. "We don't have much time. I should clean this thing out but…never can seem to make myself do it."

Belle helped him rearrange a few smaller boxes, noticing a pack of letters and some pictures. "Is it hard to let go of your parents' stuff?"

"Harder than I thought, yes. I kept what's here and what I have in my closet back at the apartment. Years of their lives and I have yet to accept fully that they're gone." He stopped and wiped at his brow. "They should have had more years together, but I guess I can fuss about that when I'm at the pearly gates."

Belle smiled at his gentle faith. Emmett presented himself as a big strong man but she could see that soft heart underneath.

"We'll all have questions then," she said on a soft note. "I'm glad I came to keep you company. I can't imagine my parents being gone."

No one should have to go through grief alone. She tried to imagine if something were to happen to her parents or siblings. How would she handle that? Hard to think about and yet, that day could come. Maybe he'd grown used to being a loner because the pain of being alone hurt so much. Tough to crack that facade.

When she heard a door opening down the way, out of habit, Belle checked the exits and entryways, then glanced out the one nearby window that had a good view of the street. Justice did the same, trained in much the same way as she'd been.

Dusk began to settle like dark velvet over the city while the last of the sunset left shadows that stretched across the eerie hulk of the nearby buildings. Outside, a hot wind whipped around corners, darting here and there in the simmering heat and blowing half-dead leaves off the trees. Traffic sounds echoed back into the open parking garage one floor below. Somewhere down the way, a car door slammed. Someone had a moving truck backed up to an open storage unit two rows over. Belle could hear the movers shouting at each other.

Emmett grunted and squinted at each container. Pushing away a table and two heavy chairs, he stretched toward the back of the square unit. "I think I see my dad's file box."

At least they didn't have to search long. Emmett's organization skills sure beat her own. Everything in this locker was neat and categorized so it didn't take long for him to find the bin marked *Emmett Marlin Gage.*

Popping the hinged lid up, he started methodically going through the batches of mustard-colored envelopes, each marked to show its contents.

Just outside the open unit door, Justice stood at attention since Belle had commanded him to guard. The big dog lifted his nose, sniffing the air with seasoned practice. He could pick up any number of scents around here, but she knew he'd zoom in on a human and alert them of any changes in what he sniffed.

She shouldn't be so jumpy, but her instincts repeated over and over that someone could be lurking around here. What if Emmett's cousin had gotten word that Emmett wanted to talk to him?

Why did she have that same feeling she'd had last

night? That someone was watching her. It had to be Johnson, but something felt different.

"You're a junior?" she asked Emmett to keep her mind from going overboard on the speculations, noting the name on the bin he'd located way up top. "I'm surprised your dad's name hasn't popped up on our radar more."

"He went by E.M. Gage," Emmett explained while he pulled out and returned envelopes. "Never did like his name but my mom wanted to give it to me. He was Emmett Marlin Gage and I'm actually Emmett Michael Gage. We have the same initials but not the same name. A compromise—just one of the many lessons I learned from my parents."

"They sound like a wonderful couple," Belle said. "My parents are like that, always offering up life lessons even if none of us want to listen. I worry about my younger brother, Joaquin. He's going through a rebellious stage so he's disrespectful to my dad sometimes."

"How old is he?" Emmett asked as he moved bins and reorganized the tiny locker.

"Joaquin is fifteen, but he thinks he's older."

"Tough age but he'll learn."

"I'm afraid of what he'll learn," Belle said, her anxieties kicking in.

A pigeon fluttered down from the top of the squat building, startling Belle. Justice's ear perked up but he didn't move.

"Joaquin thinks he knows everything," she added.

"Ah, I remember that age."

Belle gave Emmett a twisted smile. "C'mon. You had

to have been a Dudley Do-Right. I can't see you acting out like my brother's doing."

"So you consider me to be that boring?" he asked, grimacing. "I'll have you know I was indeed an upstanding citizen but I did have one of those summers a boy never forgets. But my dad never forgot, either. After those rebellious few months, he made sure I had a job lined up at the end of each school year."

Belle could imagine him as a teenager. Tall, with that sandy-blond hair and those piercing eyes. "I'm thinking you were a real charmer. Could have gotten into a lot of trouble and talked your way out of it."

"Actually, I have a hard time lying," he admitted. "I got in trouble, but I always fessed up. Took the rap to cover for a lot of friends who later turned out to be not-so-good friends. I wanted to be cool and wild, but my mom told me that God had a plan for me and it didn't include me trying to be something I wasn't. I guess I *am* a straight arrow. Boring but loyal." Then he grinned at her. "With the occasional rogue streak."

"Loyalty is a good trait," she replied, thinking her ex Percy Carolo hadn't had a loyal bone in his body but he had the rogue thing down in a bad way. Percy had wanted to be in law enforcement, but his hotheaded attitude didn't go over very well during training. "I'll take loyalty over being too wild and out of control any day."

"You seem loyal to your team," Emmett replied. "But you also seem very in control."

She moved another bin and then checked on her partner. Justice stood waiting patiently. "I love what I do. It's easy to be loyal when you want to do the best you can."

"A good trait." Then he gave her a determined

glance. "But this kind of work takes its toll. Makes it hard to settle down."

"I hear that," she said, a deep disappointment coiling through her system. This man was heavily commitment shy.

Even though the place was climate-controlled, Belle noticed the sheen of sweat popping out on Emmett's upper lip and forehead. She also noticed that he was in good shape. Not an ounce of extra weight on him and mostly muscle. With a grunt, he lifted out one last filing envelope.

"Bingo." He held up a thick file envelope held together with strong bands. It was marked with the name *E.M. Gage* and the word *Private*.

Emmett shifted a few more boxes and containers. "I think it should all be in this one file I found. Might not be anything much in here, but Dad kept a few records and notes on cases he'd worked. If he knew anything of the McGregor murders, it might be in here. Okay, so are you ready to go somewhere and dig through this folder?"

Justice glanced back at them and then lifted his nose again. Belle heard a noise, like someone running on the industrial gray hallway floors.

Emmett put away the container and then tucked the file under his arm. Then he guided her out and secured the keypad on the door. In the next instant, Justice gave a soft woof of warning and then a shot rang out followed by a ding. A bullet pierced the top of the folded metal door.

Justice stood his ground and growled low while Emmett tugged Belle down into a crouch and automatically shielded her. "Are you okay?"

"Yes," she said, her weapon drawn, her eyes searching the long row of identical storage units but the hall light was muted, causing all of the shadows to merge and dance. "Do you think Lance Johnson followed us here?"

"Somebody did," Emmett replied on an angry growl of his own as he held her close to the floor. Pulling his shirt up, he shoved the file against his stomach and then tucked his shirt back in. "Let's get out of here."

Holding his weapon up as he scooted toward the other side of the unit, he whispered, "I can't see anyone. We need to get to the truck."

"What about the few people in here?"

Emmett checked the keypad again. "Let's move along each row on this floor and try to find any bystanders. I know where a staircase to the left can take us down to the street level on the backside. Once we have people out and safe, we can circle back around."

"I can cover you," Belle said, eying both ends of the long aisle and the exit a few feet away. "You can make a run for it and warn people."

"I can do that," Emmett said, keeping his voice low. "But I'm not leaving you in here alone."

"Excuse me," Belle said. "I have Justice, and this is my job."

"I get that, but if we leave together, we have a better chance. What if the shooter isolates you in here? You'll be a sitting duck."

"Okay." Belle positioned herself on the other wall, by the door. "I'll get in place first, then motion to Justice. Justice can lead us out. He'll pick up any scents on the aisle or the stairwell. But we might have to split up to get help and we need to get everyone out of this building."

"Stay down and let's go." Emmett nodded and turned toward the first exit, a few yards away. A shot echoed over the building. Screams and people shouting soon followed.

Emmett went to his knees behind the container of files. "Those people are close by. That's not good."

"And we need to find this shooter fast," Belle said.

"Agreed."

Belle scanned the alley where they crouched in the narrow doorway of a closed closet. Another shot came close, hitting the ground at Emmett's feet. Justice waited in his position across from Belle, then barked and looked north. Belle heard people shouting and prayed they'd take cover until she and Emmett could help.

"I'm calling for backup," she whispered. "Then we move in."

Emmett nodded and watched while she made the call. "10-10. Shots fired inside City Wide Storage." She named the address and their location.

Justice barked again, his nose in the air. Then he glanced back at her, eager to go.

"Good boy," Belle said, shifting low to the ground. "I agree."

The shots were coming from inside the building and most likely this floor. Someone must have followed them and waited for an opportunity.

Emmett managed to dive into another corner across from them. "I can't see anyone."

Another shot rang out, pinging the concrete between units.

"I'm taking Justice along the open catwalk," Belle said. "You try to sneak out the back exit."

"Belle?"

"Emmett, let me do my job."

He nodded and scanned the corners. "I'll cover you until you're out of sight."

Lifting her head, she accepted that, then made another move. "Go," she ordered Justice. "Go. Find."

Justice started up the catwalk and then sniffed to the left, two aisles over. Giving him the silent signal to halt, Belle crouched down, then peeked around the row of storage closets and saw a movement on the other side of the long aisle. The shooter, inching closer.

A bullet whizzed past her head and Emmett returned fire from behind her. Belle moved to the next corner, Justice following close, and waved Emmett to go. Then she sat back a few minutes and listened to running feet and shouts. She was about to make another run for it when she heard someone around the corner.

Justice emitted a low growl that told her he'd picked up the scent again. "Stay," she said, giving him a hand signal to back it up.

Belle lifted around the corner to peek.

A round of fire came at her and she retreated back, bullets pouncing and pinging past her and hitting the catwalk floor and concrete sides near the open air.

Then Emmett came up behind her, returning fire. "Belle, let's go!"

Belle lifted and took another glance. The man dropped down and rolled around the corner.

"I see the shooter, Emmett. I can circle around."

"No, I've alerted the manager and he's getting everyone out. They're all headed away and down the back stairs. That leaves us and him until backup gets here." Motioning to where the shots came from, he added, "We need to wait and let him come to us."

She didn't want to put anyone else in danger and if she went after the man now, he could grab a hostage to get him out of here. But she could go around and between units to get closer. But by the time she could sneak up on the shooter, they should have help surrounding the perimeters of the building.

"Let's try again," Emmett said when the sound of footsteps and voices settled down.

"Behind you," she said to Emmett. Then she shot once and did a quick sprint to the next set of units. She pointed to the last few rows of units across from them. "We can't get out unless we make a run to the very end units. And he'll be running that same way."

"Copy that." Emmett glanced up. "We need to make the stairs and get on a floor over him. Spot him from the catwalk."

Belle motioned okay. But footsteps took off up the way. "There he goes."

Belle saw a man dressed in dark colors moving in a crouch along the row where they'd planned to hide around the corner. "I think I can get in a shot." She got down and belly crawled as close to the corner as she could. "I'm going to send Justice in and then I'll make a move."

"Dangerous," Emmett said while sirens wailed in the distance. "Wait for backup."

"Justice can take him," she retorted. "I have to get over the fear of him being hurt again. He's trained, same as me."

Justice barked an agreement on that.

Belle lifted up and then shouted, "Attack."

The dog hurled through the air with teeth bared, but the man spun up and took off, his heavy footsteps echoing between units.

Justice followed in a fast, eager trot.

Belle hurried along with him, not sure where Emmett was since she'd taken off without him.

She made it around the corner and spotted the man going down the stairs to the parking garage. The opposite direction of where the manager had led the people away, thankfully.

Justice stayed on the man's trail with Belle sprinting behind him.

The man stopped at the bottom of the stairs when she and Justice reached the landing. "Stop," Belle called out. "Put the gun down." He fired but missed. Then he took off running.

Emmett came up behind her and fired after him. They spotted the man as he reached the other end of the parking lot where a sign stated Employee Parking Only. He hurled over barriers and sprinted toward a navy-colored car, Justice racing after him.

Justice kept barking and snarling. The man turned, his features shadowed by dusk, and shot haphazardly into the air. Then he opened the battered car door and jumped into the vehicle. A moment later Justice jumped up against the driver's side door, all teeth and bark.

The economy car had seen better days, but it cranked

and revved before heading out of a small exit on the east side of the building.

Belle shouted to Justice to halt and ran with all her might, praying Justice wouldn't get shot or hit. But the car peeled out and skidded around a corner before she could get in a shot.

"Come," she called to Justice. Justice snarled but he retreated back toward her. Belle heard the car's squealing tires as it sped away.

"Did you get the license number?" Belle asked Emmett as he came hurrying behind her.

"No, I couldn't make it out in the dark," he said, stopping to catch his breath. "We should have chased him in the truck."

"We wouldn't have made it, anyway," she said, gulping in air. "Justice almost had him."

Belle sent a description out over the radio. Officers came running and surrounded them. Belle and Emmett quickly gave an update. Reports of officers in pursuit came back.

After they'd secured the building and made sure everyone else was safe, Belle turned to Emmett. "At least I got a good look at that messed up door on the driver's side."

"Did he look like your man?"

"I can't say," she admitted. "He had on gray baggy pants and a lightweight hoodie and big sunglasses. Could have been anyone."

"But only a few would shoot at us. Namely, two that I can think of."

"You mean the two men we're after?" Belle asked as they turned toward Emmett's truck.

"Yep." Emmett made sure she and Justice were both inside before he got in and put the vehicle in drive. "Lance Johnson and Randall Gage."

"But Randall doesn't know we're looking for him," Belle said, wondering again if Emmett had been in touch with Randall.

"If he's in the area and he's seen us together, it wouldn't be hard for him to figure out. He might have been warned by someone in cahoots with him. I've put out the word so people might have been asking around."

"Would your cousin shoot at us just to scare us? Or would he shoot to kill? Because we know Lance Johnson is a lousy shot and so was this person today."

"Who knows at this point," Emmett said. "They both might have motive to keep us quiet. But you're right. That person had every opportunity to shoot to kill and he missed."

Belle let that realization soak in as they headed out of the storage lot. She could see Lance Johnson wanting to kill her but Emmett's cousin? And would he really shoot his own relative?

If he killed once, he could easily kill again.

Then word came over the radio that they'd lost the car in pursuit. Apparently, whoever this was knew his way around Brooklyn enough to elude a police chase. Where had he gone?

"I'm liking Lance Johnson for this," she told Emmett. "Let's find Randall and bring him in before we jump to any more conclusions," she suggested. "It's a stretch that this could be him, but he did live here once and could be tailing us, too."

"Yeah, same as it was a stretch that you'd find one

of my relatives who might be involved in a cold case from twenty years ago?"

Emmett had a point. What were the odds?

She needed to keep this case and all the facts front and center and get the job done. They had to find both Lance Johnson and Randall Gage soon. Because not only was she in physical danger on all sides, but her heart was becoming more and more open to getting to know Emmett better, too.

She sure didn't need to add dealing with an interesting, hard-to-read man to her to-do list.

SEVEN

By the time they went their separate ways, Belle was too tired to focus on anything but sleep. Her boss had called her and reprimanded her heavily about not listening to orders. "I'm not telling you again, Belle. Stay home tomorrow or I'll put you filing away evidence down in the basement."

"Yes, sir," she'd replied while they stood inside Gavin's office. "I didn't think this would turn into an ordeal."

"Someone is trying to kill you, Belle. *That* is an ordeal and one you need to take seriously. You went out with the marshal when you were supposed to be off duty and recuperating."

She didn't argue that she also wanted to take Randall Gage seriously. But she did want to stay on the case and since she didn't want to lose this job, she had to settle down and wait for at least twenty-four hours or risk being in even worse trouble.

"I'll look these files over tonight," Emmett told her back at the precinct, once Sarge was done with her. "If I find anything helpful, I'll call you tomorrow."

"Did he let you have it, too?" she asked Emmett.

"Not in the same way. He mostly glared at me and then asked about the shooter. But he did say he's got people searching for the car we described. It seems to have disappeared off the face of the earth."

"I should be out there, too."

"No. You're supposed to go home. Don't push it, Belle."

Emmett hadn't exactly ordered her around. The concern in his voice held her steady. That and the exhaustion taking over her whole system.

"Okay," she said in sharp acceptance. "I'm leaving right now. Justice and I will watch an old movie."

"Now I know you're tired. You didn't argue with me."

She smiled and then made a face at him. But he was right.

Her throat muscles were still sore, tight and burning and her whole body seemed locked in a death grip she couldn't shake. She'd held it all in but now it shouted at her with every step she took. Plus, she needed to see her family. She'd been making excuses since the other night when Emmett had come to her apartment with her. Had that only been last night?

Usually, she'd poke her head in at breakfast, grab a piece of toast or a bagel and head out to work. Then she'd stop by at night and nibble on leftovers and give her parents a kiss before crashing in her own place. Her mother started speculating if she didn't show.

Sure that Cara had reported the whole scene of her and Emmett in the dark kitchen of their parents' home, Belle needed to make an appearance before she could go to her own apartment and get some sleep. Her mom would come looking and then Belle would get a lecture about settling down and getting married. Her mother prayed she'd give up her dangerous job and find something more suitable. That would never work. Belle wasn't cut out to be an office worker or a stay-at-home mother. She needed to be out in the city, helping other people.

Around nine o'clock, she entered her parents' apartment, using the key she always had on hand, Justice following excitedly since he loved her family.

"Belle, is that you?"

"It's me, Mamá."

Gina Montera lapsed into Spanish, fussing over her oldest daughter and telling her to sit. She needed to eat.

"I'm not hungry," Belle replied, slipping down onto a dining chair, the feeling of being home and safe overtaking her. "I just wanted to report in. Things have been kind of wild at work this week."

"I'm your mother, not your boss," Gina pointed out, her short dark curls framing her oval face. "You don't check in with me, you come by to see your poor mother, show me you are alive and okay. This is my one rule." Pulling out sliced turkey and sandwich bread, she shoved a plate in front of Belle and then stared at her neck, her dark gaze slamming against Belle's face. "What happened to you? And don't tell me you have some stalker but I'm not to worry about it. Mothers worry."

Belle cringed and chewed on a chunk of spicy turkey. "I got into a fight with a bad guy and I don't think he's done with me."

Gina shook her head and put a hand to her mouth.

"He did this to you? Is he the one who left that envelope? The one you warned us about?"

"I think so, but I'm fine," Belle said, lifting her collar a bit. "And I have people watching over all of you, too." He grabbed me at the park, but I had help."

"The man your sister saw you with last night?"

"Sí." Belle nibbled the bread, then took a drink of tea. "He's a US marshal who's helping me with a cold case. We had a meeting and he came along just in time."

"I'm thankful for that." Gina flicked Belle's uniform collar. "As if you could hide that from your mother. You need to settle down and get married. This is not the work for you."

"We've discussed this," Belle said for the hundredth time. "I like what I do. I like protecting people."

"But not yourself." Pointing to Justice, she asked, "Where was this one when you were attacked?"

Justice's ears went up and his dark eyes widened as if he wanted to explain but felt too fuzzy to do so. He let out a soft whimper and then put his head back on his paws.

Belle didn't want to go into detail about Justice getting hit with a tranquilizer dart because she'd get another round of fear and condemnation. "Nearby, but Justice did his best and between him and my friend, I'm here and I'm okay. Sorry I missed dinner again."

She stood and stretched. "Is Papá in bed already?"

Gina nodded. "He's tired. Your brother and he had words again."

"About?"

"Joaquin seems to think he can run around with

whomever he pleases. The crowd he's with now is not a good one."

"I'll talk to him again," Belle said on a frustrated note. "He could get into serious trouble if he keeps this up. I won't always be able to run interference." She thought about Randall Gage and felt sure Emmett's father and Emmett, too, had done their best to help him when they could. But the man was in his sixties now and could be getting away with murder.

How did a person live with that kind of guilt?

"We both try to tell him this," her mother replied, tears in her eyes. "But your brother thinks he knows more than we do. He is stubborn and determined."

"Well, so am I," Belle replied before she kissed her mom on the head. "Anita and Cara?"

"Up in their room, supposedly going to bed early since they start summer jobs this week working at Uncle Rico's café."

Belle nodded at that. She remembered earning money working at Rico's Café just around the corner from their apartment building. Her uncle had encouraged her to follow her dreams and never forget her roots.

"I'm glad they're working and close by at that." Then she pushed her plate away and took a long sip of her mother's tart lemonade. "Has anyone come around this week? Asking questions? Anything like that?"

"No, but we're watching carefully, just as you said."

"I'm so sorry, Mamá. I don't want it spilling over on all of you."

"You'd tell me if there's more right?"

"I'll tell you if you need to know, yes, Mamá."

Gina shook her head. "Now I'll worry."

"Don't. You know I watch out for all of you."

"What about you?" Gina asked. "Does your new friend watch out for you?"

"He tries," Belle admitted, thinking about how she and Emmett had somehow meshed in spite of being forced together in a strange way. "If I let him."

"You need to start letting more," Gina reminded her. "I want grandchildren before I'm too old."

Belle accepted a motherly kiss and then went down to her place with her mother's parting words in her head. Did she want children?

Emmett came to mind again and she shoved that image away. She would not put a man like Emmett Gage in the same thought with a passel of kids. She'd only met him a little over twenty-four hours ago. Not much time to plan out a future.

And way too soon after she'd dumped Percy Carolo, a man who wanted to be a police officer but didn't want to accept the rank-and-file authority that required. She wouldn't compete to prove her worth with another law enforcement man, even if this one actually knew what he was doing and seemed to treat her equally.

Nope, she wouldn't go there. Not tonight. Too tired, sore and sleepy. But her mind whirled with why Lance Johnson had it in for her. Then she moved to the puzzle of Emmett's cousin Randall and why he might murder a married couple and leave the young child, Penny, who'd been home at the time, unharmed. Could he have done the same thing again two months ago with the Emerys and little Lucy?

The two couples had little in common and didn't know one another. She knew based on her video phone call with the Emerys' landlords, the O'Malleys, that the couple had been rowdy renters who were behind on their bills. Lucy, appearing unkempt, had often been seen playing alone in the yard. Bradley and Penny McGregor hadn't had a stable childhood, either. Both sets of parents were neglectful. But that didn't constitute murder unless the killer thought the parents deserved what they got and had a soft spot for children. Seemed far-fetched, but all ideas for motives were welcome.

That made her think of Emmett again. He'd be good with children. He had a strong work ethic and a solid faith.

Your parents would be so proud of you, Emmett.

Why did she feel that Emmett had something to prove and that something meant he didn't want to settle down?

Maybe tomorrow or weeks from now, she'd let that image of Emmett's silvery eyes and nice smile slip back into her psyche. But for now, they had a lot of work to do and none of it involved him being in her future.

Her phone buzzed at seven the next morning.

"Hello?" Belle said, still sleepy.

"It's Emmett. I got called out on a case. An escapee we've been trying to locate for six months. We've got a strong tip that he's hiding out in Long Island. Not sure when I'll be done here."

"Go," she said, "And be safe."

"How are you?"

"I was good until someone woke me up."

"Sorry, just wanted to check. I'll call later."

"Okay. Meantime, I'll do some online research and

try to behave." Then she said, "Hey, Emmett, would Randall go out of his way to protect a child?"

A pause and then, "Maybe. He had a tough life with a tough dad. Are you onto something?"

"I don't know. Just wondering why the murderer left Penny there with a stuffed animal. I could ask the same about Lucy Emery, but since we only have DNA evidence from the McGregor murders, I'm focusing on the cold case."

"Good question." Then he let out a breath. "You know, Randall did some work as a carnie. He worked one of the games where the prizes were stuffed animals."

Belle jotted that in her notes, remembering Emmett's earlier reminder that Randall liked to collect toys and trinkets. "So he loved stuffed animals and also had access to them. Interesting. I'm going to pretend to be resting while I try to piece things together."

"Right. You're something else, Montera."

Belle hung up, wondering what that *something else* might be. A good something or a pain-in-the-neck something? He'd given her enough warnings to show her he was unavailable. Or at least, emotionally unavailable.

She actually smiled. Maybe she should date more just to prepare her for when the really good ones came along. She had a feeling Emmett was a good one but that was beside the point.

She stretched and got up, then turned on the coffee pot. Throwing on a robe over her nightgown, she let Justice out into the dog-run and gave him some playtime in the small square yard with the tall white fence.

Belle had a nice Adirondack chair with soft cushions to sit in when she wasn't chasing Justice around. Now she sat there with her coffee and took in the scent of her mother's roses and the neighbor's breakfast.

"Belle?"

She glanced up to see her twin sisters smiling down from the fire escape, their long dark hair falling in silky waves around their faces. "Hey."

"Mamá says come eat breakfast. She made blueberry pancakes and your favorite scrambled eggs."

"I'll be up soon," Belle said with a grin.

"Where did you meet that hunk that Cara caught you with?" Anita asked with a smug smile.

"At work."

"Are you two a thing?"

"No, we are not a thing. He's on a case with my unit."

Cara grinned. "So? You've been on a date?"

"No date. I just met him like two days ago and we were after a very nasty person. That doesn't qualify as a date."

Her sister shrugged. "It could, if you flirt a little."

"Hey, I don't flirt at work."

"Maybe you should," Cara suggested.

They both whirled when their father called out in his gruff voice, "Time to eat."

Belle got Justice in and they both trudged upstairs to enjoy an early breakfast with the whole family. Except Joaquin.

Apparently, he was sleeping late now that school was out.

Since Belle had the day off, she intended to have a strongly worded talk with her brother.

EIGHT

Belle was back at work in the training yard the next day, taking Justice through the paces. Her partner seemed as anxious as she was to get rolling again, despite the unsettling talk she'd had with her brother last night. Joaquin didn't want to listen to her warnings about finding a summer job and staying away from the group of kids who roamed the streets looking for trouble night and day.

She'd have to keep on him whether he liked it or not. Right now, she wanted to finish this workout and get back to her desk to try to find more information on the two thorns in her side—Randall Gage and Lance Johnson.

Justice must have felt her anxiety. The German shepherd was all in on running through the obstacle course out in the training yard. It was hard to keep a good working dog down.

"That a boy," she called as the eager K-9 showed his worth by walking across ladders and flying over low walls before searching through barrels and containers for hidden evidence. Then they practiced circle-and-bark and worked on reasonable force. The circle-and-bark was just that—he'd keep circling the cornered suspect and bark until he had further instructions. The reasonable force meant Justice wouldn't bite until ordered to do so as a last resort. A well-trained K-9 meant less unnecessary injuries and fewer lawsuits for the department. And that meant she had to be on high alert all the time, too. Justice trusted her to make the right calls.

Wishing they could have cornered the perp in the storage warehouse yesterday, Belle gave Justice due credit for trying to capture the man, at least. Justice would have taken the shooter if she'd shouted the attack order in time. But the man had sprinted to the car and that was that.

She made up for her mistake this morning by pushing both Justice and herself to the limit.

"We've still got it," Belle told her excited partner once they'd gone through the paces. "Playtime now."

Justice knew what that meant. After a short game of tug-of-war to show him that he would always be rewarded after hard work, they freshened up and Belle hurried to her cubicle. "Time to find the truth."

Emmett was waiting for her, dressed as usual in his dark polo shirt and khakis, his badge hanging from a lanyard around his neck, his dark baseball hat on the desk in front of him.

"Morning," he said, standing when she reached her chair. "I brought fresh coffee."

"You're going to give me a bad rep," she said, gratitude in her tone. "My team members will be jealous and call me a diva."

"You, a diva? I doubt that." He opened his own coffee and took a sip. "I saw you two out on the practice field. Pretty impressive."

Justice lifted his head and shot them a doggy smile.

"Yes, you, too," Emmett said, grinning at the big dog.

Belle wanted to smile, too. So he'd been watching them? That made little tingles of awareness move down her spine. It had been a while since a handsome man had shown her any interest, even if it was only the professional kind.

"We have to do a certain amount of training each week to stay on track and stay certified," she explained. "Can't slack off or get too complacent."

"No, because the bad guys never do."

"Well, I'm thinking the one who's after me has some issues there. He's kind of trigger-happy but also haphazard. He'll mess up soon enough."

"Just remember he has serious upper body strength," Emmett replied, touching a hand to his collar. "I didn't enjoy seeing his hands on your throat."

"Good point. I'm going to check the gyms around his apartment. The man obviously works out. Probably did in prison, too. I don't remember him being so beefy the first time Justice and I took him down."

"I guess he remembers you, though."

"Too well. I guess prison didn't suit him so now he blames me. Too bad he's going back there."

Belle finished her daily workout report and then gave her full attention to Emmett. "So first, did you find the escapee?"

"Yes. He's back in a warm, cozy cell with a nice downtown view of nothing but bars. He won't be roaming around on the sly anymore."

"Good, and second, did you find anything in your dad's files?"

Emmett sighed and leaned back in the chair across from hers. "Yes. In fact, I'm waiting to talk to see—"

"Marshal Gage, Belle, a word," Gavin called from his office.

"Him," Emmett finished, getting up and waiting for her to do the same.

"Coming, sir," Belle called after giving Justice the sign to follow.

Gavin stood waiting for them and then shut the door. "Deputy Marshal, what did you find last night?"

Sarge was obviously still sore at them for going rogue the other day. Belle wanted to hear what Emmett had to say so she refrained from apologizing again.

"I went over the few bits of information I could find," Emmett explained. "My father never brought home official files, of course. He always logged in any evidence or notes and put them in the evidence room just like any good officer would."

"But?" Belle asked, wondering.

"But he kept a personal notebook to back up what he saw each time he made an arrest or got involved in a case."

"Just as a reference?" Gavin asked, his scowl not so sharp now.

"Yes," Emmett replied. "And because, unfortunately, he worked with some pretty shifty cops at one time."

"Do any of those shifty cops have a place in our investigation?" Gavin asked.

"No, but I'm trying to establish that he had his reasons for keeping thorough notes and that served him well for many years."

Gavin nodded. "Your dad sounds like a good cop. What did you find?"

Belle gave her superior a slanted glance, but Gavin remained as stoic as a rock. He wanted answers.

Emmett sat up and pulled out a black notebook. "I have a few notations. *April 20, 2000. I got a call from Randall today. Haven't heard a word from him in five years. But he didn't have much to say when push came to shove. Seemed nervous and rambled a lot. Just said that he was heading out.*"

"Heading out?" Gavin took the notebook and studied the handwriting. "This would have been around the time of the McGregor murders."

Emmett nodded. "Could have been Randall's way of telling my dad he was leaving the state of New York. I did some digging and found out that's the first time he went to Pennsylvania. Worked around the farms there, even worked with the Amish a few years. But he drifted away and lost contact, as I've already reported."

"What else do you have?" Gavin asked, handing the notebook back to Emmett.

"Another reference right before my father retired. *Randall's in trouble again, but I can't help him. He won't tell me what he's done but he's in a bad way about something that happened long ago. Couldn't get him to meet with me.*"

"That was in the fall of 2015," Emmett continued. "My dad passed away a couple of months after that."

"That's not much to go on," Belle said. "It shows your dad tried to keep in touch with Randall but if Randall told him anything regarding the cold-case murders, it went to his grave with him."

Gavin nodded. "Why would your father leave such cryptic notes? Maybe he was noting times and dates while he protected Randall, maybe even knew he was on the run and where he was headed."

Emmett shook his head and stood up. "You didn't know my dad. He was straitlaced and hard-nosed. He went by the book, always. Never had a speck of scandal in his thirty years of being in law enforcement. You can easily verify that."

Gavin stood, too. "We have to consider every angle. Trust me, I've been through this and it's not easy." Shrugging, he said, "Even the best of us try to do the right things for the wrong reasons. If your dad had a soft spot for Randall, he might have overlooked or purposely left out some important details."

Emmett shook his head. "I'm telling you—it's not like that. You both said you didn't find any connection in the official files that could show my dad was aware of these murders. This murder case might have been common knowledge, but my dad was never part of the investigation. So stop going down that rabbit hole."

Gavin shot Belle a reluctant glance. "Duly noted but we all need to stay on this and go back over every detail. Maybe your father destroyed a few journal entries."

Emmett scrubbed a hand down his chin, his expression sharpening with anger. "I'll keep reading my dad's notes but I'm telling you both, he wouldn't have covered up a double homicide even if his own mother had done it."

Belle reached out to him. "Emmett, I'm sorry."

"Sorry?" His eyes narrowed. "You people tracked me down and questioned me, made me feel like a suspect even though I had nothing to do with this and now you're starting in on my father? We can't help that Randall is related to us and none of us—not my dad nor me or my mom—has any inkling that Randall could have been involved in something so horrible. I understand you need my cooperation and you need me to find Randall so I can get fresh DNA to verify what you've found. I'm on that. But you need to lay off my dad. Keep him out of this."

Pointing his finger at the notebook in his other hand, he said, "If my dad had heard word of him being a suspect, he would have noted it here and he would have at least kept the news clippings, or anything to tie to Randall. Then he would have worked to bring him in. But the news reports and the official reports all indicate *suspect unknown*."

He gave Belle a frustrated stare and then whirled toward the door. "I have my own cases to get back to but I'd appreciate it if you'd keep me informed if you find Randall. And I'm duty bound to do the same—I won't cover for him or help him escape. He needs to pay if he did this, but he is innocent until proven guilty. Understand?"

Belle glanced from his departing back to Gavin's shocked face. "Sir?"

"Let him go for now. He's right, of course. We just need to find something on Randall Gage. Anything that can either clear the man or condemn him. We're stalling out here."

"I'll get back on it," she said, motioning to Justice.

"But we just lost a strong contact. I don't know if Emmett *will* come around anymore."

"We've established enough to do this on our own, Belle."

"Have we?" she questioned.

"Are you disputing me?"

"No, sir." She shrugged. "He was kind of growing on me, though. He was a good resource."

Gavin gave her one of his measured stares, but Belle met his gaze with one of her own. "The man saved my life. We kind of bonded."

"Well, that's good," Gavin replied on a dry note. "Once you've solved this case, you can be friends with the deputy. How 'bout that?"

"That might work, sir," she said. Then she hurried out the door, hoping to find Emmett.

But Emmett Gage was long gone from the Brooklyn K-9 Unit headquarters.

Would she ever see him again?

Gavin didn't give her much time to think about Emmett. He ordered her and Noelle Orton, a rookie who used to be a K-9 trainer, to search once again for Lance Johnson. Noelle had been taking less public assignments since her K-9 partner, Liberty, had broken up two major gun-smuggling operations at the airport. Because of that, a gunrunner had put a bounty of ten-thousand dollars on Liberty's head. So neither of them had had much street time lately.

"A car matching the description of the one you and Emmett saw last night at the storage warehouse was located near a building in Canarsie about thirty minutes ago. It's not far from Johnson's last known address. He might be around. Take Noelle and Liberty with you. Noelle can use the experience and Liberty needs to stay sharp, too. Since this is a low-profile case, they both should be safe."

Now Belle and Noelle along with their partners were walking the perimeters of the older neighborhood. Noelle was tall and strong, her long dark hair in its usual low bun below her cap. Her yellow Lab, Liberty, had a telltale black splotch on her ear, which made the targeted K-9 all too easy to identify. They'd have to be vigilant for Liberty's sake. As they walked, Belle spotted the car immediately and took a picture. Justice sniffed the vehicle and turned to give her a doleful affirmative.

"Dark navy economy car. Damage to the driver-side door and a deep white gash along that side of the vehicle. That's the car the shooter used to get away yesterday," she told Noelle. "Has to be the same one."

After radioing confirmation and the car's license plate number, she turned to Noelle. "We can't search it without a warrant, and I didn't get the license number yesterday. So we'll have to wait to find out who owns the vehicle. But we can check Johnson's apartment building again."

Noelle's green eyes widened. "Let's go."

Liberty appeared to be just as eager to get some action.

The valiant Lab didn't know she was in any danger from gunrunners who wanted to stop her from being so good at her job. She was always ready and willing to take down criminals. Justice trotted along beside Liberty, obviously smitten.

"I hear that," Belle said to Noelle's gung ho attitude. "I want this guy off the streets."

They walked back to the big old square brick apartment building. "The super is not friendly," she warned Noelle. She'd already told her colleague about the super wearing a ring that looked like the one her attacker had been wearing. "We'll see if he has on jewelry today."

But they never made it up onto the stoop. Gunfire raged all around them, sending Belle and Noelle running up the cracked concrete steps to hide behind the stone railings.

"Stay down," Belle told Noelle. "I'm going to see if I can get a visual on the shooter."

She ran to the other side of the porch, thinking being shot at was getting tiresome. But after scanning the area, she couldn't see anyone hiding on a roof or lurking around a corner.

The whole neighborhood went quiet as people slammed their doors and turned down their music and televisions. Belle waited a couple of beats and then moved to the other end of the porch.

When she heard footsteps in the alley behind the narrow building, she signaled for Justice. He came charging and waited for her next command.

Then she motioned to Noelle and pointed toward the other side of the property. "Around back."

Noelle and Liberty headed in one direction and Belle took Justice over the railing on her side of the house.

When she rounded the corner, she saw a figure dressed in dark clothes running away. "Go," she ordered Justice. They both took off running to the right.

Belle called out. "NYPD. Stop!"

But once again, the shooter eluded them. Justice ran to a high wooden fence and barked. Belle caught up but found the fence chain-locked from the other side.

Noelle and Liberty came running. "What happened?"

"I think they went over this fence. Or had some help getting inside," Belle replied, irritation coloring her words. "I'm not enjoying being shot at every time I turn around."

Noelle's eyebrows lifted as she glanced around the hot, dank alley. "What if that shot wasn't for you, Belle?"

Noelle pointed to Liberty. "You're not the only K-9 officer in danger these days."

"You think they came here for Liberty?" Belle asked, a chill going down her back.

"I don't know," Noelle replied. "But the first shot hit pretty close to where Liberty was standing." Shrugging, she said, "We were both in plain sight and the shot hit near my partner. I try to take her out only on support cases, like this one, but maybe someone is following me—someone who wants the bounty on Liberty's head."

"Thankfully the shooter missed," Belle replied. "Let's get a team out here to scavenge for bullet fragments and any prints we can find."

"Like that'll be a piece of cake," Noelle replied. But she made the call.

Shaking her head, Belle wondered when they'd gone from protecting the public to trying to keep each other alive.

NINE

"So the vehicle does belong to Lance Johnson," Belle told Noelle later that day after they'd gone back to the precinct. "But of course, he's nowhere to be found. Nor was the building super today, either."

They'd gone inside after the shooting and found the office door locked and the reception area empty. None of the residents wanted to talk much about anything.

"Maybe they're in cahoots," Noelle said, letting out a tired breath. "Or maybe today's shooting had nothing to do with your suspect."

"I'm glad Liberty is okay," Belle told her friend when they walked up to the vending machine to get a snack since they'd missed lunch. "Hard to believe someone could be so evil as to try to kill a dog."

"Not just any dog," Noelle replied. "But a trained officer of the law. If Liberty's gone, these gun smugglers win. They tend to forget, however, we train dogs to work with us all the time. I'm going to protect Liberty with all I've got but if they harm her, I'll work with another K-9 in Liberty's honor to find them once and for all."

Belle lifted her chin in acknowledgment. "You're a good officer, Noelle. Liberty is blessed to have you."

"I feel the same about her," Noelle said. "But speaking of that, what happened to that hunky shadow that's been following you around for the last few days. You haven't mentioned Emmett at all today."

Belle tugged the potato chip bag out of the ornery machine and lowered her head. "Nope. We're still hoping he can help us track down the one cousin who lived in Bay Ridge at the time of the McGregor murders. But the deputy marshal is not happy with us since he thinks we may taint his father's memory. He was a police officer."

"Will you?"

"I hope not. It's been hard on Emmett. I think he regrets not keeping up with his cousin."

"Family is complicated," Noelle replied. "But you and the marshal seem chummy."

"We're friends," Belle said. "And we have to get this case figured out. Not to mention, the man's saved my life twice now."

"Sounds like a good person to have in your corner."

"Emmett is a good person," Belle said, something in her heart hurting too much. "He's doing his job right now, nothing more."

Noelle shot her a glance. "Have you two grown close?"

"Yes, I guess almost being choked to death brings out my friendly side."

Noelle shook her head. "I'm glad Emmett came along when he did."

"So am I," Belle admitted. "For more reasons than one."

* * *

Belle took Justice home and fed him. Then she took him out back for a while. Justice ran off to explore while she sat down in her bright blue chair and enjoyed the last of the warm sun on her skin.

"Hi," her sister Anita said, trotting down the outside stairs to the yard to join Belle.

"Hi, yourself," Belle said. "How ya doing?"

Anita, the quieter of the twins, sank down in the grass and twirled a strand of her long dark hair. "I guess I'm okay. I like working for Uncle Rico's café, but Cara flirts with all the busboys. It's embarrassing."

"Your sister is a bit more outgoing than you."

"You think?"

Belle laughed at that. "I know she's a pain at times, but you two are to always stick together coming and going to work since Uncle Rico put you on the same schedule."

"We are for now," Anita said. "But I want extra hours and Cara wants the least amount of hours. So…"

"Have you noticed anyone strange hanging around?" Belle asked, fear for her sisters on her mind. "I need to hear daily reports."

Anita shrugged and tugged at a tear in her jeans. "I don't know. I mean, maybe. We've been working there all week but today, this creepy guy kept sneering at us. He even asked why there were two of us."

Belle's antenna went up but she stayed calm. "What did he look like?"

Anita made a twisted face. "Big. You know, the kind who hangs out in the gym a lot? Thick hair but he wore weird glasses."

"Sunshades?"

Anita nodded and adjusted her baggy tank top. "The kind that go from light to dark. Kind of freaked me out."

Could her attacker have been wearing glasses with transitional lenses?

That would explain the sunshades the other day, Belle thought. The late afternoon sun had been bright right before that rain had hit in the park.

"So he didn't take the glasses off when he came inside?"

"No. They were dark and then they got light enough for me to see his eyes before he shoved a hat on his head. Do you think he's the one who's after you, Belle?"

Belle always walked a fine line between keeping her family safe and keeping them unaware of most of what she dealt with on a daily basis. So she had to tread lightly here. She'd sent someone to watch the café but she'd heard nothing. If Gavin would let her, she'd stake out the place herself. But she didn't want her sisters in further danger.

"He sounds like him," she explained to Anita. "He's got it in for me so he could try to harass any of you, too. He's kind of bulky, like you mentioned, and he wears dark sunshades. Never takes them off." Calling to Justice, she worked hard to keep her voice normal. "Do you remember the color of his eyes?"

Anita twisted her chin. "Hazel, maybe?"

Grabbing her phone, she showed her sister the mug shot she'd been using to ID Johnson. "Is this the man?"

Anita took the phone. "That could be him, *sí*."

Lance Johnson's rap sheet described him as having dark shaggy hair and hazel eyes. But when he'd attacked her in the park, Belle remembered his hair as being shorter. She needed a positive ID.

"Do you think he'll try something?" Anita asked, apprehension coloring her question.

"I don't know. But we have to check every lead. You just let me take care of this. I'll speak to Uncle Rico, too. You both might need to stay away from work for a few days, or at least continue to be driven back and forth."

"Okay," Anita said. "Uncle Rico watches out for us, anyway. He's afraid the waiters will hit on us, you know?"

"I do know," Belle said. "I worked there a few summers. You find him if this man returns or call me on my cell, okay?"

Anita nodded. "I will, I promise."

Stretching to hide the fear clawing her insides, Belle added, "Just be aware and stick together. I have a patrol car watching this street. Don't go anywhere on foot until this is over. I need to tell Joaquin that, too, and make him understand."

"That sounds serious," Anita relied.

"Comes with the territory." Then she knocked on her sister's arm with a gentle fist. "Remember what I've always told you and Cara. Be aware and use all the self-defense tricks I've taught you. Understand?"

"Sí, bonita."

Belle's cell buzzed while she smiled at the endearment. "I need to answer this," she told Anita as she stood. "And Justice should get inside and get settled. Wanna come in?"

"No, thanks." Her sister hopped up. "I'm reading a really good book. After dinner, I'm going to finish it."

Belle nodded as Anita took off up the stairs. Then she scanned the small yard and street behind their building but didn't see anything out of the ordinary. "Justice, come," she called before hitting Accept. "Belle Montera."

"Hi. It's Emmett."

His grainy voice shouldn't have made her pulse get so jumpy, but the man seemed to have a strange effect on her.

"Hi," she replied after shutting the door and locking it. Trying to sound unconcerned and nonchalant, she asked, "What's up?"

He let out a breath. "I wanted to apologize for storming out on you and Sergeant Sutherland this morning. This whole business has ruffled my feathers and made me see that I don't have much family left. It's hard to accept Randall might be a killer."

Belle's heart stopped jumping but the jitters were replaced with a steady throbbing beat. She felt sorry for Emmett. He didn't have anyone close in his life from what he'd told her.

"Hey, you want to come over so we can talk?" she asked against her better judgment and being bolder than she'd ever been with any other man. "I didn't like how we left things this morning, either."

"Are you sure?"

"Of course I'm sure, Emmett. We've been through a lot together this week. How about tonight we just hang out like friends do?"

"Friends? Are we still even that?"

"Hey, once you've been chased and shot at together

a few times, I think there's a rule about it making you friends for life."

His chuckle kicked down her backbone. "I didn't know about that rule."

"Well, it triples when you save my life not once, but twice."

"I didn't save you, Belle. You're good at saving yourself."

"Then it's my turn to save you from being bored and lonely and concerned about all of this. Come on over and we'll relax. Maybe watch a corny movie."

"I haven't watched a movie in years."

"How about *The Fugitive*?"

"You're funny, you know that. I'll be there soon. Want me to bring dinner?"

Belle thought about her empty refrigerator. "Yes. Surprise me."

"I can do that."

She ended the call and hurried to call Gavin regarding what her sister had told her. By the time Emmett arrived, she was clean and wearing a blue T-shirt, old well-worn jeans and slip-on sandals.

He'd just walked in with two bags of Chinese takeout when Belle saw her mother coming down the stairs. She couldn't shut the door in her mom's face.

"Belle, come up for dinner," Gina said, stopping when she saw Emmett standing there.

Belle cringed as her petite mother's eyes moved over Emmett until she had to lean her head back to actually see his face. "Oh, you have company?" Then she added in Spanish, "*él es muy guapo.*"

Belle cringed again, knowing that Emmett spoke

Spanish. But her mom was right. The man was very handsome. She rolled her eyes.

He grinned and said, "Is this your beautiful mother, Belle?"

Gina's dimples went into overdrive. "*Sí*, I am her mother and whatever you have in that bag, bring it upstairs and we'll share our food if you'll share yours."

"Mom, I don't think that's a good idea," Belle said, motioning Emmett inside.

"No, I think that's a great idea," Emmett said, clearly enjoying this. "I bought enough fried rice and dumplings to feed a large crowd."

"We have a large crowd," Belle said on a defeated note. "Which you will soon find out."

She shouldn't subject the man to her family all at once. But Emmett needed people and her family was friendly and loving if nothing else. She'd set them all clear on why Emmett was here later. Friends. They were just friends.

"I can't wait," he replied. "Mrs. Montera, may I escort you up to dinner."

Her mother actually giggled. "You certainly may. And a gentleman, too," she said over her shoulder to Belle.

"Don't worry. I know the way," Belle said, motioning for Justice to follow them.

She wanted to update Emmett on what her sister had told her but that would have to wait. She'd called Gavin almost immediately and he had an extra patrol car canvasing the area around her uncle's café and keeping tabs on Johnson's apartment. Lance Johnson was good at hiding and sneaking in and out of places, but he'd slip up one day.

And Belle would be there waiting for him when he did.

Right now, she had no choice but to follow Emmett upstairs.

She was hungry, and he had their food.

This could get interesting, but the smile on his face was so worth the trouble her family would put them both through. She only hoped that once they had criminal matters under control, they could still hang out together. He needed people, and she needed a good friend. Nothing more.

But what if there could be more? Did she want that?

TEN

Emmett listened to the conversation flowing around him in both English and Spanish, glad he had a general understanding of what was being said. It had been a while since he'd been surrounded by a big, loud family.

Belle kept glancing across the table at him, checking to see how he was holding up. So far, her family had gone on with their meal as if they'd known him for a long time. But he could tell they were curious. Probably wanting to ask him a million questions, most of which he couldn't answer.

Her father, of course, had given him a steady no-nonsense once-over before shaking his hand. Her twin sisters had giggled and mumbled things to each other, Anita with a shy smile and Cara with an inquisitive direct stare.

Her brother's eyes stayed hidden behind thick inky bangs. Joaquin glowered at Emmett and remained sullen and quiet while he ate the food his mother had prepared and ignored the food Belle and Emmett were sharing.

"So you two are working together?" Mr. Montera asked now, his tone level even while his dark eyes shot out an intense laser-like inspection.

"Yes, sir," they both replied at once.

Belle smiled at Emmett and then gave him a quick warning look. "A cold case that we need to clear up after a new development. And that is all we can tell you."

Gina Montera did a motherly eye roll. "Her work. Always secretive and dangerous. I worry for her, but she is brave and works hard. I'm also proud, of course."

"And you should be," Emmett said, glancing at Belle. "She's dedicated."

"Are you the one who came to her rescue?" Belle's mom asked, her dark gaze lifting and pinning Emmett.

"I did help Belle recently when someone got ornery with her while she was on her way to meet me. But she's brave and she held her own. Your daughter knows her job."

Anita's wide-eyed gaze moved from him to Belle. She looked as if she wanted to say something, but Belle tilted her chin slightly and Anita looked down at her plate.

That subtle exchange didn't get past their keen mother, but Mrs. Montera let it slip, too. It had to be hard for them, knowing Belle put herself on the line every day.

Belle's mom shifted her gaze to her daughter. "Then I thank you for coming to her aid and I am proud that she is able to handle herself out there."

Mr. Montera's frown deepened as he looked from Belle to his wife. "Belle, you are safe, right?"

"The man just told us she can take care of herself," Mrs. Montera said, patting his cheek. "You look tired. Want some ice cream?"

"Maybe later," her dad replied, his gaze on Belle. "I

have to leave soon for my management meeting with one of the supers"

"Ah, *sí*."

Soon, dinner was over, Mr. Montera had left for his meeting and the girls cleared the table.

"I'll wrap up the leftovers for you," Belle's mom said.

"No. You should keep those," Emmett replied. "I did crash your meal."

"Nonsense. You are welcome here anytime."

Joaquin pushed through the kitchen. "I'm going out."

"No, you're not," Mrs. Montera said. "Just because your father had to leave doesn't mean you get to roam the streets, especially now when your sister has warned us about the man who attacked her."

Joaquin's frown shouted teenage defiance. "My friends are waiting."

Belle touched her brother's arm. "You know we're being extra careful right now. Why don't you hang around? You can come down to my place and we'll play a video game."

Joaquin tossed his bangs and rolled his eyes. "I want to go out."

"No, Joaquin," Belle said. "Not tonight."

"You can't boss me around, Belle."

"I can and I will if it means protecting you," Belle said, sending her mother a worried glance.

"I don't need your protection," her brother shouted before heading up to his room. "I know how to take care of myself."

"I'm sorry," Mrs. Montera said to Belle and Emmett. "He has a very bad attitude these days."

"Teenagers," Emmett said, trying to lighten the tension. But the danger out there was real.

When they were back down in Belle's apartment, he watched her putting away food and then turned to face her. "I guess I should head home."

"No," she said too quickly. "We didn't get a chance to talk. I need to tell you something."

"Oh, okay then, I can stay for a while."

He didn't want to leave, anyway. His place was lonely and too sterile without a woman's touch. Belle's apartment was homey and full of color and flowers. Kind of like her personality.

He should leave. Like now. And he needed to remember how this was a bad idea on so many levels, the first being he might have to help her put Randall away. After that, their heavy work schedules could ruin a good friendship.

She offered him a mineral water over ice and then poured herself one, too. "We can sit out back. I'm sure Justice could use one more break before bedtime."

They went out on the tiny stoop. Belle motioned to a folding chair off the porch and Emmett grabbed it and opened it so he could sit next to a bright red table with glass tiles covering the round top. Belle sat in her comfortable chair. Justice took off to the far corner where a gate to the alley completed a solid wooden fence that enclosed the rectangular yard.

"Nice out here," he said, enjoying the coolness of the summer evening while he scanned the yard several times. "This heat wave has everyone frazzled."

"Yes. New York in summer. Brings out the worst in people."

"Sure does." Emmett leaned in, ready to get down to business. "What did you need to tell me?"

Belle glanced up, then said on a low voice, "My sister Anita told me this earlier." She went on to explain about a man coming into the café where Anita and Cara worked for their Uncle Rico.

"He's taunting my family, Emmett. I've warned all of them and I called Gavin to ask for more protection. My Uncle Rico is aware and my dad is being diligent, too. But is it enough? Noelle and I were shot at again today."

Emmett didn't like this latest news. He wouldn't overreact, however. Belle knew her work, so he had to stay neutral even if apprehension seared through him. "I'll help you in any way, you know that."

"I'll go over his background and see what else I can find—check out gyms around his apartment and go back and confront his cagey landlord once again. Johnson's got it in for me and it goes deeper than my catching him assaulting a woman."

"Hatred like that is dangerous," Emmett warned. "He probably blames you for sending him to jail and ruining his life, but he did that all on his own. Just be careful."

"I'm going to set up camp near his apartment," Belle said. "He's got to show up sooner or later."

"I'll go with you."

"You don't need to do that."

Before she could dispute him, Justice stopped near the back gate and growled low.

Emmett held a hand on Belle's arm as they both became alert.

Belle nodded. "Let's see if anyone tries to get through that gate." She stood. "Got to get to my weapon."

Justice growled again as the gate started shaking.

Emmett stood and moved away from his chair. In the next second, something heavy came barreling down from the rooftop three floors up and landed in the chair where he'd been sitting. The chair's webbing ribbed apart.

The chunky piece of concrete had gone through the flimsy webbing and landed on one of the stone steps with a loud crack that sounded over the neighborhood.

Justice started barking now, his eyes still on the gate.

The pressure on the gate ended as Belle rushed forward. Emmett heard footsteps running away. Belle called Justice back and then reached for her cell to call for backup.

"Are you all right?" Belle said to Emmett after she got off the phone. "That could have hit you."

"Yeah, if I'd still been sitting there, it would have knocked me out." Looking toward the gate, he frowned. "Two of them?"

"The roof," she said, whirling to hurry toward the fire escape on the side of the building. "One at the gate and one on the roof."

"I'll take the fire escape," Emmett said. "You know the stairs inside better."

"I'll grab my gun on the way."

Belle took off, Justice leading the way. Emmett hurried up the rickety fire escape, worried that Belle would run headlong into a would-be killer. But she was capable, and she had Justice. He had to remind himself she'd been at her job long before he came into the picture.

He made the rooftop at about the same time she came bursting through the door. Justice bounded out with her and ran to the far corners but returned and stood at her feet.

After scanning the entire roof, she threw up her hands in frustration. "Impossible. How did they get away?"

Emmett glanced around. The roof was empty. "Is there another way into the building from here?"

"No. Just this door to the inside and up the fire escape. This door is usually locked, and we were right there by the fire escape."

"So they had someone distract us with the gate rattling and then came in through the front?" Emmett examined the heavy door to the roof. "This lock is intact."

"They had to have had access to the key at the front door," Belle said, her eyes going wide. "Emmett, that means they can enter this building anytime they want."

"That or someone you know let them in," he said, his tone grim.

"But my family members are the only ones who know about the key and where we keep it."

"Your immediate family or extended family, too?"

"My mom's sister and my dad's brothers might be aware," she said. "I'll have to ask around."

The door pushed back and her mother stood there, staring at them. "Belle, want to tell me what's going on? I heard a loud noise and then saw you flying up the stairs to the roof. Did your stalker try to get inside here?"

"Someone was here," Belle said. "I called for backup, but they're probably long gone."

Before Belle could explain what had happened, her sisters came running out onto the roof. "Joaquin is gone. He's not in his room."

* * *

An hour later, Belle and Emmett finally found her brother sitting in a park not far from their building. He was with a group of boys gathered on an old picnic table.

Justice alerted and barked, picking up her brother's scent right away.

"This is not good," Belle said, her heart dropping. "I've already had to tell my parents we might have an intruder who wants to kill me and now I might have to arrest my own brother for loitering."

"We'll handle it," Emmett told her, his eyes on the boys in the park.

Belle had to admit, it felt good knowing someone was willing to help her on all sides. She'd always had her family but Emmett saying that caused her whole system to come alive. She was beginning to really care about him. But she had to push that acknowledgment away for now.

When they pulled Emmett's big truck up to the curve, the boys all turned in surprise. Someone shouted, "Cops!"

They took off running, dropping trash on the sidewalks while they scattered in all directions.

Except for Joaquin. He stood there, glaring at her.

"Joaquin, what are you doing?" she asked, checking him over to make sure he wasn't high or hurt. Justice stood with his nose in the air.

"Having some fun," her brother said on a sneer. "Something you should try sometime."

"Hey," Emmett said, stepping in front of Belle. "You

had your whole family worried. If another officer had come along, you'd all be in trouble for loitering."

Her brother looked nervous and for good reason. But that didn't stop his attitude. "Man, you can't come in here and tell me what to do."

"Yes, he can," Belle told her brother. "I'm going to give you a warning this time but next time, remember the loitering laws. This park is off-limits after dark."

Joaquin glanced around, then lowered his head.

"Yep," Emmett said. "All your buddies swarmed away. Left you having to explain things."

"They were scared," Joaquin said in a weak defense. "I'm the one who told them the cops were here."

"They were cowards," Belle retorted. "You can't keep doing this. It will only lead to trouble. They'll leave you holding the bag and I don't want it to be a bag of drugs." Reaching out, she touched his arm. "Because I won't be able to protect you if that happens."

Sullen, Joaquin looked out from underneath his bangs. He almost said something, but then clamped his mouth shut. "Can I go home now?"

"Good idea," Belle said. Then she wrapped her arm across her brother's shoulder. "Did any of those boys have drugs on them?"

"I can't say," Joaquin replied. "Okay? Just let it go."

"For now," Belle said, her voice low. "I won't tell Papá but if you mess up again, I'll have to let him know. Especially since I've warned all of you about a suspect who has it in for me—and my family."

Emmett remained silent, letting her take the lead. Another thing she liked about him. He wanted to protect her, but he also gave her the space to do her job and handle things on her own. Completely the opposite of her ex.

After they got back to her place, she turned to Joaquin. "We had an incident here tonight. Someone managed to get on our roof and drop a chunk of broken concrete down near where Emmett and I were sitting on my back stoop. Mamá and Papá and the girls are all okay. What time did you leave?"

Her brother stared up at the house. "I don't remember."

Belle sent Emmett a glance, then turned in her seat. "What do you mean? You don't know what time you snuck out?"

"I didn't look at a clock."

Shaking her head, she asked, "Did you notice anyone hanging around when you left? Did you make sure the front door was closed tight?"

Joaquin slapped at the back of her seat, his eyes downcast, causing Justice to yelp at him. "Let me out. I don't know anything about any of that."

Belle got out and let the seat down so her brother could scoot out of the jump seat. Joaquin hurried toward the house.

She stood there, watching, and then turned to Emmett. "My brother is not telling me the truth."

"Nope." Emmett glimpsed toward the house. "I think he might know something about what happened here tonight."

"Me, too," she said. "And it'll be up to me to find out what."

ELEVEN

Belle hadn't confronted Joaquin last night. When she'd gotten back inside, her parents wanted to talk to her.

"Did you find him?"

"Yes," she told her mother. "He was with some boys in the park. We broke it up and brought him home."

"I'm grounding him for a month at least," her dad said. "He'll do dishwashing duties in the café and he'll help me paint and clean apartments."

"Good idea but he might give you a hard time."

"Hard work will cure that," her father admonished. "It worked for my brothers and me."

"Now about you and the man stalking you," Mamá said. "What more should we do?"

"Change the locks, for starters," Belle said. "Sarge is going to send round-the-clock patrol cars to monitor our street and the café."

"I'll keep up our watch, too," her dad replied, nodding. "I'll alert all of your uncles again and we'll escort your mother and the girls everywhere they go. I'll keep Joaquin with me."

"This is why I wanted you to be aware," Belle said.

"But please don't take matters into your own hands. That will only lead to more trouble."

"We take care of our own," her father said. "But I won't make a move without letting you know first."

That was the best she would get from him. Her father wouldn't do anything violent, but he would stand his ground.

Now, she was with Emmett in her SUV, Justice in his kennel in the back. "Today, we start with the fitness centers and gyms around Canarsie," she told Emmett. "I've reported everything to Sarge so he's aware of what I'm planning."

Emmett gave her a questioning glance. The man sure looked good first thing in the morning, all fresh and woodsy smelling, that crisp, close-cut hair shimmering a dark gold.

"Exactly what are you planning?" he asked, bringing Belle out of her crush.

"You sound worried, Marshal Gage."

"I am worried. I've seen you in action."

"I told you, first these places and then we'll revisit Lance Johnson's charming building super, Albert Stein, and get the truth out of him, at least. For all we know, he's in on this with Johnson."

Emmett absorbed that and said, "So Johnson's car has been impounded for illegal parking?"

After checking traffic, she weaved in and out of lanes.

"He didn't pay so yes, his vehicle has been removed from the lot. I hope we'll get a warrant to search it since I IDed it as the car we saw the other day at the storage unit."

Emmett glanced over at her. "I can back you up on that, at least."

"His parole officer is looking for him, too. So you might get to serve him a warrant yet."

"I'd like nothing more," Emmett said, his tone grim. "In fact, I'll alert my division and ask for that assignment."

Belle knew he'd get it done. Emmett seemed to have the respect of everyone who knew him. Too bad his cousin hadn't fared so well.

"Okay, so there are three different workout places within walking distance of Johnson's apartment," she said. "Let's start with this one."

She pulled into a beat-up parking lot and squeezed the SUV into a tight space between a sports car and a big sedan. "Well, the clientele certainly drives nice vehicles."

"Not like Johnson's at all," Emmett replied. "He abandons both his home and his vehicle. He must have someone hiding him."

"And helping him to harass my family."

Belle shuddered each time she thought of that chunk of concrete coming down so close to Emmett and her.

"Here we go," she said, using her key fob to open the back door of the SUV. "Justice will make sure no one tries to bully us."

Emmett followed her into the stifling hot gym where boxing rings warred with heavy weightlifting equipment and a musty smell permeated the air. Belle showed Lance Johnson's picture to a man who said he was the manager.

"Yeah, I remember him. He came in here a lot a couple years ago. Didn't pay his monthly dues so I kicked him out. Haven't seen him since. He was a trouble-maker, anyway."

"One down and two to go."

The next fitness center looked new and smelled a little better than the last one. It had a yoga room and a spin class. "Not Johnson's type," she said to Emmett.

They talked to a woman who wore a zip-up light-weight jacket and matching workout leggings, her gym shoes designer status. "I've never seen that man in here," she said with her nose in the air. Then she checked the books. "No record of him, either."

When they were back outside, Belle said, "Okay, one more."

Belle drove about three blocks past Johnson's apart-ment building and pulled around the back of an old brick building that could have been a garage at one time.

They entered the big industrial doors and saw a true weightlifting arena. "We need to see the manager," she told the young man who greeted them at an old beat-up metal desk.

A burly man with a shaved head glared his way to them. "What can I do for you, officers?" he asked, giv-ing Justice a narrow-eyed glance.

Belle pulled out the picture of Lance Johnson. "We're trying to locate this man. We think he might work out here. Do you know him?"

The man whose name tag said Perkins nodded. "Yeah, that's Lance Johnson, all right. He comes and goes and he owes me money. What kind of trouble is he into now?"

"The kind you don't want to be involved in," Emmett replied. "When was the last time he was here?"

Perkins went to the desk and pulled up a sign-in sheet. "About three weeks ago. That's the night I told him to either pay up or find another place to lift weights."

"It seems Johnson owes money to everyone we talk to," Emmett said on a droll note.

Perkins sneered in agreement.

"I'm definitely seeing a pattern," Belle replied as they left with Perkin's assurance that if Johnson came in, he'd personally make sure to give them a call.

Next, they went to see Albert Stein for round three.

"You two again?" he asked, his jitters causing him to shuffle too many papers. "I told you, Lance Johnson skipped out on the rent he owes me and now I hear his car's been impounded. I don't know where the man is and at this point, I really don't care."

"Where's your ring, Albert?" she asked, her gaze steady on his ring finger.

"I don't know what you're talking about."

"Yes, you do." She edged closer, Justice by her side. "You see, Lance Johnson was wearing that ring the night he attacked me and I noticed you had on a similar ring when we talked the other day. Now it's not on your finger. I want to know why."

"I don't have to explain that to you," Albert replied, crossing his meaty arms over his chest in defiance.

"But you do," Belle replied. "I was here the other day with another K-9 officer. We found Johnson's car and then someone started shooting at us. You didn't seem to be on the premises. Did you fire on us, Albert?"

Albert's beady eyes widened and filled with shock. "No, I didn't fire any shots. I don't know anything about that. I was at the doctor's office all day. Gout." His expression filled with self-pity, then he turned ugly again. "You can't pin that on me. People shoot at each other in this city all the time."

"But you might have to explain a lot to a building inspector," Emmett said, pointing to the flies gathering at the overflowing trash can and a raw wire hooked up to several different electronic appliances behind the front desk.

Albert's ruddy face turned deep red but he dug in his pocket and pulled out the ring and held it up. "Okay, all right. I took the stupid ring from Johnson's apartment after he got behind on his rent. Figured it might be worth something since he liked to flash it around all the time. But the pawnbroker I took it to said it's worth about twenty-five bucks, tops. That's the honest truth."

"Why would Johnson buy this ring?" Belle wondered out loud.

"He's a show-off," Albert replied. "He likes the finer things, but he doesn't have the finesse to pull that off and he sure doesn't have the money. He's a loser."

"He's gonna be a prisoner again when I get my hands on him," Emmett replied. "You'd better let us know if he shows back up here or you'll be in a whole mess of trouble, got it?"

"I got it," Albert said. "That man has been nothing but a pain in my neck."

Belle lifted her chin. "I need that ring for evidence."

"It's mine," Albert whined.

"It's stolen," she reminded him after she pulled a couple of tissues out of a box on his desk.

Albert reluctantly handed over the ring. "If you people will leave me alone, I'll gladly give it to you."

"Good idea since technically you stole it and I don't want to take you in for lifting this cheap thing."

"I don't need that, either," he said, shaking his head.

"Thank you, Albert," Belle said with a smile. "And remember, you call us if Johnson shows his face around here."

Albert nodded and sank down on his rickety chair.

"I kind of feel sorry for him," Belle said after they'd left the building. "He's obviously not in good health and he has to deal with the likes of Lance Johnson."

"He's a survivor," Emmett replied. "He'll land on his swollen ankles, trust me."

Belle glanced over at the man who'd stood by her since the night he'd helped save her life. She did trust him, which surprised her. She wasn't a paranoid, distrustful person to begin with but this job demanded that she couldn't fall for any sob stories or excuses until she'd studied all the evidence and found the truth. She trusted her coworkers, but they all had a silent code that kept them at a distance, anyway. It worked like a protective shield around all of them.

And yet, she knew anyone in her unit would stand by her same as Emmett was doing. But would he be willing to take things further than just having her back?

"Well, we've accomplished a few things today," she said later after they'd grabbed a pizza from a favorite hangout down the street from the K-9 headquarters.

They strolled back to the unit, the last of the sun's heat turning toward sunset.

Belle held up her index finger. "Everyone who knows Lance Johnson has it in for him, so that and the fact that he didn't follow through with his probation officer has him hiding out. We should be able to get a warrant to search his vehicle now."

"His ring didn't amount to much, but Albert confessed all and should do the right thing now," Emmett added.

"But we still have two wanted men on the loose."

"I'm going to deepen my search for Randall," Emmett said. "I can't help but think he's around for some reason. He might have heard on the news about the current murders, which were so similar to the cold-case murders. Maybe he came back to find out what was going on."

"So you think the Emery murders were the work of a copycat—and not the same killer?"

Emmett shrugged. "I wish I knew. If my relative did commit the first murders, I sure hope he didn't come back to kill again on the twentieth anniversary."

"I don't know, either. I hate to say this, Emmett," Belle started. Motioning to a bench underneath a young oak, she sat down. Justice did the same. "But what if he came back because he's afraid someone's naming him for the McGregor murders? Regardless of whether he killed again or there's a copycat. What if he wants to tie up loose ends?"

Emmett rubbed a hand down his chin and glanced at the street. "I hate to say that, too, but yes, I have thought it. I don't know what's going on inside Randall's head but he has to be messed up. If I can find him and get him to talk, maybe it'll stop him from doing something stupid like killing again."

"But what if he's already killed again? What if he *is* responsible for these new murders?"

"Then our best shot is to prove that," Emmett replied, a tinge of anger in his words. "Not an easy task, but it's my job, Belle. You have to know I'll do what's right."

"I believe you will."

Belle dropped it for now. Her heart beat with sympathy for this good man trying to deal with a troubled relative.

"Hey, you know I'm on your side, right?" she said, aware of other officers passing by. "You can talk to me about anything."

Emmett's eyes shimmered like a blue lake. "Can I talk to you about the way you make me feel?" he asked, his eyes on her.

Belle's pulse quickened while her body buzzed with a sweet surprise. "How do I make you feel?"

"Like I want to get to know you better," he admitted with a sheepish grin. "You're a beautiful distraction. All of this is new for me. I tend to keep to myself." Then he gave her another quick glance. "I quit dating because of work and I pledged to never date a woman in law enforcement. Too complicated and I figure I'd go full protection mode and she'd wind up resenting me."

Belle couldn't hide her surprise. "Well, that pledge explains a few things. I've been getting mixed vibes from you since we met, but I figured you were married to your work and…you'd always be hands-off." Shaking her head, she said, "You can relax, Marshal. I'm kind of hands-off right now, too. I'm still recovering from a man who tried his best to control me."

"That's the problem," he said, the sounds of traffic all around them. "I don't want to control you, Belle. I just want to be around you and that goes against my vow to stay away."

"And I threw you right into having to search for a relative who might be a killer and protecting me from a dangerous man. Not to mention my family's chaos."

"It's a beautiful chaos," he said. "I miss that." Then he shrugged. "As for the rest, yes, we need to get these cases out of the way."

"Okay," Belle said, getting that particular vibe loud and clear. He didn't want to take things further. Well, she didn't want that, either. "Glad we cleared the air."

She stood at about the same time he did and they crashed. Emmett grabbed her to keep her steady, their eyes meeting, his hands on her arms.

Emmett tugged her close, his gaze moving over her face. "I guess we could test that theory."

"What?" She could barely breathe. Her heart fluttered away and a sweet longing stirred her soul.

Emmett kissed her right there on the street, around the corner from the front door to the precinct building. Belle should have pulled away. Too many officers coming and going, too many emotions hitting at her resistance.

But she couldn't let go.

Emmett ended the kiss way too soon. But when he stepped back, realization flared and put out the other flame between them.

"That was a mistake," he said. Then he quickly

amended. "I mean, not that kissing you was a mistake. I liked that part. But I know better. I'm sorry I put you in a bad position."

Belle had to find her voice and get her brain settled. "We can't do this. Our work, the crazy hours, the cases we're working on together. Fraternizing is never a good idea. You just said that and then you kiss me?"

He glanced around and so did she. "I'm sorry, Belle. I shouldn't have."

Thankful that no one was walking by, Belle called to Justice. "I have to get back. It's late and I have reports to file."

Emmett nodded. "I should go home and book an appointment to have my head examined."

"Why? Are you sick?"

"No, but I know better."

"Emmett, this threw me." She shrugged. "I don't have a very good record in the relationship department and you obviously don't want a relationship with anyone."

"Threw me, too, and threw my self-imposed pledge right out the window. But I liked kissing you and I want to kiss you again."

Belle wanted to allow that but hesitated. "Again, not a good idea right now. We've been thrown together on two cases and we're not thinking straight."

"So you're determined to avoid the obvious?"

"No, I'm just cautious. I like you and I owe you my life."

"Is that why you kissed me back? Because you feel obligated, filled with gratitude?"

Belle laughed and started back around the building.

"I can assure you, Marshal Gage, that right there was not gratitude."

He caught up with her. "So you're saying if we went on a real date and were walking through a park, you'd let me kiss you again."

She grinned. "As long as I'm not being mauled by a criminal, yes, I'd let you kiss me again. But I'm going to have to think about this, a lot. Kissing you is one thing. But watching you walk away is another."

A fire of frustration roared across his face. "I'll see you around, then, Officer Montera."

"I'll be right here, Deputy Marshal Gage."

She watched him walk to his truck, then turned to go inside.

And ran smack into Sergeant Gavin Sutherland.

TWELVE

"Uh…hello, sir," Belle said, her skin burning red with embarrassment. Her gaze moved from Gavin to watching Emmett walk around the corner to where he'd parked his vehicle.

Gavin inclined his head and glanced to the street. "You and Gage seem to be on good terms."

Not knowing what Sarge had seen, she bobbed her head. "Yes, we get along great."

Gavin's eyebrow twitched but he didn't say anything to her about what he might have heard or seen. "Any work-related news for me?"

"We're after a warrant to search Lance Johnson's vehicle and we found the ring he was wearing." She explained about Albert Stein. "So that verifies that Johnson had to be my attacker since it was his ring that Albert swiped. I sent it to the lab to check for DNA and fibers." Tugging at her bun, she added, "With the fibers and epidermis particles the techs scraped from my fingernails, added to this new information, we're building a strong case against Johnson."

Gavin crossed his arms and pursed his lips. "That's all great, but we need to *find* your attacker."

"I'm on that, sir. He's good at hiding but we do have people at his old hangouts watching out for him. None of them want him back, either."

Gavin scanned the area and nodded. "And Randall Gage? No one seems to be able to get a handle on him, not even a trained US marshal who happens to be his relative."

"Emmett's trying, sir. He's good at his job and I know he wants to find out the truth. He's put out feelers and asked around all over Bay Ridge and beyond."

"We need to track down and verify any leads, Belle."

"We will, sir. We're meeting up tomorrow to explore Randall's work records, if we can find any. He works for pay under the table a lot from what Emmett's dad left in his notes."

"Keep your focus."

"Yes, sir. I will. Emmett and I might be becoming friends but that's it."

"Right." Gavin's hard-edged face softened. "I remember saying that about Brianne and me, and you see where that got me."

"You two make it work somehow," Belle replied, smiling.

Gavin's usually stoic expression turned into a broad grin. "Yes, we do. In spite of the odds. With her help, I've come a long way in learning how to deal with people. She's part of why I'm here today. She believed in me when it seemed no one else did." He jingled his keys. "Speaking of that, I'm going to go get Tommy from the groomer and then I'm going home to my wife."

"Have a good night, sir," Belle said, Gavin's words buzzing in her head. She believed in Emmett even when some on the team didn't trust him. She couldn't blame Bradley or even Penny for having doubts. Emmett reminded them of the man who could have possibly killed their parents.

Whirling, she took Justice and headed to the reception desk. "Hi, Penny," she said. "Can I ask you something regarding your parents' case?"

Twenty-four-year-old Penny's brown eyes took on the guarded wariness everyone around here was used to seeing. "I guess." Her freckles looked more pronounced when she got anxious, Belle noticed.

"I know you've been asked this over and over, but I was wondering if you can go over with me what you remember about the man who murdered your parents."

Penny shifted in her chair. Her mouth set in a firm line tightened and her brow puckered. "He had on that horrible clown mask with blue hair. But…his eyes. I can't say for sure what color they were—maybe greenish—but if I ever saw him again, I think I'd know him by his eyes."

This was all in the file, of course, and Penny had answered these questions many times the past few months since the second murders. But Belle kept hoping Penny might suddenly remember something, anything. "Okay. Maybe his eyes struck for a reason. Did you ever think you might have seen him someplace else?"

Penelope shrugged. "Bradley used to pick me up at the day care. I guess he could have been someone who dropped off his own kids there, if he even had kids. I don't remember much but…he had to have known my parents. Why else target them? Why else leave me alive and well? And give me a toy?"

Belle nodded sympathetically. "What was the name of the day care?"

"Happy Day. No. Happy Child," Penelope replied. "Although I don't remember being very happy there. I always wanted to be home with my parents." Then Penny stopped, her lips twisting. "I've answered a lot of questions, but I've blocked most of that time. I think there might have been a man who always brought toys to us."

Belle halted, remembering the picture Emmett had found of Randall as a little boy holding a stuffed dog. "What else do you remember? Can you describe the man?"

Penelope shook her head. "No. I mostly noticed the cute little stuffed animals," Penelope said. "Whoever killed my parents gave me a little monkey wrapped in plastic. I don't like monkeys very much now."

Belle found the picture of Randall she'd sent to Gavin that first night. It was a longshot; Penny had been only four years old then. "Does this look like the man from the day care?"

Penny studied the picture, her expression darkening. "I can't be sure. It's been so long."

"Thanks, Penny," Belle said, wishing her friend didn't have to go through this again. What a nightmare.

Belle and Justice headed home. Tired but alert, Belle kept an eye on the rearview mirror and thought about Emmett, her brother and her family. Then she thought about Bradley and Penny and what they'd been through. She prayed for all of them.

"Father, take care of the people I love. And please help Emmett get through this."

Justice listened to her spoken prayers and woofed an Amen.

She loved her partner so much.

Why couldn't humans be so easy to love?

When she got home, her sisters were sitting on the inside stairs, waiting for her.

"Belle, we need to talk," Cara said. "Inside your apartment."

"Okay." Cara looked so serious. Belle's heart rate increased tenfold. "Is everything okay?"

Anita shut the door and nodded at her sister. "Tell her."

Cara twisted her braid and said, "When Uncle Rico brought us home today, we saw Joaquin talking to a man. It looked like the man gave him a wad of money."

Belle froze, her heart dropping like a brick. "Where was this?"

Cara scuffed her pink sneakers against the wooden floor. "Near the old park down the way where you found him the other night."

"Did Uncle Rico see him?"

"No," Anita said. "I poked Anita and we both watched him but didn't say anything." Shrugging, she looked up at Belle. "We decided to tell you first."

"You did the right thing," Belle replied, her mind spinning ahead. "What did the man look like?"

"Like the one you described." Anita pushed at her long hair. "The same man who came into the café the other day."

Belle tried to keep the panic out of her voice. "Text me when Joaquin gets home. I want to talk to him."

"Don't tell him we said anything," Cara said in a low voice. "He gets really mad when we mess with him."

"Well, he can get over that," Belle said as she fed Justice and gave him fresh water before letting him out back. "I won't say who told me, though."

"Oh, and there's one more thing," Anita said. "The man got into a car that we think we recognized."

"What kind of car?"

"One like your ex Percy used to drive. Black. An old BMW."

Belle's heart did flip-flops and her whole system went still again. "Are you telling me that the man who tried to choke me to death got in a car with Percy Carolo?"

"It looked like Percy," Cara told her. "It happened fast while we were stopped at the traffic light by the park so we could be wrong."

Belle motioned to her sisters and took them into her arms. "You did good. This is very important information. Don't mention this to Mamá and Papá, okay? I'll talk to them in private. Joaquin could run away if he thinks we suspect him."

"We won't," Cara said, her hand reaching up to push Belle's falling hair out of her eyes. "What do you think he's doing with that man?"

"I don't know," Belle said. "But you don't need to worry. I have a lot of people watching out for us and Justice will protect this whole house."

She kissed her sisters and sent them upstairs. "I'll be up for dinner after I freshen up."

She almost called Emmett after they left but she needed to process this. Why would Joaquin be taking money from Lance Johnson? And why would Johnson have any reason to be hanging out with her vindictive, bitter ex-boyfriend?

At a tense dinner where Joaquin picked at his food and ignored everyone, Belle tried to keep the conversation flowing while she prayed the whole time that her sisters wouldn't blurt something out. Her mother watched all of them with a hawk eye but remained quiet. She'd probably question the twins and Belle later. After helping with the dishes, Belle came back to her apartment and immediately did a background check on Percy Carolo.

They'd met years ago at the police academy and had hit it off instantly. Percy was one of those beautiful men who had a lot of charm but no substance. Belle had realized that too late, however. They'd had to be careful while in training, but they'd dated and things became serious pretty quickly. When graduation time came, things took a turn for the worst.

Belle had passed with flying colors but Percy had failed due to a bad attitude and a constant fight with authority.

"I can't believe this," Percy had said by way of congratulating her. "You get through and leave me in the dirt?"

"Percy, we both had the same training. You know how hard I worked for this."

"What about me, Belle? I worked hard and still got

shot down at every turn. It's not fair. I'm every bit as qualified as you."

"Of course you are," she'd replied, hoping to soothe him.

But Percy couldn't be soothed, and he didn't have the grace to be happy for her.

He hadn't taken things very well at the time, but because she'd seen his good side when they'd first started dating, Belle believed she could make it work despite how he'd started trying to undermine her and manipulate her. She went on to become a rookie officer while he got odd jobs here and there and finally wound up in security.

But he was never happy being a mall cop or a night watchman and claimed he would have been better at her job than she was. Which made no sense. He had no patience with humans or animals and scorned all of his superiors and coworkers. A lot of talk and no real action.

She'd ended the bad romance when they'd gotten into a fight on the day she should have been celebrating getting on with the Brooklyn K-9 Unit. Angry and jealous, he'd come at her and almost hit her. Taking him down and knocking him flat on his back hadn't helped matters.

That ended her long run with a confused, abusive, hotheaded man who'd almost ruined her self-confidence and could have cost her a career if she'd stayed with him. Being with Percy had made her distrustful toward other men.

That's why she'd held back with Emmett. But Emmett wasn't anything like Percy. Emmett was confident and brave and went beyond the call of duty. He knew his job well and he got along with just about everyone. He just didn't want to commit to anyone. Especially someone like her.

Belle couldn't consider anything beyond friendship until she was out from under this cloud of fear for her family and for herself. Emmett obviously didn't need her in his life. He had to find his cousin. Emmett was closed off and shuttered, maybe because he'd lost both his parents and his grief had hardened his heart. He lived for his work. Period.

Remembering their kiss, Belle tried to clear her head and get back to business.

Now she wondered if Percy had been keeping tabs on her since the day they'd broken up. She hadn't seen Percy since she'd left his apartment that night. Where had he been for the past two years?

After searching for over an hour, Belle knew exactly where Percy had been. More odd jobs and short stints at various places around Brooklyn. The man couldn't hold down a job.

Then she found something that set her hair on edge and made her pulse burn.

Percy Carolo was currently employed as a security guard at City Wide Storage. The very storage unit where someone had shot at Belle and Emmett a few days ago.

Her stomach roiling, Belle stared at her laptop screen and wondered if her ex had somehow teamed up with Lance Johnson to harass her and her family. How could that even be possible?

What were the odds?

Then she reminded herself that while she lived in a

big city, small neighborhoods had their own grapevines and ways of communicating. Anything was possible.

Unable to sleep, she made notes and set up a timeline to see if she could match a cross section between Percy and Lance Johnson. They could have easily moved in the same circles—the gym, piecemeal work habits, bars where angry bitter men hung out and picked fights with each other. Somehow, she had to find a way to connect them.

And she would definitely plan to do a little surveillance at the park up the street. Because now, they'd possibly gotten her baby brother involved and there was no way on earth she would let Joaquin go down that road.

Not without a fight, anyway.

THIRTEEN

Emmett walked into the 646 Diner and searched among the many NYPD uniforms to find Belle in a corner booth with Justice lying at her feet.

All around, officers sat in clusters in the old booths and chunky tables enjoying the greasy-spoon menu, laughing and discussing life. Some of them noticed him and waved since he'd somehow become a fixture around these parts lately.

Maybe he'd get his photo up on the wall, too, he thought with a wry twist.

"Hey," he said as he settled down across from Belle in the booth and removed his dark cap. "What's up? Your message sounded kind of frantic."

"I am frantic," Belle admitted, her pretty eyes dark with apprehension. She told him about her sisters seeing Joaquin taking money from a man in the park. "They said the man looked like Lance Johnson, the same man Anita saw in my uncle's café."

"Okay, so why would he give your brother money?"

"That's the question," Belle said, staring at her half-eaten eggs and toast. "I didn't get to corner Joaquin last night, but I explained what was going on to my parents. We're all on edge. The girls and I were tense and worried at dinner and Joaquin barely ate."

Emmett didn't like the sound of this. "The boy's in trouble, Belle. We need to question him."

"I am, today, somehow." She lowered her head and then whispered, "There's more. The girls saw Lance Johnson get in a car with someone I know."

"Okay? Who?"

"My ex-boyfriend Percy Carolo."

"Your ex?" Emmett touched a hand to his coffee cup. "You've never talked about him much."

"And for good reason. The man messed with my head and tried to mess with my career. He didn't take it well when we got in a fight about my making it in law enforcement when he couldn't. He came at me and I dropped him on his back."

A heat flared in Emmett's gut. "Did he abuse you?"

Belle glanced away and then back to him. "He tried. Not so much physically but he tried to undermine me and make me feel bad about myself, whined at me for getting a promotion and constantly implied he would do better at my job than I ever could."

"Did he also work for the force?"

She shook her head. "No. We met in the academy and trained together but he flunked out and had to settle for pick-up work here and there—security mostly. From what I've gathered, he subs a lot in security and works crowd control at big events, whatever he can find."

"Okay, so why would he be with Lance Johnson?"

Belle sat still, her eyes holding Emmett's. She couldn't seem to bring herself to say the words.

So Emmett did it for her. "You think those two have partnered up to attack you and harm your family, Belle?"

"It looks that way," she said, letting out a breath. Then she told him what they'd found out so far. "If Percy's involved, he'll play Lance Johnson like a fiddle and have the man doing his bidding. And if he's got my little brother involved, I'll go after both of them and make them pay dearly."

Emmett touched his hand on hers in a brief display of assurance. "Steady. Don't go rogue here. We do this by the book, and we'll bring 'em both in. Together."

"You shouldn't have to deal with this, Emmett. You've got enough just trying to find Randall."

"I'm in it," he said, his tone firm. "I'm in it for you and I won't leave you on your own. This is dangerous."

"Well, there's one more piece to the puzzle," she said, her wary expression showing the stress of the last few days. "Percy works at the City Wide Storage warehouse where you keep your parents' stuff."

Emmett let out a breath. "Are you kidding me?"

"I wish. He's either been watching me and saw me there with you or…he saw us and called Lance to come and do us in. I don't know yet. But… I'm going to find out."

"*We're* going to find out," Emmett corrected. "Don't do this without me."

She nodded, gratitude in her eyes. "Thank you, Emmett."

He gazed over at her, his own concerns deepening and turning stormy. "Belle, what's going on with us?"

"I don't know," she admitted. "But one day, when

this is all behind us, maybe we can figure that out together."

"If you can trust me," he said. "This Percy left you in a mess, didn't he?"

"He did. I haven't dated much since him because I love my work and some men just can't handle that."

"I'm not one of those men," he said. "I admire you and see you as a valuable part of the NYPD. Don't you ever forget that."

"You're a good man, Emmett."

"Don't forget that either, then," he said, giving her what looked like a genuine smile. "Now, let's get to work."

Both of their phones buzzed as if on cue.

Belle answered hers first. "Belle, it's Lani."

"Hi, Lani," Belle said. She liked Lani Jameson even though some thought she got special treatment because she was married to a chief from another K-9 unit. But Lani had joined *their* team to avoid any conflicts and worked hard to prove herself. Sometimes Belle got together with Lani and Noelle for girl talk. "What's up?"

"We could use your help," Lani replied. "We've tracked a stray dog who recently had pups to an old two-family brick home not far from the precinct. She's under the house with her puppies and we're trying to lure her out since we heard the house has been condemned. I thought you might be able to help since you're so good with soothing the dogs when they're in training."

Belle thought of all the things she needed to be working on but she couldn't turn down Lani or a hurting animal. "We'll be there in fifteen minutes," she said. "Emmett Gage is with me."

"Oh, okay," Lani replied. "So you and Emmett—seeing a lot of each other these days?"

"Working on a case, as I've said," Belle reminded Lani, lifting her gaze to where Emmett stood, taking his own call. She could just picture Lani's blue eyes going bright with interest. "For now."

"Okay, we'll talk later," Lani said. "Thanks, Belle."

Belle ended the call and took one last sip of coffee. Dropping some bills on the table, she motioned to Justice and they met up with Emmett at the front door.

After explaining that Lani needed some help, she asked, "Do you want to come with me? We can work on these new developments after we see about this stray dog."

"Yes," he said. "I told you I'm in this. Unless I get called away, I'm going to shadow you as often as I can." Then he added, "And that call I got? A friend on the force thinks he spotted Randall at a diner near where he used to live. Couldn't be sure it was him since it's been a while since my friend has seen Randall, but I'm going to case the place and see if he shows up again. My source said he was there earlier. Goes there a lot for coffee, if it's him, that is."

Surprised, Belle said, "Should you go?"

"No, Randall's not there now. My source confirmed that. I can help you today. But tomorrow morning, I'll be at that old diner and let's hope I see Randall there."

"Meantime, I'll let Sarge know," she said as they loaded up Justice and headed toward the street Lani had named. "He can put someone on the diner, too, for now."

"Yeah, he'd want to know," Emmett said on a gritty

note. "No reason to give him anything else to chew on while he wonders if he can trust me or not."

"We all trust you, Emmett. It's just that trust comes hard when you're dealing with murder and mayhem."

"Yeah, well, we both have that problem," he replied.

But the look in his eyes told her he wanted her to know he was dependable.

Belle believed that, at least. She could depend on Emmett to finish what he'd started. But she couldn't trust him to start something with her and then not break it off when he decided he couldn't handle it.

The noonday heat beat down on them like falling embers, but Emmett was determined to get this dog and her pups out from under this collapsing house. He had a lot to think about and he'd rather be casing the neighborhood where his cousin might possibly be but he'd promised Belle he'd help with this stray and her little family. Only it was taking longer than they'd planned.

"Got any more ideas?" he asked Belle after an hour of sweating and calling and offering treats to the scared, scrawny German shepherd.

Lani told them she'd named the mama dog Brooke, short for Brooklyn, and that best she could tell from shining a light down in the hole was that five puppies were with Brooke. They could hear the furry puppies yelping and crying out where they were embedded in the deep hole their mama must have dug to protect them.

Belle refused to leave them there.

"It's supposed to storm later," she told Emmett. "Look at the sky. Dark. They'll get wet when the water comes down from the roof."

"Well, we're running out of ideas," he said as he belly-crawled as close to the dogs as he could get. "If I get stuck, you'll have to ply me with treats, too."

Belle laughed at that. She looked adorable with her hair falling down and dirt on her sweaty nose. Her love for animals showed in her concern for these little ones and their mother.

That kind of commitment made Emmett want to be around her even more. She surprised him on a daily basis, something his jaded mind couldn't comprehend. But their conversation last night had set a new pace between them, one that kept things on a professional level. But then he'd gone and kissed her, which had blown away his theory of not getting involved.

"How about we put some dry food in water and soften it?" she said, causing him to come back to the present. "Maybe she's too weak to eat a chew treat."

"Whatever might work," he replied. Like everything else involving her, Emmett was beginning to go all in.

Belle went to her SUV and got water and a bowl. Justice followed back and forth with his eyes but remained sitting where she told him. She didn't want her partner to scare the frightened mama dog. But Justice was trained to stay on task, so he took it all in with wide eyes and perked up ears.

After she'd soaked the kibbles, Belle slowly slid the bowl close to the tight opening under the crooked porch, brushing at spiderwebs and old wasp nests.

"C'mon, Brooke. Sweet girl, let us help you," Belle said, her voice soft and reassuring. "We'll take you and your babies to a safe place where you can all thrive." Smiling, she kept cooing and speaking in a calm voice.

"I think your little fluffy balls of fur can be trained to become some of the best of the best. What do you think? Your five cuties becoming NYPD K-9s? Pretty impressive, huh?"

"They do look like full-blooded shepherds," Emmett noted. "You might be right on that, Belle."

"We think so," Lani added. "Just need to get them in and let Doc Mazelli have a look."

Behind her and Emmett, Lani stood trying to do her best to help, her blond messy bun even messier now. "Belle, do you want me to take over?"

"Nope. Let her get used to me," Belle said. "Just keep Justice happy so he doesn't scare her."

Lani called to Justice and ruffled his fur. Her K-9 partner, Snapper, was nearby so she ordered Justice to stand with him. Belle's partner seemed to take it all in stride. Emmett wished he could.

"She's moving toward the bowl," Belle said, handing him a short leash. "Emmett, as soon as she eats a bite or two, you'll have to throw this leash like a lasso and hold her by her fur and tug her out so we can get her in a kennel."

"I'm ready," Emmett said, amazed at Belle's dedication.

The mama dog finally took the bait and dove toward the waiting food. Belle let her eat several bites while she kept petting the hungry mama on the head and reassuring her. Then she moved the dish closer to the opening, allowing Emmett a chance to grab the dog and drag her out.

Emmett was careful to be gentle as he roped the soft fabric across the dog's head and tugged on her middle.

She growled and tried to nip at him, but he held her steady. "Got her."

He passed the yelping dog off to Lani and Noelle, who got her into a kennel and gave her more water, all the while talking to her in soothing voices.

Belle went in and grabbed the first of the puppies and soon they had all of them out, one by one, until all five were accounted for. They were dirty and skinny but still alive, their big black eyes bright with fear.

By the time they'd finished up and had the puppies in a separate kennel in Lani's vehicle, the sky had turned dark and big drops of rain hit their sweaty faces.

"Thank you for helping," Belle said once they were headed back to the precinct. "I need a good shower and I'm sure you want to get on with your day."

Emmett glanced over at her, his mind in turmoil with protecting her and needing to hunt down his cousin. "I do. You need to follow up on the connection between Lance Johnson and your ex."

"Yes, that I will do."

"I'm going home to get cleaned up," Emmett said, watching as Lani and Noelle took Brooke and her puppies to the training center, where the vet would give them all examinations and clean them up. "Then I'm going to swing by the diner where my friend thought he saw Randall. How about I check back with you later and we can compare notes?"

"Okay," Belle said. "I'll be here, catching up on paperwork and calling around to find out what's up with my ex and Lance Johnson. They had to have run into each other somewhere. I need to prove they've been seen together recently beyond what my sisters told me."

"You'll be careful, right?" Emmett asked. "Don't go out alone. Take a buddy if I'm not back."

Belle shook her head. "You tend to forget what I do for a living, Marshal." Then she put her hands on her hips. "Let me rephrase that. You know exactly what I do for a living."

"Yes," he replied. "I haven't forgotten that for a moment since I met you." And now that she knew how he felt about things, she wouldn't forget it, either.

She slanted her eyes at him as she bent her head to one side. "I get it now. We met under unusual circumstances and now we're forced together until this ends. At least I know where I stand with you."

"Nope, you have no clue where you stand with me, Belle."

Emmett left the building, well aware that Belle's coworkers were watching him like a hawk. If he didn't produce something soon on Randall's whereabouts, he might get asked to leave and never return. He was in too deep with Belle even after he'd tried to explain his stance.

He and Belle might not have a chance to finish what they'd started on a personal level. He should have been glad about that.

Since he didn't plan on letting her go despite his stupid pledge, he decided he'd work double time to solve both of these cases.

And he'd stay close to Belle, no matter the outcome.

FOURTEEN

After Belle reported what her sisters had seen to Gavin, he suggested she stay put for today. "I'll send someone else to ask around about your ex. Makes sense he might have hung around the same locations as Johnson and somehow, they started comparing notes."

Belle wondered how, then a thought dropped into her brain. "This case, sir. The cold case."

"What's that got to do with this?" Gavin asked.

"It was all over the news, in all the local papers. We were on the news when the second set of murders happened. That's probably how Lance found me again. If he was in a place with Percy, and the news report was on television, they could have compared notes again."

Gavin nodded. "And not in a good way."

"No, sir. They both have grudges against me."

"Okay, you stay here. I'm sending someone to the storage warehouse and back to the gyms and bars around Johnson's neighborhood. Let's pull up a photo of both of them so they can show them around."

Belle did as he asked, glad she could do her own checks and wait here for Emmett. Sarge was right. She'd been seen and recognized and now it was even more dangerous for her family.

She still had to talk to Joaquin, too. That would be the hardest part. But her sisters had reported that he was working with Papá today.

So she sat at her desk while Justice got in some practice with a handler in the training center. Going back over her time with Percy was like opening a jagged wound but Belle had changed and grown since then. No man would ever intimidate her again.

She thought of Emmett and how he'd helped her and Lani and Noelle today. He hadn't complained much at all and he'd done his part in bringing Brooke and her pups to safety. Maybe they could name one of the pups after Emmett. Why did she want to be with him even when she was afraid to even try?

That made her smile.

He made her smile.

"You're smiling."

She looked up to find Brianne Hayes-Sutherland giving her an amused look. "Hi, Brianne," she said, getting up to hug Gavin's wife. "How are you?"

"I'm good," Brianne said, her face splitting in a grin. "I'm supposed to be having lunch with my husband."

"He's in his office," Belle said. "But Penny probably already told you that."

"She did." Brianne shrugged. "It's my day off so I'm stealing him for an hour or so."

"Good plan," Belle said, noting Brianne's street clothes and loose hair. "How's Miss Stella?"

"Stella is amazing," Brianne said, referring to her partner, a yellow Lab trained in bomb detection. Stella had been gifted to them pregnant, and Liberty, Noelle's partner, was one of her now-grown pups. "Has the best instincts. I love working with her but lately, things have been quiet for us. Thankfully."

They chatted a few more minutes, then Gavin came out and kissed his wife. "I need to talk to Belle a minute and then I'm yours for the next hour or so."

"I like that," Brianne said, her dark eyes sparkling.

After she moved on to visit with other officers, Gavin turned to Belle. "One of the officers I sent out said the gym owner you and Emmett talked to the other day recognized the photo of your ex. Said he came in with Johnson a few weeks ago."

Belle's stomach lurched as if she'd eaten something that had gone bad. Her skin became clammy and heated. "Then they do know each other."

"Yes," Gavin said. "He remembered snippets of their trash talk. Seems they met when Percy Carolo worked as a guard on a short stint at Rikers Island Prison. A very short stint from what I found after I verified that."

Belle's whole system buzzed, concern for her family and everyone she knew gnawing at her. "So they might have gotten to know each other there."

"Yes. Seems that's a good start. Carolo got fired after only a couple of weeks—for being a hothead and for associating with the inmates a little too much."

"I can attest to the hothead part," Belle said. "Apparently, that hasn't improved since I left him. I think he belongs on the other side of those bars now."

Gavin gave her a serious look, his brow puckering. "This is getting more and more dangerous. With two of them against you, you're not safe anywhere."

"I just want my family safe," she said. "I need to find my brother and get him to talk to me."

"Not alone," Gavin replied. "Get someone to go with you or call Emmett back in if that makes you feel better."

She stared at him in surprise. "Yes, sir. We're supposed to meet up later to see if he spotted his cousin at the diner where he might have been seen this morning."

"As long as you have a partner," he said. "Now if I don't get Brianne out of here, I'm going to be in the kennel with Tommy and Stella tonight."

Belle nodded at that and watched as they walked away, laughing with each other. They were really in love.

When she looked up from the computer an hour later, Emmett was walking toward her in plain clothes. "I thought I'd check in."

Her frustrations regarding this new development lifted like a mist. "Yes. I have an update on my situation."

He listened as they headed to get Justice.

"Gage, why don't you just apply and become a K-9 officer with us?" K-9 Detective Henry Roarke asked, his brown eyes full of a knowing gleam. "You're in here about as much as I am these days."

Henry was on modified duty due to a pending investigation regarding him possibly using excessive force when dealing with a twenty-year-old suspect. So he'd been stuck here filing papers, answering the phone and doing some training with the K-9s, waiting for internal affairs to send in a new investigator. The last one had recently had a heart attack.

Emmett grinned and shook Henry's hand. "I just might do that before it's all over. This is not a bad place to hang out."

"You'd change that tune if you had to deal with what I'm dealing with." Henry shot Belle a wry smile, shook his head and kept moving. Belle and he were good friends so he liked to rag on her about her love life. He'd been down lately so she tried to visit with him when she could.

"He's going through a lot right now," Belle told Emmett as they were leaving. She'd explained to him about Henry when she'd first introduced them. Now Henry kept a keen eye on her and Emmett.

Emmett's silvery gaze moved over her face. "You all seem close. I like that."

"How about you and your people?"

"Oh, we get along and work hard but we're so scattered and always on the go. Hard to get too intimate." Shrugging, he said, "Hard to get close to anyone."

Belle heard that as, yet again, a warning to her. Was he really going to deny that kiss and how he felt for her? Well, she'd denied it over and over, so could she blame him?

"And that's the thing," she replied. "The work comes first and right now I have a lot to accomplish."

He gave her an understanding glance, a dark longing in his eyes. "Agreed. So what's the plan?"

"I want to see if I can talk to Joaquin before I do anything else. He was asleep when I left this morning and my dad had plans for him to help paint apartments all day. He's supposed to stay at home tonight."

She glanced at her watch. "It's still early so I should catch him when they come home around four or so."

"Okay. Meanwhile, I'll catch up on some paperwork."

"Sorry you came by. You could have called."

"Maybe I wanted to see you."

"Why, Emmett?" she asked, wishing he'd really open up to her.

"I don't like how we left things last night."

Belle shook her head. "Oh, you mean that kiss, after you'd told me in no uncertain terms that you have a steadfast aversion to dating anyone, especially another law enforcement person. This kind of work and all of that?"

"Yeah, that."

"I'll check in with you later," she replied, determined to stay on track.

"Belle?"

She whirled to face him. "What?"

"Never mind. Just be safe, okay?"

Belle headed home, anxiety for her brother front and center in her mind. But getting used to having a man like Emmett around sure was tempting. After Percy, she'd concentrated on work and hanging out with her family and friends. Emmett made her realize that might not be enough. Funny, he'd made her see that but he couldn't see he needed people in his life, too.

When she got home, her mother met her inside the entryway, her eyes red-rimmed, her hand clutching her blouse.

"I'm so relieved you're home early, Belle. Your brother is missing again. You have to find him."

* * *

Belle circled the park again, telling herself Joaquin had to be all right. He might have come here, but had he left with Percy and Lance?

When she saw a dark pickup, she let out a sigh of relief. She'd texted Emmett and he'd insisted on coming to help her. She'd also called in the patrols that had been watching her building.

"We didn't see your brother exit your house," one of the patrolmen told her. "But he could have gone out the back."

It was impossible to keep someone on him 24/7, Belle knew. Her brother wasn't stupid. He'd probably timed the rounds the patrolmen made and managed to sneak right by one of them.

She parked her vehicle and used her key fob to open the back door for Justice to jump out. He'd be needed on this search.

"Hey," Emmett said, putting on his official cap while he scanned the deserted park. "Nothing?"

"Not yet. I have one of his shirts so I'm going to let Justice sniff it and hopefully we can locate him." She lifted her head to the dark clouds that had dumped rain off and on all day. "We have to find him."

"We will," Emmett said. "How are your parents?"

"Frantic and angry. They didn't raise him to turn into a hooligan."

"He's not there yet, but things could go bad if he's listening to that duo harassing you."

"That's the part that driving me nuts," she admitted. "I brought this on my family, Emmett."

"Hey, now, you were doing your job and you also

were wise to dump Percy. Don't beat yourself up. These two aren't wired the same way we are, Belle."

"No, they're not. That's the scary part." She lifted her gaze to meet his. "We're wired to do this and everything else is secondary."

They started walking the perimeters of the rundown park. Belle let Justice smell the shirt she'd brought and then loosened the leash so Justice could get to work.

When she saw a cluster of teens, she flagged them down and showed them a recent picture of her brother. "Have you seen him today? And don't try to bluff me. It won't work."

One of the boys gave her a confused stare, his sandy bangs falling over his eyes. "I think I saw him maybe two hours ago, talking to two men."

Belle swallowed the bile in her throat and tried to breathe. "Did he leave with them?"

"No. They all walked that way."

The boy pointed to an overgrown area of the park by a small dark pond.

Taking Justice back out, Belle tried to focus on her training and not the horrible thoughts running rampant through her mind. The trees were heavy with humidity, the wind hot on her clammy skin. Every twig that snapped set her senses on edge.

"Hang on," Emmett said, his steady presence holding her together. "We'll find him, Belle."

His reassurances helped, but Belle's worst fears pushed her like a hot breath on her skin. What would her parents do if something had happened to their only son?

"Justice, let's go."

The big dog sniffed the air and the ground, moving slowly at times and picking up the pace at other times, his ears up and his gait full of energy. They moved on a grid back and forth, past rusted-out swing sets and crooked piping hot metal slides. A wobbly merry-go-round moved eerily in the wind, whining a forlorn moan with each circle.

The desolate undergrowth of the heavily wooded corner of the park only added to Belle's concerns. She looked for lurkers around the bushes and old trees. The swaying oaks hovered like sulking giants ready to attack. The wind hissed a hot warning that rasped at her soul. Remembering the feel of her attacker's beefy hands on her neck, she closed her eyes and prayed for her brother.

God would protect Joaquin even if Joaquin seemed to scorn God these days.

I hope he calls out to You, Lord, she prayed.

They came up on an old shack—probably used for storage. Justice held up his head, his nose in the air, his body quivering with an intensity that had Belle's hair standing on edge. Justice knew her brother's scent as well as he knew her own and all of her family's.

Belle glanced at Emmett, every fiber of her being dreading what she might discover in that shed. Bracing herself, she swallowed and breathed, determined to keep moving. Somewhere over the trees, lightning hit the tepid air. A roll of thunder boomed a shattered stomp of urgency.

"Find," she said to Justice.

The German shepherd trotted to the shed and stood at alert, a soft whine whispering through his clenched teeth. Then he turned and looked back at Belle.

A sure sign of confirmation he'd honed in on her brother's scent.

Emmett stepped forward and touched a hand to her arm. "Let me go in first, Belle."

Belle couldn't breathe, but she had to keep moving. "I'll be right behind you," she said, conceding that she really needed Emmett to help her do this.

Emmett gave her a grim nod and then silently walked toward the shed, his weapon drawn, his body coiled in a low crouch. When he pushed at the rickety metal door, it fell open with a noisy groan and several howling screeches of protest.

A dove cooed and flew off the roof of the old building, the fluttering of his wings only matching the beat of a heavy pulse hitting at Belle's temples.

Emmett stuck his head inside and looked down. Then he stepped into the darkness of the building. "Belle, he's here."

Belle rushed forward, her heart in her throat, the worst images running through her mind.

Emmett went down on his knees.

Belle's gaze followed him. Justice leaped inside and then she spotted her brother lying still on the floor. "Joaquin, no! Joaquin?"

Emmett gently tugged at her brother and rolled him over. He groaned and blinked, his gaze unfocused and dull.

"Hey, Belle," Joaquin said, his eyes bruised and swollen, his lip bleeding. "I guess I'm in big trouble, huh?"

Belle fell down beside him. "Joaquin." Then she took him in her arms and hugged him tight, tears burning at her eyes. "Yes, you are so in trouble. But… I love you. Always, I love you."

FIFTEEN

Belle paced outside the hospital room, her mind roiling between anger and fear. Her parents were in with Joaquin. Once they could see that he was okay despite the many bruises and cuts on his face and body, she'd go in and get the truth out of him.

Pushing at the bun she'd long ago forgotten, she glanced up to see Emmett coming toward her with two coffees and a white paper bag.

"I found some croissants in the hospital diner," he said. "You need breakfast."

"I need answers," she replied, realizing they'd never had dinner last night. "You eat that."

"I had some food already. And I called and checked on your sisters."

"Are they okay?"

"Your aunt said they're sleeping. They won't go into work at the café today."

Belle let out a sigh of relief. "This has to end. After I talk to Joaquin, I'm going after Lance Johnson and Percy Carolo. I'm going to put them both in a prison cell."

"I can't blame you, but keep calm and let me help,"

Emmett said. "I've already asked around. There's a traffic camera near the park that could show us if Johnson and Carolo were there."

"That's good," she said, still out for blood. "But I know they were there. I feel it in my gut."

Her parents came back into the waiting area, both looking aged and exhausted.

"He won't tell us anything," Papá said, his gaze close to accusing but he quickly went blank on that. "Maybe he'll talk to you."

Belle stood, every muscle in her body protesting and her heart filled with guilt that she'd let this go so far. "I'll try to get him to tell me what happened." She handed Emmett the coffee she'd barely touched. "I'll see you when I come out."

Emmett touched a hand to her arm. "I'll be here unless I hear something about Randall."

She found Joaquin staring up at the ceiling tiles, a single tear moving down his right cheek.

"How are you?" she asked as she pushed at his thick black hair.

He tugged away. "How do you think?"

"I think you're blessed to be alive," she admitted, hoping bluntness would make him open up to her. "You suffered a near-concussion and you have a cracked rib. Which is probably going to cause you quite a bit of pain for a few weeks."

"The doctor gave me a report, Belle."

"Okay then, this means you can't go running all over town with your former friends, got it?"

"I don't have any friends."

That confession surprised her. "You can have good friends if you're careful."

He didn't respond to that.

"Joaquin, you have to talk to me. I had to report this so we need a statement and—this is very important—you need to tell me the truth."

Her brother's frown crashed against his skin. "I don't want to talk about anything."

Belle shook her head and tugged at her hair. "You have to be honest with me. It's the only way I can help you. Were you with Percy and another man today?"

His dark eyes widened, first in surprise and then in panic. "Who told you that?"

"I'm a cop, little brother. I ask around. People talk, see things. Lance Johnson has made it clear he wants me dead and he's using you to terrorize our family and me. Is that what you want?"

Her brother didn't need to know that she hadn't verified any of this yet. But she needed him to tell her how he'd become involved with these ruthless people.

"No."

The one word came out like a whispered wail.

"Then you'd better start at the beginning and don't leave anything out."

Joaquin swallowed, his fingers clutching the blankets. "Percy found me in the park. Told me he missed seeing the family. Missed you. Asked a lot of questions about you."

Belle managed to keep a blank face even while her jaw muscles tightened. "What did you tell him?"

"That you were still a K-9 cop and you still had an apartment at our house. Stuff like that."

"How did Lance Johnson get involved?"

Joaquin stared at the ceiling again. "Percy came back around and he was with him. A friend, Percy said." He looked into Belle's eyes. "I didn't know, Belle. I didn't get it."

"Get what?" she asked, her heart bumping, her nerves sizzling.

"They told me Emmett wasn't good for you. Stuff about how he was investigating our family and that he was using you. Told me they'd pay me to make him go away."

Go away? They wanted to harm Emmett to get to her?

"What happened, Joaquin?"

"They gave me a hundred-dollar bill to…to scare him and you."

"Scare us? How?"

"The roof, Belle. The chunk of concrete."

Belle stood up and put a hand to her mouth. "You did that? You went onto the roof and threw that broken concrete down at us?"

He nodded, his face contorted with shame and rage. "I wasn't going to hurt either of you, really. I waited until he moved before I dropped it. I just wanted the money."

Belle gulped in air. "You don't worry. I'm going to make sure those two pay much more than a hundred dollars. You could have killed Emmett, Joaquin. You have to know they were lying to you."

"I know that now," he said, his voice rising. "When they came to me again and wanted me to—"

"To what?" she asked, standing at the foot of the

bed, her knuckles turning white from gripping the steel frame.

"They wanted me to poison Justice," he blurted out, tears misting over in his eyes. "I couldn't do it. I refused to do it."

White spots of anger dotted Belle's eyes. "So they beat you?"

He nodded. "I got away and hid in the shed."

Belle came around the bed and tugged her brother into her arms. "I'm going to take care of this, understand?"

Joaquin bobbed his head. "I'm sorry."

"I know you are," she whispered. "Now you've learned a valuable lesson. You use this lesson to change your life, okay? To do better, to do good things."

Joaquin looked up at her. "You're not going to arrest me?"

"No, not this time."

Then she let him go and stood. "But I am going after the men who did this to us. You can count on that."

When Belle came out of Joaquin's room, Emmett was gone.

"He got a call. Something about work," her mother said. "Tell me about my son."

Belle pulled her mother close. "He's going to be okay." She explained what had transpired between her brother and her ex. "He told me everything and… I think you'll see a change in him, Mamá. Right now, I have to go."

"Belle, you realize these men have come after our family," her father said. "I'm proud of you for being honest with us and I know you're trained to do this work, but if you don't handle this, I'll find a way."

"No, you will not," her mother said, taking her father's hand. "Enough. Let our daughter bring these two evil men to justice. She's been trained to do that."

Belle appreciated her mother's pride. "She's right, Papá. Stay here and be kind to him. He's afraid and ashamed."

"You check in with us," her mother said.

"I will. I have to pick up Justice and get to work but I'll make sure an officer stays here with you until I can return. Hopefully, this will be over soon."

Emmett approached the greasy-spoon diner on foot, taking his time to notice the exits and the area around this desolate part of Bay Ridge. One of his informants had seen Randall here again. Emmett had had no choice but to leave the hospital and get here as quickly as possible. He hoped Belle would understand.

He'd called Gavin right away for backup so someone could guard her brother in case she had to leave, too. But Gavin told him Belle had already called in for an officer at the hospital.

"Did she say why?"

"No," Gavin had replied. "Said she'd explain later. Sounded urgent but I think she got a lead. Don't worry. I sent backup to find her."

Now Emmett's thoughts moved from finding Randall to worrying about Belle. He had to remind himself Belle had been doing okay up until now and she'd probably go in with guns blazing to take out the criminals who'd beat up her brother.

If she'd managed to get the truth out of the boy.

Now, he eased his way around the diner's storefront with the appropriate name of Last Stop Hop since it was situated underneath several overpasses. He spotted an NYPD patrol car across the street.

The sound of traffic constantly buzzing against the steel girders and beams overhead blurred with the street noise of people shouting and laughing, moving, always moving. Finding a spot where he had a clear view inside the dingy windows, he searched the sparse mid-morning crowds.

And spotted his cousin Randall sitting at a small table toward the back. Randall wore a Mets cap pulled low over his brow but Emmett knew it was him from his jawline and brawny shoulders. He turned toward the patrol car and nodded to let them know he'd located Randall, then pivoted around.

Before he could make a move, Randall glanced up and saw him, their eyes meeting. Emmett waved and prayed Randall wouldn't bolt out the exit on the other side of the building.

Instead, Randall surprised him by waving and motioning to him.

Emmett entered the diner and took in the few patrons—an older couple arguing about pancakes and traffic. A young mom trying to deal with a crying baby and an older toddler. A bleary-eyed couple in party clothes who looked like they'd been out all night.

The smell of burning coffee and fried bacon assaulted Emmett's senses followed by a musty smell of old, overused furniture and an even older greasy kitchen.

And then there was Randall. He stood when Emmett approached and reached out a calloused hand but he was as jumpy as the grease hitting the hot griddle behind the long counter. "Well, as I live and breathe, Emmett Gage. I haven't seen you in I don't know how long."

"Long time," Emmett said, shaking Randall's hand and noting the tremor that shook it. "How've you been?"

"I've been better," Randall admitted, motioning for Emmett to join him, his eyes darting to the door and all around. "Just having a cup of this mud they call coffee."

The waitress came over, her expression curling in a sneer that pretended to be a smile. "What can I get you?"

"Coffee's fine," Emmett said, glad they served it in real cups. Because he planned to nab Randall's cup somehow.

The weary woman shifted away. Emmett looked over at his distant cousin. "Do you still live around here?"

"Nah, I come and go," Randall allowed, his fingers tapping a nervous jig on the battered tabletop. "Just passing through."

"Where have you been?"

His cousin grew wary, his eyes filling with a dark dread, his hands shaking. He took a sip of coffee and spilled a couple of drops. Randall took the dingy white cloth napkin by his plate and rubbed it over his mouth, then wiped up the spills.

Emmett would bag that, too.

"I've been moving around. Hard to find work anymore at my age but I get by."

But it seemed Randall wanted to hear about Emmett. "What are you doing here, anyway, cuz? How's the family?"

"My parents are both dead now," Emmett said. "I live in Dumbo with two roommates." He explained about his work.

Randall's jitters increased, panic racing across his expression faster than the constant trains at the nearby 59th Street Station jarring the earth as they hummed by.

"Yeah, well, law enforcement runs on your side of the family," Randall said on a bitter note. "Never caught on with my old man. Nor me."

"So you're working still?" Emmett asked, laughing.

Randall bobbed his head, his grin showing two missing teeth, his cough ragged and rough-cut. "I got a friend up in the Catskills. Gives me work here and there in construction and such. He sends me to Brooklyn sometimes to do odd jobs here, too."

They sat silent for a minute while a newsbreak came on the television blaring from a wall-mounted television.

Out of the blue, a report about the Emery murders came on. The pretty newswoman told the tale in a crisp, practiced voice.

"No new leads on the bizarre murder case that rocked Brooklyn a few months ago, but the latest report from the NYPD is that they are getting closer to finding out if the same killer is back in town. Deemed the Emery murders, this heinous crime involved a couple murdered in their home. But the killer left their small child unharmed, even giving the three-year-old girl a stuffed animal."

She went on to talk about the similarities between

this case and the cold case from twenty years ago—the McGregors and the little girl the killer had also left behind with a stuffed animal—Penelope McGregor. "The NYPD is currently following a lead on a DNA sample and will check out any and all leads on this case."

Emmett listened and then turned back to Randall, hoping his cousin would say something. But Randall's only response was a telling one.

"I gotta go, man." He got up so quickly the table shifted and people stared. Pushing past Emmett, he said, "I need to get back to work, you know. Good seeing you, Emmett."

"Randall," Emmett said, grabbing his arm. "Wait. You can talk to me. I can help you. If you need anything—"

"I don't need your charity or your pity." Randall yanked away, his congenial mood changing as swiftly as the rainy weather left over from last night. "I need to get outta here."

Emmett tried to block the door, his hand inching toward his weapon. "Randall, I need to talk to you."

Randall pulled a gun from underneath his baggy shirt and waved it in the air. "Nah, I know how this works. They sent you to bring me in."

Emmett held his hands up to calm Randall. "It'll be better if you just go with me to answer some questions."

"I don't think so," Randall said, his hands shaking, his weapon wobbling. Then he turned the gun on the mother and her two suddenly quiet children. A collective gasp went out over the diner. "Let me go, Emmett. I don't want to hurt no one."

Emmett held up his hands again, not about to pull out

his own weapon now. "I don't want you to hurt anyone, Randall. But I believe you're in trouble."

"Trouble's been shadowing me all my life," Randall retorted as he backed toward the door, waving the gun at anyone who moved. "You just pretend you never saw me. That's the best thing you can do for me now."

Emmett stood still, keeping watch on all the people who could be in the line of fire. "Randall—"

Randall waved the gun again. "I said, stay back!" Then he gave Emmett a hard glare. "And call off whoever's out there waiting for me. Or I'll have to shoot someone."

Everyone in the café ducked and crouched, afraid for their lives. Emmett tried to see past his cousin to warn the other officers. "Take me, Randall."

His cousin backed out the door, his gun pointing from target to target inside the diner before he held the gun on Emmett. "Let's go."

Emmett went in front of Randall. Randall shoved Emmett with his gun. "Sorry, man. I can't let you take me in." Then he jabbed the butt of his gun against Emmett's head and shoved him against the pavement before he took off on a run, shooting toward Emmett. "Stay away."

Emmett tried to stand but dizziness overtook him. He tried again, pressing his hand against a lamp post. Then he opened the door to the diner.

"Don't clean this table," Emmett called to the wide-eyed waitress as he pulled his gun and spun around after Randall. "I'm coming back."

He spotted Randall heading west and called again,

this time with more anger than compassion, his head throbbing with pain. "Randall, stop."

Two officers ran toward them. One shouted, "NYPD. Drop your weapon."

Randall stopped and shot into the air near Emmett and took off around the corner. Then he turned and fired again.

Emmett dived down, frustration heating his gut, dizziness overcoming him. Then he called to the officer. "Go after him."

Dragging himself inside the diner, he held his badge up. "No one leave. The NYPD will need to question you." Then he stood and grabbed the table where he'd been sitting with Randall. "Bring me a plastic bag."

The waitress gave him an evil eye but did his bidding, her scowl now full of fright.

Emmett took a clean napkin and quickly poured what was left of Randall's coffee into the other cup, then bagged the empty cup and the napkin Randall had used.

"Hey, where you taking that mug and napkin?" the waitress asked, her hands on her hip, her tone bullish.

"To the police," Emmett said, deciding that should be explanation enough since he'd flashed his badge and he was bleeding from his temple. He dropped a twenty on the table to take the edge off.

The woman shrugged and grabbed the money, her attitude already rearranging itself.

Emmett pushed away the help the manager offered, took the bagged items and hurried to search the weed-infested empty lot next to the diner. Then he scanned the streets and sidewalks. When he saw one of the officers heading back, shaking his head, dread froze him on the spot. His cousin had disappeared right out from under him. Should he have injured Randall so he could bring him in?

The Brooklyn K-9 Unit might believe he'd let his cousin go. But he had made contact, and from the way Randall had acted, Emmett's gut told him his cousin was the killer of the McGregors.

Gage DNA matched what they'd found on that old watchband and Randall's actions today sealed the deal.

"Sorry, Marshal Gage," the officer said. "He slipped over a fence and then we lost him."

Emmett gave a report to the young man, refused to see a doctor for his busted head and then hurried to his truck. His dad had tried to help Randall and so had he. But he had to remind himself that sometimes a person went beyond wanting to be helped.

And that made his job too tough to handle at times. This would be one of the worst of those times.

SIXTEEN

Emmett sat inside Gavin's office, exhausted and weary, his mood as grim as the rain clouds outside.

Gavin came back in and sank down in his squeaky office chair. "All the witnesses panned out—said the man you were with pulled out a handgun and held it on a woman and two children, then waved it around, threatening everyone in the diner. The waitress said you saved them all by letting him take you out the door with him. The patrol officers saw it all through the window and watched him hit you on the head and run. They tried to capture him—one going one direction and the other following him. He gave them the slip, too, so don't be so hard on yourself."

Emmett shook his head and touched a hand to the bandage he'd found in his first aid kit. "Well, at least I won over the waitress." Then he stared out the window. "I could have shot him."

"You could have," Gavin replied, his tone blank. "But you might have shot him in the back and killed him."

"You know my aim would have been spot on."

"I assume that," Gavin said. "You could have injured him enough to bring him down. But you had others to consider."

Emmett studied Gavin's wall of photos, taking in his wife, Brianne, and their K-9 partners, Tommy and Stella. Other photos of the team showed honors and awards and more wedding moments.

"I hesitated," Emmett admitted. "I wanted to gather evidence and bring him in, not shoot my own kin."

Gavin rubbed his face and studied the papers on his desk before leveling Emmett with a hard glare. "You assured us you'd do your best. I think I should send someone from my unit next time we get a tip on Randall. You're too close to this case. Maybe you need to back off."

A knock at the door brought Belle inside, Justice with her. "Sir, I heard the report."

She spotted Emmett sitting there, his hands cupped, his bandaged head down. "Emmett, are you all right?"

Emmett held up a hand. "I'm fine. Just a scratch."

Gavin came around and shut the door. "We were just discussing what happened."

"I heard you kept Randall from shooting up a whole diner," Belle replied, her tone full of fire as she glanced at Emmett.

"That's true," Gavin said. "He took control of a bad situation, but Gage still got away."

"I can speak for myself," Emmett said, sitting up in his chair. "I bagged his cup and napkin. Your lab is analyzing them and we should know soon if the sample on the watchband found at the McGregor murder site is a true match for his DNA."

Belle sat down in the chair beside Emmett. "I should have been with you. Together and with Justice, we could have caught him."

"I almost had him," Emmett said, "but I had to protect those people in the diner." He held his hands together. "I had a clear shot when he fired at me and the other officers, but this injury made me question my judgment."

Belle glanced over at Gavin. "So what now, sir?"

"Well, we've put out a BOLO on Randall Gage and we'll keep turning over rocks and searching the streets. But I'm suggesting Marshal Gage steps back to let us handle this."

Emmett stood. "I agree. I messed up. I had one chance and I blew it. Maybe I am too close to this."

His eyes held Belle's. He'd become too close to her, too. He needed to take some time and space and get his head together.

Belle's gaze moved from him to Gavin. "Sir?"

"It's for the best, Belle," Gavin replied. "Whatever you two do on your own time is your business."

Emmett got up. "I'll talk to you later, Belle."

Then he turned and stalked out of the Brooklyn K-9 headquarters, his mind in turmoil, but with a new determination to go back to the work he knew best—tracking wanted criminals.

And he'd start by trying to find his cousin, in his own way.

Belle sat out in the backyard at the family compound, watching Justice sniffing around the yard. She'd sent her parents, sisters and Joaquin, newly released from the hospital, to stay with Uncle Rico until the threat to all of them was over.

"Why aren't you coming with us?" Joaquin had asked when she called to check on him right before his release, his attitude now demure and subdued.

"I won't put any of you in danger again," Belle told him. "I'm trained to handle these types of situations and Justice will alert me if anyone breaches our property."

Joaquin had nodded. "Uncle Rico said he has people watching out for you, too."

"Oh, yeah, is that right?" Belle's Uncle Rico carried a lot of weight in this neighborhood but in a good way. People respected him and, yes, everyone watched out for each other, per his encouragement. "Tell Uncle Rico I love him," she'd said before ending the call.

Now she sat there thinking that this plan just might work. She'd gotten her family out of the way. Emmett was off trying to find Randall, she knew without him telling her so. She'd seen it in his eyes when he'd left Gavin's office.

She was alone just as she'd been in the park that late afternoon. But this time, she was ready.

"Come and get me," she said into the night. "Because I'm waiting."

These two wanted to slither around like snakes and she was ready to catch one or both of them.

The night cooled down very little but at least a soft breeze kissed at her warm skin. Belle lifted her hair off her neck and took a sip of lemonade. Justice came back and hunkered down beside her. Normally, this was their favorite time of day.

They'd come out for Justice to take a break and then

he'd roam for a while before they headed back inside. Now, her little yard took on a sinister feel—shadows sparing with each other, trees shifting as branches scratched and moaned. Voices out on the street around front.

Her phone buzzed, jarring Belle out of her watchful visual.

"Belle Montero."

"Hey."

Emmett. "Hey, yourself. How are you?"

"I've been better," he said. "I told myself to stay away, but I kind of miss you."

"I miss you, too," she admitted. "And I told myself the same thing, but I hope you know you don't have to drop out of my life just because Gavin told you to stay off the case. I know there are boundaries but…we can be friends."

"I'm not dropping out of your life, and I'm certainly not letting this case go. I want to bring in Randall as much as anyone does so I'm casing the areas where he's been seen." He hesitated and then said, "And I'd like to come by and see you. I can still watch out for Johnson and Carolo, too. I have their stats and photos on hand, so I'll know them when I see them."

"Emmett, remember how you warned me to be careful?"

"Yes."

"You do the same."

"I will. What are you doing?"

"I'm sitting on my tiny porch with Justice, enjoying the quiet."

"How is Joaquin?"

"He's fine. He's with my family at my uncle's house about three blocks over. I sent them there for the weekend and I've got a patrol car monitoring them."

"Belle, are you alone?"

"Yes. Is that a hint that you should come over?"

"Do you want me to come over?"

Belle thought about that. She really liked this man. Should she say yes when she'd put herself out here, hoping to lure her attacker?

Could it hurt to have someone watching her back? Or should she give herself and Emmett some time to think this through?

Her stomach tingled with awareness, and then her instincts kicked in. "I'll be okay, Emmett. You don't need to come."

"No, you shouldn't do this alone. I told you I wasn't going anywhere."

"You also told me you can't commit to me," she reminded him.

"That's not exactly what I said, and you know it."

"I heard it, though. You're warning me to stay at a distance and now you're off the case. I have to go."

She ended the call and looked over at Justice. Then she sighed. "I shouldn't have pushed him away, because I think he needs us, boy. We just have to show him that, right?"

She put down her phone, thinking she'd told him the same thing—that she wasn't ready for a new relationship. Even with Emmett, she couldn't break that rule. He might think he could, but she'd believed in Percy's promises and he'd almost destroyed her.

Even with a good man like Emmett, she wasn't ready to risk it again.

So she sat in the dark and wished things could have worked out for them and she also accepted that they might not be able to stay friendly, after all.

A few minutes later Justice stood, startling her. Then her partner growled low and lifted his head toward the alley. Belle shot up out of her chair and scanned the yard. The streetlight behind the fenced wall shimmered an eerie yellow glow. She stilled and listened. When she heard a rustling and what sounded like the gate shifting, she knew someone was behind that fence.

"Seek," she whispered to Justice.

Justice took off toward the fence, barking and snarling.

"That didn't take long," Belle said.

She had her gun ready as she slinked along the fence line and listened, her breath held, her lungs tightening. The fence butted up to the building on each side but there was a gate on the side of the building by her porch. A locked gate.

Justice lifted and scratched at the other gate across the small yard. A gunshot roared through the night and then the gate popped open.

Justice leaped toward whoever had entered. Belle called out, "Attack! Bite!"

Justice followed her command but in the muted light, Belle saw the man. He was dressed in a protective suit.

The kind the team wore in training sessions.

Justice held on, but there was no way he'd get a firm grip on the intruder.

Then she heard another noise.

Someone was trying to scale the fence nearest to the porch.

They were both coming after her.

Emmett had finally secured a parking spot on the street when he heard a shot ring out. Taking out his weapon, he jumped out of his truck and bounded up the porch stoop. "Belle?"

Justice's snarls echoed out over the night. Emmett hurried around the house.

No gate on the right side.

He ran to the left and saw a dark figure running away.

"US Marshal. Stop!"

The man darted over a small chain-link fence into the next yard over and kept running.

Emmett heard Belle's voice. "Justice, halt. Release."

Emmett looked around, trying to figure out how to scale the high wooden fence and then he saw the gate and tried to open it. Still locked. He was halfway up, grunting and trying to find a toehold to jump the fence when he heard Belle again.

"NYPD. Stop," Belle shouted.

Then a gunshot and Justice barking again, angry, snarling barks. The gate at the back of the property slammed shut with a whack.

"Belle?" Emmett called out, his heart dropping, his mind swirling with the worst-case scenario. "Belle?"

The front door swung open with a clatter. "Emmett?"

He dropped away from the fence and rushed around the corner of the yard. Belle stood on the porch, the door open behind her.

Emmett leaped onto the stoop and gathered her close. "Are you all right?"

"Yes. He ran away when he heard you."

"Did Justice injure him?"

"Tried," she said, her breath coming in gulps. "He was wearing protective gear. The other one was trying to come over the front fence."

"I heard a shot."

"I got one in to bring him down. Think I hit his leg but with that gear on, who knows if it went through."

Emmett held her tight while lights came on and people came out of their houses. The whole street went quiet and the night seemed to stand still.

"What are you doing here?" she asked against his shoulder.

"I ignored you telling me to stay away," he said. "Did you honestly think I'd let you do this alone?"

"You got here so quick."

"I'd been circling the block for an hour. I called you from my truck."

"Stubborn."

"Let's get inside," he said, only now catching his breath.

"I have to get Justice in. He's guarding the backyard and people are on the way."

"Okay." He followed her into her apartment but then turned to check the hallway doors. She'd locked all of them, including the one she'd just come back through.

Soon, she had Justice inside and drinking water. Then she turned to Emmett. "I almost had him. I called off Justice and rushed at the man, but he shot and then I shot back. He turned and whirled out the gate, shooting one more time."

She shook her head. "But he screamed at me and told me I'd cost him the woman he loved when I put him in jail. Said he'd get me one way or another. I'm guessing Lance's girlfriend finally left him and now he's blaming me. I think he started watching my routine the minute he got out of jail."

Emmett checked her over and pulled his hand across his moist forehead. "I almost had a heart attack trying to get over that fence. I heard Justice barking and snarling."

"The fence is built to protect and to last," she said, taking him into her arms again. "We rarely unlock either the front or back gates."

Emmett looked down at her and pushed her hair out of her eyes so he could check to see if she was hurt. Then he leaned down and kissed her, savoring the warmth of her lips and the soft sigh that pushed through her body.

Belle held on to him and then pulled back. "This isn't how I usually do things."

"What do you mean?"

"I've never gotten close to a man during two active cases before. I've never actually had two active cases at one time and I've never been threatened in such an aggressive way."

"There's a first time for everything," he whispered against her ear. "I guess you've never kissed a man who's also involved in such cases before, right?"

"Right. And such a determined man at that."

"Let's try it again, then."

He pulled her back into his arms and kissed her completely and thoroughly. "I think my heart is racing more now than it was before."

Belle nodded in agreement. "How do we handle this, Emmett?"

"Do you want to be with me? To know me?" he asked.

"I don't know… There's so much going on. I didn't think I'd get involved with anyone. Not after my ex did a number on me." Looking up at him, she said, "And I'm not so sure about you. You're too good to be true. I'm waiting for when the bad stuff comes."

Emmett wasn't buying her logic. "First of all, your ex is a horrible example of what love really is. He was pretending at wanting to be a policeman, and even now, he's one of those shadow people who hang around bragging but never actually accomplish anything."

"Except trying to get even with me."

"He hasn't succeeded yet," Emmett reminded her. "He's tried all the ploys and yet, you're still here. Thankfully." Holding her back so he could look into her eyes, he went on, "And second, I'm not perfect. I have doubts and now you know that. I'm a loner and set in my ways. I travel a lot and I never wanted to settle down with anyone."

"I think that's the part I'm having trouble with. How can I trust that you won't resent me and my work one day?"

"I had a plan, a solid commitment to not get involved with you. But here I am, Belle. I'm not like Percy."

"No, you're not," she said, slapping at his arm. "But I have to be absolutely sure."

He was about to kiss her again to reassure her when they heard voices echoing throughout the hallway.

Belle sighed and laid her head against his chest. "That would be my relatives coming to check on me and just in time. I'm sure the neighbors called my dad since he alerted them that no one would be here tonight. News spreads like a flash flood around here."

"You have a lot of people who love you," he said. Then he thought about that. Could he be one of those people?

SEVENTEEN

They were all talking at once.

Emmett tried to absorb Belle's family moving through the house and up and down the stairs while he also worked to keep up with the two members of her unit who'd shown up to search her yard, coming and going while they talked into their radios. He had sensory overload since his parents had been stoic, quiet and stern most of the time. That had taught him to savor quiet and solitary moments. He felt in the way and out of place here amid so much action, but he also knew the procedure. Emmett had to get back out there, and he might have to do it on his own.

If he could find a way through this crowd.

"You're going to get yourself killed," Belle's mother kept saying, her hands waving more and more with each repetition. "This is too much, Belle." Then she lapsed into Spanish, explaining why Belle needed to get married and settle down.

Emmett didn't think that would happen anytime soon. She would have stopped him from kissing her back there even if her folks hadn't shown up. And all because he'd told her the truth—falling for a woman as bold and brave as her could be the most dangerous thing he'd ever done.

Belle looked as if she wanted to scream.

"Belle, we need you outside," K-9 Detective Tyler Walker, who'd brought his golden retriever, Dusty, to help track the intruders, called out. Her friend Noelle had also arrived on the scene with her K-9, Liberty, but Gavin assigned her to crowd control in the house. Others were canvassing the yard and streets and knocking on doors to see if anyone had seen two suspicious men lurching about.

Looking relieved, Belle started toward the back door.

"Belle, why did you stay here like some lamb to be sacrificed?" her father asked, his salt-and-pepper hair standing straight up in a jagged ruffle on his head.

Her twin sisters sat on the stairs, leaning on each other, tired and worried. Every now and then, they'd both shot a look at Emmett, their dark eyes pleading for answers.

"I'm fine," Belle said to her parents. "I have to get to work."

"Work. Work to do. That is her way." Mrs. Montera threw up her hands one last time and stalked toward the stairs. "I'll go up and make everyone something to eat."

Belle kissed her father and then turned to head back out.

Emmett stood staring after Belle, wishing they hadn't been interrupted earlier. But neither of them was ready to admit anything. Plus, they had to gather evidence and track footprints and try to find these aggressors.

He knew that better than anyone. So he turned and started out the back door, determined to work his own grid like he'd done a hundred times with criminals.

"Hey." A voice called out behind him. Emmett turned to find Joaquin standing in the hallway, his hands in the pockets of his jeans.

"What's wrong?" Emmett asked, wondering if the boy was still keeping secrets. He looked dejected and... guilty.

"I might know something," Joaquin said, lowering his head.

"Something like what?" Emmett asked.

"I heard them talking once, arguing, when they were trying to beat me to a pulp."

Emmett saw the black eye and cuts still healing on the boy's face. "What did you hear?"

"Percy said something about a house over near the park. I think it's abandoned but he's been sneaking Lance Johnson in and out. He said something about getting the stuff they needed and hiding it there." Brushing at his hair, Joaquin finally looked up at Emmett. "They planned to dump me there, you know, after they'd killed me."

Emmett heard the fear in the boy's words. "Have you told anyone else this?"

"I didn't remember at first. Things keep coming to me now, though. I know the address."

After he memorized the address Joaquin gave him, Emmett stepped closer and moved the teenager out onto the porch. "Listen, I know you're scared but you can't live in fear. You have to tell the truth, or this could get worse."

"How can I do that now?" Joaquin said. "I almost died over trying to make easy money."

"You learned a hard lesson," Emmett said. "Take that and make something out of it. Walk inside the light—no more trying to make easy money."

"What can I do?"

"You keep remembering things that might help us and we'll keep fighting them. They'll mess up sooner or later and we'll end this."

Joaquin's shoulders lifted. "I'll do my best. I love my sister."

"I know you do. You just watch your back," Emmett told him. Then he handed Joaquin his card. "And you call this number if you ever need me, understand?"

The boy nodded and put the card in his pocket.

"Joaquin?" His sister Anita's voice lifted out over the night.

"Coming." He gave Emmett a shy glance and hurried inside.

Emmett glanced around and remembered the front fence where one of the intruders had been trying to break in. He headed over to examine it, using his flashlight to see what he could find.

Footprints on the ground all around the gate, but then he'd stepped in this same spot so his would be there, too. Holding the light up to the worn wood, he noticed a strip of fabric dangling from a crooked nail.

Emmett held the light close and noticed the print on the material. Tugging in his pocket for some latex gloves, he put his light down long enough to put them on. Then he gently lifted the torn material off the fence.

Part of an emblem or patch clung to the torn material. A uniform maybe. Then a memory came to him. A uniform from a certain storage unit located across town? He squinted in the sharply focused light. It just might be a match.

He'd give this to the crime scene techs. Maybe they could find some DNA on this and match it to Percy Carolo.

That would be another win for the growing pile of possible evidence linking Belle's ex to her attacker.

The fence had held and thankfully, when he'd shown up, they'd both run away like the cowards they were. They thought they could take Belle, but she'd proven them wrong.

That thought scared him enough to make him see that he did care about her and with more than just a feeling of friendship. That also meant he had to keep her safe, whether she or these intruders liked that.

Belle stood at attention the next morning when Gavin entered his office. Her colleagues and friends Lani Jameson and Jackson Davison stood with her. They'd been called in for an assignment.

Belle liked having Lani and her partner, Snapper, with her, and Jackson worked with Belle in Emergency Services. He looked fresh and clean, his dark hair crisp and his green eyes always flashing in that guarded way she'd come to know. His chocolate Lab, Smokey—one of Stella's famous pups and now trained in cadaver detection—sat on his haunches by Jackson's side.

Were they going to search for bodies?

Lani shot Belle a questioning glance while Gavin came around his desk, her blue eyes bright with questions.

"Sit," Gavin said as he eased into his chair. Then

he looked directly at Belle. "I called you three in this morning because we've gained new evidence regarding the roving harassment team of Johnson and Carolo."

Belle leaned in. "Did the techs find something last night, sir?"

"Your friend the marshal found something," Gavin said, his tone firm while his eyes softened. "He gave a scrap of material to one of the crime scene techs. Turns out it's from a uniform. That, added to your brother's testimony and all the information you've gathered, should be enough for a warrant to enter Percy Carolo's home."

Belle took in his words and wondered why Emmett hadn't come to her about this. But then, he'd gone off on his own last night and she'd been busy with the techs and keeping her family calm. Had her family drama scared him away?

Or had their kisses scared him in the same way they'd scared her?

"What did the material show?" she managed to ask.

"A lot, all things considered. It's from a uniform that Percy Carolo obviously still had on. From the City Wide Storage unit."

"Bingo," Jackson said. "That's the one right, Belle? Where you and the marshal were ambushed?"

"Yes." She couldn't believe Percy would go to such lengths to get even with her. "So Johnson had on the protective suit and Percy planned to come through the front and probably take me down while Justice was distracted."

"That's what we believe," Gavin said. "After your brother gave him a location near the park he'd heard the two men talking about, Emmett came up with his own plan of attack. He wants to bring these men in so he can get back to finding his cousin."

"Emmett?" Belle shook her head. No way Emmett would take over this case. He had no right. "This is my case, sir. I can handle this. He shouldn't have come to you since he's off the cold case, per your request."

"He wants you to be safe," Gavin said, keeping his voice neutral but controlled. "He gave me the evidence and suggested a plan to put a surveillance team on the abandoned house they've been using. The man does know how to capture criminals, Belle. I never doubted he'd keep searching for his cousin, but on his own time."

Belle tried to digest this, her heart screaming right along with the thoughts shouting inside her head. Emmett wanted this over so he could get back to finding his cousin? But he wanted her safe. Did he care about her? Their kisses indicated he did, but was he just doing his duty since he'd been involved from the beginning? He was the kind of man who'd do the right thing, even when he wanted to be elsewhere.

"He can't keep me out of this," she finally said. "Whatever he's planned without me, I want in."

Gavin let out a sigh and lifted his eyebrows. "That's why you're here, Officer."

Belle settled back. "So what's the plan?"

Gavin glanced up and nodded. "I'll let him tell you himself. Come in, Marshal Gage."

Belle whirled to find Emmett standing there. She'd get to him later. "Why don't you go ahead, sir," she said to the chief.

Emmett stepped farther into the room and spoke instead. "After I checked out the house and found it empty, the plan was to have Lani and Jackson patrol the park and the house where these two miscreants hang out, hoping to nab them. But—"

"But I'm the one who needs to do that, sir," Belle said, turning from Gavin to glare at Emmett. "And I don't care what Marshal Gage thinks about that. I want in on this. Lance Johnson came after *me* and then he hooked up with the worst person possible—a man who's had it in for me since I walked out of his life a few years ago. He finally found a way to get back at me."

Then she stood and dared anyone to argue with her. "But I'm going to take them both down and I hope you'll allow me to do that." Her gaze centering on Emmett, she added, "To do *my* job."

Gavin stood and they all followed suit. "You heard my officer, Marshal Gage. She's in. No discussion. I'd like to believe I'm still in charge of this unit, after all."

Emmett looked at Belle and then nodded at Gavin. "Sorry I overstepped. Of course, Officer Montera would want in on this. After all, she's the target."

He said that in a way that expressed concern and acceptance. He wanted to protect her, but Belle had to do this herself. Had he planned this whole thing so he could be in on capturing these men with her? To show her how much he cared? Or to make a point that he knew better than her?

She wanted to believe he cared and she also wanted to believe he understood she was perfectly capable of handling this. Right now, her brain couldn't deal with all the emotions roiling over in her stomach. She had an assignment. She would follow through.

"Yes, I'm the target," Belle said, whirling away from her coworkers to confront Emmett. "And I'm going to be the bait this time."

She saw the flare of concern in his beautiful silvery-blue eyes, but she ignored it. He wanted to protect her, and she wanted to do the same for him. How could they ever compromise and have a relationship when they lived with danger each and every day? Maybe this was more proof that they didn't belong together.

Emmett gave her a resigned appraisal. "Then let's come up with a plan." He briefed them on the location of the house and went over the plans for the park.

Belle felt both relief and dread wash over her. This had to end so her family would feel safe again. And so she could finally explore her conflicting feelings for Marshal Emmett Gage.

EIGHTEEN

"Remember, you're patrolling the park, nothing more," Jackson reminded Belle later that day. "We've put out the word that we're cracking down on illegal activities in this particular park and we have people watching the abandoned house. A kid was attacked here, and the NYPD wants to put an end to that kind of violence."

Her brother—the kid who was attacked. But they hadn't put out his name, thankfully.

"Got it," Belle said as they pulled up and parked off-site, both their partners waiting in the back of the SUV. "You'll patrol with me, but I'll be on the other side of the block where I can see you at all times." Belle took a deep, calming breath.

"Yes, and Emmett and Lani will be dressed in plain clothes, a couple out walking their dog."

"Except their dog is Snapper, and the highly trained German shepherd is good at his job," Belle added with a streak of vengeance.

"It's going to be over soon, Belle," Jackson said. "We'll all make sure of that."

Her phone buzzed. *Emmett.*

"Belle Montera," she said in her most professional voice.

"I know you're mad at me but—"

"That is correct, and I can't talk right now."

"Belle, I want you safe."

"Because you want to move on to the bigger concern. I get it."

"No, you don't get it, but you will," he said. "When this is over, I'll show you what I mean."

"I'm not planning on that."

"Stay safe, Belle. For me, okay?"

She had to admit the plea in his words got to her.

"I'm going to do my level best."

She ended the call and glanced over at Jackson.

"You okay?" he asked, a slight smile on his face.

"Never better. Let's get this over with."

They got out of the vehicle, and Jackson hit the key fob to let their partners out. This was a sign to both dogs that it was showtime. Smokey danced in excitement and Justice stood staring up at Belle, his dark eyes curious and full of anticipation.

"You two are the best," she said to the smart animals. "We're going to do our jobs, and I want you to stay safe."

Jackson nodded to her. "You do the same, Belle."

They parted and Belle started along with Justice, allowing him a loose leash in case he spotted someone. He'd pick up on the familiar scents of the men who'd tried to break into her family's property and she had to remember Justice was trained to do his work, too. Since he'd been hit with that tranquilizer dart the night she met Emmett, she'd feared for her partner. Thankful that her attacker hadn't killed Justice last night, she prayed for strength and courage.

And protection.

Your unit members are listening in, she reminded herself. *Justice will be safe. I have to trust in God's protection, too.*

She had a whole community praying for her since her mother had a very long prayer chain.

They'd purposely waited until an hour before dusk since that was prime time for park gatherings around here. Belle walked along at a casual pace, glancing here and there to see if she was being followed.

When a group of teenagers appeared near the old basketball court, Belle took notice. Justice sniffed and deemed them not what he was searching for, so she did a crisscross through the park and stopped here and there so the kids would know she was official. They scattered, mumbling to themselves. Belle recognized a couple of boys who hung out with Joaquin now and then.

Thinking her brother had been very brave by telling her the truth and giving Emmett more information, she prayed for him, too. It was tough being a teen in this neighborhood, but she'd survived. She wanted her only brother and the twins to do the same.

After an hour, the sun began descending through the trees to the west. Belle was about to give up.

"I got nothing," she said into her mic, pretending she was talking to Justice.

"We're still here but no word from the house." *Emmett.* He'd been trying to talk to her, but she wasn't in the mood. Belle had watched Emmett and Lani, laughing and talking as they sat on a bench across from where she patrolled, Snapper calm by Lani's side. Then they'd walked around the perimeters of the park and ignored her as she'd done the same. Yet, she felt his eyes on her, knew he was watching through his sunshades. She'd have to forgive him. His intentions were good, after all. And truth be told, she did feel safe with him nearby.

She had to admit, she was falling for the man and she'd fought it every step of the way.

She rounded a corner and came close to where they'd found Joaquin in the old shed. Her heart pumped with fear for her brother as she flashed back to that night. Emmett had been right there with her.

Emmett.

He'd been with her through this whole ordeal and he'd come to her rescue over and over. But she'd acted like an ungrateful brat today.

She couldn't say that with others listening in.

"I'm not giving up," she said to anyone who could hear. "I mean it."

"I'm not, either," Emmett replied.

Had they just made their peace?

Before she could relax on that thought, Justice bristled.

Then a flash exploded, and smoke shot out everywhere. Belle's eyes filled with the thick, cloying gray fog, burning so she couldn't see. Her throat clogged with the stench of chemicals, mainly sulfur. Justice barked and snarled. A smoke bomb!

Jackson called out behind her. "Belle?"

Someone grabbed her and forced the leash out of her hand.

"You're mine now. It's good to have you in my arms again, Belle."

Percy.

Belle tried to squirm away, but he put something over her face and she passed out.

Her last thought was of Justice and Emmett. Her two protectors. Would they be able to save her this time?

Emmett heard a man's voice over the static of the radio. "Something's wrong." He tore away from Lani and took off toward the smoke rising across the park. He figured it was a smoke bomb before he saw the cylinder-style container lying on the sidewalk.

Lani reported their status and hurried after him, Snapper leading the way.

Jackson sprinted across the park, calling the location as he ran. Smokey barked and hustled along with him. "I was a few yards behind her. He took her."

Emmett stopped where the smoke still hung heavy in the air, the heavy fog settling into his lungs.

"She's gone," he said, glancing around to find Justice's leash lying on the broken sidewalk near the shed where they'd found Joaquin a few days ago. "They took her and Justice."

He couldn't believe he'd let her do this—put herself out there like this—knowing these two men wanted her dead.

He'd never forgive himself if he couldn't find her.

Lani came back from the old storage shed and touched his arm. "Think, Emmett. She's not in the shed but the dogs are restless. Whoever took Belle might still have her nearby."

"You're right," he said. Then he heard a dog barking. "Justice."

They took off past where Jackson still worked the shed, searching inside and all around. "Nothing here to help," he said, following them.

They found Justice hidden behind an old oak with what looked like a fishing net thrown over him. Someone had tied him to the tree. Justice struggled to get loose. Emmett quickly freed the big dog, glad he wasn't harmed.

Lani took over. "Justice, find."

Justice knew what to do. He took off into the bramble and the saplings, his barks loud and anxious.

Emmett and Lani followed while Jackson stayed behind to alert the first responders.

"The house," Emmett said as they sprinted into the weeds and underbrush. "The abandoned house. They must have taken her there." He shouted out the address again.

Someone responded. "We've got movement inside the house."

"Justice must be taking us there," Lani replied, her blond bun bouncing as they jogged.

Thankful for her long legs, Emmett kept up with her while they searched the surrounding houses. But Justice kept trotting, glancing back to make sure they were following.

Emmett prayed the dog had the right scent.

He had to find Belle before it was too late.

Belle woke, disoriented and groggy, sick and nauseated.

Blinking, she looked around the dank, stifling room and wondered where she was. Then it all came back.

The park, the smoke bomb, Percy drugging her, knocking her out.

She tried to move and realized her left hand had been cuffed to a flimsy chair back.

Struggling to sit up, Belle tried to get her bearings. She reached for her radio. Gone. Her phone. Also gone. Her weapons had been removed from her uniform.

"Hello?" she called, her pulse drumming heavily against her temple, her breath coming in great huffs while she tried to think, to find a way out.

The windows were covered with tan paper—the kind used to wrap boxes for mailing. The scents of body odor and stale food assaulted her, along with the smell of decaying wood and old leaves and moist dirt. Sweat moved like a clawing hand down her back and across her shoulders.

"I have to get out of here," she whispered.

"I don't think so."

Lance Johnson walked through some old tattered curtains from another room. "You're hard to kill, Officer Montera. But now I have you right where I want you."

"Where's Percy?" she asked, knowing this would not go well.

"Oh, so you do miss your ex? He told me all about you two."

Johnson knelt by where she sat on the old mattress. "He said you like to put strong men in their place. Made him feel less than with all your bluster and bragging. I know how that feels since you wrongfully sent me to prison."

"You were guilty," Belle pointed out. "I caught you beating up your girlfriend."

"My ex-girlfriend now," he said, grabbing Belle by the arm. "I swore I'd get even with you when she broke up with me and left the city."

"Well, you've certainly made a mess of that," Belle retorted, her need to survive overcoming her anxieties. She knew her team members would show up and she certainly knew that Emmett would be with them. Justice would find her.

Her prayers held tight, surrounding her, filling her head.

We do not live in a spirit of fear.

Johnson shoved her against the back of the chair, causing her neck to snap and her head to hit hard against the old wood. "Percy is going to pay me a big amount of money for helping him to find you. He wants to talk to you, so he'll be here soon."

Bile rose in Belle's throat. Percy would want revenge, too.

"Tell him I'll be waiting," she said, spitting each word out in a rage that left her breathless.

Johnson laughed and whirled to leave.

"Wait," Belle called. "Was that you on the motorcycle?"

"Yes. But it's long gone. Turned into scrap."

"So you used a stolen motorcycle to spy on me and you followed me to the park that day?"

His smug grin showed malice. "Easy to do. Just watch and wait."

"And you waited at the precinct later that night and tried to run me down on that same bike?"

"Maybe."

He didn't lie very well.

"I have to get out of here," he said. "Percy made it clear he wanted me gone before he comes back."

Belle watched him go, then took in her surroundings and went to work on getting herself free. The old high-back chair didn't have the strength to hold her, so she managed to twist around enough to start poking at one of the skinny posts. They'd cuffed her with enough of a chain to give her a little movement, so she used that to her advantage by standing in a stooped position. Each kick and jab seared her cuffed wrist, the digging pain shooting all the way up her neck to make her wince. But she would not die here in this desolate place.

Emmett's heart pounded with all the intensity of bullets hitting concrete. He had to find Belle. The images in his head weren't good ones. He'd dealt with enough deranged, vengeful men to know how things could go. Carolo and Johnson would taunt her and then kill her.

Dear God, help us all now.

They moved through woods and yards and stomped through messy drainage areas, but Justice didn't stop. The big dog seemed honed in on one scent, one thing, one way.

All around, Emmett heard others roaming through the dusk, shadows deepening, voices carrying, people shouting. Neighbors staring at them and calling out. The SWAT unit pulled up around the corner, ready to roll.

He kept going, focusing on the steps, putting the horrible thoughts out of his head. Wishing he'd told Belle how he felt about her, wishing he'd said so many things to so many people.

But he had to find Belle and be honest with her. He wanted to stay around her, spend time with her. Love her.

Yes, he could admit that he'd fallen and hard. Never saw that coming and not so quickly, either. They still had so much between them, but he was willing to wade his way through all of it for her.

Emmett stumbled over a broken crack in the sidewalk.

Then he looked up and found Justice standing alert, his head up, his ears pitched forward, his gaze on the old abandoned house on the corner, back from the street. The address Joaquin had given him.

Emmett held up his hand to those all around. Then he pointed to the dog and the house.

Shouts came over the radio. Locations. Positions. "Move in the SWAT team. Get here ASAP."

Please, get here fast. That thought echoed in Emmett's head as he slowly made his way toward the boarded-up, beaten-down house.

NINETEEN

Belle heard a noise in the other room. Quickly, she positioned herself on the chair, willing her heart to settle. Her bruised wrist throbbed against the cuff.

But she was ready now.

The curtains curled back, crackling with age and mold.

"Well, well, it's been a long time, hasn't it, sweet Belle?"

Percy stood there in jeans and a dark T-shirt, his black eyes burning with hatred and rage, his inky ebony hair long and rakish. "I know you must have missed me a little bit."

"Not all that much," she retorted, so ready to end this even while her heart rate accelerated. "And by the way, chasing me, threatening me and hiring some lowlife to try to kill me didn't make me any fonder of you, Percy."

"I don't know what you're talking about."

"Yes, you do," Belle said as he inched closer, the smell of his cheap aftershave making her gag. "You put the envelope underneath my door, didn't you? Because you kept a copy of the key I gave you, right?"

"Well, I did help you install the security system years ago, and I figured you'd changed the code and the lock.

But I sent Johnson to do the job. Slipped right in after your brother opened the front door and jogged right on upstairs without a clue."

"We do have a new key code now," she retorted. "And better security. I'm a different woman. Stronger, more secure, a lot smarter."

"You might think you're smart," he said through a hiss as he yanked her up and shook her shoulders. "But you're the one cuffed to that chair, aren't you?"

Belle waited until he was leaning over her and then she lifted her now uncuffed hand away from the broken chair spindle she'd managed to stick back up against the old backing. "Not anymore, Percy."

Then she grabbed the spindle and hit him hard against the head. She knew she hadn't done too much damage but it was enough get him away so she could squirm up and run. Running as fast as she could, she almost made it to the front door.

Then barking outside and a commotion stopped her. Justice!

Belle screamed out, her hand on the doorknob. If she could open it, Justice would be able to help. Her adrenaline high, she called out in hope. "Justice, Attack."

But Percy tackled her, and her hand slipped away from the locked door.

Emmett heard a faint scream and then watched as Justice leaped into the air and put a bite-hold on the man trying to sneak around the corner of the house.

Lance Johnson cried out in pain, screaming and begging Justice to let him go.

Jackson hurried by, headed toward the dog and the

man writhing in pain on the ground. "I got this, Marshal Gage. Go in and find Belle."

Confused, Emmett realized Belle wanted Justice to come into the house. But the K-9 had done his job out here. He'd captured Lance Johnson. So that meant someone else had Belle inside the house.

The grim weight of that hit Emmett in his gut. Percy Carolo would enjoy tormenting Belle, especially if he knew her entire unit was right outside.

Emmett was headed up the cracked steps when he heard a voice through one of the broken window panes where stained paper hung tattered and shredded, leaving partial views into the house. "Don't come any closer or I'll kill her."

Emmett saw the silhouette in the waning shadows. A man holding a woman against his chest, a gun pressed against her rib cage.

Belle.

"What do you want?" Emmett called out, holding a hand behind him to warn the others. "Just tell me."

Percy Carolo chuckled hard and fast. "I want my Belle back."

"I don't want *you*," Belle said to Percy, her eyes on Emmett. She spoke firmly, a cut on her lip, blood seeping down her face. "Percy, you need to let me go or things will only get worse for you."

"Worse?" Percy yanked her closer, one hand pressed across her chest. "How much worse could it get? I hired an inept stooge to help me get to you, and he failed at every attempt. He couldn't even kill you in the park before I met him."

Emmett inched closer, not daring to take his eyes

off them. But darkness was settling like a moldy blanket all around this house. He couldn't let this man take Belle away.

Behind him, Lance Johnson cried out. "Carolo made me do all of it. Hired me to harass her and kill the dog, talked her brother into helping. I told him I tried to get rid of her in the park, but he wants her all to himself before he does the job."

"Shut up," Jackson told the bleeding man as he hauled him toward where an ambulance waited. "You can spill your guts in court."

Emmett called out again. "What do you really need right now, Carolo? Time's wasting out here."

"I got what I want."

Emmett gritted his teeth at that comment. But he pulled himself together. "Then I'll stay right here because we have you surrounded, Carolo. And your buddy Lance is squealing like a pig."

Carolo shoved Belle toward the window, then stood behind her, his weapon pointed at her. "I told you, I'll kill her if you do anything more than breathe."

"I'm not doing anything," Emmett said, praying Belle's unit members had things under control. "But I can't speak for the Brooklyn K-9 Unit and the SWAT team moving in now. You see, I'm a US marshal and I'm trained to bring in people who break the law." He paused, let out a sigh. "And we all plan to bring you in for assault and battery on an officer, attempted murder and kidnapping. That's just the first page."

"So you'll bring me in—and you don't care if I shoot her first?" Percy cursed and shouted, "You tell all of them to back off and let me alone. I need to think. I mean it. If anyone comes close to this house, it's over. If I die, so does she."

Emmett held his breath, his mind whirling. He knew Justice was standing guard behind him. But how did he get the K-9 into the house?

"I'm backing away, Carolo," he called. "But I'll be nearby. Everyone else has moved away."

"Keep them back," Carolo called. "I have to come up with a new plan."

Emmett had to do the same. Come up with a new plan.

How did he save the woman he'd fallen in love with from a madman who only wanted to make her suffer before he killed her?

Belle clung to the sure knowledge that Emmett was on the other side of that door. She'd been so close to escaping when Percy had grabbed her and hauled her back, slapping her hard for daring to try.

Now he held her there by the window as a shield while he watched the night shadows outside, threatening anything that moved. It hurt so much to know people she cared about were close and she couldn't reach them. But she wasn't going to sit here all night with a man who'd gone from bitter to irrational.

Where was Emmett?

"Your new man is out there," Percy said, as if reading her very thoughts. "I don't get you, Belle. I thought we had something special." He rubbed his dark hair and gave her a perplexed stare. "When I saw you with him going through a storage unit, I went berserk all over again. Right there under my nose but as it turned out, a perfect coincidence."

"So you called your new friend and my enemy, Lance Johnson, to help you take out both of us?"

"I knew Johnson would leap on that," Percy said. "But he's an idiot. Can't shoot anything but his own foot." Then he changed, his voice whining and soft. "We could fix all of this if you'll just go away with me."

Belle gave him a look of disbelief. "Percy, you were abusive to me and you hated that I got a promotion. We had nothing special." Then she raised her voice. "I'm not going anywhere with you."

He leaned down and stared in her face, waving his gun in the air where he forced her to sit in a chair centered in the window. He could pace in front of her knowing the sharpshooters wouldn't shoot through her. "You're wrong. We had everything until you left me. Lance told me you did the same thing to him, caused his girl to leave him."

"He beat her. You came close to that with me, remember? Women don't put up with that stuff these days."

"No, no. We just had a little spat. Baby, you know I love you. I'll always love you."

Belle didn't respond to that. The man was seriously deranged. But she did watch his every step and she counted how many steps she'd need to jump through that shattered window and get away. If she just gave him time to move to the other side of the room, she thought she could make it.

It might be her only chance to get out of here alive.

Emmett stood with Jackson and the rest of the team. They planned to charge the house but…they had to find the right time. He'd studied the layout enough to know the bottom floor held a kitchen and large living room, where Percy had taken Belle.

"We can storm in there and hope he doesn't hurt her," Gavin told them earlier. "Or we can wait it out. SWAT is ready to do whatever we need."

"Negotiating won't get us anywhere," Emmett said. "We can't sweat him out, but he might get hungry."

"He might start making demands," Gavin said. "It's been two hours and he hasn't made a move other than pacing in front of that window. But we can't shoot him—too risky with Belle there as his shield."

"He knows I'm not alone," Emmett said, the thought of Belle getting shot making him want to go into action. "He's keeping her alive for some reason. I'd like to believe he has a soft spot in that black heart."

Or the man just wanted to drag out the torment and fear.

Emmett stared toward the house. The yellow glow of a street lamp showed the true hero. Justice sat hunched at the bottom of the steps. The dog refused to leave without his partner.

Emmett looked around at the people who'd gathered here, their emergency lights off and their vehicles out of sight. "There is one other thing that could happen."

"What's that, Marshal?" Lani asked.

"Belle might be waiting for the chance to save herself. And that scares me more than anything else."

Gavin stared back at the house and then glanced back at Emmett. "You're right. She's capable of doing that, but just in case, when she does, we'd better be ready to move in."

* * *

Belle had to make her move. They'd been inside the house for three hours now and Percy's agitation was growing by the minute. "I can get us both out of here," she said, trying to stand.

Percy whirled, his gun pointed. "I'm not falling for that trick. You and I both know how this works. If I open that door or make a wrong move, I'm toast. They probably have a sniper on me right now just waiting for the command to take me out."

"I haven't seen a red spot on your forehead yet," Belle said, thinking the same thing. "They don't want to kill you, Percy. They have Johnson. He's going to blame you. But they want you alive to hear your side of things."

Percy pushed at his damp hair, then jabbed a finger in the air. "He started this. I just met him while he was in prison. I worked there briefly as a guard, but man, I hated working at Rikers. They never saw my worth. After Lance got out, we met up again at the gym and then we went to a bar and put two and two together. All he talked about was how he'd make you pay. I wanted in on that."

"I thought you loved me," she said, knowing he never had loved her at all. "But instead, you decided to threaten me and my family and now you want to kill me?"

"I do love you, Belle," Percy said, pushing her back against the wall. "Enough to kill both of us and end it here."

Belle stared at him and, even in the moonlight, saw the hatred in his eyes. "Neither one of us needs to die and… I can help you get away."

Percy's eyes widened. "Do you mean it? Have you had a change of heart?"

Belle thought of Emmett and willed her expression to soften. "Yes, a big one."

"So what's the plan?" Percy asked, his hand touching her hair, his dark eyes burning with a madness she couldn't tolerate. "'Cause if you're playing me, I'll know it."

Belle held back the cringe that rumbled down her spine and gave Percy her best smile. "Just this," she said, rising out of the chair, her hands on his meaty arms guiding him so he had to face away from the street to keep her near. She motioned him toward her, a smile hiding the revulsion coiling through her.

As he moved close, she pressed against the opposite wall behind her in the tiny room. Just as he lowered his head to kiss her, Belle shoved him hard and lifted one of her legs with a high kick to Percy's midsection. He flew back toward the front window where he'd been holding her and dropped his gun. Grabbing the weapon, Belle put it in her belt. Then she hurled herself at Percy and flipped him down onto his back underneath the open window, stomping her boot in his back while she lifted the chair and smashed the remainder of the window into bits. A gaping hole of fresh hot air greeted her. Freedom.

"Justice," she called, her boot still digging into Percy's back while he moaned. "Come. Attack."

Her partner lifted into the air and sailed through the open window to land a foot away from where Percy moaned on the floor.

Justice then added to the moans when he bit into Percy's jeans.

Belle let out a shuddering breath as the house exploded with K-9s and their partners. The dogs surrounded Percy so she called Justice off and then turned as Emmett rushed in the door and parted the crowd. Giving her a quick glance, he kept moving toward the man curled in a ball in the corner.

He lifted Percy Carolo off the floor and snarled at him. "Let me do the honors, please." Then he told Percy he was under arrest for harassing and assaulting an officer, for the attempted murder and kidnapping of said officer, just as he'd stated earlier. Then he read him his rights and cuffed him before shoving him toward Jackson.

"I'll get him out of here," Jackson said, grabbing Carolo by his sweat-soaked collar.

"Belle, you betrayed me again," Carolo shouted. "I will kill Lance Johnson when I find him."

Belle gave him a look of pity but decided he'd find out soon enough how things worked with the law.

Belle stood by the window while the EMT checked her out, her adrenaline sliding away with each breath she took. Lani hugged her and let her be. Jackson nodded to her and did his job. Gavin came in and stood staring at her.

"I'm all right," she kept saying, her eyes always shifting to Emmett.

Emmett moved around the officers filing through the house and hurried to pull her into his arms. He held her there until both of their hearts beat a new rhythm.

Together.

TWENTY

Belle woke up late the next morning, her body sore, her mind at peace. It was over. Lance Johnson would go back to jail for a long time and even if he got out, he wouldn't dare mess with her again.

Percy Carolo would probably meet the same fate since they had enough evidence to put him away for a long, long time. He'd still blame her, but both Emmett and Gavin had explained to him in no uncertain terms that if he ever came near Belle again, he'd regret it in a big way.

Last night, they'd all gone to the precinct to file reports and question both of her attackers. Her ordeal was over but Sarge had announced that someone had tried to run over Liberty, the yellow Lab K-9 with a bounty on her head, last night while several of them were trying to save Belle. Noelle had taken her partner for a walk when it had happened. Now Noelle's street and home would be monitored around the clock. Belle wanted in on that.

She said a prayer for Noelle.

She rolled over and saw Justice lying in his home kennel near her bed. She'd left the kennel door open because he seemed to want to follow her around, still in protection mode.

But she had to wonder about her other protector. Would he stick around now that the danger was gone? He'd made it clear he wanted to get back out there and find his cousin. But where things stood between them, she couldn't say.

Emmett had brought her home after she'd given her statement and Gavin had ordered her to take the rest of the week off.

Emmett waited while she took a shower. Her mother sent down food but left them alone. Emmett told her to eat.

Then he went upstairs and explained to her parents and siblings about what had happened, assuring them she was okay and they were safe. Uncle Rico could call off his guards.

Emmett came back and held her close for a while, silent and strong and sure. "We can talk later," he told her. "We have a lot to talk about. Right now, you need to rest and sleep."

Belle loved being there in his arms. She did fall asleep on the couch, her head pressed against his chest.

After a while, Emmett lifted her up and tucked her into bed with a kiss. "I'll see you soon, I promise."

Then he kissed her one last time and headed to the door.

Belle could only nod, her emotions and the letdown that always came after a big arrest being twice as difficult this time. She wanted to tell him that she'd thought about him the entire time she'd been held in that house with Percy.

But she couldn't be sure if Emmett wanted the same. He must. He'd stayed there outside the house, watching over her.

He'd come back to her, wouldn't he?

He had to give her some space. That had been the hardest thing to do. Leaving Belle last night had torn Emmett's heart apart, but he still had some unfinished business out here.

Emmett had work to do, but he wanted to see Belle and make sure she was all right. She was tough but even a tough person could only take so much.

She'd been chased and harassed and shot at over the last couple of weeks—and almost killed. How did a person put that behind and get on with life?

And how did they stop these careening emotions and feelings that had exploded between them in the heat of the chase?

Could they sustain those feelings now that things had settled back down? He wanted that, wanted to be with Belle. But he had to find Randall first.

After checking in at his office and getting ribbed for hanging with the Brooklyn K-9 Unit too much these days, Emmett filed a report and talked to his superiors regarding his cousin. He had permission to continue the hunt for Randall Gage, but he wouldn't overstep with the K-9 unit again.

He still had informants all around Brooklyn, so he expected one of them to alert him. But first, he had to see Belle and tell her how he felt.

He was on his way to do that when his phone buzzed.

Speaking of informants, Decker Palmer had been with him a long time. Emmett watched over Decker since the man was trying to get his life back together after losing a lot of money with gambling and stocks and then becoming an alcoholic. He lived in a halfway house in Bay Ridge. "What's up, Deck?"

"Hey, man, I saw your cuz about ten minutes ago. He was walking toward the apartment he used to live in—the one in Bay Ridge you told me to watch. Only now it's a laundry or something. He looked real bad. I heard he's been hanging out at a homeless shelter nearby there."

"Thank you, Deck," Emmett said.

His informant hung up without another word.

Emmett put his truck in gear and turned around to head to Bay Ridge. If Randall was around, he intended to find him.

But he had to go by the book this time. So he called Gavin Sutherland and asked for assistance.

"I'll send Max Santelli and his K-9 Rottweiler, Sam. Sam's trained in suspect apprehension. A patrol officer will be with them."

Emmett had met Max once. He appeared intense and aggressive but was well liked, according to Belle. He gave Emmett the location. "Let me go in first and see if I can talk him into turning himself in."

"Okay, but… Max and Sam will be close by."

When Emmett arrived on the street where Randall had lived, Emmett parked his truck and started walking. Randall liked to hang out in diners since he never had gotten a good meal at home. Emmett's heart went out to his cousin. Randall had had a hard life, but that didn't give anyone the right to murder another human being. He wondered if the shelter had a soup kitchen.

He checked a few places but things had changed over the years. Finally, he saw a sign at the corner of 5th and 77th Street. Not far from the M-Train station.

Shelter from the Storm. Soup Kitchen All Day.

Emmett entered the building that had once been some sort of two-story retail store from the looks of it. Following the signs pointing to the kitchen, Emmett breathed a sigh of relief since the place wasn't packed with hungry people. He spotted Randall sitting alone in a worn armchair, watching an old Western. This time, he'd do things differently. He went in and sat down and looked over at his cousin. "Randall, don't run. I'll have to shoot you."

His cousin looked shocked to see Emmett and then he looked resigned. "Shooting me might be the best thing right now, man."

"I want to help you," Emmett said. "Let's walk out together, without any fuss, okay?"

"I haven't had breakfast," his cousin said, a stubborn gleam in his eyes.

Emmett leaned close. "Get it to go."

Randall shook his head and went to the open counter from the kitchen. "I need to get out of here. Can you wrap mine to go?"

The attendant nodded and brought him his food and gave him a to-go cup of coffee.

Emmett breathed a sigh of relief as they left the soup kitchen. He glanced around and spotted the NYPD cruiser parked up the street. "I'm not going to cuff you, but I'm going to take you to the Brooklyn K-9 Unit precinct," Emmett explained. "They want to ask you some questions regarding the McGregor murders twenty years ago."

Randall glared at him. "I didn't do anything, and I don't know what you're talking about."

Emmett could see the lies in his cousin's eyes. "Okay, then you shouldn't have anything to worry about."

They made it to the truck and Emmett moved to make sure his cousin got in. But Randall had other ideas. He whirled and threw hot coffee at Emmett. It hit his chest in a scalding fury, the bag of food following. The flimsy bag smashed into Emmett's face and fell to the ground, the bacon-and-egg sandwich splattering on the hot sidewalk.

Randall took off running.

The cruiser cranked and hurried up the street. Max came around the corner with a barking Sam.

Emmett knew the dog could apprehend and hold Randall, but he hesitated. "Max, bring Sam and follow me."

Emmett sprinted after Randall, his weapon drawn. He checked the street and watched helplessly as Randall swerved to the right into a crowded Starbucks. Emmett went in and searched. No Randall.

Then he turned and saw his cousin rushing out the door. Emmett pushed through the crowd and kept his eyes on Emmett as he hit the subway station.

And disappeared inside.

Max and his partner were right behind Emmett.

"I can track him from here," Max called.

Emmett took a breath. "Go."

Max took off toward the subway station and got lost in the crowd. Would he find Randall?

Emmett called in the report. "I had him, and he gave me the slip again. But Officer Santelli and Sam are in pursuit." He gave the location and the train route. What else could he do? He wasn't even supposed to be on this case.

And he didn't need to be on this case. He tried to never shoot in public places but with Randall, he'd hesitated twice now and twice his cousin had managed to get away.

I should have cuffed him right then and there.

It wouldn't happen again. He would pass this on to the people who were trying to find a killer. The Brooklyn K-9 Unit could finish their cold case without him.

Dejected, Emmett went back to his office and wrote up a report and then he called Gavin Sutherland and told him he was done.

"I should have cuffed him or at least held my weapon on him but I was hoping he'd cooperate. I can see I'm too close to this. I'll stay out of the way from now on."

Gavin let out a huff of breath. "Relax. You did call for backup, but Randall got on the subway and they lost him. So it's not all your fault. The man knows his way around the streets of Brooklyn and he seems to have an uncanny ability to hide rather quickly. Don't beat yourself up, Marshal Gage."

"I'll try to remind myself that I do sometimes fail."

"And what about Officer Montera?" Gavin asked in that firm tone of his. "Are you going to fail at that?"

"I'm not done with Officer Montera yet, Sergeant Sutherland. That's between her and me."

"Fair enough," Gavin said. "I wish you the best, Marshal Gage."

"Will you keep me posted on Randall?" Emmett asked.

"Will you do the same for us?" Gavin countered.

"Of course."

"Then we'll call it even," Gavin said.

"You need to stop moping."

Belle gave Cara a stern stare and wished she'd stayed in her apartment. This family dinner would be full of questions. "I've had a long day. I can mope if I want to."

It had been two days since her ordeal. Two days and no word from Emmett.

This morning, she'd been called into the precinct to talk to Lieutenant Olivia Vance from Internal Affairs. Belle had to vouch for her colleague and friend Henry Roarke who was on modified desk duty. He had been accused of using excessive force when a twenty-year-old suspect had tried to grab Henry's weapon. With a body cam on the fritz, there was no proof of how things had gone down.

Olivia, a pretty but tough brunette, had taken over the position when Lieutenant Jabboski had a mild heart attack. Belle, tired and irritated that her friend had to deal with this, had answered the lieutenant's pointed questions to the best of her ability. Now she was worried about Henry.

Detective Bradley McGregor, who'd been with Henry that night, had tried to assure Henry he'd be cleared. "I didn't see what happened but, man, I know you. No way. And I told that overly confident IA woman the same thing."

Belle had agreed with Bradley. "You're solid, Henry. Everyone knows that."

Henry's dark eyes had looked doubtful. Shaking his shaved head, he'd said, "Belle, you know the odds are against me."

Belle had touched his bronzed arm. "But you've beaten those odds over and over. Don't give up." Shrugging, she'd added, "Look at me. I've survived the worst."

That had made him smile. "And I thank you for coming in when you're supposed to be resting. I appreciate you, Belle."

She'd then slipped in and out of the precinct quickly because she hadn't wanted to answer any questions about Emmett and her.

But now Belle worried for her friend Henry and feared Emmett wouldn't ever come around again. Or maybe she was just letting her anxieties do their thing and run wild.

"It's not like you, though," her sister said while she shook out her still damp mane and then went back to folding napkins. "You got the bad guys and we're all safe again. It feels good. You're a hero, Belle."

Belle snapped back to attention. "I'm nobody's hero," she told Cara, following behind her with silverware for each place setting. "I got involved with the wrong man and made sure another abusive idiot went to jail. But they found each other and they both wanted revenge on me. That almost got me killed."

"But you survived and you fought back and maybe

you found the right man," Anita chimed in, looking cute in a plaid tunic over black leggings. "Don't you think that's good for us to see?" Then she poked Belle's arm. "You are not the criminal, Belle. You went after the criminals and brought them down before the rescue team could get to you. You're kind of a big deal."

She needed to listen to her own advice. She'd reminded Henry of how she'd survived. He'd do the same. Henry was tough and always in control. Same as all of them.

"You're our role model," Anita said, grinning at her.

Belle reached her arms wide. "This role model loves you both." Her sisters hugged her and giggled.

"Don't tell me you're both going into law enforcement," she said as they finished putting her mother's meat loaf on the table.

"No, but I am," Joaquin said with a soft smile from where he stood pouring tea into their dinner glasses.

Mamá put her hands on her hips and whirled to stare at her son. "This is news to me."

"Is it true?" Papá asked, his eyes glistening with fear and pride. "Have you thought about this, Joaquin?"

"It's what I want," Joaquin said. "I don't have to think about it. I've lived through it but on the wrong side. I'm going to finish school and then I'm going to apply to attend the police academy."

Glancing at Belle, he said, "I hope you'll give me some pointers."

Belle's emotions shifted like a roller coaster. "I'd be happy to do that."

Their mother lapsed into Spanish, and not in a good way.

They all laughed and hugged her while she ranted on.

Finally, Joaquin grabbed his mother and gave her a big kiss. That won her over. She held him close, tears in her eyes. "I suppose I should be proud, *si*?"

"Si," her children all retorted. Then they all rushed to find their seats.

The doorbell downstairs rang.

"I'll get it," Anita said. "And yes, I'll check the peephole first."

Belle went about passing potatoes and corn, thinking it was probably her uncle coming to check on them. He'd been so good about having the neighborhood watch members patrolling around their block.

But when she turned to see who Anita had brought up, her heart fluttered and came alive.

Emmett, with flowers and chocolate.

"Are those for me?" her mother deadpanned with a smile.

"No, ma'am, but I'm sure Belle will share with you," he replied.

Belle rushed to take the wildflowers and the box of chocolate. "Nice," she said. "Very nice."

"Cliché, but I was desperate," he whispered. "Can we talk?"

"First you eat," her mother announced, her tone undisputable.

Belle gave him a beseeching stare.

"I am hungry," he said with a grin. "Is that meat loaf?"

And so they ate, Belle's gaze hitting Emmett's when she thought no one was watching. But everyone was watching.

"So what's the deal with you two?" Cara asked in her sassy way.

"Cara!" Her sister gave her a be-quiet glare. Then Anita turned to Belle and Emmett. "But…we all want to know."

Belle stood. "That's it. Marshal Gage and I are going downstairs to my apartment for some privacy."

"We'll want details," her mother said, shoving two dessert plates at them. "Coconut cake."

Emmett took the plates with another grin. "I could get used to this."

After they were in Belle's apartment with the dead bolt on, he took their dessert plates and put them on the counter. Then he turned to face her.

Pulling her into his arms, he said, "Hi."

"Hi," she replied. "I missed you."

"I had to figure out some things," he replied, his hand moving through her hair.

"About us?"

"No, I've pretty much decided that I'm in love with you."

Belle's heart did a little dance, a mixture of awareness and anticipation. "That's good, because I've pretty much decided I'm in love with you, too."

"I can get used to that, too," he said, kissing her.

Belle enjoyed the kiss and then lifted her head back. "But…you have to deal with Randall."

"I did try to deal with him again yesterday," he told her. "But he got away again."

She listened while he filled her in. "Emmett, I'm so sorry. It must be hard, knowing he's the only family you have left around here. I think it's good that you're stepping away."

Emmett's eyes held hers, the misery in his words showing in his expression. "I have to step away, but I won't stop thinking about him or hoping he'll do the right thing. But I can't be the one to bring him in. I'm too close."

"I understand," she said. "But this won't be in our way, will it?"

Emmett looked into her eyes. "You mentioned my not having family here, but Belle, when I'm with you and your family, I feel at home. I think I've found my people, my person. I want to be with you."

"And my family?" she asked, tears in her eyes.

"Yes, oh, yes." He lifted her and twirled her around. "I get meat loaf and coconut cake. Are you kidding me?"

Belle laughed while Justice woofed a happy bark.

"And you get me, Marshal Gage."

"That's the best part of all." He touched his finger to her chin. "I want to marry you and come home to you and get in arguments with your siblings and…be here to guide them and help them. I want to spend the rest of my life with you."

Belle kissed him and then said, "We'll need the rest of this floor."

"For our family?"

"Yes." She ruffled his hair. "For our family."

"I might have rescued you that day in the park," Emmett said, "but you saved me."

Then he kissed her again before they both dug into their cake and smiled at each other.

Justice sighed and sank down on his haunches. His work here was done.

* * * * *

Terri Reed's romance and romantic suspense novels have appeared on the *Publishers Weekly* top twenty-five and Nielsen BookScan top one hundred lists, and have been featured in *USA TODAY*, *Christian Fiction* magazine and *RT Book Reviews*. Her books have been finalists for the Romance Writers of America RITA® Award and the National Readers' Choice Award and finalists three times for the American Christian Fiction Writers Carol Award. Contact Terri at terrireed.com or PO Box 19555, Portland, OR 97224.

Books by Terri Reed

Love Inspired Suspense

Buried Mountain Secrets
Secret Mountain Hideout

True Blue K-9 Unit: Brooklyn

Explosive Situation

True Blue K-9 Unit

Seeking the Truth

Military K-9 Unit

Tracking Danger
Mission to Protect

Northern Border Patrol

Danger at the Border
Joint Investigation
Murder Under the Mistletoe
Ransom
Identity Unknown

Visit the Author Profile page
at Harlequin.com for more titles.

EXPLOSIVE SITUATION

Terri Reed

Trust in the Lord with all thine heart; and lean not unto thine own understanding. In all thy ways acknowledge him, and he shall direct thy paths.
—*Proverbs 3:5–6*

Thank you to my family for all the support and love.

ONE

A prickle of unease tingled at the base of K-9 detective Henry Roarke's neck. Squirreled away in the records room of the recently formed Brooklyn K-9 unit with his bomb-sniffing beagle, Cody, lying at his feet and dozens of his fellow officers in the building, he knew there was no reason for the unsettling sensation of being watched. Yet it was something that he had been feeling the past several months. Even before the incident that had landed him in hot water.

Eyeing Cody, who lifted his head but made no sound, Henry couldn't decide if he was being paranoid or had just been cooped up in here too long, especially with the humid July heat adding its own special brand of oppression to the windowless room. Yet he couldn't shake the disquiet alerting his senses.

With slow, deliberate movements, he set down the file folder he held, straightened his spine and turned around, fully expecting to find an empty doorway. Instead, his gaze collided with the amber-colored eyes of Internal Affairs Lieutenant Olivia Vance. He suppressed a groan of frustration.

She stood tall and regal in a black pantsuit with her brunette hair pulled back into some sort of fancy bun, which emphasized the slender column of her neck visible above the collar of her white shirt. Her tawny skin had the glow of health and her full lips were tinged a slightly rosy color that emphasized her very feminine and pretty mouth. He jerked his gaze back to her eyes.

The woman exuded a professional aptitude that would normally draw Henry in. He liked women who were confident and sure of their place in the world—not that he'd dated much the past six years. After his long-term girlfriend Kathy's refusal to bond with Riley, he'd made a vow not to let anyone in his life until his sister was on her own.

Except this woman was here to dig into his life, not start a romance. Olivia was tasked with determining whether the allegations brought against him by a twentysomething-year-old punk, who'd resisted arrest and made a grab for his sidearm, were reason enough to recommend to the review board that Henry be brought up on assault charges. Charges that would end a career he loved.

Sharply turning back to the mound of folders he was organizing, Henry asked, "Can I help you, Lieutenant?"

"I need to interview you."

He slanted a glance at her.

"If you would please accompany me to an interrogation room." She gestured to the open doorway and empty hall behind her.

Jaw clenching, Henry marshaled his irritation as best he could. "With all due respect, ma'am, I've already spoken to Lieutenant Jabboski. Can't you read his report?"

Olivia's delicately dark, winged eyebrows rose. "I'm sorry to inform you that Lieutenant Jabboski's skills as an investigator were lacking. He made few notes and relied heavily on his gut feelings. I, however, do not."

The original Internal Affairs investigator had recently suffered a mild heart attack and retired, leaving the investigation to be completed by the recently promoted Olivia. Though Henry had never met the woman, he'd known of her for years. He was friends with her two older brothers, both officers working out of Manhattan precincts and also knew one of her sisters, a paramedic. Each had described Olivia as a taskmaster, meticulous and overbearing. Traits that lent themselves to the career she'd chosen.

"Because I am basically starting from the beginning," the lieutenant continued, "I need to hear from you regarding the events that took place on the night in question."

Henry's coworkers had already been interviewed by the Internal Affairs lieutenant. And no matter how much each one had assured him that the investigation wouldn't amount to anything, anxiety twisted in his chest. Now it was his turn to fall under this woman's scrutiny. "I'd like my union rep to be present."

After a second's hesitation, she inclined her head. "That is your right. I will wait to hear from you and set up a time in the future. Meanwhile, have fun with your file folders—though I seriously doubt any of them are about to explode."

Henry drew back his chin at the jab. "Excuse me?"

She shrugged and gave him a smile that didn't reach her eyes. "I was told you were chomping at the bit to get back to full duty. Apparently, I was misinformed." She turned to go.

"Lieutenant, wait!" Henry was indeed eager to reclaim his position on the bomb squad. He was tired of the menial assignments and there was only so much training he and Cody could do in a day before the dog needed a break. "I've changed my mind. We can do this now. Here."

He'd talk to her without his union rep because he hadn't done anything wrong, but he wasn't about to let her put him in an interrogation room like he was some criminal suspect.

For a moment, she seemed to consider his words, then nodded before withdrawing a small notepad and pen from her suit jacket. She stepped just inside the doorway. "Okay, then. Tell me about the night of March twenty-seventh."

Resigning himself to repeating what he'd told Jabboski, Henry said, "A call came in about a possible bomb threat at Owl's Head Park's skate park. When we—"

The chime of an incoming text on his cell phone filled the room. Henry grabbed the device from the top of the filing cabinet. He hoped the text was from his sister saying she had made it safely home from her summer class at Brooklyn College.

He still wasn't used to the idea of his baby sister going to college. She'd elected to take summer classes to jump-start her freshmen year. Plus, it would keep her busy because her regular summer job of nanny for the neighbors was on hold while the family was out west visiting relatives.

"Excuse me," Olivia's voice snapped. "We're in the middle of an interview."

Henry met her gaze. "I understand, ma'am. This will only take a minute."

He opened his text messages, aware of Olivia's displeasure emanating from her like daggers poking into his skin. He turned his back while he read the text. It was from Riley. She was on her way to Coney Island. Her class had ended over an hour ago. No doubt she was already at the boardwalk and texting him had been an afterthought. She was in so much trouble.

He blew out a breath as he quickly typed a response, reminding her they'd discussed her going straight home after her class. She may be eighteen and technically an adult, but until she was on her own and not living under his roof, she still had to abide by his rules. And she'd just broken one.

He pinched the bridge of his nose as he set the phone back on the filing cabinet. His head throbbed with a brewing headache. Why had no one told him parenting a teenager would be so difficult? He didn't regret taking in his half sibling after the death of their father and her mother six years ago. But there were times when he pondered what it would be like to be free of this constant gnawing worry.

"Can we proceed?" Olivia's voice was edged in impatience.

"Yes, ma'am." He couldn't believe he had to go through this again. He had had complete confidence that Lieutenant Jabboski would have told the review board that Henry had acted appropriately. Now the investigation was starting from scratch. And with the disapproving glare that this woman was serving him, he doubted she would find much in his favor.

Reining in his frustration, he said, "When Cody and I, along with Detective Bradley McGregor and his K-9, arrived—"

His phone chimed again with another incoming text. He cringed. Now what? He hoped Riley was saying she was headed home.

Olivia cleared her throat. "Can you please put away your phone and set it to silent?"

"Sorry. It's my sister, Riley." He snatched up the phone.

Family came first for him, always.

Only this wasn't from Riley. The incoming text came from a number he didn't recognize. His mouth dried as he read the words.

Knock knock. Who's there? Joey Yums. Joey Yums who? Joey Yums goes kaboooom—at 3:20 LOLZ

Henry's stomach dropped. Joey Yums was a hole-in-the-wall falafel joint at the far end of the Coney Island boardwalk and one of his sister's favorite places to eat when they visited the area.

He checked the time on his phone and panic exploded in his chest, making his body shake. It would take twenty to thirty minutes to reach the restaurant from the station, depending on traffic—barely time to arrive and remove people from the vicinity, let alone disarm an explosive device. But he had to try. Riley was in danger. His veins flooded with adrenaline. He quickly sent her a text warning her to stay away from Joey Yums and go home. Now. He grabbed Cody's leash. "Time to work."

He pushed past Olivia and hurried out of the records room in search of his sergeant.

"Excuse me!" Olivia's voice rang out with indignation. "We're not done here. And you aren't allowed to work."

"I have to go. Lives are in danger." He went straight to the front desk, leaving Olivia staring after him, her gaze like a heavy weight on his shoulders.

"I need Gavin now," he told Penny McGregor, his friend and colleague, and Bradley's younger sister.

"He's out on a call," she told him. "But I can contact him."

Having no other choice, Henry had to make sure his sister and everyone else was safe. "You do that. Tell him Joey Yums restaurant in Coney Island. A bomb threat. We're on it. Alert the sixtieth precinct to meet us in front of Joey Yums."

Without waiting for a reply, he headed out the door as his fingers flew across his text message screen, writing to his boss. He had to let Gavin know what he was doing. Henry had no doubt he'd end up in hot water, but at the moment, he didn't care. Riley was his only family and innocent lives were at stake.

He reached his vehicle, a large white SUV with blue lettering identifying the K-9 unit. The back passenger area was outfitted with a large compartment for Cody and a smaller passenger space for suspect transportation. Behind that was cargo space for his and Cody's equipment.

A question ricocheted through his mind: How had this bomber managed to get a hold of his personal cell phone number?

A good dose of irritation, annoyance and stunned outrage engulfed Olivia as she raced to keep up with the towering, fast-moving officer while stuffing her notebook and pen back into her suit pocket.

The summer sun glistened off his shaved head and deepened the bronze angles of his handsome face. He presented a formidable adversary with a well-toned, muscular body beneath his dark blue uniform. His shoulders were wide and his bearing that of someone who was used to being in control.

Which irked her to no end.

Her late husband had wanted to control her and that had caused issues in their marriage, which left her with a bitter taste in her mouth. She was done with controlling men.

Olivia caught up to him at his vehicle. "Where do you think you're going? You're on modified duty. Which means you are not to leave the station."

He opened the back passenger door and lifted Cody into the K-9 unit's caged compartment.

The moment he shut the door, Olivia planted herself in front of the driver-side door. The intensity in his dark eyes was both daunting and frightening, but she had two older brothers who had mastered the art of intimidation. Henry's ire didn't faze her. She blew out a breath. "Your refusal to obey orders doesn't bode well for you."

"With all due respect, this investigation is a sham. The kid is lying. I didn't hurt him. And I know how to follow orders. I'm former Army."

She'd read in his file that he'd served. Combat soldier with a medal of valor. Impressive, but she couldn't let that sway her. "Then you should stay put and let someone else deal with the situation."

"I can't." He reached past her, his hand grabbing the door handle. He was taller than her by at least four inches, which was a lot considering she was almost six feet tall. His arm brushed against her shoulder, the friction disconcerting.

"Why? Where are you going?"

"Coney Island," he said sharply. "That second text was a bomb threat."

Her stomach contracted with a wave of anxiety. A bomb? "There's a bomb hidden somewhere on the Coney Island beach or boardwalk?"

"Yes." He faced her. His dark eyes filled with worry. "I don't care if you take my job away. My sister is there, and she's in danger. I'm going. As a police officer or not. Time is of the essence. Come with me or not, the choice is yours."

Stunned by that bit of news, Olivia understood now why he was so anxious to get to Coney Island. And his sister was involved. She understood family loyalty.

Her two brothers would react the same way, not caring that they were risking their lives or their careers, if one of their three sisters needed them. Apparently, Henry was the same. Grudging respect filled her and she mentally tucked away the knowledge.

Without another word, she ran around the front of

his vehicle, keeping her hand on the hood to make sure he didn't leave without her as he jumped in and started the engine.

She quickly climbed into the passenger seat. She'd barely shut the door before he peeled out of the parking lot behind the K-9 unit building with sirens blaring. Even with her seat belt fastened, she had to hang on with both hands to keep from being thrown about the inside of the cab as he drove out of the Bay Ridge neighborhood like a man on a mission. Which she supposed he was.

Everything about this man was sharp. Sharp edges, sharp tongue and sharp anger. She'd done her research before confronting him today. His fellow K-9 officers spoke highly of him. All trusting his judgment. His superior had said Henry was top notch. One of the best.

Even his instructors at the police academy praised him and his dog.

But the man sitting beside her didn't appear to be a man in control. More like a man desperate to protect someone he loved. What had happened the night of Davey Carrell's injuries? Had Henry lost his cool as Davey claimed, bending Davey's wrist to the point of breaking and elbowing the kid in the neck, causing strain to the muscles there?

She had to admit Henry drove with skill and focus. Even at this breakneck speed, she felt safe. For both herself and the child growing inside of her.

His phone blew up with incoming text messages. He ignored them and concentrated on the road. She had to admire his commitment to no texting and driving. "Should I read your text messages?"

He sped through an intersection. "Yes. Please."

She plucked his phone from the pocket of his shirt where she'd seen him drop it. Leaning close to him, she got a whiff of his spicy aftershave that momentarily stalled her hand. The scent was something she'd never smelled before. Unusual and very masculine. Giving herself a shake, she looked at the lock screen, thankful he didn't have a privacy setting. The texts were all from his boss, Sergeant Gavin Sutherland.

Swiping up, she was able to read the furious missives from his boss. "Your sergeant says he's dispatched a local bomb squad and will meet you there."

She studied Henry's profile. His jaw was clenched so tightly she was surprised she didn't hear his teeth cracking. He didn't bother to glance away from the road, but gave a sharp nod of his head. "I need you to text my sister again. Tell her to leave now if she hasn't already and meet us at the corner of West 12th and Bowery. And to stay away from Joey Yums."

She scrolled through his text contacts until she found his sister Riley's name. She read the last two texts. The one that had come in at the beginning of the interview and the one he sent back, reprimanding her for not going straight home after her classes, the tone more fatherly than brotherly.

Considering he'd raised his sister alone for the past six years, she wasn't too surprised, but somehow the idea of this man as a father tugged at her in unexpected ways. Giving herself another mental shake, she quickly sent a text to Riley giving her the information.

No answering text came in. Olivia stared at the device as if she could will the teenager to respond. She sent up a silent plea heavenward for God to prompt Riley to look at her phone. Was this what parenthood would be like? Worrying, waiting and praying?

She needed to talk to her brothers' wives and ask how they coped with motherhood.

Henry brought the vehicle to a screeching halt at an angle at the curb of West 12th and Bowery. The iconic state park was bursting with activity along the famous boardwalk, the amusement park rides were filled with tourists and locals alike, and the sandy beaches sported sunbathers on blankets or children and adults frolicking in the waves.

He jumped out and slammed the door. Quickly, she followed suit. By the time she made it around to his side of the vehicle, he had Cody already leashed up and was talking to him in a quiet, soft voice. She wouldn't have deemed him capable of such tenderness, especially in the midst of a bomb threat. Another aspect of him to tuck away for further analysis.

She handed Henry back his phone. "She hasn't replied." His distress ratcheted up her own nervousness. "She probably put her phone in her purse and can't hear it." She hoped that was the case.

Henry tucked the phone in his pocket.

"Where to now?" she asked.

"Joey Yums."

She had no idea where that was, or even what it was, for that matter. "I'm coming with you."

If she stuck close to him, she could observe and record his behavior for her report. Seeing him and his dog in action would help her to better form an opinion of his work habits and ethics.

He hesitated, concern etched on his handsome face, then he said, "Let's go." He and Cody took off at a run.

She hurried after them, glad she'd worn her flats today with her suit. She couldn't imagine running on the planked boardwalk in heels. Huffing with the speed at which she ran to keep up with Henry and Cody, she was thankful when the pair slowed outside of a restaurant.

Two police officers from the local precinct stood nearby. From the fresh face of the younger officer, Olivia guessed him to be a rookie. Protocol was for the first on scene to wait for the supervising agency, in this case the Brooklyn K-9 Unit, to arrive before starting evacuation, because opening doors without having them checked by explosive experts could result in disaster.

Henry halted at the older officer's side. "Set a perimeter while we evacuate the restaurant." Henry pointed to the eating establishment then glanced at his watch. "According to the text message we have seven minutes before detonation. We have to clear the place."

Olivia's lungs squeezed tight. "You can't go in there, Henry."

Had she just called him Henry instead of Detective? The texts from his sister, his worry, the imminent danger made this suddenly more…personal.

He stared at her for a heartbeat. "May I call you Olivia?"

She lifted her chin and then nodded.

"Olivia, we're trained for this. Waiting will result in destruction."

He was right. Civilian lives were at stake. "Go." She prayed she was making the right decision.

Henry and Cody hurried forward. Cody sniffed

around the entrance without alerting before they disappeared inside.

Staring after them, worry wormed through her. Within moments, a stream of people rushed out of the restaurant. She and the two officers hustled the crowd away. She was thankful to have something useful to do while Henry and Cody searched for the bomb. And she was just as thankful the smells of Coney Island weren't causing her stomach to rebel. She was glad to be done with the morning sickness that had plagued her the first trimester of her pregnancy.

More officers arrived. A man in a full explosive ordnance disposal suit headed for the entrance to the restaurant. She quickly ascertained the officer in charge and explained that Henry and Cody had already gone inside. Officers set up a barrier around the restaurant, asking people to vacate the area.

Not knowing what else to do, Olivia joined in. "Please back up. You need to leave the boardwalk."

Many people moved back but several remained to watch, and some scurried off. Her gaze scanned the growing crowd of onlookers. Was the bomber among the gawkers?

Henry's boss and his partner arrived on scene. Olivia recognized Sergeant Gavin Sutherland and his dog, Tommy, a brown and white springer spaniel. She rushed to him and brought him up to speed on what was happening.

"He did the right thing, you know," Gavin said.

She nodded. Even though he'd disobeyed orders, she couldn't fault him for putting the safety of others ahead of his own interests. Something her late husband would never have thought of, let alone done.

A moment later, Cody and Henry walked out. Henry held up his hands in a gesture of confusion and shaking his head. "Nothing. Cody didn't alert on anything."

"We'll take it from here," Gavin said. "You cooperate with Lieutenant Vance. We need you back on duty!"

"Yes, sir," Henry replied, though his troubled gaze scanned their surroundings.

Gavin and Tommy walked back toward the restaurant.

"Has your sister responded?" Olivia asked.

His anxiety obvious in the tightness around his mouth and the concern in his eyes, he shook his head. "Do you mind if we search for her?"

Deciding neither of them would be able to concentrate until they were sure his sister was safe, she nodded. "Let's find Riley."

Figuring Riley had headed for Luna Park, Henry and Cody led Olivia at a fast clip toward the amusement park rides. He kept an eye out for any sign of Riley among the throng of summertime visitors. His phone chimed. Finally. He read the message and his stomach dropped. Same phone number as before. His steps faltered as the words on the phone's screen registered like a loud clanging in his ears.

Oh, did I say Joey Yums? I meant the garbage can. Kaboom! LOLZ

A fresh wave of panic hit Henry. There were several trash bins on the boardwalk and inside the park. "Cody, seek!"

"What's going on?" Olivia asked.

"Another bomb threat," he told her as he and Cody hustled toward the nearest garbage can. Nose working the ground and the air, the beagle moved past the round metal containers. Then he let out a loud bark and strained against his leash. Clearly he'd picked up a scent.

Running to keep up, Henry let Cody lead him down the boardwalk. Cody's feet scrabbled on the wooden planks as he neared a garbage can that had been moved from the center aisle and placed beside a bench where a young couple sat kissing.

The dog halted in front of the trash can and stared at it. His signal that he'd found an explosive.

Fearing for his dog, Henry gave a sharp whistle, Cody's signal to return. The dog immediately responded. Running toward the couple, Henry waved his arms and shouted, "Off the bench! Run. Now!"

The garbage can exploded.

TWO

Muted screams penetrated the ringing in Olivia's ears. Crouched, she protected her head with her hands. All around, people were taking cover. Trash and sand rained down, stinging her back and hands.

Peeking around her elbows, she watched Henry, a few feet away, scoop up his dog and cradle Cody in his arms. Henry's back had taken the force of the blast. The young couple who had been sitting on the bench beside the garbage can had heard Henry's warning and were halfway over the railing separating the boardwalk from the beach when the bomb detonated. Now both were lying in the sand.

The world settled into a stunned silence as the echo of the explosion dissipated. Olivia cautiously rose, assessing any injuries to her person and deemed herself unharmed. The baby moved, the slight sensation reassuring. She rushed forward. "Detective Roarke? Are you hurt?"

Henry set Cody on the ground then straightened and faced her. His dark eyes blazed with anger and concern. "I'm good. You?"

"Fine." Though her heart raced at a fast clip.

On the beach, the couple sat up and appeared to have minor injuries. Henry headed toward the spot where half of the bench had been ripped away and a charred circle remained on the ground where the garbage can had once stood. Now the can rested on its side a few feet away. There was a ragged hole where the explosive device had ripped through the metal.

"That could have been my sister," Henry's horrified whisper tugged at Olivia. "I have to find her."

"It seems a bit too coincidental that the bomber would contact you at the same time your sister is in the vicinity," Olivia stated aloud. She hadn't put the two together until now. Were the Roarkes being targeted?

Pressing a hand over her abdomen where the small round bump pressed against her clothing, protective instincts surged through her so strongly she shivered.

The thought of something happening to the child growing inside of her... Nausea, different from her previous bout of morning sickness, rolled in her stomach. She lifted a silent prayer to God for protection and glanced up to find Henry's intent gaze locked on her like a laser. She dropped her hand away. At his raised eyebrow, heat infused her cheeks. The man noticed way too much. The last thing she needed was for him to realize she was pregnant. She didn't want anyone treating her differently because of the baby.

Finding her voice, Olivia said, "How do we find your sister?"

His eyebrows dipped and for a moment she was afraid he was going to ask questions that she'd rather not answer. Then he pulled his phone out of his shirt pocket and typed in a text.

Sirens punctuated the air. The officers who'd converged on Joey Yums now flooded the boardwalk, quick to preserve the area for the crime scene investigators.

An ambulance rolled to a stop nearby and two paramedics jumped out. Olivia met the surprised gaze of her youngest sister, Ally.

After saying something to her partner, Ally grabbed a big red box and jogged to Olivia's side. "What happened? Are you okay? The baby?"

"Shhhh," Olivia hissed and shot a quick glance at Henry to see if he'd heard. His gaze was trained on the crowd that had gathered to watch. She prayed he hadn't been paying attention to her sister's questions.

Ally was shining a penlight into Olivia's eyes. "What?"

Batting her sister away, she said, "I'm fine, Ally. It's those two I'm worried about." She pointed to the two young people sitting on the sand, now flanked by officers.

"Jake, we've got two injured on the beach," Ally called out to her partner, who nodded and headed in that direction.

Ally turned her brown gaze to Henry. "Whoa, Henry, you have a cut on your head." She opened her box and pulled out gauze and tape.

Olivia wasn't surprised that Ally and Henry were familiar with each other. Despite the size of the Brooklyn borough, first responders and law enforcement were a tight-knit community. Except when it came to Internal Affairs.

She'd experienced firsthand the cool disdain most everyone in uniform held for the division that investigated its own. It was uncomfortable, at best, and downright disturbing most of time. Not to mention lonely and isolating. And no matter how much she tried not to let the drawbacks to the job get to her, there were days she regretted the professional track she'd chosen.

Henry put his hand to the back of his head and pulled it away to reveal dark red blood smeared on his palm.

Olivia sucked in a breath. "You *are* hurt."

He gave a negative shake of his head. "I barely feel the wound."

Stubborn man. Of course he wouldn't admit to any pain. That would be too much like admitting to being human.

"Well, I need you to sit so I can bandage your laceration," Ally told him.

Olivia pointed to the nearest bench. "Sit."

Henry's startled gaze met hers. "Yes, ma'am."

Henry took a seat so Ally could dress his wound.

"You should make an appointment with your primary doctor to make sure there's no concussion," Ally said as she finished up.

"I will," he promised. "But I have something I need to do first."

Olivia put her hand on his shoulder, keeping him from rising. "Take a breath."

Ally rose, gathered her things and said to Olivia, "I'll let you tell Mom and Dad about this."

Olivia grimaced. "Thanks. Honestly, they don't need to know."

"You really think Dad won't hear about this incident?" Ally shook her head, her golden-brown ponytail swishing. "I better go help Jake." Taking her red supply kit with her, she hurried away.

Olivia glanced at Henry, who stared at his phone as if willing it to ding. Cody sat at his feet, waiting patiently for his next job.

Her sister was right. Their father, a captain with the NYPD, would learn that his oldest daughter was at the scene of a bombing. Not a usual day in Internal Affairs. She'd worked hard to make the rank of lieutenant and hoped to make her parents proud. But after the death of her husband, her life had spun out of her control. She wasn't quite sure how to handle the grief, the betrayal, the anger. Most days it was easiest to pretend she didn't feel anything at all.

Henry stood, bracing his legs apart for a moment as if to steady himself.

Concern arced through Olivia. She put a hand out to help him then thought better of it, letting her hand drop back to her side. She empathized with his worry and could only imagine the strike to his head hurt, but giving into her natural inclination to support and comfort wouldn't serve her position as an Internal Affairs investigator well. And that really was a source of irritation that she needed to suppress.

"Henry." Sergeant Gavin Sutherland jogged to their side.

Henry squared his shoulders and faced his boss. "Sarge."

"Lieutenant," Gavin greeted with a nod.

She returned the gesture of respect.

Eyes narrowed on the white bandage on Henry's

scalp, Gavin said, "After you write up the incident report, take the rest of the day off. Visit a doctor. I don't want you back at the station until Monday."

"Yes, sir," Henry said. "I have to collect my sister and then I'll stop by the precinct to write up my report. Can you give Lieutenant Vance a ride, sir?"

Olivia gaped at Henry, pretty sure she looked like a fish landing on the dock of her family's vacation spot. He was trying to get rid of her. Not so fast. "That won't be necessary. I'll go with you to find your sister. You took a nasty blow to the head. I wouldn't want you to collapse on the boardwalk."

"I'm not—" he protested but she held up a hand.

"I insist." She smiled sweetly to soften her words. She outranked both of these men. "I still need to interview you."

A frown pulled his dark eyebrows together. "I'm sorry, can't that wait?"

"No. Why else do you think I came with you?"

Gavin stared at her a moment before saying, "Do as the Lieutenant wishes, Henry. Someone has to be there in case that hard head of yours decides to explode."

"Har, har, Sarge," Henry muttered, tossing his boss a small smile. All the K-9 officers at the Brooklyn K-9 Unit had grown close in a short time, and a little ribbing on one another, even from Sarge, always helped with tension. He turned to Olivia and said, "By all means," then addressed his dog. "Let's find Riley."

Cody gave a sharp yelp as if in agreement.

Olivia nodded to the sergeant, then fell into step with Henry. "You and Cody were very brave back there."

"We were doing our job," he said. "Which we're good at, by the way."

"I know you find this process arduous but it's necessary," she said. "Allegations of police brutality must be taken seriously."

His jaw firmed but he made no comment as his stride lengthened. The beagle had no trouble staying in step with his handler and it was obvious Cody's nose was working, sniffing through the various odors permeating the air. She had to move quicker to keep up.

They entered the Luna Park amusement area filled with rides for all ages, a variety of foods, games to play and shopping. All around them, people had gone back to their fun as if the exploding garbage can on the nearby boardwalk hadn't happened. She didn't understand it. "Don't any of these people realize how close they came to disaster?"

Henry glanced at her, then away. "In my experience, most people view danger as something that happens to others. As long as it doesn't interfere with their own lives, they ignore what could harm them. Besides, considering last week was the 4th of July, most of these people probably figured the noise was leftover fireworks."

She supposed he was correct. Still, the danger had been real. Once again, the protective instinct to cover the child inside of her with a comforting hand on her abdomen flooded her veins, but she refrained.

Henry placed his hand to the small of her back and guided her around a line waiting for the roller coaster. Cody sniffed each person he passed. Henry's gaze scanned the crowd. She was glad he wasn't looking at her because she was sure her expression would give away her shock at his touch.

"Finally. There's Riley."

Following the line of his gaze to a pretty young woman with dark ringlets and a wide smile standing near the front of the line of the roller coaster with some friends, Coney Island Cyclone, Olivia smiled. The resemblance to Henry was unmistakable. They shared the same deep bronze skin, dark wide eyes and high cheekbones. Both were tall, though Riley still had the gangly look of a teen while Henry was all muscle and strength.

If Henry pulled Riley out of line now, the teenager would be both embarrassed and angry. Olivia turned to Henry. "Let her have her ride."

Doubt clouded his eyes but then he sighed and nodded. After having Cody sniff the perimeter of the ride and those standing in line and seeing no sign of alert, Henry and Olivia moved to the shade of a tree to wait for his sister to come off the roller coaster. Cody sat at Henry's feet as if waiting for his next command.

Seizing on the opportunity, she took her notebook out of her pocket and, with pen poised, said, "You were telling me about the night at Owl's Head Park."

Henry folded his arms over his chest, his gaze scanning the area as he spoke. "Cody alerted to a backpack sitting off to one side. The owner of the backpack tried to take the bag and leave. We detained him and he resisted. Then he made a grab for my sidearm."

She scribbled as he talked. Glancing up from her notes, she said, "That is the point when Mr. Carrell sustained his injuries?"

"Allegedly," Henry bit out. "I didn't break that kid's wrist."

"Then can you explain how the injury happened?"

He shook his head. "I have no idea. If I was going to break something on the suspect I would have gone for his elbow. But I didn't."

A shudder at the image his words evoked rippled through her. Eying his muscular arms, she had no doubt he could snap a bone.

"He also sustained an injury to his neck," she commented, forcing herself back on track. "I suppose you didn't do that, either?"

His gaze flicked to her, hard and unyielding. "Olivia, I used a defensive tactic to prevent the suspect from relieving me of my duty weapon."

"And Detective McGregor witnessed this altercation?"

The muscles in Henry's neck tightened. "Bradley was managing the crowd."

"Right. So he didn't actually see Mr. Carrell grab for your weapon."

"No. If Bradley had been able to corroborate my story, none of this would be happening."

That was true. And unfortunate for Henry that Bradley McGregor hadn't witnessed the altercation. "How did you secure your weapon?"

"The way I was trained," he replied. "I grabbed his right hand, which held my weapon, while wedging my other forearm into the curve of his neck and pushing him backward until he released his hold on my sidearm. Would you like me to show you?"

She blinked, intrigued by the offer. Would a demonstration of this tactic support Henry's version of the story? "Maybe that would be a good idea."

His head jerked back and he stared at her. "Really?"

She suppressed a smile at his surprise. "Yes, really. But we will have to table that for another day. For now, we'll stick with questions. You didn't find an explosive device in the backpack, correct?"

He heaved a beleaguered sigh. "No, we did not."

"But Cody alerted?" She'd witnessed the dog in action today. Both the dog and handler were competent. They worked well together. She could understand why his sergeant wanted him back on duty.

"He did."

"A false alert?"

"No way. The NYPD's forensic specialist found non-visible trace amounts of particulates on the bag."

"But you did not find a bomb."

"No. However, that doesn't mean there wasn't some sort of incendiary device inside the bag at one time. The department searched the residence of his parents where he said he was living. His parents seemed confused, but they corroborated that he was their son and that he had a room at their home." He let out a scoff. "At least that was the report I heard from my coworkers. Since I was not allowed to question anyone or investigate the case."

His frustration was palpable but couldn't be helped. "Had you ever had a run-in with Mr. Carrell prior to this?"

"No, I had not."

"Has Cody ever given you a false alert?"

The dog's ears perked up as if he, too, waited to hear the answer.

Henry clenched his teeth together. "One time. During training."

"Ah. He has a record of giving a false alert." Surprising after what she'd seen today, but she made a note.

"Only the one time during training in the early days."

His sharp tone had her lifting her eyebrows.

He dipped his chin, as if checking his attitude. "Sorry, Olivia."

Abruptly, Henry shifted, taking a protective stance in front of her as his gaze swiveled and he slowly turned in all directions as if expecting a threat. Cody seemed to read his master's mood because the beagle stood, his nose in the air.

Henry's sudden anxiety caused a cascade of alarm to flush through Olivia. She placed her hand on her sidearm hidden beneath her suit jacket. "What's wrong?"

"I don't know." His words came out measured, as if he were barely breathing.

"Something has you spooked." She glanced around. Was the bomber here? Would another text come in telling them an additional bomb had been planted in the vicinity or somewhere else?

After several tense seconds, he grimaced. "Paranoia."

"Or a cop's instincts." Olivia kept her own gaze vigilant.

He gestured to where Riley and her friends were exiting the roller coaster ride. "Here we go."

They approached the trio of teens.

"Henry? What are you doing here?" Riley gasped. "What happened to your head?"

"We need to leave," he barked.

Riley pulled a face. "Why?"

"I've been texting you," he said.

"My phone's in my bag. I haven't checked it lately. What's going on?" Riley's gaze bounced to Olivia and back to her brother.

Henry told the girls about the bomb on the boardwalk. "For whatever reason, this bomber has decided to communicate with me. I would rather you were home safe so I don't have to worry."

"Henry," the young woman's voice rose with pleading. She glanced at her friends, clearly embarrassed by being brought to heel by her older sibling, yet there was no mistaking the concern in her dark eyes.

Olivia could appreciate the conflicting emotions warring through the young woman. Being the eldest girl, many times the responsibility for her siblings landed on Olivia's shoulders. A point of contention with her brothers and sisters. Moved by the need to diffuse the situation, Olivia stepped forward and extended her hand. "Hi Riley, I'm Olivia."

The girl blinked then took her hand. "Olivia? Aren't you the Internal Affairs officer investigating my brother?"

"I am," she confirmed, sliding a glance at Henry. Obviously, he had talked about her. Probably disparagingly.

That was the way of it for most IA personnel. The rank and file weren't fond of those who chose to police the police. And though she fought to not let the wariness and resentment directed toward Internal Affairs affect her, it did. The solitary nature of the job was beginning to grate on her nerves.

Stifling a sigh, she said, "I was with your brother

when he received the threatening text. He was very concerned about you being in the vicinity of the bomb."

Riley's gaze darted to Henry and back to Olivia. Realization shined bright in the young woman's dark eyes. "Were you hurt because of me?"

Shaking his head, Henry was quick to say, "No. This is not on you."

Riley turned to her friends. "I'll catch you all later."

"You both should go home, as well," Henry interjected. "If I had my way, the whole park would be shut down."

Riley's two friends exchanged a glance then said in unison, "Yes, sir."

Henry nodded. "We'll walk you to the subway."

Riley turned to him eagerly. "Can I go home with them?"

He shook his head. "No. You'll come with me."

Disappointment flared in her eyes, but she didn't argue. "Fine. But I'll walk with my friends."

After making sure Riley's friends were safely on their way home on the subway, Henry hustled Olivia, Riley and Cody back to his vehicle where he secured Cody in his specially designed compartment and gave him some water.

"I can take the back seat," Olivia said to Riley.

The girl shook her head. "Naw. It's fine." Riley sat in the space reserved for suspect transport and slumped down in the seat, putting her head back and closing her eyes.

Shrugging, Olivia climbed in front. "We should head to your doctor's office."

Starting the engine, Henry replied, "They're closed by now."

"You heard my sister," she reminded him.

"I'll follow up with the doc tomorrow," he said.

Needing the reassurance that he would, she asked, "Do you promise?"

He met her gaze, confusion lighting the dark depths of his eyes. "Sure."

Hoping he was a man of his word, she settled in. He no doubt wondered why she cared enough to elicit the promise. If they were truly colleagues instead of adversaries, would he be confused by her concern? Not likely. It aggravated her to no end that everyone in the police bureau treated her and the other IA officers as the enemy in every situation.

All she'd ever wanted to do was help. But she'd allowed herself to get caught up in the need to achieve and make her family proud. There were days she wasn't sure the status was worth it.

The ride back to Bay Ridge was quiet inside the SUV. Henry brought the vehicle to a halt in front of the K-9 Unit headquarters, an attractive limestone, three-story building that once housed a police precinct that had outgrown the space.

Hunger pains gripped Olivia's stomach in an audible symphony. Embarrassment heated her face.

"Hey, anyone want to grab a pizza?" Riley gestured toward Sal's Pizzeria two doors down from the K-9 Unit.

"I shouldn't." Though Olivia's mouth watered at the thought of gooey cheese, pepperoni and veggies.

Riley hopped out of the vehicle. "Why not? You have to eat, right? And I'm starving."

"I can wait until I get home," Olivia offered. Her stomach rumbled once again, denying her claim.

Henry's mouth tipped up at the corners. "I'd appreciate it if you'd accompany Riley. I have to write a report and feed Cody. I really don't want her to be alone."

The congenial tone of his voice wrapped around Olivia. The baby inside of her wiggled as if affected by him, as well. Henry trusted her with his sister. She couldn't deny the pleasant sensation sliding over her limbs. Telling herself it wouldn't be a bad thing to get to know Riley and gain some more insight into Henry, Olivia threaded her arm around Riley's. "I could eat a whole pizza by myself."

"Me, too," Riley said with a laugh.

Henry waited until Olivia and Riley entered the local pizza joint, known for being a favorite with the police officers in the area. Established by a retired officer and his wife long before the K-9 Unit landed nearby, Sal's was as safe as the precinct as far as Henry was concerned. The men and women in blue would keep an eye on his baby sister. Though he questioned how Olivia would fare. IA officers were rarely popular.

He turned to go inside when the hair at the base of his neck prickled with apprehension. He glanced around, searching for the threat. No one seemed overly interested in him and Cody. Still, he couldn't shake the unease prickling his skin.

Movement across the street caught his attention. A guy in a hoodie emerged from between two buildings.

He was of medium height and wore dark sunglasses and jeans. The stranger paused and glanced Henry's way before sauntering in the opposite direction.

Rubbing the back of his neck to dispel the unnerving sensation, he headed inside the building with Cody at his heels and went straight to tech guru Eden Chang's desk.

She blinked up at him. "Henry, what is this I hear about a text and a bomber?"

He handed over his phone and explained the situation.

Eden scratched Cody behind the ears. "You're a hero, boy." She took the device from Henry and plugged it into her computer console. "I'll do what I can. If the bomber used a burner phone to text you, then we won't get too much information. Unless it's still on, then I can ping it for a location. And I can definitely check the unique identifier number to learn where it was bought. And from there determine if we can find the person who made the purchase. But let's hope it's somebody's personal phone and they're too dumb to realize that the police can trace it."

Henry chuckled. "I couldn't be that fortunate."

She grinned at him. "Well, it's worth praying about."

"This is true." And he would be praying mightily. "Any breakthroughs on recovering anything off my body camera from the incident in Owl's Head Park?" He appreciated all the extra time Eden had put in on that.

She frowned. "No. Nothing more than what I had before. There's clear video of you walking into the park and clear video of you leaving the park. But the in-between is fuzzy."

"That is interesting and disturbing." The one piece of evidence that would clear him of the excessive abuse charge.

"Exactly my thought. I still maintain that if a strong enough electromagnet got close enough to your body cam, it could cause this issue." Eden's intense gaze met his. "I believe you're being set up."

His stomach clenched at the disturbing idea that someone had gone to a lot of trouble to orchestrate a setup like this. If only he could talk to Davey Carrell himself and coax the guy into being honest about what happened. But Henry was going to have to rely on Olivia to ferret out the truth. "I wish you would tell Lieutenant Vance that."

Eden nodded once again, reaching to scratch Cody in his sweet spot. The dog leaned into her. "I told Lieutenant Jabboski and I will tell Lieutenant Vance when I talk with her. She left a message earlier today asking if we could meet."

"Thank you." It was good to have someone else on his side. "Hey, so about that bombing this afternoon... Can you pull up any video footage from around the entrance to Coney Island, Luna Park, along the boardwalk and the Joey Yums restaurant? At least two hours before the bomb detonated and maybe another two hours after. You know bombers, they tend to hang around to view their handiwork and the damage they've done."

"I'll work on it over the weekend," she promised.

He hated that she was going to give up her personal time for this, but it was a priority. "I really appreciate that."

"No sweat."

"Thanks." He gave her a salute. "I look forward to learning what you find out for me on Monday."

"Have a good weekend, you two," Eden said as she turned her attention to his phone.

Henry and Cody walked out of the tech room and into the station office. The place was pretty empty. There was a light on in Bradley McGregor's cube. Henry made Cody stay on the dog bed at his cubicle before heading to see his friend. Bradley's dog, King, a large Belgian Malinois, laid curled on a round bed. King lifted his head to watch as Henry stepped in to the cubicle. The tall, muscular detective swung around and smiled. "Heard you had an eventful day."

"You could say that."

"At least you, Riley and… Lieutenant Vance, are safe."

Ignoring the subtle ribbing in Bradley's tone, Henry said. "That's true." He'd never forget the relief that had flooded him when he'd realized Olivia was unharmed after the explosion. "What about you and Penny? How are you two holding up?"

The siblings had had a tragic childhood and there had been a recent double homicide that matched the modus operandi as the murders of their parents twenty years to the day. The brother and sister were understandably rattled.

Bradley took a breath. "Some days are better than others. I'm worried about Penny, though. She's taking it hard. Especially with another little girl being left alive at the scene."

Just as Penny had been left alive as a young child when her parents had been brutally murdered. The killer had dressed as a blue-haired clown and given each little girl a stuffed monkey in a plastic bag.

Bradley had been at a sleepover with friends at the time of his parents' deaths. Back in the day, the police had considered Bradley a suspect and that he'd snuck home and killed his mother and father because the then fourteen-year-old had been outspoken about how negligent they'd been toward four-year-old Penny. That was never proven. Because it couldn't be true. To Henry, Bradley was as solid as they came. The unit was investigating both murders now.

"How's it going with the IA investigation?"

Henry blew out a compressed breath that left him a bit disoriented. "Honestly, I can't tell. When Lieutenant Vance first showed up this morning, she was ready to rumble. She believes that I'm capable of hurting someone without justification."

Bradley shook his head. "Man, I'd give anything if we could go back and I could've just witnessed the altercation."

"You and me both, brother." Henry rubbed his chin as he debated his next words. "And I know this is going to sound totally bizarre and like I'm losing it, but I believe somebody's been following me."

Bradley stood, radiating tension. "Listen to your gut. It will never steer you wrong. Sometimes God talks to us in a small voice and sometimes in the loud clanging of a bell. You've got to honor it."

"I hear you, man." Henry had often listened to what he believed in his heart to be God directing him. Was that the case here?

Bradley clapped Henry on the back. "Anything I can do to help?"

Appreciating his friend's offer, Henry said, "I'll let you know."

"I'm here for you." Bradley leashed King and they left for the night.

Henry made quick work of writing up his report about the exploding garbage can while Cody ate his kibble. After a quick stroll on the grassy area between the unit headquarters and the training center next door, Henry kenneled Cody in the training center and then headed to Sal's.

From the doorway, he saw his sister and Olivia seated in the back corner. Their heads were bent close as they talked. He took a moment to study this woman who'd inserted herself into his life. What was her story?

He'd heard her sister Ally ask about "the baby" at Coney Island. He'd wanted to ask Olivia about her pregnancy, but then decided not to delve into her life. Better to not become emotionally embroiled with the IA investigator, no matter how attractive he found her. Because whether he liked it or not, she literally held the fate of his career in her hands. And any sort of personal relationship between them was strictly forbidden. Not that he was looking for a relationship. Especially not with a superior officer. They'd probably be hauled over the coals as it was for this innocent jaunt to the pizzeria. It bothered him that he had to second guess his every move.

"Hey, Roarke, what's IA doing with your sister?"

The question stopped Henry midstride as he made his way through the Friday night crowd at Sal's. His neck muscles braced as if taking a blow. He noted his sister pick up a carrot and dip it in dressing before taking a bite. Hmm. She wasn't one to normally eat veggies. Had that been Olivia's doing? He'd have to thank her.

With effort, he turned his attention to the man who'd asked the question. Henry tipped his chin to his colleague, Emergency Services officer Jackson Davison. "Jackson."

The imposing man sat at the counter. His green eyes were narrowed on Olivia. For some reason, irritation swept through Henry. He didn't understand his reaction to Jackson's query but wasn't about to analyze the emotion. "Looks like Lieutenant Vance is eating."

Jackson's gaze shot to Henry. "Obviously. But why? I thought she was investigating you."

Acid churned in Henry's stomach. "She is." The admission rankled. He couldn't wait for this debacle to be over. He'd always worked hard to be one of the good guys. His reputation was important to him and now it had been sullied.

"You better be careful," Jackson warned. "Riley might say something that the Lieutenant could use against you."

Drawing back, Henry stared at his fellow K-9 handler. "Like what?"

Jackson's eyebrows rose. "Like you have a temper."

Flexing his fingers, Henry made a face. "Ha. Just because I called foul on your play at the last basketball pickup game doesn't mean I have a temper."

Jackson grinned. "Dude, you threw a basketball through a window."

Grimacing, Henry said, "Purely accidental."

It was true he'd had a bad day on the court and had let a spike of anger get the better of him. In his defense, he'd just been put on modified duty and his sense of justice was riled up. It wasn't fair that Davey Carrell's unsubstantiated claim could cost Henry his job.

Shrugging, Jackson turned back to his slice of pizza. "I'm just saying. If it were me under IA's microscope, I wouldn't be fraternizing with the enemy or let her anywhere near my family."

He clapped Jackson on the back. "Yeah, thanks."

As Henry moved through the restaurant, he noticed more people giving Olivia the eye. He wanted to tell everyone to mind their own business. She had just as much right to be in Sal's as anyone else. She'd paid her dues on the force before moving to Internal Affairs. Though he understood the need for oversight, most officers operated under the assumption that Internal Affairs rejoiced in taking down other officers. Unfortunately, there was no way he could dismiss decades of distrust between officers and IA. The fact that he wanted to defend Olivia didn't sit well. Her goal was to prove his guilt. Why did he care if she was treated with wariness and resentment?

Because she'd been nice to his sister. And had understood how important it had been for him to find Riley at Coney Island today. Olivia had shown compassion and concern. She was human, after all, not just a robot out to find fault.

Shaking off his disturbing thoughts, he slid onto a stool beside his sister and took a carrot stick. "Ladies."

"Our pizzas should be ready any moment," Olivia said.

"Pizzas as in two?" He assessed the two women.

Both were healthy and vibrant, but he doubted they'd eat that much. "Hungry, are we?"

Riley pointed the end of her carrot at Olivia. "Her idea."

Olivia shrugged. "Leftovers for tomorrow."

"Ah." Henry smiled. "That's reasonable."

"I can be reasonable," Olivia stated, her gaze direct.

"Glad to hear it," he countered, holding her gaze and pondering the defensive tone in her voice. He could only imagine the kind of flak she received doing her job. And the fortitude it took to accept that hostility.

"Vance, your pies are ready," a deep voice called out.

"I'll get them," Riley offered, sliding off her stool and hurrying to the counter.

Henry waved his hand at the salad and stack of carrot sticks sitting on the table. "Thanks for this, Olivia."

She slid the large salad bowl toward him and handed him a plate and fork. "Help yourself."

"Thank you for getting Riley to eat carrots."

"I know a thing or two about coaxing kids to eat their veggies. Smother them in dressing."

A small smile played at the corners of her lush mouth, drawing his attention. It hit him like a subway car that she was not just a lieutenant in Internal Affairs who could end his career, but a tempting, beautiful woman. The last thing he needed in his life right now. Not to mention becoming entangled with Olivia would put them both at risk of losing their jobs and being publicly reprimanded.

Forcing his gaze to the task of putting salad on his plate, he said, "You're one of six kids, right?"

"I am."

Sensing her gaze, he said, "I have just the one."

"One what?" Riley asked as she set the two pizzas on the table.

"We're talking about siblings," Olivia said. "I have two older brothers and three younger sisters."

"Wow." Riley grabbed a slice of Canadian bacon and pineapple and plopped it on her plate. "That's a lot. I couldn't handle more than Henry."

Henry shot his sister a mock glare. "Excuse me? Who has to handle who?"

Olivia's soft chuckle settled in his chest. He liked the sound of her laugh. As the evening progressed, Henry settled back, enjoying the way Riley and Olivia were hitting it off. Riley needed a female influence in her life. Raising a teenage girl alone had been difficult and if not for the advice of his female coworkers, he didn't know how he and Riley would have survived.

After eating their fill of pizza and chatting about the latest superhero movies, Henry had the remaining slices boxed up. One box for Olivia and one for him and Riley.

Outside of Sal's, Henry turned to Olivia. "Are you parked close?"

"I didn't drive," she said. "I'll call a car service."

His sense of honor and duty wouldn't allow him to accept that. Leaving her waiting on the street corner was unacceptable. "Can we give you a ride home?"

She hesitated a moment. "Actually, that would be great. I live in Carroll Gardens."

"Let me collect Cody and we'll be set to go." He led the way as Jackson's warning about trusting Olivia rang inside his brain. Was he making a mistake that could cost him his job?

THREE

With her hunger satisfied, Olivia marveled at the turn of events. When she'd arrived at the Brooklyn K-9 Unit earlier today, she'd expected to question Henry and then move on to meet with the unit's technology specialist, Eden Chang, to find out if there was video footage near Owl's Head Park that could help her track down as many of the young people who'd been at the skate park the evening of the incident involving Henry and Davey Carrell. Lieutenant Jabboski hadn't believed tracking down anyone from that night in the park was worth his time.

She still needed to meet with Miss Chang, but that would have to wait until next week. After surviving an exploding garbage can, conducting her interview near the roller coaster on Coney Island and eating nearly a whole pizza, Olivia only wanted to get home to change out of her clothes and put her feet up. Though having dinner with Henry and Riley certainly beat eating left-over pot roast alone.

After swiping his keycard on the security pad, Henry held the door of the training center open for Olivia and Riley to enter. Olivia had never set foot in the building before and was surprised by the cleanliness of the facility. She followed Henry and his sister into a large room that housed multiple hard-sided kennels. A few were occupied but the majority of the thirteen crates were empty.

A woman with shoulder-length auburn hair and brown eyes behind silver-framed glasses greeted them with a smile. "Cody's been sleeping, but I'm sure he's ready to go outside."

She opened the kennel door and the beagle shot out and raced to Riley. She knelt down and accepted slobbery kisses with a laugh. Olivia watched the exchange with a pang of tenderness. Clearly, the dog and young woman were bonded, though in a different way then Henry and Cody. Watching the two in action today had been impressive.

"Gina, this is Lieutenant Olivia Vance," Henry said. "Dr. Gina Mazelli is our vet in residence."

Olivia shook the other woman's hand. "It's nice to meet you. Do you always work this late?"

"Likewise. I'm living in the building temporarily. We had a stray German shepherd give birth to five puppies in April. I'm fostering them and figured it would be best to keep them here. The mama, Brooke, is going to be trained for service. We'll see about the pups."

"I admire your dedication," Olivia said.

Gina shrugged. "I love animals."

"It shows." Olivia respected the other woman's devotion.

"Could we show Olivia the puppies?" Riley's hopeful expression was contagious. "They are so cute."

Excitement danced in Olivia's chest. "Would that be allowed?"

With an easy smile, the redheaded veterinarian nodded. "Of course it's allowed. The puppies need to be socialized."

Gina led the way to a small room where an extra-large dog exercise pen had been set up and cushioned with colorful blankets. The mama German shepherd reclined in the middle of the five little fur balls.

A couple of the puppies slept, while the other three roamed around the space. Olivia's heart swelled with tenderness.

Soon she'd have her own little one to cuddle. Her arms ached to hold her infant. There was so much she was looking forward to about being a mother. Reading to her child and teaching her little one to sing, to read and to dance with joy.

The future stretched before her and yet she had no idea how she was going to manage once she gave birth. Her parents had offered to help. But Olivia wanted to be there for every moment of her baby's life, from crawling to walking across the stage at her or his high school graduation.

She wasn't going to miss any firsts or special moments. She just hadn't figured out how to make it all work yet. She would, though. That was a promise she made to her baby the day she learned she was pregnant.

Riley went down on her hands and knees and crawled toward the pen, drawing Olivia's focus.

"Hello, you little cuties," Riley cooed.

Gina opened the wire gate so Riley could enter the pen. "Brooke, let's get you some food."

Brooke rose and gingerly stepped over the puppies, pausing to lick Riley's face before following Gina out of the room.

The runt of the litter stumbled on wobbly legs toward Riley. She scooped the pup into her arms and nuzzled him. "Hi, Maverick. It's good to see you again. You're going do great things. I just know it."

Olivia noted the sad wince pulling at Henry's expression. "What's wrong?"

"Maverick's life has been touch and go. Still is, truth be told," he said in a low voice. "The little pup is frail and has health issues. But he's getting the best care possible. He has a fighting spirit."

"Come on, Olivia, hold a puppy," Riley called.

"Go on. They won't bite." He wagged his eyebrows. "Much."

She wrinkled her nose at him and then moved closer, sitting on the floor. Riley handed her Maverick. The tiny body quivered in her hands. She lifted him to look into his dark eyes. "It's okay. I've got you." She pulled him to her chest. Another puppy, twice the size of Maverick, crawled up her leg. She laughed, reaching out to stroke the soft fur.

Cody nuzzled his way into the pen to sniff the puppies, who pawed playfully at him.

Henry folded his frame to take a seat next to Olivia. He scooped up a puppy trying to escape. "Oh no, you don't."

"What will happen to them?" Olivia asked.

"Each will be tested soon to see if they'd be good working dogs or therapy dogs."

"And if they aren't?" She stroked her hand over Maverick. The pup had settled against her and seemed to be content in her arms. Would this be what it felt like to hold her child? Tenderness swelled in her chest and an ache of longing to protect this puppy, and the child growing inside of her, burned the back of her eyes.

"I'm sure Gina will find them homes."

The urge to take Maverick home with her pulsed in her veins. She wasn't set up to care for a puppy, or a baby, yet. But soon. She needed to put together the crib she'd ordered online, as well as the changing table and wash all the little clothes her family had been buying in neutral colors. She wasn't sure if she hoped for a girl or boy. Honestly, she didn't have a preference.

With Maverick's warm body snuggled against her chest, Olivia relaxed and a yawn escaped. Cody came over and nuzzled the puppy before giving Olivia a quick swipe of his tongue as if in approval. She couldn't help the laugh that escaped her.

"Ready to leave, Lieutenant?" Henry asked, his gaze bouncing between his partner and her as if he were surprised by the dog's behavior.

Though Olivia didn't want to admit it, fatigue was setting in. The stress of the day had taken a toll. Her emotions were rubbed raw. She'd let down her guard and become comfortable with him. "Yes. Thank you, Henry."

They put the puppies back in the pen, latching the gate so they wouldn't escape. They said goodbye to Gina on the way out.

When they left the center, Cody was put in his compartment and Riley climbed in back of the SUV while Henry opened the side passenger door for Olivia. She smiled her gratitude and slid on to the seat, putting the pizza box on the floor at her feet. She appreciated he'd offered to drive her home. She doubted many officers who were being investigated would be so solicitous. It spoke volumes about his character.

When Henry settled in the driver's seat, he handed her his phone, open to the maps app. "Punch in your address, please, Olivia."

Too tired to argue and say she could just as easily tell him how to get there, she put her address into the device and handed it back. He pressed Start and a British female voice emanated from the phone, giving him directions. Thirty minutes later, he pulled up in front of her building, a four-story brick structure built in the 1920s.

When he moved to get out, she put her hand on his forearm. Warmth radiated up her arm and wrapped around her. She quickly drew her hand back. "You don't need to walk me in."

This wasn't a date, though she suspected his gesture stemmed from the overprotectiveness she'd seen glimpses of rather than some gallant offer of chivalry. Besides, she could take care of herself and her unborn child. She didn't need his or anyone else's protection.

Well, except her family…but that was different. Family helped each other out. Stuck together. She wished someone had told Roger that before he betrayed their marriage vows.

A frown showed Henry's concern and warmed her from the inside out. She had to admit he made her feel cared for, even though both were aware how dangerous forming any emotions for each other could be for their careers.

"We'll wait for you to enter the building," he said. "Which apartment is yours?"

She pressed her lips together to suppress the amusement of being proven right. He had a wide streak of chivalry. Even for someone he undoubtedly considered the enemy. Deciding to go with it and appreciate his thoughtfulness rather than cling to her independence, she said, "Bottom right. I'll wave from the window."

He gave a satisfied nod. "Okay. Good night, Olivia."

"Good night, Henry." She popped open the door and found Riley waiting to take her place in the front seat. "It was really nice to meet you, Riley."

"You, too," the younger woman said. "I hope I see you again."

Taking one of her business cards from her suit jacket pocket, Olivia held it out. "My cell phone is on this. You call me if you ever need anything. Even if it's just to chat."

Riley palmed the card. "Thank you."

As Olivia withdrew her hand, Cody let out a soft bark.

Riley laughed. "He says good-night, too."

Smiling, Olivia hurried to unlock the building's front entrance, then went to her apartment door and unlocked the double bolt that her father had installed when she'd moved in right after Roger's death. She hadn't wanted to stay in the ultra-modern condo they had shared. Too many memories, most of which she didn't want to keep.

Once inside her small one-bedroom unit, she secured the door, flipped on the lights and went to the window. Drawing back the curtain, she waved at the vehicle idling at the curb. Henry waved back before driving the SUV away.

A stark and cold sense of isolation invaded her, making her insides quiver. Not since the night her late husband had stormed out of her life had she felt so alone.

But soon there would be a little bundle of joy for her to love. Until then, she had to deal with the loneliness disturbing her sense of peace.

With a sigh, she dropped the curtain and faced her apartment. The quiet surrounded her, unnerving in its completeness.

"Kitty?"

A soft meow came from the bedroom. Her faithful companion couldn't be bothered to come greet her. Maybe she *should* get a dog.

Henry pulled away from the Carroll Gardens apartment building. He kept an eye on the curtain of Olivia's window as it fluttered closed. She had moved away from view. He didn't like leaving her knowing she was alone. He'd heard about the death of her husband, but it hadn't seemed quite the appropriate topic to discuss. Not that he wanted to discuss it. He didn't want to get involved with this woman. She was an irritation. A burr under his flak vest. Even if he did feel sympathy for her loss and had, surprisingly, enjoyed her company tonight.

Watching her with Riley and having Cody give her his stamp of approval with the lick at the training center created conflicting emotions within him. There was something so very vulnerable about Olivia. Yet formidable, too.

Maybe it was the fact that he suspected she was pregnant, if what her sister had said was true. Or that Olivia was a widow, still grieving her late husband. Or maybe it was the stress of the day getting to him, stirring up uncomfortable feelings he had no business entertaining. She was a superior officer and investigating him. How much more taboo could any feelings for Olivia be?

Yes, it had to be the stress of the day or the blow to his head.

Well, more like the stress of the past three, almost four months, to be exact. Ever since the night Davey Carrell tried to grab Henry's sidearm. The ever-present frustration reared as Henry merged into traffic, heading toward their Cobble Hill neighborhood. Bright headlights moved in behind the SUV, causing apprehension to slither over his flesh.

His paranoia was getting the better of him. On the way to Olivia's apartment there had been a moment when he'd suspected they were being followed. But the silver sedan had veered away and turned down a side street. Then the car reappeared at the next block, turning into the driveway of a parking garage a half block past Olivia's apartment. Clearly, he was losing it.

But as he drove into his neighborhood, he was sure the car behind him was the same silver sedan that had been tailing him since he left Olivia's apartment. Just to make sure, he went right at the stoplight and headed away from the street where his two-story condo was located.

"Where are we going?" Riley asked.

Watching the rearview mirror, Henry replied, "Just circling the block."

He was halfway down the block when the silver sedan made the turn.

Heart rate doubling, Henry turned down another block. Sure enough, the car followed. As they passed beneath the illuminating glow of a streetlamp, he caught a better glimpse of the silver sedan and the empty space where the front license plate should have been. Tensing, he made another quick turn.

"Henry?"

Not wanting to scare his sister, he said, "Being cautious."

Who was driving the sedan? Why was he, or Riley, being targeted? Did this have something to do with Davey Carrell? He tightened his grip until his knuckles hurt. Rounding the block, he kept a vigilant eye on the rearview mirror. The sedan didn't follow.

Shaking his head, he sped home and parked in his designated spot. He climbed out, retrieved Cody from his compartment and ushered Riley, along with the pizza box, up the steps to their condo. He made her wait at the front door while he and Cody cleared the place. Once he was satisfied there were no dangerous surprises waiting for them, he said, "We're good."

Silently handing him the pizza box, she headed to her room, but he'd glimpsed the anxiety in her dark eyes as she passed him. His chest tightened. He'd do everything in his power to keep her safe. After letting Cody out in the small fenced-in side yard of the condo, Henry secured the premises for the night.

Too wired to sleep, he kept the lights off as he stood guard, pacing between the windows at the front of the condo and the ones lining the balcony. Cody whined, wanting Henry to go to bed. But he couldn't. He was going to listen to his gut. If it was God talking to him, he had every intention of paying attention.

In the wee hours of the morning, a low growl emanated from Cody, raising the fine hairs at the back of Henry's neck. He bolted upright from the living room recliner. When he reached the kitchen, he found Cody standing at attention in the moonlight streaming through the glass insert of the balcony door. His tail raised high, his ears back.

A shadow passed by the door, momentarily obscuring the ambient light.

Henry's heart jackknifed with adrenaline.

Someone was on the balcony.

FOUR

Heart hammering in his chest, Henry didn't want to alert the intruder as he spoke softly to Cody, "Good boy. No bark."

For a second, Henry debated retrieving his weapon from the gun safe in his bedroom. But it would take precious time and he wanted to act now. Hurrying to the hall closet, he grabbed his dad's Louisville Slugger. Hefting the bat in his hands and staying in the shadows, he returned to the kitchen. With Cody at his side, he approached the door leading to the balcony and quietly unlocked the door, then wrapped his hand around the knob.

On a deep breath, he yanked open the door and hit the light switch, throwing the five-foot-wide balcony into sharp relief. The platform, guarded by a wrought iron railing, ran the length of the condo's second floor. A medium-height, slender man wearing dark jeans, gloves and a black hoodie that cast his face in shadow stood outside the window to the room Henry used as an office.

"Halt, police!" Henry yelled and rushed toward the

prowler. Cody scrambled past Henry, his teeth bared as he growled menacingly.

The hooded man dropped to a crouch for a split second as if he could hide before jumping to his feet. Cody latched on to his pant leg. With a vicious kick, the intruder dislodged Cody. The sound of fabric ripping filled the air as Cody tore away a chunk of the pants. Once free of Cody, the man grasped the railing with his gloved hands and swung over the side, dangling there for an instant before dropping away.

"No!" Henry reached the spot where the prowler had just been. Bracing himself, because he was positive the guy would have broken a leg or something from the fall, he leaned over the railing just in time to see the would-be burglar shimmying down the drainpipe to the ground below. "Hey!"

Without looking up, the man scaled the side yard fence and disappeared out of sight. Then his pounding footfalls echoed through the still night as he ran away. There was no way Henry would catch him. Frustration beat a steady rhythm at his temples. After checking that Cody hadn't sustained an injury from the kick, Henry darted back inside and called the precinct. He explained the situation to the night dispatcher.

"I'll alert patrol to be on the lookout for anyone matching that description," the dispatcher promised.

Doubting they'd catch the guy, Henry said, "Can you send a CSI team to my residence? Specifically Darcy Fields." She worked often with the K-9 team and was an ace forensic specialist. If there was any evidence that could lead to the intruder's identity she'd find it.

"Will do, Detective Roarke."

After hanging up, Henry went to wake Riley with Cody at his heels. He cracked opened her bedroom door, allowing the hall light to spill into the room and flinched at the mess. Clothes hung half out of her dresser drawers and shoes lay haphazardly on the floor like little traps for him to trip over. Stacks of books, six to ten high, appeared ready to topple if he so much as breathed on them. Her messiness was another source of contention between them. He didn't understand how Riley could operate in such chaos.

Carefully, he and Cody picked their way across the room to her full-size bed. She lay twisted in her covers, her sweet face relaxed and her arms wrapped around a large stuffed animal that Henry had won for her at Coney Island several years earlier.

Tenderness filled his chest as he sank onto the bed. Cody sat at his feet. "Hey, munchkin," he said, using the childhood nickname their father had coined when she was an infant.

She stirred, rolling to her side away from him. He gently nudged her.

"What?" she asked, though her eyes remained closed. "I'm sleeping."

"We have a situation," he said. "Someone tried to break in."

That grabbed her attention. She twisted to face him. Her dark eyes went wide as she blinked away sleep. "Break in?"

"A crime scene unit will be here soon," he told her. "You don't have to get up. I just didn't want you to be frightened if you woke up and heard noises."

"Are we safe?"

He smoothed back her hair. She looked so much like her mother, Susan. Henry had always liked his step-mom. She'd tried hard to forge a relationship with him, even though he'd been less than receptive until he'd become a young adult. "Yes. We're safe. But if you'd feel better I can leave Cody here with you."

"Don't you need him?"

"I'll be fine," he assured her. "He's already done his job tonight." For which Henry was grateful. Cody was better than an alarm system…but he might have one installed anyway.

Riley scooted over to make room for the dog. "Okay."

Henry patted the bed. Cody jumped up, sniffed at Riley and licked her face before turning in a circle and settling down beside her. Riley slipped her arms around Cody much the way she had been hugging the stuffed toy.

A sharp knock at the front door had Henry rising to his feet. "I'll let you know when they've gone." He reversed his trek through the minefield of her room, leaving Cody curled by her side.

At the front door, he greeted Darcy Fields, a petite blonde with pale brown eyes and dimples in her cheeks. She carried a case filled with her equipment and wore her uniform of khakis, dark blue polo shirt with the NYPD logo and dark shoes, now covered with paper booties. Her team of two male techs filled the space behind her.

"Hi, Darcy. You got here quick."

"We were just finishing up at a crime scene nearby when I received the call. Came straight here. Not much in the way of traffic at three o'clock in the morning." The forensic specialist led her team into the condo.

"I appreciate you coming," he said. "The prowler was on the balcony." He led the way through the condo. Stepping out to the terrace, he said, "He must have climbed up from below." He told her how the man had swung over the railing.

"Agile trespasser," she commented. "Was he wearing gloves?"

"Unfortunately, yes. But Cody snagged a piece of his pant leg." He pointed to the scrap of material on the ground where Cody had dropped it.

She quickly bagged the evidence, then turned to the two men with her. "Head to the ground level and see if you can find any footprints in the soft dirt of the flowerbed that we can use."

The two men nodded and retreated out the front door.

"I'll dust to see if there's any pattern in the grain of the gloves the suspect wore," Darcy said. "It may or may not be helpful. And I'll look for stray hairs or epithelia on the material. Let's pray we get a match in one of the many DNA databases."

"I should have tackled him," Henry muttered.

Darcy gave him a sharp glance. "Aren't you being investigated for excessive force?"

Henry flinched. "Yes." Though he didn't see what that had to do with this situation.

"Then it's probably better for you not to have any physical contact with a suspect," she said.

He grunted, not liking the accuracy of her statement. He had to trust that Darcy's crack skills would produce some evidence to lead to the intruder. But until the guy was caught and brought in, Henry would remain in the dark about why he had wanted into his house. What had he been planning to do?

Henry gazed out at the darkened street and vowed he'd do everything in his power to keep his sister safe.

The next morning, Henry awoke from of fitful rest. The only reason he'd been able to get any sleep was the assurance that two patrol officers were watching the condo building. After checking in with the officers and letting them know he was up and about and they could go have their day off, Henry made a strong pot of coffee. He didn't particularly like the stuff, but there were days when he needed it.

His head hurt where he'd sustained a gash from the flying debris after the garbage can explosion. He really needed to go see the doctor and have the bandage changed. But thankfully no blood had seeped through. That was a good sign.

He popped a couple of over-the-counter painkillers with some water as the coffee percolated. Just as he was pouring himself his first strong cup, he heard Riley's door open and the pad of Cody's feet coming down the hall. Leaving his coffee on the counter, he grabbed Cody's leash and collar from the basket near the front door.

"Here, boy." He opened the front door as Cody hurried up to his side and sat patiently waiting for him to put on his collar and lead. They went outside so Cody could have a few moments on the grass. The early morning air was just beginning to heat up with the promise of another hot July day. There were few people out and about. Saturdays were generally quiet. Still, Henry kept a vigilant eye out for any sign of the silver sedan or for strangers who didn't belong in the area.

When they returned to the apartment, Riley was dressed and making scrambled eggs. Henry unleashed Cody and made sure there was fresh water in the dog bowl. The dog sniffed at Riley's pink backpack sitting on the edge of the couch before jumping up on to the cushion and lying down. Henry wandered back to his cup of coffee, which had grown cold. He dumped it out and poured himself a fresh cup. He leaned back against the counter. "You're up early."

"Nicole called and woke me up," she replied with a quick glance. "We're making plans for the upcoming concert. We thought we'd get ready at Kelsey's place." Riley's expression turned hopeful. "You aren't really serious about going with us to and from the concert hall, are you?"

He rounded the corner of the counter and sat back on his stool. "Dead serious. Especially now. With bomb threats and someone trying to break into our condo. We have to be vigilant and use caution."

Her shoulders slumped as she dished eggs onto plates. When she sat the plate in front of him, it bounced slightly with her agitation. "I'm eighteen. I don't need a babysitter. Nicole's nineteen and Kelsey's eighteen, like me. We're adults now. I don't need your permission. And I certainly don't need you as my shadow."

There was so much in her statement to unpack and pick apart, he couldn't decide where to start. "First off, you may be eighteen, but you live under my roof. When you move out and start adulting, I will have no say in your life. But until then, you have to abide by my rules."

She huffed and rolled her eyes. "That's so lame."

A flash of memory hit him along with a sense of déjà vu. Though he couldn't recount the exact words, he was certain he'd had a very similar conversation with their father when he was Riley's age. Arguing with her about this wouldn't be productive. So he chose to go with the more obvious issue. "We can't ignore the danger."

"What does that have to do with me? You're the cop, the one putting his life on the line. Not me. I'll be fine." She glared at him as she dredged up an old argument.

From the day she realized what his job entailed, Riley had resented his career. He understood from the grief counselor they'd both seen after the tragic death of their father and her mom that Riley's anger was a mask for the fear of losing him, too.

He rubbed a hand over his whiskered jaw. There was no delicate way to give her a reality check. "Did you forget what happened yesterday? You were within striking distance of a bomb."

He recalled Olivia's comment that it had been an unlikely coincidence that Riley was at Coney Island the same time as the bomber was texting Henry. Had the bomber known his sister was there? Had she been targeted? Or was it a strange fluke that they intersected? He wished he had answers to the questions plaguing him.

"I barely heard the explosion," she shot back.

Frustration tightened the muscles of his shoulders. He steered the conversation back to the original topic.

"If you want to go to the concert," he said slowly, "This is what we are doing."

"It's not fair." She stabbed her fork into the fluffy eggs on the plate in front of her.

"Life is not fair, Riley. God never promised it would be. The sooner you get that through your head and accept it, the better. Because expecting life to be even and square will only frustrate you."

She set down her fork and stared at him with tears clouding her dark eyes. "You sound so much like Dad."

His heart twisted in his chest. Riley's grief was always near the surface, especially when they were arguing. But this was the first time she'd compared Henry to their father. Her words were both a compliment that made him proud and a wound that sliced him to the quick.

Their father, James Roarke, had been a man of integrity who'd provided a good life for his children as an accountant. Henry's mother had abandoned Henry and James when Henry was six, disappearing and never contacting her son again. For many years, it had just been Henry and his dad until his dad had met Susan Cantor. They'd married and soon had Riley.

Even as an infant, the little girl had had their father wrapped around her pinky.

Taking a bracing sip of coffee, Henry stalled a beat as he wrangled his own grief. Swallowing, he said, "Riley, I love you. But you're not going to that concert without an escort both to and from."

She threw up her hands. "That's just mean."

Holding on to his patience by a thread, he said, "Riley, it's not mean. It's being protective."

"You're smothering me." She grabbed her plate and scraped the last of her eggs into the disposal before setting the plate in the dishwasher. She slammed the dishwasher door shut.

Cody let out a startled bark and jumped off the couch. He trotted over to investigate the commotion while Riley moved into the living room. Her phone chimed with an incoming text. She glanced at it and rolled her eyes. Snagging her backpack from the couch, she said, "I have an anthropology assignment that's due Monday. I'm going to the Museum of Natural History."

He slapped a hand to his forehead. "You're not going to the museum by yourself. You're going to have to wait for me and I will take you."

"I don't need you to come with me."

He stood up, marshaling his frustration and irritation, and stared her down. "Riley, someone tried to break in last night. You're not going to win here."

"You're impossible." She stormed down the hall, slamming her bedroom door shut.

Henry slumped back onto the counter stool. He understood her desire for more freedom. He was exactly the same age when he left home for college. But times were different. Their father hadn't been a cop. Riley didn't understand that he couldn't risk her safety. He'd seen the worst of humanity. How did he make her understand that it wasn't her he didn't trust? It was everyone else.

He cradled his head in his hands and lifted up a prayer asking God for guidance and wisdom because he didn't know how to navigate this young adult stage. In fact, he wasn't sure he'd ever know how to do the parent thing. And had no plans to again. Raising Riley was enough for one lifetime.

Putting on her sunglasses, Olivia stepped out of her Saturday morning exercise class when her cell phone rang. She paused on the sidewalk to dig the device out of her bag. She glanced at the caller ID and didn't recognize the number. Hefting her rolled exercise mat beneath one arm and her gym bag over her shoulder, she stepped out of the flow of traffic into the alcove of a restaurant that wasn't open yet.

"Hello?"

She heard a sobbing hiccup and then a weepy female voice, "Olivia? I mean, Lieutenant Vance?"

The voice struck a familiar chord, but Olivia couldn't place it. "Yes, this is Lieutenant Olivia Vance."

"This is Riley, Riley Roarke."

Olivia's stomach clenched. "Is everything okay, Riley?"

"No, it's not. Henry's a tyrant. I just can't live like this anymore. Can you help me?"

The dire note in Riley's tone slid along Olivia's limbs. Henry wouldn't hurt Riley, would he? He seemed to dote on her. "Are you safe?"

"Yes. Will you come?"

What was going on? Had Henry lost his temper with his sister? Did Henry really have an anger issue? After yesterday, she'd started to think not. But now Olivia was doubting herself. She needed to make sure there was no credence to the excessive force allegations by seeing what Henry was like with his family at home, she decided. She took off at a fast clip toward her apartment. "Can you text me your address? I'll be right there."

"Okay, please hurry."

When the text came in from Riley, Olivia's eyebrows shot up when she saw the Cobble Hill address. Pretty swanky on a police officer's salary. How could Henry afford such a nice condo?

At home, she quickly freshened up and changed into work clothes. She exchanged her workout equipment for her purse and made sure Kitty had water, then hustled back out the door. Squaring her shoulders with determination to get to the bottom of what was going on, she called a car service. She lifted up a prayer that she would be able to diffuse whatever was going on.

FIVE

Henry returned from the doctor's office with a new bandage on his head and a prescription for pain pills that he wouldn't be taking. Over-the-counter pain medication would do just fine. He wasn't about to take something stronger that would impair his judgment. Not when there was so much at stake. His sister's life, his life and the safety of the neighborhood. The safety of Brooklyn.

Riley was still in her room, no doubt pouting, so he took Cody outside again. The late-morning July sun beat down on his head. Staying inside would be a good idea today. A perfect time to go with Riley to the museum.

Back inside the condo, Henry knocked on Riley's door. "Hey, sis? I'm ready to go to the Museum of Natural History whenever you are."

"Whatever," came her muffled reply through the door.

Blowing out a frustrated breath, he shook his head. Was she really going to do this? She wanted to be treated like an adult, yet when she didn't get her way, she acted like she had at thirteen. Experience told him he had to wait her out. He headed back to the kitchen and finished loading the dishwasher, setting it to run. To keep himself busy, he wiped down the counters and cleaned out the fridge.

A knock at the front door set Cody scrambling from his bed. Tension constricted the muscles in Henry's neck as he hung back a second to watch his partner. Cody would give a passive alert indicating if a bomb waited on the other side of the door. The dog sniffed, then scratched at the door, apparently not detecting a dangerous scent.

Still, Henry used caution and pressed his eye to the peephole. Lieutenant Olivia Vance stood on the other side, looking very professional in a black pantsuit and crisp white shirt.

He drew back in surprise and rubbed a hand over his stubbled jaw. He usually didn't shave on the weekends. Then he shrugged. She was at his house on a Saturday. She could hardly expect him to be uniform-ready. He opened the door and braced himself. "Olivia. What brings you to my house on a Saturday?"

Adjusting the strap of her purse on her shoulder, she took a moment to respond, as if collecting her thoughts. "I need to speak with Riley."

His gut knotted. "Why?"

Her gaze hardened. "Riley called me. I want to talk to her and make sure she's okay."

Henry groaned. "Seriously? She called you? I'm sorry she bothered you. We had an argument but after the attempted break-in last night—"

"Wait," Olivia held up a hand. "Someone tried to break in here?"

"Yes. But Cody alerted and the perpetrator ran away. And now Riley's upset at the restrictions I've set and she's being overly dramatic. It's what she does."

Olivia's face softened just a tad. "I'm glad to hear none of you were hurt. I'd like to see her, please."

With a sigh of aggravation, he stepped aside so the Internal Affairs lieutenant could enter his condo. "By all means. Come in."

She glanced around his space. Suddenly, uncharacteristic insecurities assailed him. Did she notice the stain on the carpet? The dust on the picture frames? The secondhand furniture he'd picked up at a yard sale? He was glad he'd at least cleaned up the kitchen area.

"Nice place." Her gaze landed on him. "How do you afford this on your salary?"

Taken aback by her direct question, he lifted an eyebrow. Apparently nothing was out of bounds for her. "It *is* nice. And it was paid for with the life insurance money from my father's estate."

Tenderness filled her eyes, making his heart skip a beat.

"It must have been very difficult for you and Riley."

"Yes. The pain is always just underneath the surface," he admitted, though why he'd tell her anything personal was beyond him. Maybe because he sensed she understood grief. "I was sorry to hear about the loss of your husband."

Sadness and another emotion he couldn't identify crossed her face. "Thank you."

Confused by the stiffness of her tone, he asked, "A small plane crash, correct?"

Her gaze shuttered. "Yes."

Did she feel guilty that she hadn't been with him at the time of his death? It wasn't unusual for those left behind to have survivor's guilt. "You must miss him."

For a moment, she was quiet, as if debating how to answer. "At times. We were married for only two years. Our careers didn't lend themselves to married life."

His eyebrows rose as he digested her statement. "What was his profession?"

"A dentist," she said. "He had a thriving practice."

There was just a hint of bitterness in her tone that raised his curiosity. Though he really shouldn't pry, he asked, "Where was he headed when he crashed?"

For a moment she didn't speak and he cringed. He had overstepped. "I'm sorry, Olivia. It's none of my business."

"It's not a secret. From what I was told, the Caribbean," she replied. "We weren't on speaking terms at the time." She clamped her lips together as if she hadn't meant to let the admission slip.

Stunned by that revelation, Henry wasn't sure how to respond. Empathy flooded him. He fought the need to soothe away the hurt lurking in her eyes. Doing so would definitely be out of bounds.

Riley opened her bedroom door and ran straight at Olivia, throwing her arms around the woman. "You came!"

Olivia's eyes went wide and her mouth opened in obvious surprise. She braced her feet apart to balance herself against the onslaught of the gangly teenager. Henry winced. His little sister was putting on quite a show.

Olivia pulled back to look into Riley's face. "What's going on?"

Riley hitched a thumb over her shoulder. "Him. He's a brute."

Henry's mouth fell open. Didn't his little sister understand that saying things like that to the officer investigating him for excessive force would hurt his career? But then again, he figured hurting him was her intent. Riley wasn't getting her way and she was acting out. Not cool at all.

Letting out a half groan, half sigh, he shook his head and walked toward the balcony door. "I'll let you two talk."

Hopefully, Olivia was smart enough to realize what was going on and not hold Riley's antics against him.

Olivia saw the play of emotions march across Henry's face before he turned away. Obviously, his sister's words were upsetting to him. From the moment Olivia had stepped inside the condo, she'd had trouble keeping her focus on why she'd come over. Henry was breathtakingly handsome today.

She'd always thought him good-looking in uniform. But dressed in khaki shorts and a short-sleeve, pale green button-down shirt, he appeared both casual and dressy at the same time. He had a crisp, white bandage on his head that was a stark reminder of the trauma they'd experienced together.

A bond that had led her to admit she and her late husband hadn't been on speaking terms. Why else would she reveal anything personal to an officer she was investigating? She pushed aside the persistent voice that whispered she liked this man.

Leaving the door open to the balcony, Henry settled

onto a deck chair with his back to them. Cody lay down beside him. Henry dangled his hand over the armrest and stroked Cody as if needing comfort. Which Olivia figured he probably did, considering his sister's state of mind.

Turning her attention to Riley, Olivia met the younger woman's red-rimmed gaze. Remembering well the emotional roller coaster her two younger sisters had trapped the family on when they were young adults, Olivia decided to tread softly. Leading Riley to the leather couch, she said, "Tell me what's going on."

Riley plopped down on the middle cushion, tucking her feet beneath her and giving a very beleaguered sigh. "He's just so overprotective. He's a helicopter parent."

Olivia pressed her lips together to keep a smile at bay because showing any sort of amusement would only lead to more drama. At least, it always had with her siblings. "And what is he being an overprotective helicopter parent about?"

"The Colt Colton concert is coming up at the Barclays Center and he insists on escorting me and my friends."

Ah. So that was the crux of the issue. Taking Riley's hand in her own, Olivia gave her a gentle squeeze. "You do realize he's acting out of love? Especially after an intruder trying to break in."

For a moment, Riley's mouth firmed into a stubborn line, then she seemed to deflate. "I know. I know he loves me. And last night was scary. But he won't even let me go to the Natural Museum of History today by myself. I'm eighteen, old enough to go into the city on my own. I have an anthropology project due on Monday and I'm supposed to go to the museum and pick a subject to write about. We can't do it online. The teacher said we actually have to go to the museum. I don't want Henry to go with me. My other classmates will be there. I'll die if I have to have my big brother tagging along."

Dizzy from the onslaught of words, Olivia held up a hand. "Again, you do realize he's trying to protect you because he loves you?"

Riley threw herself against the backrest of the couch, her gaze on the ceiling. "Yes."

At least the young woman was acknowledging the truth through her dramatics.

Suddenly, Riley sat straight up and stared at Olivia. "Will you come with us? If you're with him, then he won't be hovering over me. You two can go off and do your own thing." She flicked her fingers as if shooing away a fly. "But he can still be there in case I need him."

From the balcony, Henry called out, "I'm okay with that."

Astonished, Olivia stared at the back of Henry's head. Really? He was okay with her going to the museum with him and his sister? Hmm. No doubt he wanted a buffer between him and Riley, too.

Was she seriously contemplating letting herself be drawn into this family's drama?

Who was she kidding? The moment she'd agreed to come over, she'd stepped into the fray. And she could be of help here. She wanted to help the brother and sister figure out how to navigate this season they were in. After all, she did have the knowledge and training. Plus, seeing them interact more outside of the home would help her understand the dynamics between them. She smiled wryly. "I'm ready to go whenever you are."

Riley clapped her hands and jumped from the couch. "I'll grab my backpack."

Henry came back inside and stopped at the foot of the couch. His gaze searched her face. "Are you sure about this?"

Misgivings filled Olivia, but she wasn't one to go back on her word. "Yes."

Henry leashed Cody and slipped a K-9 Unit vest over his small, round body.

"You're taking your partner?"

"It's a perfect opportunity to do some real world training. Besides, better to be prepared in case the texting bomber strikes again."

A shiver rippled over her flesh. She couldn't argue with that logic.

The trek into the city via the subway was uneventful. Riley buried her head in her phone, apparently texting with her classmates. Henry remained standing the whole ride, his gaze hard as he studied each passenger. Cody sniffed everyone he passed but showed no signs of alerting.

Seated next to Riley, Olivia fretted more with every mile that clicked beneath the rails. A bubbly sensation in her belly made her wonder if the baby sensed her anxiety. She breathed deep in an effort to calm herself and the baby. Yet her mind nagged at her—what if somebody from one of the precincts saw the four of them and realized they were on an outing together?

She could claim this was work-related, though would anyone believe her? She hated to acknowledge it, but she was jeopardizing her own career by fraternizing with the officer she was investigating.

However, it was her day off, even if she was treating it like work. A rebellious streak she rarely let loose clamored that today she was not an Internal Affairs investigator. Today, she was just a woman accompanying a teenager and her older brother and his dog to visit the museum. Nothing more. And if anybody actually bought that rationalization, she had a really nice piece of swampland in the middle of Manhattan to sell them.

With her stomach tied in knots, she followed Henry, Cody and Riley off the train and to the entrance of the American Museum of Natural History.

Bypassing the electronic ticket kiosks, Henry stepped up to the ticket counter, showed his badge and explained that he and Cody would be doing some training.

The ticket agent shrugged.

"Two adult and one student," Henry said.

Oh no, he was not going to buy her ticket. That would definitely be crossing a line. Olivia put her hand on his arm. "I can pay my own way."

He frowned but nodded and turned back to the ticket agent. "One adult, one student, then."

The agent handed Henry his tickets and then stared expectantly at Olivia. She dug into her purse and produced the right amount of cash for her ticket.

"You really didn't have to buy your ticket," Henry said. "You're doing us a favor by being here."

Riley linked her arms through Olivia's and Henry's as they moved past the ticket counter. Wedged between them, her gaze bounced back and forth. "That's right, Olivia. You're doing Henry and me a great favor. When we get inside, you two take Cody and just toddle off in the opposite direction of me, okay?"

Henry shook his head. "Uh, no."

Riley detached herself from them with a huff.

Olivia spoke up. "We will stay discreetly in the background. Won't we, Henry?"

"Yes, we will," he said. "We'll stay within striking distance."

Riley halted. "No, no, no. You have to stay at least thirty feet behind me."

Olivia laughed. "We can do that."

"Hey," Henry said. "I'm not sure about that."

Olivia's tucked her arm through Henry's. "Henry, we need to chat about a little thing called letting go."

Henry's heart hiccupped. *Okay, Lord, so this is your answer?* He eyed Olivia. For her to bring up the subject of letting go, after he'd prayed earlier that morning asking God for direction on how to let Riley grow up, had Henry's mind reeling. He tightened his hold on Cody's leash. The dog, attuned to Henry, stared up at him as if questioning what had his handler upset.

Henry took a shuddering breath and tried to reduce the storm raging within him. Purposely, he relaxed his hold on the leash, giving Cody more slack.

Riley picked up speed, heading into the nearest exhibit. Henry guided Cody and Olivia in his sister's wake. So far Cody hadn't caught any scents that he associated with explosives.

Before they stepped into the exhibit room his sister had entered, Olivia put pressure on his arm, forcing him to stop. "You need to give her some space."

"Olivia, how exactly do I do that with some maniac out there who set off a bomb while she was in the vicinity and then someone tries to break in?" A chill of residual fear swept down his back. If something had happened to Riley, he didn't know if he could survive.

"We have to trust that God will keep her safe and give you the means to protect her."

He drew in a breath, glad to hear she trusted God. In this moment it was easy to forget she was IA. He hadn't realized he needed a friend with whom he could discuss the situation. "You're right. But sometimes it's so hard to do."

"Agreed. Believe me, when you have an issue with control, faith can be a challenge."

"You, too?"

She gave him a sheepish smile. "Oh, yes. More than I care to admit. We'll walk in there in just a moment and we'll be able to keep an eye on her. Really, Henry, she *is* eighteen. You're treating her like she's six."

He ground his back teeth. "Now you're going to start in on me? I can't help it. There's no playbook for me to consult. I'm doing the best I can."

"And you're doing a great job. I know it's hard," she said. "Being stuck in the middle of my siblings with two very busy parents, I took care of my sisters and corralling my older brothers."

"Your brothers are both really good friends of mine. You did a good job with those two. I only know Ally on an acquaintance level. I haven't met your other two sisters. Though I've heard the one in the DA's office is—" He stopped, searching for a polite way convey what he'd been told.

Olivia laughed. "Maria is a shark. It's okay. I know. Even as a kid, she had a strong sense of justice and the determination to make the world a better place."

There was affection in her tone and he smiled. He liked this side of her. "I don't know if I could ever go through this again."

"You don't want children of your own one day?"

He shrugged. "I hate to say never but right now, no, I don't."

She looked away and appeared fascinated by the plaque on the wall. There was a tension in her shoulders that hadn't been there before.

Not sure what he'd said to upset her, he nudged her. "Okay, so what kind of wisdom do you want to impart to me?"

She started them walking in the direction that Riley had disappeared. Henry scanned the exhibit room and caught a glimpse of his sister as she read the plaque for a display.

Olivia stopped him so that they could pretend to view an exhibit on sea turtles. "Henry, here's the thing. There's a fine line between letting go and giving up. You don't want to give up. That's not okay. That's how many teens and young adults end up in trouble. But letting go means you stop treating her like a child."

He opened his mouth to protest, but Olivia held up a hand. "I don't mean that you shouldn't protect her from imminent and real danger. But you have to stop rescuing her. She's in college now. It's time for her to take responsibility."

"I get what you're saying but sometimes when I look at her, I still see that scared, traumatized twelve-year-old."

"Becoming the parent of a preteen overnight must have been very hard for you. Now, you have to transition to being a marvelous big brother who lets his little sister grow up and make mistakes."

He nodded as he digested her words. Could he be a brother and not a parent? He had no idea how to go about making that sort of switch in his thinking now. Especially with the threat of a bomber targeting their little family unit.

Riley moved on to another exhibit. After a several moments, they entered into the large mammal section. Riley was about fifteen feet away, looking at the mummified remains of baby woolly mammoth. The two girls who'd been with her at Coney Island had joined her.

Stopping to look at the fossil display of a Lestodon, he said to Olivia, "You must've been a real blessing to your parents."

Her mouth quirked. "I hope so."

"You're good at this, you know."

She arched an eyebrow. "At what?"

"Giving out wise counsel. And the way you dealt with Riley... I was impressed. If you hadn't joined the force, you'd make a wonderful guidance counselor."

An expression mixed between pain and surprise crossed Olivia's face before her attention shifted away from him. Why did his praise upset her?

"Who's that talking to your sister?"

His gaze landed on a young man not much older than Riley. All of Henry's senses went on alert as he recognized the expression of panic on Riley's face.

In long strides, with Cody close at his heels, Henry

reached Riley's side in time to hear her say, "I've already told you, I can't. Please, stop asking me."

"What's going on here?" Henry asked, planting his feet wide, his hands at his sides, ready to drop Cody's leash and scrabble with this kid if he didn't back down. Cody sniffed at the younger guy and lost interest.

The young man turned dark eyes on Henry. There was a flash of disdain in his gaze before he stepped back and held up his hands, palms out. "Hey, sorry. I go to school with Riley. No harm. I was just asking her some questions."

"What's your name?" Henry asked.

The kid backpedaled a few steps. "Parker. Ask her." He gestured to Riley. "We're in the same anthropology class."

Henry turned his gaze on Riley. She nodded but kept her lips clamped together. Not sure why his sister was so freaked out, Henry regarded Parker.

The kid looked like he'd skipped too many meals. Slim with baggie jeans and a T-shirt that hung on his long-limbed frame. His dark hair needed some attention. The kid looked vaguely familiar, but Henry couldn't place where he'd seen him.

"Well, you best get on with your assignment then," Henry said. "Let Riley do hers."

The kid shrugged and sauntered away, disappearing into another exhibit.

Riley hiked her backpack higher on her shoulder. "I had it handled."

Sure didn't look that way to Henry. "What did he want?"

"Nothing." Riley stepped around him and trotted off to join her friends.

"That didn't look like nothing," Henry muttered. He didn't like that Riley was keeping secrets. A warm, soft hand on his arm drew his attention to Olivia.

"She might open up to me," she said.

He stared at her for a long moment. "You could be right. She likes you. Maybe later, you can take a run at her. Unless, of course, you think that's too smothering of me."

"Not smothering at all. Just a concerned big brother." She patted his arm before stepping away. "If you'll excuse me, I'm going to the ladies' room."

Henry watched her walk away, torn between the need to escort her and keep Riley in sight. Olivia was an officer of the law and could take care of herself. He and Cody hurried to find his sister.

Olivia checked her reflection in the restroom mirror one last time. Her baby bump was a bit more pronounced today. And she was feeling a bit queasy for other reasons. Like the way she'd let her guard down around Henry. She couldn't deny how nice it was to relate to him in a friendly manner. But she would have to remember to keep up the emotional barrier that her job demanded or there would be a steep cost. One she wasn't sure she was ready to pay.

Adjusting her purse over her belly, she stepped into the hall. Rough hands grabbed her from behind and pushed her up against the wall, knocking the breath from her lungs.

Panic for her unborn child speared through her. She

was thankful her purse provided a cushion of sorts against the hard wall.

An arm pressed against the back of her neck and a hand pressed on the middle of her back, holding her in place.

A male voice spoke close to her ear. "It's not fair. You better find him guilty of hurting Davey Carrell or someone else is going to get hurt."

SIX

This wasn't a drill. Olivia had been trained by the best. She knew what to do when attacked from behind. Though her blood pounded in her ears and panic threatened to render her immobile, Olivia focused despite the adrenaline spike and gripped her right fist with her left hand. Using momentum and exerting every ounce of strength she possessed in both arms, she rammed her right elbow into her assailant's gut. He let out a loud groan.

Not satisfied with her effort, she followed her defense tactic with a hard heel stomp on his instep. The assailant cursed, released his hold and danced back. Olivia spun in time to see his retreating back and head covered by a dark hoodie. The guy pulled the fire alarm before he rounded the corner and disappeared from sight.

Covering her ears with her hands against the loud shriek of the alarm bouncing off the walls, Olivia gave pursuit, but there was no sign of the hooded figure among the now-panicked crowd rushing toward the exit. He'd escaped.

She had to find Henry and Riley.

Stepping out of the path of a woman dragging her school-age son toward the exit, Olivia grabbed her phone from her purse and shot off a text to Henry, telling him to meet her at the West 77th Street exit.

Within moments, Henry, Cody and Riley hurried toward her, dodging through the crush of people intent on vacating the museum.

"Are you okay?" he asked, his hand touching her elbow in a comforting way that rendered her speechless for a second.

Riley's eyes were huge with fear. "The museum is on fire!"

Regaining her wits, Olivia shook her head. "No, it's not." She told them what happened.

"What?" Henry put his hand on her shoulder. "Did he injure you?"

With a gasp, Riley clutched at Olivia. "You were assaulted? In the museum?"

"I'm fine," Olivia assured the siblings. "He threatened that someone would get hurt if I don't find you guilty of the charges."

"Can you ID him?" Henry's hands clenched and his gaze scanned the area.

"I didn't get a look at his face. He pulled the alarm and ran off. I looked for him, but he'd escaped."

Riley shivered. "That's scary."

Anger flashed in Henry's dark eyes. "We have to talk to security. They'll have video footage. Maybe we can identify the guy and see where he went."

All around them, people, mostly tourists, hurried toward the exits. The elevators were left open. People flooded down the staircases from the upper floors toward the doors leading out of the building.

Henry led the way through the crowd to the security offices near the ground level entrance in the Theodore Roosevelt Memorial Hall.

"Sir, you and your party need to exit." A guard stopped them and pointed to the nearest doors leading to the street.

Henry reached into his pocket and flashed his badge at the man. "There's no fire." He explained the situation. "I need to speak to the person in charge."

The guard shook his head. "I have to follow protocol. Everyone out until the fire department makes the determination that it's safe."

Riley tugged on Henry's arm. "Please, let's just go." The young girl grabbed Olivia's arm. "Come on."

Sensing the depth of Riley's distress, Olivia said to Henry, "You can check the video footage later. We should get your sister out of here."

Henry took a breath then nodded. "Yes. Though you'll need to give a statement about the assault."

Heart thumping in her chest, she said, "I will. But not here."

They hurried through the exit door and out on to Central Park West. Seeking shelter in the shade of a tree as a fire engine came to a halt at the curb in front of them, they watched as firefighters in turnout uniforms spilled out.

Two uniformed officers approached and took Olivia's statement.

"Stay here," Henry said. "I'm going to talk to the fire chief." He and Cody hurried away.

Riley moved closer to Olivia. "I don't like this. We need to go home."

Olivia slipped her arm around Riley. "Don't worry. Your brother won't let anything happen to you."

"But who's going to protect Henry?" Riley asked. "Someone's out to get him."

Olivia's gaze sought out the man in question. There was no refuting the girl's words. Someone wanted to take Henry down. And were willing to hurt other people to make it happen. Why?

A wave of protectiveness coursed through her. She would do what she could for Henry. But she also had a job to do. She'd have to write up a report about the threat and explain her reasoning for being with Henry and Riley at the museum. She hoped her boss would see the value of spending time with Henry outside of the department atmosphere. She was gaining a better understanding of him as a man, which would be incorporated into her assessment for the review board. And though she prayed she'd be able to prove him innocent, she couldn't get emotionally involved, no matter the outcome. Unfortunately, doing as she should was proving harder with every moment she spent in Henry's presence.

Henry kept an eye on his sister and Olivia where they stood together under the shade of a large tree. His heart pounded in his chest like a runaway subway train. He'd known the moment he caught sight of Olivia hustling back from the restroom that something had been wrong. Her eyes were large and her pupils dilated.

Agitation revved through his system. He wished he'd

been there to catch Olivia's assailant in the act. Unfortunately no one close to him was safe while he was being targeted.

Even now, he didn't like being very far away from either of the women. He told himself he was doing his job where Olivia was concerned. But honestly, he couldn't say there was any discernible difference between the fear he experienced for Olivia's safety than the fear he had for Riley's safety. It didn't matter that Olivia was a trained officer who had proven moments ago that she was more than capable of taking care of herself. He couldn't curb the protective instinct any more than he could keep from breathing. He was coming to care for this woman, despite knowing he shouldn't if he valued his career.

He shook off his thoughts and forced his mind to focus on what was happening around him. People continued to stream out of the museum. Cody's head swiveled in an arc, his nose in the air but still no sign of alarm.

Henry searched for anyone matching the description that Olivia had given of the hooded man. If only she had seen his face, rather than just his back as he'd run away. He could've ditched the hoodie at any time. The guy could be watching them now.

This had to be the same man who'd tried to break into the condo. Especially hearing that the assailant insisted Olivia find him guilty in her investigation. Henry needed to question Davey Carrell and find out which of his friends would be bold enough to act with such malicious intent.

Unfortunately, Henry couldn't go near Davey.

For now, the best thing that Henry could do was take his sister and Olivia as far away from this area as possible. He would call his sergeant and request that someone question Davey.

After talking to the fire chief and touching base with the head security guard to request he send any relevant video to the K-9 Unit's tech, Henry ushered Olivia and Riley back to Brooklyn. They took a cab rather than the subway.

The cab bounced along the road with the three of them squished in the back seat and Cody on his lap. Riley sat in the center and snuggled up against him.

"Did you get enough material for you to complete your assignment?" Olivia asked Riley.

"I did," she answered with a shudder. "I'm really glad you both were with me." She nudged him with her elbow. "We should have a barbecue," she said. "Invite Olivia and maybe the McGregors and the Jamesons."

He was glad Riley liked his colleagues. "Soon. But not today. I think adding anyone else into the mix right now would be unwise. I'm being targeted and those around me apparently are, as well." His stomach clenched with dread.

It was no coincidence that Riley had been at Coney Island when the bomber reached out to Henry. And now Olivia had been attacked. He didn't want to draw anyone else into the line of fire.

Olivia turned to look at him, her gaze intense, and then she said to Riley, "It's very sweet of you to want to include me. But I really need to get home. My kitty has probably clawed her way through the door of the pantry trying to get to her food."

Riley's eyes grew big and she clapped her hands. "You have a kitty? I love kittens. Henry won't have one with Cody around."

Olivia's gaze jumped to Henry, then Cody. "Cody doesn't get along with cats?"

Henry shrugged. "I don't know. We've never encountered one up close."

"Henry doesn't like cats," Riley said.

He met Olivia's gaze. "It's not that I dislike them so much as never been around them."

"Can we come to your house and see your kitten?" Riley asked.

"She's not a kitten," Olivia said. "But I'm sure Kitty would appreciate a little love and attention."

"You named your cat Kitty?" Henry asked.

Olivia's nose twitched. "She's two years old, I think. She adopted me a few months ago. Just showed up at the apartment complex one day and wouldn't let anyone else near her but me. I tried to find her owners, because she's a unique type of cat, but no one claimed her. And yes, I named her Kitty because I could never decide on anything better."

"She adopted you?" Riley clapped her hands together. "That's so sweet."

When they reached Olivia's building and she led them inside, Henry was surprised by the small one-bedroom apartment. He'd wasn't sure what he'd expected, maybe more of a minimalist sort of vibe, but instead the place was very artsy with lots of personality.

Her walls were covered with paintings of beautiful landscapes and there were sculpted pieces on every available space. The blue suede couch and red and white accent chair invited one to sit down for a cozy chat.

One corner of her living room was devoted to crafting, with a table and bins filled with all sorts of materials he recognized because Riley was also into crafting. Though Riley didn't keep her supplies as neat and organized as Olivia. This was a different side to the lieutenant and reminded him that she was an attractive woman with depth. In other circumstances, he'd want to explore the many layers she possessed. But he couldn't. And wouldn't.

"Here Kitty, Kitty," Olivia called.

From the bedroom they heard a soft meow. Cody's ears perked up and he cocked his head, listening. How would the dog react when confronted with a cat in close quarters?

"Can I go get her?" Riley asked.

"Hold on a sec." Olivia dug into a box of treats and handed several pieces to Riley. "She may be hiding under the bed. She's really sweet. But just be cautious because she doesn't know you."

Concern arced through Henry. "Maybe she shouldn't be handling a cat that doesn't know her."

"I'll be fine," Riley said. "I know how to handle animals."

Olivia stayed Riley with a hand. "Your brother's right. It might be better for me to bring her out." She hurried down the hall, disappearing into her bedroom.

Riley whirled on him. "Really? Now the cat's unsafe?"

"You heard Olivia, she doesn't know if how the cat will respond to you."

Riley rolled her eyes and walked over to the crafting corner. He blew out a breath. There didn't seem to be any winning with his sister. Her phone chimed. She looked at the text, her mouth pulling at the corners.

"Everything okay?" Henry asked.

With another roll of her eyes, she put her phone away. "Yes."

Henry had the urge to stick out his tongue at her. That would be acting just as childishly as her, but sometimes she brought out his inner twelve-year-old.

A few moments later, Olivia arrived back into the living room carrying the strangest creature Henry had ever seen. "What is *that*?"

Cody lifted his nose toward the animal in question, sniffed, then lost interest. He settled down at Henry's feet.

"A sphynx, or Egyptian hairless cat," Olivia said. "Though they aren't really hairless. Their skin is covered with a fine layer of down. Like a peach." She held the cat out. "Pet her."

He'd never seen a cat of this breed in real life. Its pink skin was wrinkled, its ears too big for its head and the cat's piercing blue eyes stared at him, unblinking.

"She looks like E.T.'s cousin." But he had to admit, as he ran his hand over her back, that her suede-like coat was velvety soft.

Riley stepped up and held out the treat Olivia had given her earlier. Very daintily, Kitty took the treat from Riley's fingers. Then she clawed the air as if trying to gain traction so she could get into Riley's arms. Olivia handed the cat over. Riley hugged Kitty to her chest, petting and cooing. Soon a loud rumble of purring filled the air.

"She likes you, Riley," Olivia said. "Can I get either of you something to drink?"

"No, thank you," Henry said. "We should get going."

Riley spun away and walked back to the crafting table with Kitty in her arms. "You're a crafter. What are you working on over here?"

Olivia joined Riley in the craft corner. Henry stood back, his heart aching as he realized that Riley was becoming attached to Olivia. No doubt Riley was starved for maternal attention.

The two women talked about mosaic glass and art. He had to admit he respected and admired the Internal Affairs investigator. And he was attracted to her. None of that was good.

Olivia would be a good influence on his little sister, but it wasn't a good idea for him and Olivia to be spending time together. Riley shouldn't form a bond with the woman.

He had to distance himself. Not only for Olivia's safety but also because his life, his career, was on the line.

He would walk a tightrope from the Chrysler Building to the Empire State Building if it meant he could continue doing the job he loved.

Long after Henry, Cody and Riley left, Olivia sat on the couch staring out the window and watching the sun set. Kitty sat curled on her lap. Every time her child moved, she was reminded of the life growing inside of her and it filled her with tender love. All in all, it had been a good day. Up to the point where she'd been assaulted outside the ladies' restroom.

But even before the assault, Henry had been attentive and caring. A true gentleman.

How was she going to find it within herself not to become emotionally involved in this case?

They drilled it into her at the academy that an Internal Affairs investigator was to stay neutral, unbiased and unemotional and she was struggling. Did it mean she wasn't cut out for this job? Or that her heart really wasn't in it? She suspected the latter. And not just because of Henry and her growing feelings for him.

She could still vividly remember her hesitation when she took the position with IA. But her family had cheered her on. Even Roger had been supportive, a rare moment for him. She'd accepted the post and had spent the first six months shadowing another investigator. If her family hadn't pushed her toward the career she wasn't sure she'd have applied. But she did find the fact finding, interviewing and presentation of cases for the review board came easily. Her father had been so proud of her when she'd made the transfer to internal affairs.

She couldn't let him or the department down.

"I can handle this," she said aloud. "I'm a professional. I can do my job and keep my emotions in check."

But was that what she wanted? And what would be best for her baby? The questions ricocheted through her mind as the night went on.

In the morning, instead of heading to her family's congregation, she took the subway to the church near Henry and Riley's house.

Yesterday Riley had mentioned where they attended services and had asked Olivia to accompany them. Telling herself she was only trying to get a better understanding of Henry and his life, she had told Riley she would think about it. She'd thought of nothing else all night.

Now here she was, walking up the concrete steps to the big arched doorway. What if Henry and Riley didn't show up today?

The thought should have brought her some relief, but it didn't. She grew more agitated as she stepped inside the doors. A sea of unfamiliar faces lay before her in the pews. What was she doing here? She should be with her family not…not what? Chasing after Henry?

No. She certainly wasn't chasing anyone. On the verge of turning around and leaving, she heard Riley call her name.

Riley waved from a pew near the front. Olivia's gaze jumped from Riley to Henry, who remained seated but had twisted toward her. For a moment, their gazes locked, his showing surprise. Then his mouth curved upward and he gave her a nod as if also inviting her to join them. Her heart did a funny little skip that left her breathless.

Drawn forward by some invisible tether, she could hear people whispering and sense the gaze of everyone in the church. Did these people know she was crossing a line?

Feeling conspicuous, she slid into the pew. Riley hugged her, then scooted around her so that now Olivia was wedged between the siblings. Cody, wearing his K-9 vest, lay at Henry's feet. The dog nudged her foot with his nose.

Henry leaned close. "This is unexpected."

Her defensiveness rose. "Riley invited me."

Riley's smile was wide. "I did invite her." She glanced away and then waved to someone. "There's my friend Nicole. I'll be right back." She shimmied out of the pew and down the middle aisle, leaving Olivia and Henry alone on the bench.

"Are you on duty?"

"Not officially," Henry said, his voice low. "But my sergeant suggested I keep Cody close until we catch the bomber. We walked the perimeter before we sat down."

"Makes sense." Though Olivia hated to think something could happen here in this sacred place, having Cody's super nose around to interpret any dangerous odors would keep everyone safe.

The clearing of a throat behind them drew Henry's attention. Olivia followed his gaze. An older couple with big grins regarded her with obvious curiosity.

"Larry and Martha Hodgeson, this is Olivia Vance. A friend," Henry said.

Surprise jumped inside of Olivia at Henry's statement. Did he consider her a friend? Were they friends? *Could* they be friends? She liked the idea way more than she should. She swallowed the trepidation of fraternizing with Henry that threatened to rob her of the moment.

Extending his hand, Larry said, "Hello, Olivia. Welcome."

Olivia shook the offered hand, appreciating the man's sincerity. "Thank you."

Martha sat forward, her brown eyes twinkling in her gently lined face. "How do you two know each other?"

"Work," Henry stated and pointed toward the lectern. "Services are about to start."

He faced forward. Sharing his apparent discomfort at the pointed question, Olivia pressed her lips together, smiled and faced the front of the church. Henry leaned close and whispered in her ear. "I wish everybody would mind their own business."

She glanced at him, not realizing he'd turned back toward her. Their lips nearly touched. Her gaze bounced from the wonderful shape of his mouth to his gaze. What she saw there made her heart pound.

"I should leave," she whispered. And regain her senses.

"Please don't. I'm glad you're here."

His words uncurled a ribbon of joy inside her. It had been so long since anyone had made her feel wanted and special. She was in so much trouble. Straightening her spine, she reminded herself she had to keep things between them professional. She was here to gather more intel on what Henry was like off duty—or rather, away from the station house—so she could make a more informed judgment on his character and conduct. Both of which were proving to be stellar.

The sermon started and Riley never returned but had decided to remain farther back in the sanctuary with her friends.

Olivia struggled to track the pastor's message. But finally the words penetrated through her distraction with stinging clarity. "Forgive those who have wronged you so that you may be forgiven." Her thoughts turned to her late husband.

Emotions clogged her chest, an ugly mix of anger, betrayal and grief. She wanted to forgive him but she didn't know how. The hurt was still so close to the surface. And every time she tried to let go, she only ended up with a headache.

"You okay?"

She didn't want Henry to see the ugliness inside of her. Shoring up her defenses, she smoothed away her inner turmoil and nodded.

When the pastor had finished his sermon, Riley returned. Riley leaned over to talk to Henry, practically pushing Olivia into his side. He was solid and warm against her and she was hard-pressed to not melt into him.

"Can Nicole come over?" Riley asked.

Henry nodded. "Of course."

With a satisfied smile, Riley sat back. "Good. Maybe the four of us could go to brunch at The Pancake House."

Oh, Olivia was so tempted to say yes. Brunch sounded lovely and was her favorite meal of the day. She had promised herself she wasn't going to become emotionally involved with these people and yet, here they were, like a family, on the brink of going out to brunch on Sunday after church. The line between professional and personal was blurring. Somehow she had to make that line more defined.

Heaviness descended on her shoulders as longing for a complete family of her own wrapped around her like a wet blanket. She pushed it away. Soon she would have her own child to lavish with the love in her heart.

And no matter how much she was attracted to Henry or how much she adored Riley, she was afraid to trust, to risk her heart again.

Riley was an adult, ready to launch herself into the stratosphere of her life. And Henry had already made it clear he wasn't interested in raising a family after raising his sister. All good reasons for Olivia to be putting the brakes on whatever it was she was feeling. Her job required her to erect an emotional barricade. Plus, after her late husband's betrayal, how could she trust again? Being suddenly reminded of her disastrous marriage served as a wake-up call. Best to guard her heart to keep from being hurt in the future.

Abruptly, Olivia stood, shaking her head. "I'm sorry, you two. I need to head home for Kitty. And then I've got a full day of—stuff to do. Errands."

She shuffled past Riley into the aisle.

"Olivia?" Henry's concerned voice followed her.

She waved and headed out the door at a fast clip, dodging people as she went, smiling apologetically instead of stopping when she realized that many in the congregation wanted her to pause so they could grill her about who she was and why she was with Henry and Riley.

She hurried out to the crosswalk. The light turned green for her to cross and she stepped into the street, heading toward the subway station.

A silver sedan pulled away from the curb, its tires squealing on the pavement drawing her attention. The car was speeding straight at her.

SEVEN

Strong hands wrapped around Olivia's biceps and yanked her backward out of the car's path, up against a hard chest. The sedan shot past her so closely the air swirled in the late morning heat. The car made a sharp left, taking the corner at the end of the street with a screech of rubber gripping the road and disappeared out of sight. The license plate was conspicuously missing.

Shock and adrenaline coursed through Olivia's veins, making her limbs shake.

Henry slipped his arms around her, holding on to her as her knees buckled. "I've got you."

His deep voice reverberated through her and she twisted in his arms to look at him. "That car—" Her voice faltered.

"—Almost ran you down." The sharp edge of his anger sliced the air between them.

"You saved me." Gratitude engulfed her along with a good dose of affection. If he hadn't followed her out…

His expression softened, his mouth tipping up at one corner in a crooked smile that snuck into her heart and gave it a squeeze.

"Are you okay?"

Suddenly aware that Henry was holding her like a man would a woman he loved and that she wanted nothing more than to lean forward and kiss him, she gasped and wiggled out of his arms. The sting of a blush heated her cheeks. She hoped Henry didn't notice. "Thank you, Henry."

He stuffed his hands into his pockets. "No problem."

"I called 911," a man from the church said.

"We appreciate your help," Henry told the man.

Olivia took a step toward the sidewalk and nearly stumbled over the curb. Henry slid an arm around her waist to steady her. Then he tucked her hand around his arm. "Riley and I will see you home as soon as we've given our statements to the first responders."

"You don't—"

"Olivia, let us do this for you."

She was shaky, and at the moment, being alone was really the last thing she wanted. She prayed that this little jolt of adrenaline hadn't hurt the baby. She'd read that that could happen. She made a mental note to call her ob-gyn on Monday.

Henry stared at her, his gaze intense. "Are you sure you're all right? I mean, considering—"

She held up a hand, stopping him from finishing his sentence. "I'm fine. *Everything* is fine. Okay?"

He may suspect she was pregnant, but she did not want to discuss her baby with the man she was investigating. If anyone found out that she'd opened up about something so personal, she might as well just turn in her badge now. And that wasn't going to happen. If, or when, she resigned from the police force, it would be her decision. She was done allowing herself to be pressured into circumstances and situations she didn't fully embrace.

Seeming to accept her pronouncement, Henry nodded. "Good." He beckoned for Riley. As they waited for the young woman and her friend to join them, Henry said, "This wasn't an accident."

Olivia shivered, wishing she was still ensconced in his embrace. "I realize that. You said you'd thought a silver sedan was following you the other night?"

His dark eyes hardened. "I did. And I'm pretty sure that was the same car. Did you get a look at the driver?"

She shook her head. All she'd seen was sunlight reflecting off the grill as the sedan sped forward, aimed in her direction. "You?"

"Not enough for a description. He had on sunglasses and the visor was down. He had black gloves and a hoodie on just like the guy who tried to break into my condo."

"Do you think this is the same guy who assaulted me yesterday at the museum?"

"We have to assume so," he said.

Which meant the man targeting Henry and those close to him was growing impatient. But what was his endgame? If his goal was to hurt Henry, why go after her when she was the only one who could ruin Henry's career?

Monday morning, Henry stopped at Eden's desk with coffee cups in both hands. He set one in front of the tech guru.

Eden glanced between the cup and him. "This is for me?"

"I didn't want you to think I was ungrateful for all the work you do."

She smiled at him, her dark eyes twinkling as she reached down to pet Cody. "Hey, handsome." She picked up the coffee and took a sip. "Hmm. Perfect. How did you know the way I take my cup of joe?"

He grinned. "A wise man takes notice of what a person wants when asking her for a favor."

"Well, I'm glad I don't have to disappoint you today." She swung around to her monitors. Her fingers flew across the keyboard. "So I pulled up all the video footage from the surrounding area where the bomb went off in Coney Island. As well as around Joey Yums, like you asked."

She pressed Enter and the video monitors lit up. The far monitor showed a perfect shot of the front of the Joey Yums restaurant. The middle monitor had a street view in front of the eatery and the third monitor showed a long shot of the boardwalk.

The time stamp on the video was from a half hour before Henry had arrived. Eden hit the fast-forward button.

"Wait!" Henry sucked in a sharp breath. Eden stopped the video on a clear shot of Riley and her friends entering Joey Yums. Five minutes later, they exited with food containers that they ate from while walking along the boardwalk, passing very close to the garbage can that later exploded. Henry's heart rate doubled. It was one thing to suspect how close his sister had come to disaster and another to see it in color.

As soon as Riley and her friends walked out of the view on the third monitor, a hooded figure wearing a backpack could be seen from the direction of the street. The guy kept his face averted as if he knew where the cameras were located. Sunlight glinted off the guy's sunglasses. He walked toward Joey Yums's entrance before doing an about-face and walking slowly down the boardwalk in the same direction as Riley and her friends.

The guy walked past the last garbage bin and disappeared off screen. Henry frowned. "He's clearly following Riley, but he's not our bomber."

Eden held up a hand. "Wait for it."

A minute later the hooded figure returned, his body angled so the camera couldn't record his face, but he seemed to be staring at the young couple kissing on the bench. Then the guy took off the backpack, lifted the lid of the garbage can and dropped the backpack inside. He shut the lid and jogged away. The couple on the bench didn't appear to even notice him. They were too entwined in each other's arms to realize that disaster was right next to them.

"I want to see this bomber again."

Eden rewound the video.

Henry studied what he could see of the man. Jeans, tennis shoes and the edges of dark sunglasses, but Henry couldn't determine the man's race. But he did notice the black gloves on the bomber's hands, just like the ones worn by the prowler at the condo and the driver of the sedan. "This has to be the same guy who tried to run down Lieutenant Vance."

Eden turned to stare at him. "What?"

He told her about the incident at the church and the museum.

"Oh, that's why the museum called," Eden said. "I haven't had a chance to return the call, but I will. In the meantime, let me see if I can find any video footage around the church for you."

He told her the approximate time and the make and model of the car. He pointed to the screen where the hooded figure stood frozen on the boardwalk. "Can you backtrack this guy's route on the street? See where he came from?"

"I can," she said. "But it will take some time. I can text you when I have something more to show you."

"That'd be great. Any chance you have any information on the phone that was used to contact me?"

"Sorry, it was a burner phone. It's turned off now. But I have a program running to alert me if it turns back on."

Henry wasn't surprised that the phone was a dead end, but he couldn't stop the wave of frustration and helpless anger roaring through him.

Eden waved at him. "I don't like when people stand over my shoulder. Why don't you go to the unit meeting? I'll text Gavin that I'm still working."

"Thanks," Henry said. "I owe you one." He seemed to owe a lot of people these days. Even his boss, Gavin, who'd promised to send someone to talk to Davey Carrell about which of his friends might be threatening Henry and those close to him.

Eden turned back to her screen as if he hadn't spoken.

Henry and Cody headed downstairs to the conference room where the meeting was taking place. Gavin was at the front of the room getting ready to call the meeting to order.

Henry and Cody slipped inside and took up a spot against the back wall.

A minute later, Olivia stepped inside the room and took a place next to him. Surprise washed over him. It wasn't usual for IA to attend a precinct meeting, but considering the encompassing nature of her investigation, he supposed observing the unit as a whole, and him specifically, wasn't out of line. Their gazes locked for a moment. He was stunned to see the flare of interest in her amber eyes before she quickly turned her gaze forward. She looked good this morning, as regal as she had on Friday, but today's suit color was a deep purple with a striped, collared shirt underneath. Her hair was in a fancy braided updo. His blood surged with a confusing mix of attraction and affection.

When he'd dropped her off at her apartment yesterday after her near-disaster with the sedan, he'd been hard-pressed to leave her alone. Only her assurance that she'd planned on staying inside for the rest of the day until one of her brothers arrived to take her to their parent's house for dinner had relieved some of his anxiousness.

He had to admit he was glad to see her this morning unharmed. He'd hate it if something happened to her because of him. The need to protect her rose strong within him. He fought the urge to put an arm around her. She would probably deck him. And he'd deserve it.

"I have an announcement everyone," Gavin said from the front of the room, drawing Henry's and the whole room's attention. All the officers went silent. "Thanks to US Marshal Emmett Gage, who was able to grab a cup and napkin from Randall Gage, his cousin and our prime suspect in the McGregor murders, we have a DNA match."

The room erupted with cheers and gasps. K-9 Officer Belle Montera, who'd been assigned to question the US marshal about his cousin in the first place, seemed both relieved and subdued. Henry knew that Belle and Emmett Gage were engaged to be married, and to have absolute proof that his cousin *was* a murderer had to be tough on the dedicated law enforcement officer. Henry's gaze sought out his friend, Bradley McGregor, his heart gladdened by this new development. The long-unsolved murders of Bradley and Penny's parents had put a horrible strain on the siblings.

Bradley met his gaze. There were tears in his eyes as his arm slipped around his sister, seated beside him. Tears ran down Penny's face and she nearly collapsed sideways out of her chair.

"Okay, people," Gavin said, reclaiming everyone's focus. "We have our work cut out for us. Now we just have to find Randall, who hasn't been seen since he bolted from the greasy spoon weeks ago. The FBI and the US Marshals are on the trail. But we need to be vigilant. This man has killed two, possibly four, people. That we know of."

Henry knew the sergeant was referring to the recent double homicide of the Emerys, parents of a little girl who'd been left unharmed. The Emerys were killed on the twentieth anniversary of the McGregors' murders—with the same MO. Had Randall Gage also killed the Emerys? Or had that been the work of a copycat? The unit didn't know at this point, and it was frustrating. Henry glanced at K-9 Detective Nick Slater, who'd gotten personally involved with the aunt of little Lucy Emery—the lone survivor of her parents' murder—during the investigation. Nick and Willow were now in the process of formally adopting Lucy, and Henry could see from Nick's tight expression how bad he wanted justice for the Emerys.

"There wasn't any DNA found at the Emery crime scene, right?" Transit Officer Max Santelli asked. He stood near the window with his rottweiler at his side.

"Correct. There was no DNA evidence found on either of the victims. Or the evidence left behind. But our forensic expert is working hard on extracting DNA from fibers found on the back door knob of the Emory apartment."

"And if we can't match this evidence to Randall Gage?" Officer Jackson Davison asked. He sat at the conference table with his cadaver dog at his feet.

A grim look entered Gavin's eyes. "Then it's possible we have an entirely different killer on the loose. A copycat."

Henry's gut clenched with aggravation. He couldn't be on the case because of the charges being investigated by Internal Affairs. He swung his gaze to Olivia. She didn't look in his direction and kept her focus on Gavin.

Henry sent up a silent plea to God that Olivia would hurry up and finish her investigation. And find him innocent so he could get back to work and keep his family and friends safe. Including, the lovely IA lieutenant.

As Olivia stood at the back of the conference room, listening to Sergeant Sutherland's announcement of the DNA match and the possibility that the second murders might be a different killer, she had an idea. Hopefully she wouldn't be overstepping by sharing her thoughts with Gavin and his team.

She waved her hand to get Gavin's attention. Like everyone else in the city, she'd been following the double homicide case. Her conscience wouldn't keep her from speaking her mind.

Eyebrows rising, Gavin said, "Internal Affairs Lieutenant Olivia Vance has something she'd like to say."

All eyes turned to her. Heat infused her cheeks, but she straightened her spine and stepped forward. "If Randall Gage is the killer of both sets of parents, then he left *two* young children alive. He may view himself as a protector of children." A murmur of agreement swept through the room. "I would suggest two things. One, look for similar crimes where a child was spared. Two, contact the FBI's Behavioral Analysis Unit profiler, Caleb Black. He's the best of the best at Quantico."

Gavin studied her for a long moment. "Good ideas, both. We've considered the child-protector angle. I will reach out to the FBI and see if they can spare Agent Black." He turned back to his unit.

The dismissal was obvious. Slightly nauseous, Olivia stepped back into the shadow of the other unit officers. She could feel Henry's gaze like a laser on her, but she held her head high. She wouldn't apologize for speaking.

Gavin went on to report about other activity in the K-9 Unit. Twenty minutes later, when the meeting broke up, Olivia hightailed it out of the room as quickly as possible.

"Hey, Olivia, wait."

Henry's voice stopped her in the station's entryway. She really wanted to get some fresh air before she lost her breakfast all over the station's floor. Slowly, she turned and faced the man she was investigating.

Bracing herself to be told she'd crossed some imaginary line, she stiffened her spine and planted her feet apart, much like she'd seen her father and brothers do when faced with an adversary. Though calling Henry an adversary didn't sit well with her. Not after he'd saved her life yesterday. As well as how often she'd thought about kissing him. Would his lips be soft and giving or hard and demanding?

And what was that wonderful cologne that clung to his skin? She'd had to resist moving closer to him while they stood together at the unit meeting.

She really needed to get a grip. The influx of pregnancy hormones was messing with her head and her heart.

Henry strode to her side. His handsome face broke into a grin that set off a flutter in her tummy. She was pretty sure *that* wasn't the baby. She was helpless to curb the unprofessional attraction rooting inside of her.

"Good job on the suggestions," Henry said. "You really have a knack for reading situations and giving good advice."

His words were like a balm to her vulnerable state of embarrassment. "Thank you." She shrugged, trying to downplay the feeling of pride swelling within her chest. "I do have a degree in criminal justice as well as psychology."

His eyebrows rose. He rubbed a hand over his now-shaven head. "Impressive. Why are you working in IA when you could be of more help as a counselor or even a criminal profiler for the NYPD or the FBI?"

His question stung. She had originally considered trauma counseling for victims, but that would have required deviating from family expectations. So she'd joined the police force, following in her father's and brothers' footsteps. She'd started out on patrol until her father had lectured her that the best way for her to earn respect and success was through Internal Affairs. Her father was a straight arrow who respected the difficult position of internal affairs and had stressed she had the goods to excel in IA.

Despite her best intentions, she'd let herself be pressured into a position she'd never really wanted, but her dad and brothers had convinced her she was a perfect fit for the job.

Now here was Henry questioning her choice of profession.

Was this some kind of tactic to get out of being investigated? She searched his dark gaze and found no hint of a hidden agenda.

Did she dare confess that she'd once considered a different path? Or that there were times when the isolation of Internal Affairs brought regret to the forefront of her mind?

Deciding that indulging in any personal give-and-take was too dangerous for her job and her peace of mind, she simply said, "I appreciate your thoughts. Now, if you'll excuse me, I have some old case files to go through." Better than confessing she was struggling with her attraction to him.

His mouth twisted in derision. "My old case files, no doubt."

Lying wasn't in her wheelhouse, so she nodded and couldn't stop the ache of regret that they were in this position. But the job was the job. No matter how distasteful she sometimes found it.

For a moment, he seemed to be wrestling with some inner turmoil and then he said, "Full disclosure, I had a previous claim leveled against me once in the early days of my career, but it was quickly ruled unsubstantiated."

Her heart sank. That didn't bode well for him. "Thank you for being up-front with me."

"Of course," he said. "I don't want there to be anything hidden between us."

Her heart gave a little jolt. She wasn't sure what to make of his statement, so she simply watched as he turned and strode away.

After taking a moment to splash water on her face in the restroom and doing some deep breathing exercises, she headed to the records room. An hour later, she found the case he'd referred to.

In looking at the date and knowing when Henry's father had died, there was no question Henry had been acting in grief during a domestic call where the wife was barely hanging on to life from a beating by her husband.

What Henry was doing on the job that day was a question she'd like answered by the department's psychologist, who'd deemed him fit for duty. But obviously the situation had triggered something in Henry, as when the male suspect had taken a swing at him, Henry had swung back.

Internal Affairs had cleared Henry of wrongdoing.

But still, the knowledge that Henry had reacted out of anger and grief was something she needed to take into account and address with him. To be fair, she wanted to hear his side of the story so she could understand his thought process at the time. And it might help her to discern what happened the night that Davey Carrell was injured.

After asking around for Henry's location, she found him in the training center next door to the precinct.

She entered a warehouse-size room filled with an eclectic mix of obstacles. Luggage pieces of various shapes and sizes were stacked in three different groupings. There was a bicycle rack with several bicycles locked up. A shrink-wrapped stack of pallets and a car-shaped cutout caught her eye. Plus multiple boxes of various shapes and sizes were intermittently scattered between all the other obstacles.

Stepping into an alcove where she could observe Henry and Cody moving through the obstacles without distracting them, Olivia watched in fascination as the beagle sniffed along the seams of the luggage, the edges of the boxes and around the pallets and would either move along or stop and sit.

A petite blonde wearing the training center uniform would clap when Cody sat, prompting Henry to pull out a toy from his pocket and play tug with Cody for a moment before resuming their activity. Olivia inferred that meant Cody had detected correctly.

Henry glanced up and met her gaze. His eyebrows lifted, then a slow smile curved his mouth as if he were pleased to see her again. An answering pleasure wound through her, making her heart thump with a yearning that made her knees wobbly.

It had been a mistake to search him out when she didn't have her emotions under control. But there was something about Henry, his vitality and his integrity, that called to her.

And made doing her job that much more difficult.

EIGHT

On the verge of retreating from the training center in a flood of embarrassment at her silly response to Henry, Olivia backed up and ran smack into the veterinarian, Gina.

Gina had Maverick, the runt of Brooke's litter, in her arms. Brooke was the sweet German shepherd a few of the K-9 officers had rescued from the streets soon after she'd given birth to five puppies. "Good morning."

"Morning." Olivia reached out to pet the pup. Gina handed him over. Olivia fumbled to hang on to the little dog. "Oh, okay."

"He responds well to you," Gina said.

Snuggling the dog close, Olivia's heart melted. She liked the sweet little guy. "Do you think one day he'll be able to train like Cody?"

"Too soon to know yet," Gina said. "Some dogs you can tell right away and in others it takes a little time to discern what kind of training, if any, they will be able to handle."

"What Cody's doing is very specialized, correct?"

"It is. Though there are now more bomb-sniffing

dogs being trained all over the country than ever before," Gina replied. "Cody is checking for chemical vapors that come off the materials of the different obstacles, searching for specific odors that indicate evidence of an explosive device."

"Vapors? I didn't realize bombs had vapors." Olivia remembered the way the beagle had behaved at the boardwalk on Coney Island. "But that makes total sense with the way that Cody had sniffed the air and followed a scent to the garbage can that did explode."

Gina nodded. "Precisely. Everything gives off an odor. Cody has been trained to deconstruct each scent into its components, picking up on the chemicals he has been trained to detect. Kind of like when you step into an Italian restaurant and you smell that delicious aroma of spaghetti sauce. We know what goes into the sauce, but our noses can't differentiate between the tomatoes, garlic, rosemary, onion and oregano. But the dog can."

"That's amazing." Olivia cocked her head as she watched the way Henry was tracing the car outline with his hand and Cody's nose followed. "What are they doing now?"

"Henry is teaching Cody where he wants him to smell."

When the pair were done and heading out of the training ring, Olivia handed Maverick back to Gina. "Thank you for letting me hold him again."

"Anytime." Gina carried the pup away.

There was something so soothing about cuddling with Maverick. Feeling calmer and more like herself, Olivia hurried to catch up to Henry and Cody. They were walking toward the men's changing room.

Acutely aware of the other officers and trainers in the area, she called, "Detective Roarke," stopping him in his tracks. "Could I have a moment of your time?"

His gaze bounced to the file folder in her hand, then back to her eyes. "It will have to be after I'm done in the training ring."

"You and Cody aren't done?"

"Not exactly." He handed her Cody's leash. "Hang on to him for a moment, will you?"

Without waiting for a reply, he opened the men's room door and disappeared inside.

Sputtering, she had half a mind to follow him inside and tell him she was not his lackey. Not that she minded hanging out with Cody, but still. But Henry wasn't one of her brothers, who she could boss around.

At last night's family dinner, her older brothers had given her a hard time for having jammed up their friend. She hated that she had to defend herself, especially when she wouldn't be in this position if not for their urging. She didn't like being the bad guy everyone avoided. But having jammed up—police term for launching an official investigation—Henry was her job.

A job that was becoming more than she could tolerate. Especially now that she was expecting a baby. The last thing she wanted was for her child to ever experience the sort of reserved animosity that was regularly flung her way.

Cody lay down at her feet, his paws on her shoe. There was no way she could be mad at the dog, at least. He was such a cutie with his floppy ears and masked face. His brown eyes regarded her with what she assumed was curiosity. The dog probably wondered why his handler had trusted her with him. She wondered the same thing and couldn't stop the spurt of pleasure crowding her chest.

Several long minutes later, Henry returned wearing a light-colored, padded bite suit and heavy boots. His head stuck out of the top, exposed, but in his hand, he carried a caged helmet.

Olivia chuckled and her earlier ire of having to cool her heels in the hallway dissipated. "You get to be the human chew toy."

Taking Cody's leash, he shot her a glance and said wryly, "It would really help if you sped things along."

A brief stab of guilt provoked her to say, "I'm sorry, Henry, but my investigation will take however long it takes."

She really needed to do a thorough job that couldn't be questioned. Her integrity was at stake here in so many ways. She couldn't be rushed or bulldozed into making a determination, not by Henry, her family or some mysterious assailant. And certainly not her growing feelings for the handsome detective.

Henry and Cody walked ahead of her into the training ring, where K-9 Officer Lani Jameson, and her large German shepherd, Snapper, waited. Lani was dressed in her uniform and the dog had on a flak vest with the words K-9 Police emblazoned across the back.

Olivia followed the pair. "Is it normal for officers to wear full gear when training?"

Henry paused as if surprised to see her inside the arena. "Yes. Especially for the dog."

The K-9 trainer who'd been in the ring earlier with

Henry and Cody hurried over to take Cody's leash. "Who is that?" she whispered, nodding toward Olivia.

"Hi, Hannah," Henry said. "Olivia, this is Hannah O'Leary, one of the trainers and very protective of the center. Hannah, this is Lieutenant Olivia Vance of Internal Affairs."

Hannah's green eyes widened. Her mouth made a perfect *o*. "You definitely don't want to be in the ring for this, Lieutenant—for safety."

Frowning at the dire warning, Olivia moved out of the large circular arena to the spectator's area with Hannah and Cody.

"How's Snapper doing?" Olivia asked Hannah, eyeing the beautiful German shepherd who sat at attention in the ring next to Lani.

Last year the entire NYPD had been looking for Snapper, who'd gone missing after his handler and partner, Jordan Jameson, chief of the NYC K-9 Command Unit in Queens, was found murdered in a park. It had taken months for the dog to be reunited with the unit and Olivia had cheered along with everyone else when Snapper was found. When Lani transferred to the Brooklyn K-9 Unit, Snapper had been paired with her to keep the beloved police dog in the family, since Lani was married to one of Jordan's brothers, who'd become chief of the Queens unit. Olivia had seen pictures of the dog in the paper, but the images hadn't done the majestic shepherd justice. He looked fierce and capable of taking down an elephant, not at all cute like Cody.

Olivia held her breath as Henry put the caged mask on. Lani gave the thumbs-up sign, prompting Henry to run toward Lani and Snapper aggressively.

Lani unhooked Snapper's leash and gave the attack command. The dog was on Henry in a flash, his powerful jaws latching on to the padded arm of Henry's bite suit. Henry and the dog seemed to dance as Henry tried to shake the K-9 off. Lani gave another command and Snapper immediately released his hold on Henry's arm and hurried back to her side.

Olivia slapped a hand over her racing heart. She'd seen demonstrations of the K-9 officers, but it was different knowing the person in the bite suit. And realizing that the thick padding was the only thing keeping the dog's sharp teeth and powerful jaw from breaking Henry's skin or bones had her stomach knotting. They went through the exercise several times with Henry baiting the pair and then running away or grabbing at Lani. Each time, Snapper did his job and defended his K-9 handler with a ferociousness that was startling to observe.

Finally, Lani leashed up the panting shepherd and they headed out of the arena to a row of water bowls. Hannah opened the ring door to let Cody loose. The beagle raced across the ring then bit at Henry's padded ankles. Olivia turned to Hannah. "Is that normal for Cody?"

"All the dogs recognize the bite suit as training time," she replied.

Henry fell to the ground, his deep laughter echoing off the walls, as Cody's pink tongue darted in and out of the caged helmet's faceguard. That was the cutest thing Olivia had ever seen.

Hannah chuckled. "But obviously it's playtime for Cody."

Then another trainer brought out the pretty former-stray shepherd, Brooke, and her puppies, and let them loose in the arena. Henry slapped his hands on the matted floor and the puppies raced to his side, crawling over him and gnawing at him, their happy, yapping barks filling the room. The littlest puppy, Maverick, only made it a few feet before plopping down on his belly. The sight of the puppies with Henry was so cute Olivia took out her phone and snapped off several photos. She was sure Riley would appreciate the pictures.

Suddenly there was a cacophony of noise, as all of the dogs in the training center grew agitated. Barking and growling echoed off the walls and down the halls. The puppies' yipping turned to piercing panic. Cody howled like he was dying. Snapper and Brooke growled and barked aggressively at the air.

Unnerved by the sounds, Olivia covered her belly with her hand. "What's going on?"

"I don't know," Hannah answered. "But something's got the dogs spooked."

Just then, a red haze flowed out of the air ducts, filling the ring and the halls.

"It's some kind of gas!" Olivia shouted to be heard over the ruckus the dogs were making.

"Everyone out!" commanded Henry as he scooped up the puppies in one arm. Olivia darted out and picked up Maverick, holding him close to her chest. His little body shook uncontrollably.

Hannah raced to the kennel room along with Lani, Henry and Olivia not far behind, where they leashed up the dogs and ushered them all outside just as the fire alarms sounded.

"We have to be careful," Henry said at the exit. He

handed the puppies off to the trainer. "This could be a ruse to get us out in the open."

Olivia's heart sank. "You think the bomber will change tactics and start shooting? Or plant a bomb nearby?"

"Hard to say." Henry opened the door with caution. "Let me step out first."

Adjusting Maverick in her arms, Olivia met Lani's grim gaze. Henry could be stepping into the line of fire.

Please, Lord, keep him safe.

Henry stood in the open, slowly turning around as if baiting a sniper to take the shot. Then he was waving for Olivia and the others to leave the training center. Thankful to realize they wouldn't be picked off like the ducks in shooting gallery at Coney Island, she hurried outside.

Hannah set the puppies down on the grass. Henry quickly stripped out of his bite suit, leaving him in shorts and a K-9 unit T-shirt, before herding the active puppies, keeping them on the grass. Even Cody joined in, nudging a stray pup with his nose until the little dog turned around and headed away from the asphalt of the parking lot. The tender care Henry gave to the puppies and the other dogs made Olivia's insides turn to mush.

The ding of an incoming text chimed from Henry's pocket and made the hairs on Olivia's arm stand up. There was no reason for the dread suddenly stiffening her muscles with tension. Still, she hurried to his side and read the text along with him.

I can get you, anytime, anywhere.

Olivia couldn't believe what she was reading. "How did this maniac get to the air ducts?"

Henry's jaw worked. He shook his head. "I don't know. But I will find out."

She wanted to soothe away his upset over the disturbing text. But she didn't know how. The urgency to wrap up this case pressed down on her, but there were still so many questions she needed answered. It didn't help that the more time she spent with Henry, the more she was convinced he was truly a kind and caring man. The kind of man she once had hoped her own husband would be. The kind of man she wanted in her future.

She forced her thoughts away from what she couldn't change. Instead she focused on the fact that she was well on her way to caring for this handsome officer.

A fact that would most likely be her downfall.

Henry clutched his phone in a tight fist. Anger at the suspect for putting the dogs and everyone else in the training center at risk burned through him like a flare.

Olivia put her hand on his bare forearm. "No one was injured, and the dogs are safe as far as we can tell. The gas didn't seem to be toxic."

Taking comfort from her touch, he let some of the tension go. "Praise God for that."

"You acted quickly."

Her amber-colored eyes were soft and full of something that made it difficult to look away. "So did you."

Blinking, she turned away and squeezed his arm. "There's the fire chief talking to Sergeant Sutherland."

Indeed, his boss and the chief were consulting. They needed to know about the text. Henry glanced around to see more officers had poured out of the K-9 unit and were now helping to corral the puppies and the working dogs.

He looked at Olivia. "Can you take charge of Cody?" The dog knew her and liked her. So did he. His stomach clenched. Had he lost his mind?

Her mouth curved. "Of course. Thank you for asking this time."

Grimacing, he said, "Sorry about that."

"You're forgiven."

Relief flooded him and loosened his muscles a little more. Thankfully she wasn't mad at him for his earlier heavy-handedness. Henry jogged over to the fire chief and Gavin and showed the two men the text.

The chief's eyebrows rose. "Not just a prank?"

"Prank?" Henry drew back, offended by the term. "This guy filled the whole training center with red smoke. Who knows what kind of damage that could have done."

"According to the fire chief, the gas was nontoxic," Gavin said. He scrubbed a hand over his face, his aggravation showing in his eyes.

"We found a couple of homemade smoke bombs in the air vents," the fire chief said. "When the air conditioning kicked on, it ignited them. They were made with a concoction of potassium nitrate, sugar and food coloring. Anyone with a computer could learn how to make one."

"We'll be sure to make those vents inaccessible going forward," Gavin said. "And look for other vulnerable areas around both the training center and the station house."

The chief nodded. "That would be wise."

For Henry, that the texting bomber hadn't wanted to hurt the dogs didn't excuse the panic the smoke had caused. Setting off the smoke bombs had been a warning to him, just as the text had been. He remembered the message delivered to Olivia in the museum. Her attacker had said she needed to find Henry guilty. "I really need to talk to Davey Carrell."

"You're not going anywhere near that young man," Gavin said. "Bradley and Tyler have interviewed him. He claims not to know who's harassing you."

Henry had full confidence that his friend and colleague Bradley along with Tyler Walker, another K-9 handler, had put pressure on Davey, but that didn't mean Davey had told them the truth. The kid was lying about his injuries. Unfortunately, Henry had no way to prove it.

"It's more than harassment, Sarge," Henry bit out. "Olivia was assaulted and almost run down. And Riley was too close to the boardwalk bomb for my comfort. Now this. A clear warning from the suspect."

Gavin stroked his chin. "I'm aware. As you requested, a patrol officer is keeping tabs on Riley. And as for Lieutenant Vance, her father has someone guarding her place at night and she's been instructed to stick close to the station while conducting her investigation. One of her brothers will be escorting her back and forth. However, you shouldn't be spending time with the lieutenant away from the station."

Henry was glad to hear precautions were in place to guard his sister and Olivia. And though he agreed keeping his distance from the attractive investigator was the best thing for them both, the thought didn't settle well in his gut. She'd already been targeted. The perpetrator had a bead on her. Henry doubted the perp would leave her alone just because Henry wasn't around her, which meant she was still vulnerable. Despite being a trained officer and fully capable of protecting herself, she was in danger because of him. He had to do what he could to mitigate the threat.

While the officers kept the dogs corralled, the fire department sucked all the smoke out of the training center fairly quickly and gave the all clear to return inside.

Once all the dogs were settled, Henry walked back to Olivia where she stood in the shade with Cody. "Okay, we can get back to your questions."

She stared at him, the unreadable expression in her eyes unnerving him. He usually could tell when she was irritated or amused. But now her emotions were shuttered from him. "Are you okay?"

She gave a nod. "But I need a breather. I'll have to catch up with you later. I do have some questions for you, but they can wait." She handed Cody's leash back to him and hurried away.

He wanted to call her back, but then decided he also needed a moment to decompress after the spike in adrenaline. After changing back into his uniform, he and Cody left the training center to find Eden. Hopefully she could trace the latest text he'd received.

Unfortunately, Eden confirmed this latest text also came from a burner phone that was untraceable. Frustrated with the lack of progress, Henry decided to check on Olivia. He discovered she'd left the station on foot. Alone.

Had she gone back to her apartment unaccompanied? Or somewhere close by? She'd been instructed to stay close to the station. He called her cell phone. She answered on the first ring.

"Henry? Is everything okay? Did something else happen?"

He appreciated that her first thought was the safety of others. "All good here. You left the station. I wanted to make sure you were all right."

There was a loud silence. Concern that he'd overstepped by admitting to worrying about her well-being, he grimaced but couldn't apologize.

"I'm fine," she finally said. "I'm at Sal's."

A measure of relief filled him. "Do you mind if I join you? For lunch. Nothing more."

"I suppose you have to eat, as well," she said, her tone wary.

"I'll be right there," he said and hung up.

With Cody at his side, Henry headed down the street at a fast clip. Normally he would leave his partner at the training center, but he wanted Cody's super nose available in case of trouble. And thankfully, Sal allowed the police dogs inside the pizzeria. His boss's warning to stay away from Olivia echoed in his head, but Henry had to put her safety ahead of what his boss wanted, even if it cost him everything. He refused to ponder why he was willing to risk it all for Olivia.

As he entered the eatery, the smell of garlic and tomato sauce filled Henry's nostrils and made his stomach rumble. But his gaze focused on the woman sitting at the corner table by the window. Olivia. Safe and sound, as she'd said.

The rush of relief and something else, something close to the sort of affection that made him very uncomfortable, rocked him back on his heels.

"Are you in line?" a woman holding a toddler asked.

"Uh, yes." He'd been caught staring but thankfully Olivia seemed oblivious to his presence. She stared into her salad as if the lettuce and veggies were the most engrossing thing ever.

He ordered a meat lover's special slice and a small bowl of carrots for his partner before heading over to join Olivia while he waited for the order.

Cody nudged her knee, prompting her to scrub him behind his floppy ear. A smile tugged at the corners of her mouth and she made an obvious, yet valiant, effort to stop it.

He grinned and she sighed. That little noise did funny things to his insides.

Gesturing with her hand to the chair, she said, "Go ahead."

He turned the chair around and straddled it, facing her and stepped on Cody's leash. The dog lay on his belly, his head resting on his paws.

"You were supposed to be sticking close to the station house," Henry stated in a firm tone.

She lifted her chin and then surprise flared in her eyes. "You were worried."

"Yes." He had no problem admitting it. "I care what happens to you." Though that last bit took him by surprise, as well.

Her lips parted in a soft inhale, drawing his gaze to her mouth. Not for the first time, his breath quickened as attraction arced through him.

"I—" Olivia cleared her throat and glanced away as if to compose herself. She turned back to him, her expression contrite. "You're right. Leaving the K-9 unit alone wasn't the best decision I've made today."

He hadn't expected the humility or the appreciation crowding his chest. "I'm just glad you're okay."

For a moment she stared at him, her expression filled with wonder. Then she looked at her salad and stabbed a piece of lettuce with her fork.

"Roarke, order's ready."

Rising from the chair, he gave Cody the stay command with his hand and then he asked Olivia, "Can I get you anything while I'm up?"

"I'm good," she said. "I'm finishing my salad."

"No pizza today?" He remembered her appetite the last time they'd come to Sal's Pizzeria.

She smiled, her eyes brightening, making him think she, too, remembered that night. "No, not today."

He went to the counter to pick up his slice. "Thanks, Sal."

"Isn't that the new IA investigator?"

Tension coiled in Henry's gut. "Yes. Lieutenant Vance."

Sal dropped his chin and stared at Henry with narrowed gray eyes. "Fraternizing with the enemy?"

NINE

Irritated by the retired officer's censure, Henry gritted his teeth and worked to calm his knee-jerk urge to reach across the space of the countertop and grab Sal by the apron strings. Sal wasn't wrong, after all.

Henry pulled in a deep breath and tried to keep his tone even. "Just eating, no fraternizing going on."

A voice in his head whispered, *Yeah, right.* He stubbornly ignored it.

Henry grabbed his food and stalked back to where Olivia was seated with Cody at her feet. He set the plate down with a clatter of ceramic on the red laminated tabletop.

Olivia and Cody jumped.

Olivia raised a dark eyebrow. "Everything okay?"

"Everything's dandy." He picked up his pizza and stuffed it in his mouth.

Just eating, no fraternizing going on.

There was a purpose to him being here with Olivia. Keeping her safe. And in the loop on what was happening. Not crushing on her. "I wanted to give you an update on the video feed from the boardwalk."

He proceeded to tell her what he'd seen on Eden's computer monitors while she pushed around her salad.

Olivia made a face. "So he was following Riley but didn't approach her and waited until she was out of the area before setting off his bomb."

"Looks that way."

"He didn't want to hurt her." Olivia's tone was thoughtful. "Do you think they could know each other?"

The bite of pizza soured in his stomach. The idea that his sister might be familiar with the texting bomber was unsettling. "I hope not."

He relayed what his boss had said about Davey Carrell. "And the burner phone used to text me has led nowhere. This guy seems to know how to cover his tracks."

"At least he was considerate enough not to put harmful smoke in the air ducts at the training center," she said. "The dogs are safe."

"Big consolation." He couldn't keep sarcasm from his voice. "It could have gone wrong if we hadn't been there to rush the dogs out."

"You were a hero today."

Her praise settled in his chest, making him feel like the hero she claimed him to be. He met her gaze. "We made an effective team. I couldn't have ushered all the puppies to safety without you."

She set down her fork. "That's not true. The others could have handled the situation without me, but I appreciate you saying it."

"It is true. I needed you today." He realized what he'd said and amended his words. "The dogs needed you."

"Sometimes it's good to be needed," she said, and her hand went to her stomach.

Henry sensed her mood shifting downward, no doubt to grief and sadness for her late husband. He reached across the table and covered her other hand before he even thought to stop himself. Her skin was warm beneath his. "You must miss him."

Her gaze jumped to his. "Who?"

Tucking in his chin, he said, "Your husband."

She jerked her hand from beneath his. "Yes, of course. He was my husband. Of course I miss him."

Her words rang hollow, as if she'd said them only to make him feel better.

"I heard the news report that he wasn't alone in the plane crash."

Her amber eyes glittered. For a second, he thought it may be tears but then he realized it was suppressed anger shining in her eyes. "That's correct."

His cop senses tingled, and he found himself searching his memory for details and pressing her. "They never identified who was in the plane, at least not publicly. Did you know who the other person was?"

"I'd never met her. But I've been told she was one of his dental hygienists."

"A work trip, then?" He hoped.

Her lips twisted. "Not unless booking a single suite in a romantic hotel on a private beach could be consider work-related."

Henry's stomach sank. There was no mistaking the betrayal in her tone. Now he understood the anger. Her husband had been going to the Caribbean with another woman. Henry's heart ached for Olivia. He could imagine how heartbroken she must be by not only her husband's death but his unfaithfulness. "I'm sorry. That must have been a shock. Do you want to talk about it?"

For a moment, she held herself stiff. Then she seemed to deflate as if all the air had been leached out of her lungs. He didn't like seeing her defeated.

She rested an elbow on the table and her chin in her hand. "I'm sure you don't want to hear my sad tale."

"You know everything there is to know about me. It would be kind of nice to know something about you."

She opened her mouth to speak, then hesitated. Her eyes widened and she straightened as if someone had poked her in the back. "No. No, no. We're not doing this."

He studied her now shuttered expression. "Doing what?"

"Getting personal." Her finger toggled between them. "You and me. I only know what the reports tell me, and what I've observed about you. We can't get personal, you know this."

He liked that the determined spark was back in her eyes, but he wanted her to be real with him because he had a feeling she didn't let her guard down often. He shouldn't pursue his curiosity—and whatever else was causing the warmth in his chest when he was around her. She was off-limits. Taboo. But what had always trying to do the right thing done for him? Couldn't he do what he wanted for once?

He set his empty plate aside and leaned forward. "Right at this moment, you're not IA and I'm not the officer you're investigating. Can't we just be two people, friends, who need to unload some baggage?"

The yearning on her face belied the negative shake of her head. She glanced around before meeting his gaze again. "No. There are too many eyes on us. On me. I can't mess this up. Not for you or anyone else."

She scooted her chair back from the table. Cody scrambled to his feet. "In fact, we should head back to the precinct so I can finish asking you questions about the previous excessive force case."

At least she was keeping her head, because he'd apparently lost his mind. Of course they couldn't get personal. Doing so put both their careers in jeopardy.

He stood up and turned the chair back around and shoved it up against the table. He had to refrain from holding out his hand so that she could hold on to him while she maneuvered out from behind the table.

For some reason, today her little baby bump seemed bigger. Or maybe she wasn't trying to hide it quite as much. He kept the observation to himself. She'd already made it clear her personal life was off-limits. Though he hated to think of the stress she must carry. A dead husband who was flying off with a woman Olivia hadn't known, and now a baby on the way to raise alone.

Not alone, he amended to himself as he and Cody followed her out of the pizzeria. She had her family. Family was everything.

On the sidewalk, he plucked his sunglasses from his pocket and slipped them on. They walked in silence with three feet separating them and Cody walking on his other side toward the K-9 unit headquarters. His phone chimed with an incoming text. His muscles tensed. Grabbing the device, he braced himself.

How many cops does it take to stop a bomber from blowing up your new girlfriend's house? None, because you can't! LOLZ

The words on the screen made his heart rate rev into overdrive. Who was the bomber targeting now?

Olivia stepped closer to Henry to read the words on the screen. Her mind raced. She hadn't seen any evidence that Henry had a girlfriend. If he did have one, Olivia needed to talk to her. And why did the thought of him dating cause a burning in her chest?

She frowned. "What's with this *LOLZ* thing? I get that this is texting lingo, but what does the *Z* stand for? I assume the *LOL* is *laugh out loud* and not *lots of love*."

Henry scoffed. "Yeah. I looked up text slang and apparently it means laughing out loud—hard. It has to be one of Davey's friends." He started them walking again at a fast clip. "And I don't know what he's talking about. A new girlfriend?" He shrugged his shoulders. "I haven't dated in years. Not since my last girlfriend gave me an ultimatum—her or Riley. I have no plans of getting into any relationship until Riley's out of the house and independent."

Conflicting emotions jumped inside Olivia. He wasn't dating anyone and he had no plans to. A true shame, because Henry would be an ideal catch. Responsible, protective, a man of faith. Any woman in her right mind would jump at the opportunity to snag him.

Not her, for course, even if she were in the market to try romance again. Which she wasn't, for so many reasons, including her chosen career. She was bringing a child into the world and her baby would need all of her focus. But wouldn't it be wonderful to have a partner to share her life with?

And his last girlfriend had given him an ultimatum? The nerve. Good riddance to that lady.

He stared at the phone as if he could find some meaning in the text. "I don't know what to make of this."

"Obviously, this suspect is mistaken. Could they be targeting the wrong person?"

Henry halted midstride. Cody turned sharply to look at his handler. With horror in his dark eyes, Henry stared her. "You. The suspect must mean you."

She scrunched up her nose. "What? Me? We're not dating!"

"I know, and you know, but the bomber doesn't. The guy saw us at the museum together and at the church together, and now here…" His gaze roamed the street. "He must be watching us. How else would he know that we're together right now?"

"You're making a big leap there. You don't know that he's talking about me." Yet she was totally creeped out by the thought of being stalked.

"You're the only woman I've spent any time with in forever."

The bomber thought they were together as a couple. Henry's logic made sense in a strange way. They had been together often the past few days. And each time something bad had happened. "Oh no. My neighbors. We have to get them out."

With his free hand, he grabbed hers. "Let's go."

Mind reeling, she ran alongside him and Cody. As soon as they reached the station, Henry ushered Olivia and Cody inside to raise the alarm. His boss was out on a call.

The station dispatcher promised to send the bomb squad and officers to Olivia's building.

Henry's dark eyes bored into her. "Olivia, you should stay here. Stay safe."

His concern burrowed deep inside of her. And as much as she appreciated his worry for her well-being, there was no way she was being left behind. "Not happening. I'm going with you. Let's hustle."

She heard his growl of frustration as she hurried for the exit.

Once secured inside the SUV, he called his boss and put it on speakerphone. Olivia's heart raced and she prayed for the people in her building. They didn't deserve to be in harm's way because she'd let herself become too involved with Henry and his sister.

"Sutherland," Gavin answered.

"Sir, we have a situation." Henry explained about the latest text, that he, Cody and Olivia were headed to her Carroll Gardens apartment building and that dispatch had already sent out an alert.

"I'm knee-deep here, but I trust you to handle this as supervisor of the scene. If that's acceptable to the lieutenant," Gavin said.

"Yes. I agree." Wholeheartedly. She trusted Henry and Cody to sniff out any sort of explosive device.

"Be safe," Gavin said.

"Yes, sir." Henry hung up and started the engine.

Olivia couldn't believe what was happening. A strange sense of déjà vu gripped her as the K-9 unit vehicle tore out of the parking lot with the siren blaring.

When they arrived at her building, two patrol cruisers were already there and had set up a perimeter. One officer was talking with the superintendent. A fire truck rolled up with an ambulance, both at the ready. None could make a move until the location of the bomb was discovered and the threat assessed.

Henry put his hand on her arm before she could climb out of the vehicle. "No disrespect intended, but please stay put. Let Cody and I do our job. If our texting bomber has really put an explosive device in or around your apartment, we'll find it."

She had no doubt about their capability to detect a bomb. But she wasn't going to sit inside the car like some timid civilian. This was what she'd signed up for. Helping others. "I'm coming with you."

His jaw firmed. "Olivia, think about—"

"No." She jumped out and hurried up the walkway to the building's entrance.

Henry and Cody caught up to her. Cody's nose twitched and he skidded to a halt. The dog sat on the stoop and stared up at his partner.

"He's alerting."

There were no waiting packages or anything out of the ordinary. The planter with the bonsai tree that the superintendent maintained appeared undisturbed. As did the welcome mat. "Where's the explosive?"

He drew her and Cody away from the entrance to where the officers and other emergency personnel stood. To the superintendent, Henry asked, "Did you come out through the front entrance?"

"I did a couple of hours ago," the balding man replied. "I just returned from the hardware store when these officers rolled up."

"We didn't see anyone suspicious around the building," one of the officers said.

"The front door could be wired. Opening it might trigger the bomb."

Urgency made Olivia's heart rate double. "There are people inside. What if one of them decides to come out the front door? And Kitty! We have to get them out."

Henry nodded. "Is there a rear exit?"

"Yes, through the laundry room." The superintendent handed over his keys.

"Keep anyone from approaching the front entrance," Henry told the officers. To the emergency squad, he said, "Come with me."

"I'll show you the way," Olivia said, not about to let him sideline her. She led the way around the back of the building to a short staircase and the door leading into the laundry room. She and the others hung back while Henry let Cody sniff around the door and surrounding area. The dog didn't alert. Henry gave the all clear.

They raced inside with Cody in the lead. They moved through the building, banging on doors as they went, telling the few people home during the middle of the day to leave through the back exit.

Olivia opened the door to her apartment and rushed inside. "Kitty, Kitty!"

Cody entered, sniffing, made a beeline for her front window and sat staring at them.

"He's alerting," Henry declared. "The explosive is attached to your apartment window. We have to get out of here!"

"Not without my cat!" Panic fueled her. She ran to her bedroom where Kitty liked to hang out. The feline was curled on Olivia's pillow. Grabbing the cat, Olivia ignored its howling protest and ran with Henry and Cody. They relayed the bomb's location to the emergency personnel.

The officers had ushered the residents to a safe distance upwind of the building.

Henry conferred with the bomb squad technicians, one of whom was dressed in an explosive ordnance disposal suit. The other technician then brought out a bomb disposal robot and used a hand controller to send the robot across the sidewalk toward Olivia's front window.

Henry urged her forward to join her neighbors. They'd only made it a few steps when Henry's cell phone dinged, stopping them both in their tracks. Dread gripped Olivia as she pressed close to Henry to read the incoming text.

KaBOOM!

No sooner had the words registered than the window of Olivia's apartment exploded in a deafening bang, spitting glass a good ten feet.

Henry folded Olivia and Kitty into his arms away from the blast, while keeping Cody safely in front of him. Olivia burrowed into Henry's chest. Despite the fear, she felt safe in his arms. Unexpected, thrilling and terrifying all at once.

The last echo of the explosion left the world muffled. Henry leaned back to meet her gaze. "Are you okay?"

Her knees were wobbly. "I am. You?"

She remembered the last time they'd been in this position and though he'd reassured her about his state of being after the garbage can exploded, in actuality he had been injured. She inspected him carefully and saw no new wounds. Thankfully, the one on his scalp was healing.

Olivia turned to see that her front window had been blown out. The rest of the building looked unharmed. The bomb disposal robot appeared undamaged. After a careful inspection to make sure there were no additional explosive, the technicians and emergency personnel rushed forward.

Henry and Olivia moved out of the way to allow the others to work.

"I don't get it." Henry rubbed a hand over his jaw. "If this has something to do with Davey Carrell's injuries, why would the person come after you?"

"Remember what my attacker at the museum said? I'm supposed to find you guilty," Olivia reminded him. "This was just to show that he could get to me as easily as he could get to you. He seems bent on destruction rather than harm."

He shot her a look filled with disbelief. "Remember the kids at Coney Island? They only suffered minor injuries and one broken bone, but still, it could have gone very differently if we hadn't arrived in time."

"True." Her stomach curdled. "But the bomber gave you time, just as he did here. He could have blown the window when we were on the building's stoop." And been cut up by flying glass.

"He may not intend to kill, but he certainly is intending harm," Henry said. "And given that you're pregnant…"

She sucked in a breath and held up a hand. "What makes you say that?" She'd known he suspected it but for him to state the fact was an entirely different matter. She'd tried too hard to conceal her growing abdomen.

"I heard your sister ask you about the baby." He shrugged. "I've noticed other things, as well."

Resigning herself to him knowing her secret, she said, "My family knows, but I haven't said anything to anyone else. My doctor cleared me for duty. I don't want anyone treating me differently because I'm expecting."

"I would imagine it's a bittersweet blessing," he said.

"It was definitely unexpected." Not wanting him to think she resented her baby, she added, "And a blessing. I know God has a plan. For me and this child. I just have to have enough faith to see it through."

"He always does have a plan," Henry said. "I love the verse Jeremiah 29:11, about God knowing the plans He has for us. I repeated it often after my father's death. Though sometimes the plan is uncomfortable and even painful."

They shared a common bond of loss. Somehow that seemed to tether her to him in unexplainable ways. She adjusted Kitty in her arms. "Roger and I were on the verge of a divorce and I had pretty much given up my hope of motherhood."

"I'm sorry to hear that," he said.

"I never imagined life would turn out so upside down. For so long, I tried to keep my marriage together, be the good wife. But nothing seemed to please

Roger. He always found fault. I couldn't measure up to his ideal."

Henry frowned. "Why should you have had to measure up? That's not how love works."

Tears misted in her eyes. She blinked them back. Was Henry a man who would accept the woman he loved as she was, without expecting her to change to meet his wants and needs? Her heart throbbed with a longing that took her breath away.

"How far along are you?"

Pulling her composure around her like a cloak to ward off the flood of emotions clogging her throat, she forced out the words. "Nearly four months. I found out a month after Roger's death." She gave a wry twist of her lips. "I thought my morning sickness was stress and grief." And anger, but she didn't like what that said about her. "My mom convinced me to go to the doctor."

"That must have been a surprise."

"Yes." She nuzzled Kitty. "I have to admit the idea of raising a child by myself is daunting."

"You have your family for support and God to guide you," he said.

"True." She met his gaze. "But he or she will be my sole responsibility."

He reached forward to stroke Kitty's head. "I have complete faith you can do this, Olivia."

His words seeped into her, filling all the bruised places. She'd always wanted a family of her own, including a husband who would love her without conditions. If only Henry could be that man. But that couldn't happen. Even if she wasn't investigating him and they were free to pursue a relationship, he'd already made it clear he wasn't interested in being a parent again.

She really needed to find a way to put some distance between them. And not just physically, but emotionally, as well.

Henry's gaze moved to the building. "Did you live here with your late husband?"

It was a fair question. "After Roger's death, I couldn't stand to be in the home we'd shared. I had movers box up everything and sent Roger's items to his parents in Maine. I sold the apartment and rented this place."

Empathy softened the hard angles of Henry's handsome face. He touched her arm in a soothing gesture that made her want to lean on him for support. She refrained. Distance, remember?

"You can't remain here, obviously," Henry pointed out. "You'll come stay with Riley and me. Until this guy is caught."

The idea of living under the same roof as Henry sent her pulse jumping. That was one sure way for them both to get fired. Her investigation would be beyond compromised. "No way. It would be a conflict of interest for me to room with you and your sister. I'll be fine at a hotel for a few days."

The screech of tires on pavement drew Olivia's gaze. A police cruiser stopped and her father climbed out. Tall, with broad shoulders, Captain Alonso Vance scanned the crowd, his gaze locking on his daughter like a missile.

Grimacing, Olivia muttered, "Uh-oh. Brace yourself."

TEN

Olivia's father's long legs carried him to her side and he engulfed her in a hug. She inhaled the spicy scent of her father's aftershave and melted against him. Kitty meowed and squirmed to be set free.

After a moment, he stepped back. "Are you hurt?"

"No, Papa," she said, using her childhood nickname for him. At that moment, she wanted nothing more than to be his little girl and know he would make the world right.

"Thank you, God. I prayed the whole way over. I needed to make sure you were okay." Her father reached past her to offer Henry his hand. "Detective Roarke. Thank you for sending word."

Henry shook his hand. "Of course, Captain Vance."

"Wait, what?" She stared at Henry.

His matter-of-fact expression let her know he had no remorse for contacting her father. "While you were giving your statement, I had someone let your dad know what was happening."

Her emotions bounced between betrayal and being touched by the gesture. She didn't need anyone rescuing her. She wasn't some princess in a tower. She was an officer of the law. And Henry's superior. He shouldn't have taken it upon himself to alert her father.

"This is unacceptable, Olivia," her father said. "This suspect has to be caught."

Like she had any control of the situation? "We're working on it, Papa."

Her father's dark eyebrows rose. "Is that so? Since when does IA investigate bombings?"

"When the one targeted is the subject of an investigation. And now I've been targeted, as well." There was a heat in her tone that she'd rarely used with her father. But at the moment, she wasn't going to let her father or anyone else make her feel bad for doing her job. "This situation ties into the assault charge brought against Detective Roarke."

Her father's brown-eyed gaze vaulted from her to Henry. "I see."

Olivia frowned, not sure she liked the assessing look in her father's eyes. What exactly did he "see"?

"Detective Roarke, I will leave it to you to make sure the lieutenant is delivered safely to her family home. I'd do it myself but I have to return to the precinct."

"Yes, sir," Henry replied, surprise evident in his eyes.

Gaping at her father, Olivia couldn't believe what she'd just heard. "Excuse me. I'm right here. I'll stay in a hotel."

"Uh, no. Your mother would be livid," her dad stated. "You'll be safest at home." He reached to pet Kitty. "Both of you."

Though she hated to admit it, her father was right.

Her parents' house was a fortress in many ways, with a state-of-the-art security system her father had installed a few years ago. Every inch of the property was covered with video cameras and motion detectors. Her father was beyond cautious. "Fine, but I can get myself home, thank you."

Her father leveled a stern look on her. "Not tonight. You aren't to be alone until this maniac is apprehended." Turning back to Henry, he continued, "You're welcome to stay for dinner. The whole family's coming. And Simone is making empanadas and *arroz con gandules*."

Since when did Mama make her specialty dishes when it wasn't a holiday?

Henry grinned. "I can't leave my sister to fend for herself."

"The more the merrier," her father said. He turned back to her. "I'll let your mother know you're all right and will be coming to stay at the house." He walked away.

Olivia stared after him. What just happened? Why on earth would her father invite Henry over for dinner?

Her dad would be first in line of those who'd want to lecture her on keeping her work separate from her personal life. Especially when it involved someone she was officially investigating.

Her brain was muddled with confusion. Maybe she had sustained a blow to the head after all during the explosion to her apartment window. Or she was just hormonal. Pregnancy could do that to a woman, right?

Because nothing was making sense at the moment. Certainly not the excitement and trepidation warring within her over Henry coming home for dinner. On the bright side, maybe having him under her parent's roof would help to clarify some of his behavior.

Or make things worse for her.

So much for keeping her distance from the too-handsome officer.

Apparently, Henry liked playing with fire. Why else would he have agreed so readily to join the Vance family for dinner?

He really should have begged off attending, but here he was. He glanced at Olivia in the passenger seat next to him. There was no reason for him and Riley to intrude on a family dinner. Olivia would be safe with her siblings and father. He and his sister's presence would only complicate matters. They would be the outsiders. Riley was already too emotionally involved with Olivia.

But the fact was, he liked Olivia and wanted to spend time with her and her family.

The thought tore through him like a bullet, blowing holes in all of his excuses.

Shaking his head at his own folly, he parked behind an older-model SUV in front of a two-story home in the Randall Manor neighborhood of Staten Island. "Nice place."

Riley, sitting in the back, leaned forward to stare out the side window. "This is where you grew up?"

"Yes, it is nice. A wonderful place to grow up," Olivia replied. She chewed her bottom lip as she too stared at her childhood home. Kitty lay curled in a borrowed cat carrier at Olivia's feet, oblivious to her human's anxiety.

Olivia hadn't said much since they'd met with Gavin

and filled him in on what had happened at her apartment before leaving the station.

Henry could tell his boss was stressed. Gavin's usually unflappable demeanor had cracked slightly as he'd made it clear he wanted Henry and Olivia to be extra careful. He'd even instructed Henry to stick close to Olivia and make sure nothing happened to her. This contradicted his earlier admonishment, but Henry hadn't pointed that out.

Instead, Henry had promised he would take every precaution to ensure both of their safety, which earned him a startled glance from the IA lieutenant. He'd expected her to protest, but she'd only nodded.

Now Henry laced his fingers through hers. "If you'd rather we didn't come in, I'd understand."

She turned to look at him, her pretty face softening and the worry dissolving. She tightened her grip around his hand. "I appreciate that. But Dad invited you and he'd be disappointed if you didn't show up."

"What about you?" Henry asked. "Do you want me—uh, us, here?"

Her lips parted and she inhaled sharply. Then she seemed to relax. Smiling, she said, "Yes. Of course. You and Riley and Cody are welcome."

Not exactly what he'd meant, but he'd take it.

They climbed from the vehicle and he hung back to let Cody wander on the front lawn on leash while Olivia tucked Riley's arm through hers and led her inside.

The neighborhood was quiet. Pleasant. Peaceful. Trees lined the sidewalks and family cars sat in driveways of dwellings similar to the Vance home. Henry had never lived in an actual house.

His parents had lived in a five-story walk-up in midtown until Henry's mother bailed. Then Henry's dad had married Susan and moved them to the condo in Brooklyn, where they lived when Riley came along. Something tightened in his chest.

A yearning for a suburban life like this caught him by surprise. What would it be like to have more space, like a garage with a workbench and storage?

The thought of her raising her baby alone made his heart ache. But there was nothing he could do for her. He wasn't prepared to take on the responsibility of parenting again, no matter how tempting it was to think of holding a baby and being there for all the early milestones.

He'd been too young and self-absorbed at sixteen to get excited about Riley's first words or steps or the first time she lost a tooth. Now she was his world.

"Cody, old boy, I think I need a vacation," Henry muttered.

"Do you?"

Henry whipped around to find Olivia a few feet away. She'd changed clothes. She now wore a loose dress that dropped below her knees to reveal nicely defined calves. Strappy sandals graced her feet. The sight of her pink painted toenails captivated him. She was such a contradiction from who he'd first assumed her to be. She could be uptight and rigid, strong and commanding, but she also had a sweetness to her that did funny things to his heart.

"Uh, yes. A vacation." Definitely needed to get away to clear his head. He shouldn't be so fascinated with Olivia. But there was so much to be fascinated by. Her regal bearing when she was working, her quick thinking, her protective instincts and her feisty spirit. She was wise and yet humble. All traits that he found appealing.

"I would agree," she said, taking a seat on the porch step. "Being targeted is maxing out my calm reserves."

Guilt poking at him, he sat down next to her. Cody settled at their feet. "I'm sorry you're in this mess."

"Not your fault. I'm doing my job. We all know there are those out there who would like to do any law enforcement officer harm. It's just a matter of time before someone bent on destruction takes notice of anyone on the job."

"Maybe, but you wouldn't be in this position if..."

If what? What could he have done or changed that would have altered their circumstances? He'd had no control over Davey Carrell and his bogus accusations nor the serious health issues of the original IA officer, Lieutenant Jabboski, which had brought Olivia into the picture.

But Henry did have control over how much time outside of the station he'd spent with the lovely IA investigator.

His gut churned with remorse for putting her in harm's way needlessly. Especially because she was expecting a child.

But he couldn't find any regret for getting to know the beautiful lady.

"Hey." Olivia's soft voice drew him out of his thoughts. "We'll get through this. All of us."

But at what cost? His heart? His job? Her life? He couldn't let anything happen to Olivia.

Behind them, the front door opened and her brothers walked out. The two men stopped and stared.

"What are you two doing?" César Vance leaned against the porch post and grinned. He was the younger of the two with a dark mustache, close-cropped dark hair and a trim build. He wore gym shorts and a T-shirt with the New York Knicks basketball logo. He looked like he was ready to head to the court.

Alexander Vance, on the other hand, looked ready for the golf course with gray shorts and a light-colored polo shirt. His frown made his rugged face rather fierce. He crossed his muscular arms over his broad chest. "Getting cozy with our sister, Roarke?"

"Knock it off, you two." Olivia rose to her feet and planted her hands on her hips. "We're just chatting."

"Chatting can lead to kissing," César singsonged.

Henry scrambled to his feet, which prompted Cody to follow suit. "Don't be rude. I respect your sister too much to jeopardize her reputation or her career."

César lifted his hands. "Whoa. Dude, I was joking."

Embarrassed by his spontaneous reaction to his friend's words, Henry scrubbed a hand over his jaw. "Sorry. It's been a rough day."

"We heard," Alexander said. He unfolded his arms and drew his sister in for a brief hug. "We're glad you're both okay."

Olivia grinned at her eldest brother. "That's good to know."

"Mom says dinner in ten," Alexander said.

"We should go in and help." Olivia tugged on her brother's arm.

"You go on in," Alexander said. "We want to talk to Henry."

Olivia frowned. "I'm not sure that's a good idea."

"Worried about him?" César arched a dark brown eyebrow.

Henry's heart tumbled. What did she think was going to happen? That her brothers were going to beat him up? Not likely. "It's okay, Olivia. We'll be in shortly."

Olivia raised her index finger and pointed it at her each of her brothers. "Be nice."

With an apologetic look at Henry, she darted inside through the front door. Cody started after her but stopped at the length of his leash. Henry didn't blame the dog for wanting to escape with Olivia.

"So what gives?" César asked Henry as soon as the front door closed. "You and Olivia?"

Facing the two men, Henry hedged. "I'm not sure what you're talking about." Though he did, in fact, realize that his growing feelings for Olivia must be obvious to everyone. Except her. Or if she was aware, she was ignoring the attraction and affection filling the spaces between them. He would be wise to do the same.

Alexander stared him down. "We may be friends, but she's our little sister. Don't mess with her. She's had enough upheaval in her life lately and becoming involved with you could end her career."

Henry raised his hands. "I'm not messing with her. There's nothing happening between us. It's a professional relationship. She's investigating and I'm trying to help her. Trying to keep her safe."

"You may be telling yourself that," César said, "but

from where we're standing, things look like they're going in a direction that she doesn't need right now."

"I know she doesn't," Henry said. "The last thing I ever want to do is complicate Olivia's life."

But that seemed to be all he had done since he'd met her. The only way to remedy the situation was to bring the suspect who was targeting him to justice. Then Olivia would be free of the danger plaguing his every move. And she'd wrap up her investigation and they could part ways.

That last thought didn't settle well with him.

The front door opened and Captain Alonso Vance stepped out. He no longer wore his uniform. Now he was dressed in slacks and a short-sleeve button-down shirt. "All right, boys, that's enough. Henry is our guest. And dinner is ready."

"No worries, Pop," César said with a grin. "We're just giving Henry a hard time. All in good fun."

The glint in César's brown eyes belied his words. Henry respected that Olivia's brothers wanted to protect her. He'd react exactly the same if it were Riley.

"That's right," Alexander said. "Henry's our friend and we know we can trust him."

He clapped Henry on the shoulder as they started to follow Alonso back in the house.

Before they entered, Alexander whispered, "Don't hurt her. Or you'll answer to us."

Henry acknowledged the words with a nod. "I don't plan to."

Once inside the house, Olivia tucked her arm through his and made the introductions. Gesturing to two women who couldn't have been more different, she said, "This is César's wife, Kerry Jo, and Alexander's wife, Rosie."

Kerry Jo was petite with wild, curly red hair and vivid green eyes. "It's nice to meet you." A heavy Texas twang clung to her voice. "Your sister is lovely."

"Thank you," Henry said. He spied Riley in the dining room helping Ally Vance set the large oval table. Having only ever seen Ally in her paramedic uniform, it was a bit of surprise that dressing in casual clothes made her look nearly as young as Riley.

"Olivia says you two work together," Rosie said. Tall and athletic, the woman's dark hair hung below her waist and she held a sleepy toddler on her hip.

"Technically, Olivia is investigating Henry." The woman who entered the living room held out her hand to Henry. "Maria Vance. Olivia's other sister."

Henry grasped her hand and was surprised by the firm grip. "Nice to meet you."

"Hmm." Maria withdrew her hand, her golden brown eyes assessing him. She wore a tailored navy dress suit, a bright red collared blouse and red pumps, appearing every inch the assistant district attorney that she was. Henry had never had an occasion to work with her at the courthouse.

"And this is our mother." Olivia indicated the elder woman wiping her hands on a towel as she entered the room. Tall, striking and lithe, Mrs. Vance moved forward gracefully to shake his hand. The resemblance between Mrs. Vance and her daughters was unmistakable.

"Mrs. Vance, thank you for including Riley and me this evening," Henry said.

"Please, call me Simone," she said. "You're very welcome. I'm glad Alonso invited you. Can I get your dog a bowl of water?"

"That would be wonderful. Thank you, Simone." Henry led Cody to the water bowl she put down on the floor for him.

Ally waved to him from the dining room. Rosie and Alexander slipped down the hall and returned a few moments later without their child.

"Take your seats, everyone," Alonso said from the archway between the living room and dining area.

After settling Cody down near the door, Henry took a seat next to Riley. Olivia sat down on Henry's other side, which caused several speculative glances. Henry wasn't sure what to make of the Vance clan, but he had to admit it was nice to be included in the gathering.

When everyone was settled in their seats, Alonso said a blessing over the food. "Lord, we thank You for this bounty and for the family and friends gathered close. We ask for Your protection, Your blessing and guidance. May we each be a blessing to You, Lord. Amen." Alonso smiled. "Dig in."

"This smells delicious," Henry said as he took an empanada from the platter Olivia passed to him.

"These are some of our favorite dishes from my home country," Simone said.

"My mother and her parents moved stateside from Puerto Rico when Mama was a little girl." Olivia explained.

"Mrs. Vance promised to teach me how to make empanadas," Riley told him with a wide smile.

Henry's heart swelled. He was grateful to the Vance family for being so welcoming to his sister.

Over the course of the next hour, he laughed, ate and swapped stories with the Vances. It was fun to see Olivia interacting in such a casual way with her family. The care and respect they showed each other was a testimony to the power of such a close-knit clan.

Sitting here with Olivia's family created a craving in Henry he'd never experienced. He liked this big, noisy family setting. He glanced at Olivia and met her gaze. The tender affection in her eyes flipped his heart over. It took all he had not to lean over and kiss her right there in front of her whole family. He was in way too deep.

After dinner, Henry offered to do the dishes. "It's the least I can to do after such a scrumptious meal."

"What a good idea, Henry," Alonzo Vance said with approval. "Gentlemen, the ladies cooked so we can clean."

"Oh man," César complained, though he gathered plates as he spoke. "Why did you have to go and offer?"

César's wife wrapped her arms around his waist. "Don't worry, honey. You won't lose your man card for doing some dishes."

Everyone laughed. Henry enjoyed doing the dishes with the Vance men. Despite the earlier tension, they had good conversations about the Mets, the Knicks and the state of the police force.

Once the kitchen was back in order, the family gathered in the living room, where Riley was looking at photo albums.

"Henry, you have to see these," Riley held up a picture of the Vance siblings as children, all dressed in matching outfits. Over the next hour, Henry was shown a history of the Vance family in photographs.

He learned that even as a child, Olivia stood out among her siblings with the regal way she held herself. Finally the evening wore down. The siblings left and the elder Vances retired for the night, leaving Olivia, Riley and Henry in the living room.

A cell phone chimed. Henry's gut clenched. With dread eating a hole through his nerves, he reached in his pocket for his phone, fully expecting to see another taunting text from their mysterious bomber.

But it wasn't his phone that had chimed. It had been Riley's. She dug her phone out and stared at it for a moment with a scowl before sticking the device back in her backpack.

"Who was that?" Henry wanted to know who could make his little sister frown so fiercely.

She sighed. "Nobody."

"Well, I'm sure nobody has a name." Henry moved from where he'd been sitting in a straight back chair to plunk himself down next to Riley on the sofa. "What gives?"

"It's just somebody from school," Riley said. "It's no big deal."

"Is someone bothering you?" he pressed.

"No." Riley grabbed her backpack and stood. "Isn't it time for us to go home?"

Henry exchanged a concerned glance with Olivia. There was definitely something upsetting his sister. Was this the same person who had been texting her multiple times throughout the last few days?

But judging from the stubborn expression on his sister's face, he decided now wasn't the time to press her further.

Olivia took his hand. "I'll walk you out."

His sister's raised eyebrows brought heat creeping up his neck, but he wasn't going to let go of Olivia until he had to.

At the front door, Olivia released her hold on him so he could leash Cody. "I'll talk to you tomorrow," he told her.

She gave a sigh that sounded resigned. "Yes. Tomorrow. Back to reality."

Riley took Cody's leash and opened the front door. "We'll step out if you want to kiss."

Henry's chest tightened. He wanted nothing more than to do as his sister suggested. But there were risks that needed to be considered. Lines that shouldn't be crossed. The stakes of giving into emotion were too high.

Olivia tilted her head up, her lips parted. An invitation?

Despite the multitude of reasons why he should step back, his head dipped, bringing his lips close to hers. He inhaled the floral scent clinging to her skin.

A sudden gasp had him jerking back.

"Henry!"

Riley's panicked voice galvanized him into action. He raced out the door and skidded to a halt. Someone had vandalized the K-9 unit SUV.

ELEVEN

Olivia sucked in a sharp breath as horror flooded her. In the glow of the porch light there was no mistaking the red paint slashed across Henry's K-9 unit vehicle. The word *pig* was spelled out in big letters on the side and the tires had been slashed. The SUV listed to the side.

Henry's gaze roamed the darkened street. "Cody and I will take a walk around the perimeter to make sure no one is lurking about or left any explosives." He met Olivia's gaze. "Keep my sister safe."

"I will." Her heart bumped against her ribs. "This had to have happened recently or my siblings would have said something as they were leaving."

"Agreed."

She tugged Riley back into the house. "Be careful."

Henry flashed her a brief smile and a nod as he shut the door behind him, sealing them safely within the cocoon of her family home. That someone would deface the K-9 vehicle right outside the front door made Olivia shiver. Was this the bomber's latest ploy? Or something entirely different?

Riley stood frozen, her dark-eyed gaze unfocused on the closed door.

Compassion urged Olivia to wrap an arm around the younger woman's waist and draw her into the living room. "Come sit back on the couch."

A few moments later Henry and Cody returned. "All clear. You better get your dad," Henry said. The grim set of his jaw spoke of his upset at the malicious vandalism. "I'll call the local precinct."

Cody settled at Riley's feet as if the K-9 sensed she needed comforting. Olivia definitely wanted to get a dog.

Leaving Riley in Cody's care, Olivia hurried to her parents' room and lightly knocked on the door. "Dad, we have a problem."

After Olivia explained what had happened, her father and mother quickly joined her, Henry and Riley in the living room.

"Cody didn't alert, so there's that," Henry said. "At least this isn't an explosive situation."

"I'll check the recordings from the security cameras I have set up," her dad said and headed to his office down the hall. Henry followed in her dad's wake.

"I'll make some coffee," her mom said. "Riley, would you help me? I think we have some hot cocoa in the cupboard, as well."

Grateful to her mother for distracting Riley, Olivia hugged her mom then joined Henry and her dad in his den. Her father sat behind his desk, his fingers flying over the keyboard of his computer. The front porch came into view on the monitor. He rewound the footage to reveal a guy in a black hoodie and a neoprene face mask spray painting Henry's vehicle. There was no way to identify the culprit. He took off on foot down the street.

"Can you send this to Eden Chang at the Brooklyn K-9 Unit? Hopefully she can compare this guy to our bomber and see if they match in height and weight," Henry said. "Then we'll at least know if we're dealing with the same person."

"Did the museum ever send over their security camera feed?" Olivia asked. "This guy looks around the same build as the one who grabbed me."

"I'll ask Eden." Henry moved away to call the unit's technology expert.

Olivia put her hand on her dad's shoulder. "I'm sorry for bringing this home."

Her father swung his chair around to face her. "Nonsense. You are not at fault. Neither is Henry."

Her stomach quaked. "My investigation into Henry's case has been compromised."

Giving her an intense stare, he asked, "Can you be objective?"

"I don't know, Papa," she admitted. She had grown to care a great deal for Henry and Riley. Could even see herself falling for him if the circumstances were different.

"You must be." The decisive tone brooked no argument. He took her hands in his. "Let the facts speak. Take your emotions out of it. You have a good head on your shoulders. And you have really good instincts."

She blinked back sudden tears at his confidence in her abilities. "Thank you." She squared her shoulders. "I will do my job."

"That's all that is required of you."

Concern for the Roarke siblings' safety stuttered through her. "However, I do think Henry and Riley shouldn't go home tonight. There's plenty of room here."

Her father narrowed his gaze and seemed to toss the idea around in his head before saying, "Agreed. I'll leave it up to you to convince him."

Twisting her lips, she contemplated what she could say to persuade Henry that he and his sister would be safer here.

She cast a prayer heavenward that God would lend her a hand.

A commotion in the living room drew their attention.

"Sounds like the cavalry has arrived." Her father stood and tucked her arm through his and escorted her to greet the local law enforcement officers filling the entryway.

After giving their statements, Olivia joined her mother and Riley in the kitchen.

"Riley was telling me about the upcoming concert she's going to," her mom said. "I remember when you went to your first concert. Let's see, the band was…"

Olivia laughed. "Maroon 5. I had a crush on Adam Levine."

"Your sisters were so jealous that you got to go without them." Her mom's eyes twinkled.

"I remember. Maria and Ally wanted every detail about the concert. And wouldn't let me get any sleep that night."

"You were allowed to go alone?" Riley asked, her eyes hopeful.

"No," Olivia said. "My two brothers and their friends took me and a few of my friends."

"Oh." Riley's mouth turned into a pout.

Henry walked into the room just as Riley's phone chimed again. She dug it out of her backpack and glanced at the screen. Her lip curled and she deleted the message.

"Everything okay?" Henry asked her.

"Yes." She tucked the phone in her backpack.

Olivia shared a concerned look with Henry. That was the second text tonight to seemingly upset the young woman.

"Is someone bothering you?" Olivia asked.

A fleeting glimpse of panic crossed Riley's face before she pressed her lips together. "Seriously, it's no big deal. I can handle it."

Henry tugged his sister back on to the couch. "Riley, what's going on?"

"I'm allowed to have a life that doesn't involve you, Henry." Her tone had taken on a sullen note.

"Yes, you are," he said. "But whatever this text was, it upset you."

In fact, she looked a little scared. Acid churned in Olivia's midsection. "Riley, have any of your friends been acting strange lately? Have any of them been threatening you?"

Riley's gaze jumped to her. "No, it's nothing like that. This has nothing to do what's going on with Henry."

Olivia covered Riley's hand with her own. "You may not think it's connected, Riley, but it could be. The bomber followed you on the boardwalk."

"What? Why?" Fear clouded her eyes. "How does the bomber know who I am?"

"That's what we're trying to find out," said Henry. "I really need you to be straight with me and tell me if you can think of anyone who'd want to hurt you."

She jumped up and pushed past Henry, hurried to the bathroom and shut the door.

Henry moved to follow her, but Olivia held him back. "Let her have a moment."

"I worry about her," he said.

"Of course you do." One of the many reasons she was falling for him. His big heart. His generosity. His kindness. *Stop it!* She had to tame her emotions. "Why don't you let her stay the night here tonight? In fact, you both can stay. There's plenty of room. And I'd feel so much better having you and Cody here."

He hesitated a moment, surprise lighting the dark depths of his eyes. "You know, that would be helpful. I think she'd feel safer here with more people around than she would at home."

Grateful that God had granted her prayer, Olivia said, "Great. I'll talk to Riley when she's calmer. I've been meaning to, but with everything that's been going on…"

"Understandable. Don't feel bad. It's been a stressful few days."

Olivia gave him a quick nod, appreciating his thoughtfulness in letting her off the hook for not following through on her word. "I've also been meaning to address that old case with you. The domestic call six years ago."

"Right. What do you want to know?"

"I read the report and noted the date was close to the

time you lost your father." She wanted to be sensitive to his loss, but she needed to understand.

Henry sat back down. "It was a week or so after."

"I would imagine you and Riley were struggling to adjust to your new normal."

"Yes. Our new normal." He seemed to ponder her words. "That first year was difficult."

"Why were you back in the field so soon?"

He frowned. "The department psychologist cleared me for duty."

"I saw that, but I wouldn't have thought you'd be ready."

He shrugged. "Not working wasn't going to help anyone. Riley and I had to keep functioning."

Her heart ached at the grief lacing his words. She understood the need to move on. Resuming her duties had kept her sane after Roger's death. "Can you tell me about that night? What happened?"

He ran a hand over his jaw. "A domestic call came in. I was on patrol with my partner at the time, Officer Maury Standeven. Maury had been on the job for twenty years, he taught me a great deal about being an officer."

He paused as if remembering. "We were the first responders. The wife had been badly beaten. I was surprised she survived. The suspect, her husband, was enraged. We managed to pull him off his wife when a young kid stepped out of a closet. The husband went berserk. Knocked Maury over in his effort to get free. I got between him and the child. The suspect took a swing at me. Missed. My only option was to subdue him, which I did."

"And he claimed you used excessive force," she said. The story sounded too familiar. Could a six-year-old domestic case and the current one she was investigating be connected?

The bathroom door opened suddenly and Riley stepped out.

Henry stood. "You okay?"

"I'm fine," the young woman said.

Riley's chin jutted out in a stubborn way that Olivia was beginning to recognize. Henry certainly had his hands full with his little sister, even if she was a grown woman now. Olivia could imagine the handful Riley had been as a young teen.

"We know you are," Olivia said. "You and Henry are going to stay the night."

"We are?" Riley appeared excited and relieved by the prospect.

"Come on, you two. I'll get you set up in the guest rooms." Olivia led the way to the two back bedrooms that had once been her brothers'. When they both married, Olivia's mom had converted their rooms into guest quarters. Alexander's old room had a crib in it for his son, Tyler. Cody sniffed every corner, then sat wagging, as if giving his approval.

"Henry, I'm sure dad has some clothes you can borrow for the night," she said. "I'll go ask him."

She returned a few minutes later with sweatpants and a T-shirt. "And the bathroom across the hall has extra toothbrushes in the cabinet below the sink. As well as fresh towels if you want to shower."

"We appreciate your hospitality," he said. He hugged

Riley. "Try to rest. Take Cody with you. For extra security."

She hugged him back. "You rest, too."

Over her head, Henry smiled at Olivia. "Thank you."

She nodded as tenderness flooded her veins. She wanted a hug, too, but that would be too much to ask for and very inappropriate. Instead, she stepped out of the room and waited for Riley. Olivia showed her to the room next door. Cody did his sniffing routine then settled down at the foot of the bed.

Pulling a large T-shirt from the dresser, Olivia handed it to Riley. "You can sleep in this."

Taking the shirt, Riley sat on the bed. "This really stinks."

"The T-shirt?"

Riley laughed. "No." She lifted it to her nose. "Maybe a little."

"I'll get you one of mine." Horrified, Olivia held out her hand for the shirt.

"I can deal with it," Riley said and hugged the shirt to her chest. "I mean what's happening. Why would someone do that to the SUV?"

"We won't know what's motivating this person until we catch him."

"I worry about Henry," Riley said, her eyes big with anxiety. "What if someone hurts him? I can't lose him, too."

Olivia sat next to Riley and put an arm around her, wanting to assure the young woman that nothing would happen to her brother, but knowing she couldn't make such a promise. "Keep him in your prayers. Put your faith in God to protect him." She gave her a squeeze. "Henry's concerned about you, too."

"I know." Riley leaned into Olivia. "He's been really good to me. It's just he can be so controlling. And annoying."

"That's the thing about siblings," Olivia told her.

Riley pulled back to meet her gaze. "You and your brothers and sisters all seem to get along well."

Olivia made a face. "We haven't always. My brothers were protective and overbearing at times. While my sisters were wild and annoying. I love them all, though, and would do anything for all of them."

"But you went to concerts when you were eighteen. I'm an adult now. I shouldn't need Henry's permission."

Ah. The crux of the matter. "I did go and my brothers went with me. But I also lived here, in my parents' home. Even though I could legally vote and was expected to be responsible for my actions, I had to follow my parents' rules until I moved out."

Riley groaned.

"Your brother isn't trying to keep you from doing what you want to do, he only wants to make sure you're safe. With everything that's been going on, can you blame him?"

Riley made a face. "No. I get it. It's just frustrating."

Olivia understood the sentiment. "I don't like being coddled either. But sometimes we have to let those who love us protect us."

"I suppose you're right."

Taking the concession as a win, Olivia asked, "Is that what the text was about? The concert?"

"Kind of," Riley said. "It was Parker Wilton. The

guy you met at the museum. He wanted to know if I was going to the concert. He keeps asking me out and I keep telling him no."

Olivia's senses went on alert. "Has Parker been bothering you?"

Riley shrugged. "I don't want to date him. He is not my type."

Okay. Olivia wasn't going to touch the "type" comment. At the moment that was irrelevant. "So he's not taking no for an answer." She didn't like the sound of that.

"No, he's not. I finally told him that I wasn't going to date until I moved out because my brother's a cop and gives my dates too hard a time."

Olivia chuckled. She was sure Henry would approve. "And what was Parker's response?"

She wrinkled her nose. "He begged me to give him a chance. Am I being childish by not at least going to lunch with him?"

"What kind of guy is he?"

"He's nice enough. At least he was in the beginning. But after I turned him down a couple of times, he kind of became pushier. He rarely ever smiles now."

Concern arced through Olivia. "Have you told your brother?"

"Are you kidding me?" Riley shuddered. "Henry's in enough trouble. He doesn't need to deal with my stuff, too." Her expression was earnest as she said, "I'm not kidding when I say Henry would give my dates a hard time. When I was in high school, I went to the prom with Gerald Hamilton. When Gerald came to pick me up, Henry was cleaning his service weapon on the coffee table. Kind of freaked Gerald out."

Olivia pressed her lips together to suppress a smile as she pictured the scenario. That sounded like something her dad or brothers would have done. "I would imagine that was very intimidating for a high schooler."

"Yeah, you could say that. Gerald wouldn't talk to me the rest of the school year."

"That was Gerald's loss." Olivia tucked one of Riley's curls behind her ear. "You know, your brother is doing the best he can."

"Yes. I just wish he'd lighten up a little. He's always had to be totally in charge and on top of things. I'm afraid to make any mistakes because he expects perfection."

Olivia's heart squeezed tight. She could relate to the sentiment. Her parents had always expected great things, if not perfection, from their children. Especially her, as the oldest daughter. "I'm sure your brother knows you are less than perfect. We all are. But Henry once told me that love wasn't about measuring up to somebody else's expectations. I think he is a rare man who loves unconditionally."

Riley tilted her head and stared at Olivia. "You're right. He would be a great catch."

The comment elicited a startled laugh from Olivia. She needed to nip any ideas of matchmaking in the bud right now. "Yes, well. I'm sure one day he will find the right person. Now, I'm going to let you go to sleep. If you need anything, your brother is right next door. And I'm on the second floor right above you."

"Thank you. Hey, I just had an idea," Riley said.

"What if you come with Henry when he escorts me and my friends to the concert? Then you two could go on a date."

Oh, dear. Riley wasn't going to give up easily. "I can't date your brother. It's against the rules. But maybe I could go with you."

"I'd like that."

Olivia wasn't so sure Henry would. "Good night." She shut the door quietly.

"Is everything okay?"

Startled, Olivia put her hand over her heart. There was just enough ambient light for her to see Henry leaning against the wall. He was wearing a pair of Alex's lounge pants and a T-shirt. His feet were bare. The scent of mint and soap wound around her. Attraction pulled at her like a riptide in the ocean.

To prevent herself from stepping into his arms, she leaned back against the wall opposite him. "Yes, everything will be fine. The person texting your sister is Parker Wilton. The guy we saw talking to her at the museum."

Henry pushed away from the wall. "He's harassing her?"

"More like trying to convince her to go out on a date with him."

Henry harrumphed. "We'll see about that."

His protectiveness was endearing. "Tomorrow I would suggest doing a background check on him, just to be safe. And maybe you should sit down and talk to Riley. She seems to be under the impression she has to be perfect for you."

He exhaled as if her words were a punch to the gut

and straightened away from the wall. "Maybe I should talk to her right now."

Olivia stepped into his path. She placed her hand over his heart. She could feel the heat from his skin coming through the T-shirt. The thump of his heart beat against her palm. Her mouth dried. She licked her lips, then said, "It's late. We all need our rest."

He placed his hand over hers, curling his fingers around it to hold it in place. "You're right. Again. You have an amazing way of grounding me."

"Is that a good thing?" Why did her voice sound so breathless?

Her pulse beat at a staccato tempo. Standing here with him, shrouded in the hallway shadows, she could almost pretend the rest of the world didn't exist. She couldn't remember ever being so drawn to a man before in such an elemental way.

She'd found her late husband attractive and had loved him, once. But he'd never made her heart pound with such giddy anticipation. She pushed the thoughts of her past away. They had no place in the here and now.

"It's a very good thing," Henry murmured. "And a dangerous one."

She understood exactly what he meant. But the thread of attraction knitting them together was stronger than her will. In this moment, she was helpless to resist the yearning deep in her soul.

Going on tiptoe, she pressed her lips to his. The kiss was sweet and gentle but electrifying in a way that brought tears to her eyes.

Then his free hand tangled in her hair, cradling the back of her head as he deepened the kiss. Some part of her realized her world was on the verge of change even as internal alarms bells clanged a loud warning.

Slowly, he eased back until their lips separated. He dropped his forehead to hers. "I better say good-night now."

She wanted to protest. She wanted nothing more than to just stay here in this space, this moment, for as long as possible.

Something nudged her ankle and a soft meow shattered the intimate circle surrounding her and Henry.

Stepping back, she picked up Kitty and cradled the feline in her arms. The cat was a poor substitute for the attractive man standing before her.

"Good night, Henry." Olivia hurried to the safety of her room upstairs.

Her cat may be a poor substitute, but at least Kitty wouldn't cost Olivia her career.

TWELVE

The next morning, Henry was awake long before the sunrise. He'd had a fitful night thinking about a certain IA lieutenant.

Because his SUV had been towed to the crime scene lab, Olivia and her father drove him and Riley to their condo. Henry changed into his uniform while Cody ate his kibble and Riley got ready for her summer class. Henry was grateful that Riley didn't protest when a plainclothes officer arrived to escort her to school.

Captain Vance then dropped Olivia, Henry and Cody off at the K-9 unit headquarters with a warning to be careful.

They stood side by side outside the entrance for a long moment after her father's car drove away. Henry understood they needed to discuss the kiss, but he was afraid if they talked about it, any discussion would somehow lessen the moment and force them to come to terms with breaking the rules.

All night, he'd wrestled with his conscience over allowing the intimacy. He'd put her career at risk. Not to mention his own. Yet he didn't regret kissing her, not when doing so had felt so right, so natural. The kiss was imprinted on his memory. Something he'd never forget. But also that he'd never repeat.

"I hope you—" he said.

"I was thinking—" Olivia said at the same time.

Henry chuckled. "Please, ladies first."

"Okay. I think we need to run a background check on Parker Wilton."

Henry studied her for a moment. That wasn't at all what he'd expected her to say, but he'd go with it. Back to work. Better to keep the professional wall up. "Okay. It might be best if we have Eden run it."

"Good," Olivia said. "I need to speak with her anyway. You can make the introduction."

He led her to Eden's office. The technology expert was at her desk and she swiveled her chair around as they entered.

"Well, hello," Eden said.

"Eden, this is Lieutenant Olivia Vance," Henry said.

Eden's eyes widened and she stood. "Nice to meet you." Her curious gaze turned to Henry. "What can I do for you?"

"We were hoping you could pull some information about a young man named Parker Wilton," Olivia responded, drawing Eden's focus. "He's a person of interest in a case."

Henry's eyebrows shot up. Did she think this kid had something to do with the vandalism last night? Or the bombing? Riley had met Parker in her summer college class, after the incident with Davey Carrell.

Eden resumed her seat and her fingers flew over her keyboard. "Let's see," Eden said. "Parker Wilton.

Age nineteen. No criminal record. Mom, Karen Wilton. Also no criminal record." She hit a button and her printer whirred, then spit out a sheet of paper. "Here's the home address."

"Thank you," Olivia said, taking the page and handing it to Henry. "I have some other questions for Eden. We need a moment alone."

"Uh, sure. We'll wait in the hall." Henry stared at the paper as he and Cody exited Eden's office. Parker lived in Red Hook. Something pinged at the back of his brain.

He grew antsy as he waited for Olivia to finish speaking with Eden. He hoped the unit's technology expert told Olivia her theory that he was being set up. Plus, he needed to have Eden do another search.

Finally, the office door opened. He pounced before Olivia could walk out.

"Eden, could you look up Davey Carrell's home address?"

"Detective Roarke." The censure in Olivia's tone echoed on the small space. "You are not going there. You know you have to stay away from anything to do with Carrell."

"Bear with me, here. I have a suspicion and I need to see if I'm right," he said.

Eden shrugged and sat down at her computer again. "Hmm. Seems Davey Carrell's family also lives in Red Hook."

"What high school did Davey and Parker attend?" Henry asked.

"Just because they live in the same section of the city doesn't mean the two young men know each other," Olivia pointed out.

Eden's fingers flew over the keyboard. "They both graduated from South Brooklyn Community High School."

Henry turned to Olivia. "We need to talk to Parker and Davey."

She stared at him for a long moment. "You're right. But you can't go near Davey. I was planning to interview him anyway. I'll go to both of their homes and talk to them."

"I can talk to Parker," Henry said.

"I don't think that's a good idea," Olivia countered.

"Hey." Detective Bradley McGregor popped his head inside the doorway. "Henry, I heard what happened to your K-9 vehicle. That's just unbelievable."

"Yeah, I doubt Gavin's going to be too happy with me," Henry said.

Olivia frowned at him. "He can hardly blame you for the vandalism."

Henry shrugged. "Still, it happened on my watch, in my possession."

Olivia arched an eyebrow. "There are just some situations in life you cannot control."

"Spoken like somebody who knows," he quipped, remembering Olivia's comment about her own need for control.

Bradley chuckled, his gaze bouncing between them with a speculative gleam. "You two are funny. Gavin's called an emergency staff meeting. He wants us all there."

Eden rose from her chair. "We're coming." She shooed Henry and Olivia out of her office. "Move it, you two. You can debate who's going where after the meeting."

Henry and Olivia followed Bradley and Eden, but when Olivia stopped in the hallway, Henry walked back to her side as the other two disappeared into the conference room.

Henry searched Olivia's pretty eyes. "Are you coming?"

She worried her bottom lip. He was captivated by the way her teeth tugged on the tender flesh and he wanted to kiss away her worry. That was so not going to happen.

"I kind of intruded on the last one."

"You didn't intrude. You made a sound suggestion." Henry held out his hand for her to take. "You're more than welcome. Come on."

She eyed his hand then gave him a very stern look. "Henry, we need to keep things professional."

Though her words stung, he appreciated that she was drawing a boundary. He saluted her. "Yes, Lieutenant."

She made a face at him. "Smart aleck."

He chuckled and held the door open for her. Henry and Cody walked in behind Olivia and edged to the left of the doorway, finding a spot to stand against the wall. Olivia hesitated, then moved to stand beside him. She gave him a sheepish glance that had him wanting to put an arm around her and hug her close.

Instead, he crossed his arms over his chest and paid attention to his boss, Gavin, who stood at the podium at the front of the room. He had dark circles under his eyes. Apparently he'd pulled an all-nighter.

"Listen up, everyone," Gavin said, drawing the attention of the group gathered. "Despite a patrol car parked outside Officer Noelle Orton's house every night for the past few months, last night someone attempted to break in to steal Liberty. Noelle called for backup and we had the house surrounded within minutes. This was a win. We caught the guy."

Henry would have liked to have been in on that take-down. Liberty was one of their best K-9s, a yellow lab whose detection work, particularly in stopping gun smugglers, had prompted the bounty. Unfortunately, the light-colored dog had one black splotch on an ear that made her an easy target. Henry couldn't stand the thought of someone hurting one of their dogs or their officers. But he had had his own incident to deal with last night.

Gavin continued, "When we interrogated the suspect, we confirmed that there is a ten-thousand-dollar bounty on Liberty's head. Of course, we've known this from informants and because there have been several attempts on Liberty's life, but this is the first time we've gotten it straight from a suspect's mouth. We cut a deal with the suspect and promised to process him out of state if his intel leads to the arrest of the person who put out the hit on Liberty. The suspect says he only knows the gunrunner by the name of Gunther and that he operates out of Coney Island."

Gavin's gaze locked on to Henry. "Henry's vehicle was also vandalized last night. Our unit is under attack. We must be vigilant at all times, people. On another note," Gavin said, "Thanks to the suggestion of Lieutenant Olivia Vance, the FBI has put Agent Caleb Black on the McGregor and Emery murders."

Beside Henry, Olivia made a pleased little noise in her throat. He bumped his shoulder into her and whispered, "Told you. Good idea."

Though she didn't acknowledge him, she smiled and kept her gaze on Gavin.

"Agent Black caught a break quickly and reported that he'd intercepted Randall Gage, whose DNA puts him at the crime scene of the McGregors' murder—"

Several members of the K-9 unit cheered.

Gavin held up his hand and waited until it was quiet. "Unfortunately, Gage managed to evade Agent Black and escaped. This happened upstate in the Catskills."

A grumble swept through the room.

"Agent Black has vowed to continue to track Gage and keep us apprised of his progress," Gavin finished. "Now, I want all of you to be extra careful out there. Dismissed."

Henry pushed away from the wall as Gavin called out, "Henry, Lieutenant Vance, hold up."

A chill of apprehension slithered down his spine. Had his boss somehow found out that he and Olivia… No, of course not. Still, tension knotted his shoulders. "Yes, sir."

Gavin waved over Officer Lani Jameson and her dog, Snapper. While Gavin conferred with Lani, Henry led Cody out of the path of officers exiting the room.

Olivia sidled up to him and asked in a hushed tone, "What do you think he wants?"

"Probably to know when you're going to file your report." He cringed at the sharpness of his tone.

Her eyebrows dipped and her expression hardened. "Soon."

"Good to know." He didn't understand his sudden irritation. Or maybe he did. Guilt. Guilt for kissing her. Guilt for having feelings for the IA investigator that could land them both in hot water. He ran a hand over his shaved head in an ineffective effort to relieve the pressure building there, warning that a migraine was brewing.

Officer Noelle Orton and her K-9 partner, Liberty, stopped beside Henry. Cody scrambled to his feet but stayed in place. The other dog, a beautiful yellow lab with a big, black smudge on her left ear, ignored Cody and sat at Noelle's side.

"Lieutenant, have you met Officer Orton?" Henry asked.

"We have not had the pleasure." Olivia shook hands with Noelle.

"Noelle is a rookie with our unit. She is a former trainer at the NYC K-9 Command Unit in Queens. Several months ago, she and her partner, Liberty, foiled two military-weapon gun smuggling operations worth millions at Atlantic Terminal. Ever since, that bounty Gavin mentioned in the meeting, has been on Liberty's head."

"Well done," Olivia told Noelle.

Noelle gave her a slight smile and nodded. Henry had the distinct feeling Noelle wasn't too happy. Though having a bounty on your partner would do that.

As soon as the room was clear, Gavin moved from the podium to stand in front of Henry. Lani and Snapper hung back as if waiting for further instructions.

To Henry, Gavin said, "You're to stick close to the station for the foreseeable future. Hannah is expecting you in the training center. You'll work with Noelle and Liberty among others today."

Henry glanced at Olivia. "But what about Oliv—I mean Lieutenant Vance?" His boss had told him to keep her safe. Henry didn't like the idea of her working alone.

"We've got that covered," Gavin said. He focused on Olivia. "Lieutenant, I've spoken to your superior officer. And he is in agreement. Lani and Snapper will provide you backup while you are conducting your investigation."

Henry rolled this new development around in his mind. He trusted Lani and had no doubt that Snapper would be protective of both his handler and Olivia. That was what the dog was trained for, after all.

Gavin continued, "Your father would like extra precautions taken to guarantee your well-being."

Olivia gaped at the sergeant. Henry winced, because he had no doubt she was livid at her father's machinations. Henry couldn't blame her father. Captain Vance had not only his daughter to protect, but a grandchild. And though Henry understood Olivia didn't want to be treated differently because she was pregnant, Henry thought an extra layer of security was a good thing. Especially because he couldn't go with her to talk to Davey Carrell. But no one had told him to stay away from Parker Wilton.

"I think it's a good idea," Henry said.

She whipped her head toward him, her eyes sparking with anger. She focused back on Gavin. "I don't need a bodyguard."

Gavin leveled an intense stare on her. "With all due respect, Lieutenant, you have become a target because of your close proximity to Detective Roarke during your investigation. No one is saying you aren't fully capable of handling yourself. Backup is to ensure everyone's safety. I trust you are close to finishing your review of the case and will be able to move on to other investigations."

Olivia pressed her lips together, presumably to keep from arguing. Finally, she nodded. "I am close to being able to present my recommendations to the review board. I have gone over the reports and interviews from my predecessor as well as my own interviews, but I have a few more questions I need answered. I'd like to interview Davey Carrell. Then I should be able to turn in my report."

"Excellent," Gavin said. "Lani will accompany you to the interview." To Henry, he said, "Training center. And you do not leave without checking in with me. Are we clear?"

Henry's stomach dropped. Tracking down Parker Wilton would have to wait. He wished he could take a moment alone with Olivia to make sure she…what? Was okay with the situation?

There was nothing okay with the situation. The faster she finished her investigation, made her recommendation and moved on to another case, the safer she would be. At least he prayed so.

With a nod at Olivia, he and Cody walked away with Noelle and Liberty. Unsure when he would see Olivia again, he couldn't quell the anxiety taking root. He lifted a prayer for her safety, even as he felt annoyance at himself for caring. Despite his best effort, his heart had grown attached to the Internal Affairs officer.

* * *

"I know you're not happy with me tagging along," Lani said as she steered her K-9 SUV through midday traffic. "I completely understand. I married to the chief of the NYC K-9 Command Unit in Queens. Doesn't exactly endear me to everyone."

Olivia sighed and reined in her frustration. "It's not you. I'm actually glad to have you with me. It wouldn't have been appropriate for Detective Roarke to accompany me to interview the person accusing him of police brutality."

Lani slanted Olivia a glance before returning her gaze to the road. "Yes, that would be a problem. You two have grown close."

Startled by the observation, Olivia's heart rate picked up. "Why do you say that?"

"Remember, I fell for my superior officer," Lani commented. "I recognize the signs. But we made it work. I transferred out."

Olivia could see herself falling for Henry if the circumstances were different. But they weren't, so entertaining ideas of a romance with the handsome detective was out of the question. Unless…she left the force. Her mind shied away from the thought.

Lani drove them through the Red Hook neighborhood of Brooklyn and Olivia pointed to one wing of a red brick, multistory structure. "That building there."

After parking, Olivia and Lani, with Snapper trotting alongside, entered the building and found the Carrell apartment on the eighth floor.

Mrs. Carrell opened the door. She was a stout woman with dark hair that curled around her face, giving her an impish appearance. Wariness entered her dark eyes. "Can I help you?"

Olivia introduced herself and Lani, then said, "I'd like to speak with Davey."

Mrs. Carrell frowned. "Why? Our lawyer told us not to let him talk to anyone without him present."

"I can certainly have Davey brought to a station house, if you prefer," Olivia said.

A tall young man wearing a neck brace and a cast on his left wrist walked out of the back room. "It's okay, Ma. I've got nothing to hide."

Olivia recognized Davey Carrell from the pictures taken the night of the incident.

Mrs. Carrell shook her head. "But the lawyer—"

"I've got this," Davey insisted.

Mrs. Carrell didn't appear happy but walked into the kitchen.

"What do you want to know?" Davey asked, his gaze straying to Snapper. The German shepherd's brown eyes watched the young man intently.

Olivia pulled out a pen and notepad. "Tell me what happened on the night of your injuries."

Davey recounted his version of the events that took place in Owl Head Park. His story was consistent with his statement given at the time of the incident. He'd been at the skate park and attempted to leave when Henry grabbed him, twisted his wrist until it broke and then injured his neck when Henry took him to the ground. Davey's words sounded wooden as if he rehearsed them, which Olivia supposed he had. But he couldn't maintain eye contact while giving his statement. A red flag or simply a sign of immaturity? "Do you know Parker Wilton?"

Davey stilled. "Who?"

Olivia narrowed her gaze. "You two graduated from the same high school."

Shaking his head, Davey said, "Nope. Never met him. Now, you should go or I will call my lawyer."

"Thank you for your time," Olivia said, and they left the apartment.

"He was lying," Lani stated in the hallway. "The way he shut down your questions once you mentioned Parker...he knows this Parker person."

"I agree. But the question is why lie about it unless he and Parker are working together?" Olivia filled Lani in on the information she had about Parker and his possible connection to Davey. "We need to find Parker." She glanced at the time on her phone. "He should be in class with Riley now. Do you mind a trip to Brooklyn College?"

"We're at your disposal," Lani said.

Olivia was glad to have the backup and couldn't wait to speak to Parker Wilton. Then she could put at least one part of this investigation to bed. The sooner she wrapped up, the better for everyone's sake. Including her own.

"Henry," Eden called from outside the training ring.

Dressed in a bite suit, Henry motioned to Officer Max Santelli and his K-9 partner, a black and gold rottweiler named Sam. "Give me a moment."

After training first with Noelle and Liberty, and now with Max and Sam, Henry wanted more than a moment's break, but he had his orders. Stay put and be a K-9 bite target.

Max took out a toy to play tug with Sam while Henry jogged over to Eden. The heavily padded bite suit made his gait awkward.

"What's up?" he asked.

"Lieutenant Vance wanted me to see if I could find any video footage of Parker Wilton at Owl's Head Park on the night Davey Carrell was injured," Eden told him.

Henry's gut clenched. "And?"

She shot a quick glance at Max before focusing once again on Henry. "Parker was there. I didn't know to look for him before."

Henry's heart rate doubled. "Have you told the Lieutenant?"

"I left her a voice message," Eden said. "I thought you'd want to know, also."

"I do. Thank you." But what did it mean? Parker had to be working with Davey. To what end? But how had the boys disabled his body cam that night in the park? Why the bombs, the threats and the vandalism? And how did Riley figure into their plan? What was Parker's endgame?

"Also, the lieutenant asked me to run facial recognition through various social media sites for that night, looking for anything connected to Owl's Head Park. I think I found something that might be of interest. You'll want to see this."

His curiosity piqued, Henry said, "As soon as I'm done here I'll come to your office."

"Okay, that works," she said. "I'll see you later."

Henry stood there a moment, his mind whirling. He

couldn't make sense of it all. He had to find Parker Wilton. Then he would have his answers.

"Dude, you okay?" Max asked. He approached with his K-9 partner, Sam.

Sam growled, clearly ready to continue with their bite work training.

"Would you mind if we take a lunch break?"

Max shrugged. "Sure. Is everything okay with Eden?"

Henry nodded. "Yes. She's helping me on a case."

"Aren't you on modified duty?" Max said.

In lieu of an answer, he said, "I'll catch you later," and jogged out of the ring to the locker room. He made quick work of changing back into his uniform and then picked up Cody from the kennel room before going in search of his sergeant.

He found Gavin in his office and told him what he'd learned.

Gavin set aside the report he'd been reading. "Let me get this straight, you think Parker is working with Davey and trying to railroad you into the assault charges?"

"I do," Henry said.

"What proof do you have?"

"I don't have proof. Just my gut feeling. I need to talk to Parker. He's involved my sister."

"How?"

"By trying to date her and not leaving her alone when she refused. I want to find out why."

Gavin contemplated the request. "Hmm. You can't compromise the Carrell case."

"I won't," Henry promised. "I'll just ask the kid what his intentions are toward Riley."

"Not alone. Take someone with you. Feel the kid out, but don't make any references to Davey Carrell."

"Thanks, Sarge." Henry backed out of the office. If his boss had noticed that Henry hadn't promised not to dig into the connection between Parker and Davey, he didn't call him on it.

He went in search of Bradley but instead found Olivia and Lani entering the building.

"Parker was at Owl's Head Park the night of the incident with Davey Carrell," Henry said, without preamble.

"We're convinced Davey knows Parker," Olivia said at the same time.

Henry digested her words. "He does?"

Olivia nodded. "Yes, though he lied to me about it. Parker was there? That's interesting. And unlikely a coincidence."

"I'm on my way to talk to Parker," Henry said.

"He didn't show up at the college today," Olivia told him. "We stopped by there on the way back."

"I'll go to his house," Henry said. "Do you want to come?"

"Of course," she said.

A throat clearing brought their attention to Lani. "I'll drive. Someone has to keep you two out of trouble."

THIRTEEN

While Lani drove the large SUV with the dogs in separate crates in the back, Henry sat in the front passenger seat willing her to drive faster. He had to find out what Parker and Davey were up to, and how Riley figured into their plan. Olivia sat forward in the back passenger seat. He appreciated her calming presence.

She didn't have to be here. Undoubtedly shouldn't be, but he was loathe to do this without her.

In a short amount of time he'd come to respect and admire the woman. His feelings ran deeper but he couldn't let himself acknowledge them. Because if he did, he didn't know how he'd ever be able to walk away.

Right now he needed to stay focused on finding out if Parker Wilton was the bombing suspect. And what the kid wanted from Riley. That had to be his priority.

Once again entering the peninsula village of Red Hook, Lani found a parking spot near the five-story walk-up where Parker and his mother, Karen, lived.

"Snapper and I will keep watch outside," Lani said as Henry popped open his door.

"If you see anything suspicious let us know and call for more backup," Henry told her.

"Will do."

He hurried around to the back of the SUV to release Cody.

"We don't want to go in there making any accusations," Olivia warned as they walked into the building.

"I'll try to keep my accusations to a minimum," Henry said. "But I can't promise."

She stopped him on the landing of the fourth floor. "Henry, you let me do the talking."

He liked her all fierce and serious. She was a woman of substance with a strong will and a sharp mind. He wished the circumstances were different. "I will do my best."

Giving him a stern look, she said, "I hope so."

They approached the door. Henry let Cody sniff the edges but showed no sign of an alert. Henry rapped his knuckles sharply on the door.

After a moment, the door opened to reveal a petite woman holding a coffee mug and wearing the waitressing uniform of a local chain restaurant. Her light brown eyes widened. "Yes?"

"Are you Mrs. Wilton?" Olivia stepped forward with her badge in hand.

"That's right. It's actually Miss. But Karen is fine. Can I help you, officers?" She tilted her head as she gazed at Henry.

"I'm Lieutenant Vance and this is Detective Roarke with the Brooklyn K-9 Unit. May we come in?"

Karen stepped aside and opened the door wider for them to enter. The apartment was small but well kept.

There were pictures of Parker on the walls, mostly school photos.

Setting her mug on the kitchen counter, Karen stared at Henry. "I remember you."

Henry was sure he'd never seen the woman before or been to this apartment. "I'm sorry?"

Karen smiled. "I know you don't recognize me. I'm not surprised. I looked very different the last time we met."

"Okay." Henry searched his memory for some recollection of this woman and came up blank. "Can you remind me?"

"Six years ago, you saved my life. And my son's."

Memories surged and Henry's heart twisted in his chest. He exchanged a glance with Olivia. This was the woman from the domestic case that Olivia had questioned him about. Her husband had accused Henry of excessive force.

"I do remember," Henry said. "But you had a different last name."

"Yes," she affirmed. "When I recovered from the abuse, I filed for divorce and took back my maiden name. And I changed my son's last name, also."

"I'm glad to know you recovered and got out of that situation," Henry said with sincerity. "Whatever happened to your husband?" Could her ex-husband be behind the bombings? Had he attacked Olivia in the museum?

"Jack died in prison."

Henry wasn't sure what to say. He wanted to offer condolences, but the words stuck in his throat. He wasn't happy that a life was lost but the man *had* beaten his wife nearly to death. It was hard to find sympathy but he dredged up what he could. "I'm sure the loss was hard for you and your son."

Karen's lips twisted. "Yes. For Parker, anyway."

Henry had a bad feeling about Parker Wilton's state of mind. "Is your son home?"

Olivia shot him a censuring glance. "We have some questions for Parker."

Karen shook her head. "Parker has an apartment with some other kids his age. I haven't been there yet. I work swing shift at the restaurant. It leaves little time for socializing."

Cody sniffed the floor and sat in front of a closed door.

Henry moved to the door. "What's in here?"

"Coats."

"Can you open it, please?" Olivia asked.

Clearly confused, Karen went to the door and pulled it open. Coats hung on hangers, shoes lined the floor. Cody moved forward to sniff and sat in front of a pair of athletic shoes. "Are these Parker's?" Henry asked.

"Yes, those are. Why is your dog sniffing his shoes?"

"Does Parker have a room here?" Olivia moved toward the hallway.

"He does." Karen hurried to catch up with her. "In case he ever wants to come home."

"May we see it?" Olivia's words were polite, but Henry heard the tension in her tone.

"Why do you need to see his room? He's not here. What is going on?"

Olivia faced the woman. "I'm sorry to tell you this,

but your son is a person of interest in the case we're working."

Karen seemed to deflate. "What has he done?"

"We're in the early stages of the investigation and his name came up," Olivia said. "I'd rather not accuse him of something without proof."

Karen scoffed. "I've tried everything I can to keep him on the straight and narrow. He just seems to want to follow in his father's footsteps." She walked forward and opened a door. "This is his room."

Henry crowded past the women to enter Parker's personal space. It was neat and tidy. Posters of sports icons decorated the walls. The bed was made with a simple blue comforter and a desk that looked like it had never been used stood under the window. Cody sniffed around the room but didn't alert.

"Do you have the address where Parker's staying?" Henry asked.

Karen grabbed a piece of paper and a pen from the desk and wrote down an address. "You can probably find him at work. He's been working at the Tire Mart over in Gowanus since he was sixteen. That's how he can afford to live on his own."

"I took my SUV there last March when I had a nail in the back tire," Henry said to Olivia.

Her eyes widened with understanding. She turned to Karen. "Does Parker drive a silver sedan?"

"Sometimes." Karen walked back into the living room. Henry, Cody and Olivia followed. "His boss has a bunch of different cars that he allows his employees to use. He's been very generous with Parker."

"Do you know a young man named Davey Carrell?" Olivia asked.

Karen tilted her head. "The name does sound familiar. Does he work with Parker?"

"Not that we know of," Olivia said. "But they may have gone to high school together."

"Oh." Karen held up a hand. "Just a moment." She left the room.

Olivia grabbed Henry's arm. "Do you think Parker blames you for his father's death?"

He'd had that same thought. "Possibly. But why pursue Riley?"

Before Olivia could speculate, Karen returned with a yearbook in hand. She flipped through the pages until she found one that had a group photo. "Okay, here you go. Davey and Parker were classmates. They both were part of the technology club."

Henry stared at the photo of the boys sitting together at a table working on electronics. "Do you mind if I look through this?"

"Not at all," Karen said.

Henry flipped through the book. Olivia pressed close to him to see the pages. Her fresh apple scent was distracting and reminded him of her sweet kiss.

Henry flipped the page to the formal senior photos and froze. Beneath Parker's image the caption read, *Oh, yeah! Life is really great. LOLZ.*

Henry shivered. LOLZ! Just like in the texts. Parker had to be the bomber.

Meeting Olivia's gaze, Henry could see she agreed by the grim expression in her eyes. She turned to Karen. "Do you mind if we take this?"

"Sure. How much trouble is Parker in?"

"It's hard to say at this moment, but we believe he's been targeting Detective Roarke and those close to him," Olivia said.

Karen's dropped her head into her hands. "This is his dad's fault." She lifted her head. "Jack sent Parker letters. I found them after the fact. They were full of hate for the police." She gave Henry an apologetic look. "And you specifically."

"But from what I understand, Detective Roarke saved you and your son that night," Olivia said. "Doesn't Parker remember that?"

Karen shook her head. "No. The counselor I took him to said he has dissociative amnesia. He remembers only the good times with his father. Parker has no memory of the abuse or the months in foster care while I recovered in the hospital."

"Selective memory loss?" Henry said. He looked at Olivia. "Is that a thing?"

"Yes, and needs to be taken quite seriously," she replied. "It stems from the effects of extreme stress as a part of post-traumatic stress disorder."

Henry mulled that over. The kid was experiencing PTSD. But that didn't excuse what he'd done so far. Nor explain why he was pushing Riley to date him.

Olivia handed Karen a card. "If you hear from Parker or he comes home, please call me. I really need to speak with him."

"Detective Roarke," Karen said when they were at the door, ready to leave. "I never got to say thank you. I'm not kidding when I say you saved my life. The doctor said if you and your partner hadn't arrived when you had and pulled Jack off me, I would've died. And I don't know what would've happened to Parker if you hadn't intervened."

Henry nodded, appreciating her words. He'd done his job that day. As he did every day. Protecting and serving the citizens of New York was the creed that got him through the worst days of his life. "I'm glad I was able to help you."

Sadness washed over him to think her son was now going to be the one in trouble.

Lani was waiting in the vehicle at the curb. After securing Cody in the crate at the back of the SUV, Henry climbed in the front passenger seat. "Any problems?"

"No," she said. "Did you get what you were hoping for here?"

Olivia filled Lani in as she drove. "Davey *did* lie to us. I'll be seeing him again, but next time in an interrogation room. But for now, I think we need to pay a visit to the Tire Mart. You okay with that, Lani?"

"Sure."

Olivia gave her the address. The SUV merged into traffic, headed for the neighborhood of Gowanus.

"I've been here," Henry said as Lani pulled up to the garage that took up the whole block. He told them about the nail in his tire. "That must be why Parker seemed familiar to me. He wasn't nearly as tall or filled out at age thirteen as he is now at nineteen, so I didn't connect him to the domestic violence case from six years ago. He must've worked on the SUV."

"And the sight of you must have brought back all of his rage and given him someone to blame, starting him on his quest for revenge," Olivia said. "Lani, you good to join us? I'm not sure how Parker will respond."

"That's what I'm here for." Lani unbuckled and hopped out.

After releasing the dogs, Henry led the way inside. The garage had large bays, with cars being worked on by men of a wide range of ages. But Henry didn't see Parker.

"We're looking for the owner," Henry called out.

"He's in his office," a man said, pointing to a glass-walled enclosure.

A man in his late sixties with a full head of shocking white hair and bright blue eyes opened his office door and motioned them in. "Morton Daniels at your service. To what do I owe this visit?"

"We're looking for Parker Wilton," Olivia said. "We understand he works here."

"Parker hasn't shown up for the past two days. He's usually not flaky," Morton said.

"We understand that you have a silver sedan that you let your employees borrow," Olivia said. "Is it here?"

"Should be parked out in the lot." They walked out of the tire center and into the back where there were five or six different kinds of cars parked. But no silver sedan. "Somebody must have it out. Let me check the logbook."

They followed him back to his office. "Hmm. Last person to check out the silver sedan was Parker. It doesn't show it coming back in." The man shook his head. "I assume since you're looking for him he's in some sort of trouble. I feel bad for his mama. She's nice."

Olivia handed the man her card. "If Parker returns, can you please call me?"

"Will do, ma'am," Morton said, taking the card and tucking it into the pocket of his work shirt.

Once they were headed back to the station, Olivia said, "This puts a different spin on things. Once we find Parker and interview him, I have a feeling we'll know for sure if you're being set up for Davey Carrell's injuries."

"Which reminds me," Henry said. "Eden found something that she thought we might be interested in seeing."

As soon as they were back at the station they went to Eden's office, but she'd left for the evening.

"We'll have to catch her tomorrow," Henry said.

"Isn't the Colt Colton concert tomorrow night?" Olivia asked.

Henry groaned. "Yes, it is. I can't let Riley go to that concert. Not until I know Parker's in custody."

"The venue has tight security with bag checks and wand detectors," Olivia said slowly. "We can alert them to be extra vigilant. And if…we accompany her, she'll be safe."

Henry blinked in surprise. He was pleased by the suggestion but not sure he should take her up on the offer. "Really?"

"Yes, really."

"Riley will be thrilled. But we'll have to clear it with the brass." Henry wouldn't admit it aloud but he was thrilled, as well. Though he was afraid spending more time with Olivia outside of work wasn't the best idea. But then again, he was an innocent man being wrongly accused, just as he'd maintained from the beginning. And if they could prove his innocence, then there would be no issue of impropriety, right? Spending more time with her was a risk, not only because she was investigating him, but his feeling for her were growing. Changing. Would it be so bad if he fell in love with Olivia? Yes it would. As long as she was IA and he part of the rank and file, they could never be together.

The next morning when Henry informed Riley of the plan, he'd been right, she was thrilled to hear that not only would she be allowed to go, but that Olivia and Henry would be going to the concert, as well. Gavin, after discussing the situation with Olivia's boss, had given them the green light. Apparently Olivia had made the case that she needed to be in attendance to observe how Henry reacted in a crowded, stressful situation.

"But you're not sitting near me?" Riley asked. "Right?"

"No, we won't sit near you," Henry assured her. But he would sit where he could keep an eye on her. Because they still hadn't found Parker, even with every patrol officer on the lookout for the bombing suspect and the silver sedan. It had been a long, worrisome night, but Parker hadn't surfaced. Henry speculated that maybe he had skipped town.

"After school, I'm going to get ready for the concert at Kelsey's. You can pick us up there." Riley put her backpack on.

"Why can't Kelsey come here?"

"Because we've already decided we're meeting at her house."

"Officer Hall will escort you to school and to Kelsey's. You don't leave her apartment until I get there," Henry said. "Understand?"

"Yes, I understand. I'm not going to do anything foolish," Riley said. Her gaze narrowed. "Henry, I really like Olivia. I think she's good for you."

Henry gathered Riley in his arms and hugged her close. "I like her, too. But I can't do anything about it because of our jobs."

Hugging him back, Riley said, "Some things are more important. Don't let her get away. She's a good catch."

Riley's words echoed through his brain. Olivia was a woman worth loving. His heart was well on its way there. And despite his assertions that he didn't want to be a parent, he wanted to be a part of her and her child's life. How out-there was that? Especially when there was no way it could happen while he was suspected of using excessive force.

Mind whirling in directions he had no business going, Henry and Cody walked Riley out to the curb where Officer Hall sat in an unmarked cruiser. He'd been assigned to drive Riley to and from school until the bomber was caught.

"Be safe," he said before shutting door. He watched the car drive away and he lifted up a prayer to God for her protection.

A few minutes later, Bradley McGregor arrived in his K-9 unit vehicle. "Heard you needed a ride."

"That I do, my friend." Lifting Cody into his arms, Henry climbed in and they headed to work. And then tonight he'd be going to the concert with Olivia. If only this wasn't a potentially dangerous situation.

* * *

Because Lani and Snapper had been called away on a pressing matter, Henry had volunteered to use one of the K9 unit's other vehicles to drive Olivia to her late morning appointment. There was a look of consternation on his face when she told him the visit was to her ob-gyn for a checkup. She quickly apologized. "I'm sorry you're having to accompany me here. I should have taken a taxi."

He frowned as he pulled the vehicle to the curb. "No, it's fine. I want you to be fine. I'm happy to do this for you."

"After all the stress and drama of the past few days, I want to be sure all is well with the pregnancy."

"Of course," Henry said as he tugged at the collar of his uniform. "Is it okay if I wait here?"

She laughed. "Yes. You don't have to come inside. That would be awkward."

Relief swept over his face. "Okay. If you need anything, call me. I'll come running."

Touched by his words, she nodded and hurried inside the building. She didn't have to wait long to be seen.

"You and the baby are both healthy and strong," Doctor Smooter said as she moved the ultrasound probe over Olivia's belly. "Are you still wanting to be surprised by the gender?"

Olivia nodded. "Yes. I think I'll need that to look forward to when the time to have this baby comes." The delivery part of being pregnant was overwhelming to think about, though her mother and sister-in-law had assured her she'd get through it just fine.

"All right." Doctor Smooter pressed a button and an

image printed. After cleaning the ultrasound gel off of her abdomen and allowing Olivia to get dressed, the doctor handed her the sonogram print of her baby. "We'll see you next month."

Taking the image with her, Olivia's heart swelled with love for the tiny person inside of her.

"Everything okay?" Henry asked once Olivia was seated in the passenger seat of the SUV.

"All good." She held up the square sheet showing the shadowy image outlining her baby's form. "It's so amazing to think soon I'll be a mother."

"You already are," Henry commented.

Right. Excitement revved through her system and her mind jumped ahead to what she would do once the baby came. Would she stay with the force? The question was one Olivia had asked herself multiple times. As single mother, she'd need an income. And her family had offered to help with childcare.

She still had several months to decide what she wanted for her and her baby's future. She prayed that God would reveal to her the right decision to make.

However, at the moment, she needed to concentrate on proving Henry was innocent of the charges leveled against him. She needed to crack Davey Carrell's story. For Henry's sake. She wanted to repay him for all his kindness to her. And her heart whispered there were other reasons, like she was falling for him, was something she had to ignore.

Later that afternoon, Henry sat in Gavin's office going over the particulars of what he and Olivia had gathered so far about Davey Carrell and Parker Wilton. Cody sat at his feet while Gavin's dog, Tommy, a brown and white springer spaniel, lay curled on the bed in the corner.

After seeing the sonogram image of Olivia's baby, Henry couldn't help but be excited for her. The image made the baby real. And stirred in him a yearning he hadn't expected. What would it be like to be a father from the beginning?

The familiar chime of the incoming text sounded, cutting off his thoughts as dread gripped Henry's insides.

Roses are red, violets are blue, concerts are the perfect place for kaaaaboom! LOLZ

Jumping to his feet, Henry read the text to Gavin. There were still two hours before the concert started. The doors would be opening soon. "It has to be Parker. We have to go to the concert hall now and secure the bomb before they let people in."

"Agreed." Gavin rose and retrieved his sidearm from the bottom desk drawer. "You ride with me and Tommy."

The sergeant made calls as they hustled to Gavin's vehicle.

On the way to the Barclays Center, Henry called Olivia. "We just got a bomb threat at the concert arena. We are on our way there now," he told her. "Can you go and secure my sister? I know Officer Hall is there, but I just want to be sure that she's okay."

Olivia promised she and Lani would go directly to Kelsey's apartment, giving Henry a measure of peace.

The concert wasn't for several more hours and Henry was grateful Parker was giving him notice. But the arena was massive. Home to the Brooklyn Nets basketball team and the New York Islanders of the National Hockey League, the Barclays Center had over nineteen thousand seats and a hundred and one suites, not to mention the many eateries within its glass and metal structure. It would take hours for them to find an explosive device even with their highly trained dogs.

Gavin alerted the center's security and then called for more bomb-sniffing dogs from all five boroughs and the explosive ordnance disposal specialists to convene at the center.

When they arrived at the Barclays Center, sirens blazing, Gavin organized the search. He had the officers spread out. With worry eating at his gut, Henry and Cody worked methodically, checking row after row of seats.

They had to find the bomb before it was too late. And he thanked God Riley and Olivia and the baby were nowhere near the center.

Olivia tried calling Riley's cell phone, but it went directly to voice mail. "Riley, call me. I'm on my way to Kelsey's now."

Trying not to be overly worried by the lack of response, Olivia willed the traffic to lighten up as Lani drove to the address Henry had given for Kelsey's apartment in Brooklyn Heights.

When they arrived and parked, Olivia noted Officer Hall's empty car at the curb. Telling herself Riley's phone was buried in her backpack and she couldn't hear it ringing, Olivia and Lani and the German shepherd, Snapper, hurried into the building. The elevator had an "out of service" note taped to the door.

"The stairs," Olivia said as she veered to the stairwell. She made quick work of the five flights of stairs, then moved quickly to apartment 5D and knocked.

The door was jerked open by Riley's friend Kelsey. Olivia recognized the petite girl from Coney Island. "Hi, Kelsey. I need to speak with Riley."

Worry clouded Kelsey's dark eyes. "She hasn't shown up yet. I've been calling her cell, but she doesn't answer."

Olivia's heart pumped with dread. Where could Riley be? Where was Officer Hall? "If you hear from her, tell her to call Olivia."

"We have to find her," Olivia said to Lani as they retraced their steps to the first floor.

"I'll call Eden and ask her to ping Hall's phone," Lani said.

"Good idea. I have to call Henry and let him know."

They headed for the exit, but Olivia heard a phone ringing. "It's coming from the elevator."

She hurried over to the closed elevator doors and banged on them. "Hello! Is somebody in there?"

Snapper barked and scratched at the metal doors.

There was a moan.

"Somebody's stuck inside the elevator," Olivia said.

Together they pried the elevator doors open and found Officer Hall lying on the floor, holding his bleeding head.

"What happened?" Olivia asked. "Where's Riley?"

"Riley and I were headed into the elevator when

something struck me from behind. I went down like a house of cards. I blacked out." He grimaced. "I don't know who took her."

Olivia stomach sank.

Riley had been kidnapped!

FOURTEEN

Henry's phone rang, the sound echoing across the cavernous Barclays Center and setting his already tightly strung nerves on edge. He and Cody were near the stage that had been set up for the concert. The large speakers and lighting equipment above and to the sides of the stage would make excellent hiding places for explosive devices.

Henry hadn't figured out exactly how Parker had managed to plant a bomb in the highly secure facility. But the priority was to find it.

He dug his phone out of his pocket and checked the caller ID. Olivia.

Just seeing her name on the small screen sent a burst of warmth through him. He answered with, "Hey, have you secured Riley?"

There was a moment of hesitation that sent his senses on alert. A chill whispered across his nape.

"No. Henry, she's gone," Olivia's voice shook.

Dread had a feral grip on his lungs. "What do you mean, 'gone'?"

"Kidnapped. Somebody knocked out Officer Hall, and Riley's nowhere to be found."

Horror flooded Henry's veins. His sister was in trouble. Possibly hurt. How would he survive another death of someone he loved?

With a quick tug on Cody's leash, he and the dog ran toward the exit doors of the Barclays Center as he spoke. "Parker did this. We have to find him before he does something to my sister!"

"I'm going back to talk to Parker's mother. I'll see if she can come up with any idea where her son might have taken Riley," Olivia said, her voice stronger.

"His mom doesn't have the address of where he's been staying. But maybe those people at the Tire Mart do," Henry said. "I'm headed there now."

"What about the bomb threat at Barclays?"

"I trust the others will find it," he told her. "Be careful. Parker may have returned to his mother's. If so, call for back up."

"I will," she assured him. "You do the same. Don't be a hero. Riley can't lose you."

He needed to find Riley. To save his sister.

He and Cody ran outside and skidded to a halt. He didn't have a vehicle here. He'd come with Gavin. He whirled around and raced back inside. He found his boss talking with the center's management.

"Excuse me," Henry said as he interrupted. "I need the keys to the SUV. Riley is missing. I need to go find her."

"We'll go with you," Gavin said without hesitation.

They ran out the door to the K-9 vehicle parked at an angle at the curb. Instead of just calling to see if Parker was at the garage, Henry gave Gavin the address of the Tire Mart. He needed to make sure Parker didn't have Riley hidden in a room there. Sirens blaring, they raced toward the Gowanus neighborhood, weaving in and out of the evening traffic.

Leaning forward with a hand on the dashboard, Henry willed the vehicle to go faster and lifted fervent prayers to God to keep his sister safe. It was late in the day and traffic was heavy. By the time they reached the Tire Mart, anxiety had a stranglehold on his insides.

Everything hurt, but mostly his heart. Gavin had barely stopped the SUV when Henry leapt out and raced inside the garage, Cody at his heels. While Gavin and his K-9 did a search of the premises for Riley and Parker, Henry found the owner, Morton Daniels, in the vehicle bay. "We need an address for Parker Wilton now."

Raising his bushy white eyebrows, Morton said, "This way. I think I might have one." He led them to his office. He flipped through some files and pulled out an address. "This is the only address I have for Parker."

It was for Parker's mother's apartment. Frustration tightened the knots in Henry's shoulder muscles. "No, he's staying somewhere else. Maybe with some of the guys here. I need to question them."

Gavin came up behind them. "We checked the entire garage. Parker doesn't have her here." He looked at Henry. "Slow down. You're not going to help your sister by charging all over the place. Be methodical and go by the book."

Forcing himself to take measured breaths, Henry nodded. He walked at a fast clip to the garage bay where several men worked on the lift-raised cars. Henry gave a sharp whistle to gain their attention. "I need to find Parker Wilton, now. If anybody has any information about where he's staying or where he'd go, I need you to come forward. This is a matter of life and death."

Back in the far corner an argument broke out between a couple of guys. One pushed the other into a stack of tires, causing the tires to fall and bounce all over, drawing everyone's attention.

Henry hurried over to the two young men. "What do you know?" Cody sniffed both of the kids and then turned his attention to the tires but soon lost interest there, as well.

The two young men, both in their early twenties, looked at each other.

"You're not in trouble," Henry assured them.

One shrugged and said, "Parker's been staying with us. We needed more roommates to make the rent."

"We need the address," Gavin said.

One of them rattled off a street address in Red Hook.

"Thank you." Leading Cody back to the SUV, Henry called Olivia as Gavin climbed behind the wheel. He gave her the address of where Riley might be.

"That's not far from where we are," Olivia told him.

The last thing he wanted was for Olivia and her baby to be in danger, too. He would never forgive himself if something happened to either of them. "Promise me you'll wait for me to get there."

"We don't have time to wait," she said. "Lani and I are on it."

He had no say in her actions but he couldn't help the ache in his chest. "Please, be careful."

After securing Cody in the back beside Tommy, Henry urged Gavin to drive faster through the commuter traffic.

Please, Lord, please, let me get there in time to help Lani and Olivia save my sister.

Before Lani had brought the SUV to a full stop at the curb in front of the apartment building, Olivia jumped out. Her heart beat in her throat and dread made her queasy. The red brick building looked like every other building on the block. But this one held Riley. She was sure of it.

Olivia ran up to the entrance.

"Lieutenant, wait," Lani called as she released Snapper from the back of the SUV.

Seconds ticking away, Olivia's skin crawled with urgency. Lani and Snapper joined her at the door. Olivia hesitated. Was the door rigged to explode? There was no reason for her to believe Parker would wire an explosive to the entrance to his own building. She reached for the door handle and rattled it. Locked. She pounded her fist against the door.

Lani put her hand on Olivia's arm. "We need to take this slow. We don't want to spook him."

Dropping her hand to her side, Olivia took shallow breaths. For a moment the world spun, then righted itself. "Of course. But what if he's hurt her?" The thought filled Olivia with an anguish so deep she thought she might be sick.

"We can't think that way."

"I'm not cut out for this," Olivia said.

She'd never enjoyed patrol, but this was worse than

anything she'd faced. The unknown, the threat to some-one she loved. It was one thing to investigate, follow-ing facts and making recommendations, but being out in the field like this was nerve-racking. Why had she ever thought that going into law enforcement was the right decision? Because everyone else in her family had, that was why.

Shaking off the self-doubt, she put a hand over her belly. She needed to stay calm for the child she car-ried. For Riley and Henry. But how could she remain calm when her heart was torn up thinking that some-thing might happen to Riley? Henry wouldn't be able to survive if his sister were hurt. Olivia's heart throbbed.

Lani started buzzing all the apartments on the call box to the left of the door, until finally someone an-swered the call.

"Yeah, what you want?" a male voice said through the crackle of static from the box on the wall.

"Police. We need to get into the building. Possible bomb threat," Lani said.

"What?" the man screeched.

"Please unlock the door and leave the building," Lani said.

The door unlocked.

Olivia paused in the entryway, torn between her de-sire to charge forward and her need to keep civilians safe. "We should evacuate everyone."

"I'll find the building superintendent and have him go floor by floor to empty the building," Lani said.

Thankful to Lani for her levelheadedness, Olivia nodded. "I'll take the elevator to the sixth floor and start the evacuation process there before we approach 6C."

With effort, Olivia remained calm as she raced to the elevator. She checked her service weapon holstered at her back. She'd never fired it in the line of duty. And she hoped today wouldn't be the first time. Regardless, she unholstered the weapon, keeping it at the ready in two hands as the elevator rumbled upward. She stepped out of onto the sixth floor and took a moment to orient herself.

Apartment 6C was at the end of the hall. The stairwell door opened behind her. She spun, her body tensing.

Lani and Snapper jogged toward her. Olivia let out a breath of relief and lowered her weapon.

"I found the building superintendent. He's evacuating the lower floors," Lani said.

"Let's get this floor emptied," Olivia instructed. They knocked on doors and urged people to quietly leave the building. Finally, Olivia and Lani approached apartment 6C.

Lani rapped her knuckles on the door.

For a long moment, no one answered. They could hear noises coming from inside the apartment. A faint scream. A slammed door.

"That sounds like probable cause to me," Lani said. "You good with that, Lieutenant?"

"I sure am," Olivia said.

Lani motioned Olivia back, then she raised her right foot and kicked in the door.

Parker Wilton ran out from a back room, slamming the door behind him. Snapper barked and growled at him.

Olivia and Lani both trained their weapons at the

threat. Parker skidded to halt and shoved his hands into his sweatshirt pockets.

"Hands up!" Lani shouted.

Not complying, Parker backed away from the snarling dog and looked past the two officers. "Where's Roarke?"

"Get your hands where we can see them!" Olivia commanded.

Parker stared at her for a moment, then lifted his hands with the fingers of his right hand curled around what appeared to be a detonator, his thumb hovering over the trigger. "Do you know what this is?" he taunted. "A detonator. Works like a cell phone. I push this button, it connects wirelessly to a bomb and the whole building goes up in smoke." He looked at Lani. "Call off your dog."

"Heel." Lani gave the sharp command and Snapper returned to her side but stayed standing, ears back and tail high.

Olivia forced air into her tight lungs. "Where's Riley?"

"She's fine." He pointed to the exit. "You need to leave."

"Not without Riley. Have you hurt her?" Olivia's voice rose and she inwardly grimaced. It wouldn't help to panic now.

Parker stared at Olivia as if she had grown a third eye. "She's okay. I would never hurt her. I love her."

Stunned by the admission, Olivia tried to make sense of his actions. "Why kidnap her? Why have you been taunting her brother and hurting people?"

Olivia heard a thump from inside the room that Parker had just exited. Olivia held up her hands. "Parker, I'm setting my weapon down." Slowly, she set her sidearm on the ground and kicked it backward toward Lani. "I'm not a threat to you. Let me see Riley." She moved cautiously toward the door, skirting around Parker.

Parker spun and grabbed Olivia by the back of the neck, opened the door and pushed her inside. He followed, slamming the door behind him and twisting the lock. Then he pushed a nightstand in front of the door.

Snapper battered the door, scratching and barking.

"Lieutenant Vance!" Lani's cry penetrated the room.

Stunned, Olivia caught her breath. "I'm okay."

Riley was nowhere in sight. Olivia stared at the photos of Henry plastered all over the walls with big Xs drawn over them with red marker. There were photos of Riley, as well. But her pictures were grouped together in the shape of a heart. Parker had been stalking the siblings for very different reasons.

Olivia faced Parker. "You haven't killed anyone yet. Everything you've done so far has been fairly minor," she said. "You need to surrender yourself, now. Before this gets to a point where there's no turning back."

Something thumped from within the closet, drawing Olivia's attention. She lunged for the door, but Parker was faster. He grabbed Olivia, pushing her down onto a chair that had been fitted with an explosive device made with wires and a cell phone.

Olivia's heart nearly stuttered to a stop. The door shook as Lani tried to kick it open.

"Officer Jameson, I'm sitting on a bomb. Stand down," Olivia yelled as fear sliced like an open wound through her. Focusing her energy on Parker, Olivia kept her tone calm. "Parker, what are you doing? Where's Riley?"

The thump came from the closet again. Parker growled and then yanked the door open. Riley sat on the floor, hands bound and black tape over her mouth. She kicked at Parker, but he scuttled backward.

"She's a feisty one," he said. "But that's good. We're gonna run off together. I have to save her from her brother. He's a bully. He makes life hard for her. But once he's dead, she'll be all mine."

Anxiety twisted within Olivia's chest. Remembering what his mother had said about his dissociative amnesia, Olivia wanted to gauge his mental state. "Why do you want to hurt Henry?"

"He put my dad in prison. He deserves to die. He took my father away. Because of him, my dad is dead. If it weren't for Detective Roarke, my mom and dad would still be married and we'd be one big happy family."

"Parker, I talked to your mother," Olivia said in an even, nonthreatening tone. "You don't remember the night your father was taken away."

"I do remember," he insisted. "I remember that officer punching my dad and then throwing him into the car. There was no reason for him to do that. He had no right to take my father from me and my mom."

"Henry saved your mother's life that night, Parker. And your life, as well," Olivia said.

"No, he ruined my life." Parker paced in front of Olivia. "He ruined everything."

"Parker, your mother was badly beaten that night. And it hadn't been the first time. Your father was going to hurt you, too."

"No!" Parker stopped and rubbed at his head as if

his brain was hurting him. He was still holding the detonator.

Maybe the memories were coming back. At least Olivia hoped so. She needed to keep reminding him of the truth. Keep him talking so he wouldn't do anything drastic. "Your mother was put in the hospital for a long time. Do you remember? You were in foster care. Your dad did that to your mother. He nearly killed her."

"It didn't happen." Parker pounded his forehead with his empty hand. "You're making that up."

Afraid she was pushing too hard, she changed tactics. "Parker, listen to me. You don't want to hurt Riley. You love her. She's a nice girl. So just let us go."

Parker froze. His gaze jumped to Riley sitting on the floor of the closet. "No. If she'd only gone out with me, things wouldn't be like this."

Riley whimpered.

Shaking her head, hoping Riley would understand, Olivia said, "This isn't Riley's fault. And it's not Henry's fault. You targeted Riley to get close to her brother, right?"

"That's how it started," he said. "Then I really started to like her."

"What's your plan?" Olivia pressed. "How will you and Riley live?"

Parker grabbed a duffel bag from the bed. "I've got money. I've been saving. We'll be fine."

He wouldn't get out of the city. And Riley could get hurt in the process. "Did you plant a bomb at Barclays Center?"

Lips twisting, Parker said, "Naw. I just needed Roarke and his dog out of the way."

Which left Riley vulnerable with an officer who wasn't expecting an ambush. "How did you get Henry's personal cell phone number?"

Parker shrugged. "That was easy." He used his thumb to point at Riley. "She left her phone out one day in class. Unlocked."

He squatted down by Riley and caressed her cheek. She pulled away from him and he grabbed a handful of her hair. "So pretty."

With his back turned away from her, Olivia inched off the chair. If she could tackle him and secure the hand that held the detonator, then she could call to Lani. The officer could break the door in and arrest Parker.

In a swift move, Parker jumped to his feet and closed the distance between them in two long strides. He pushed Olivia back down on to the chair. "Oh no, you don't!" he yelled. "You're gonna stay right there."

Parker grabbed Riley by the biceps and pulled her to her feet. His dark eyes were malicious as he stared at Olivia. "You get off that chair again and I push this." He waved the detonator at her. "And then we all die."

Olivia shared a panicked glance with the younger woman. "You don't want to do that. You don't want to hurt Riley, remember?"

Olivia could hear Lani talking on the other side of the door, then muted male voices answering. Olivia recognized Henry's deep timbre. Hope blossomed in her chest. And yet she was afraid Henry's presence might push Parker over the edge. She needed to keep Parker distracted. "What about Davey?"

"What about him?" Parker said, seemingly oblivious to the voices outside the bedroom door.

"How did the two of you disable Detective Roarke's body camera at Owl's Head Park?"

"That was easy," Parker said. "An EMP. Any dummy could do it."

The unit's technology expert had said an electromagnet could have interfered with the feed. Apparently Parker had built himself an electromagnetic pulse device. "No," Olivia countered. "You're smart, Parker. Smarter than most. You know there's no way you're leaving here with Riley."

A sudden pounding on the door jolted through Olivia. Parker whipped around and stared at the door.

"Parker Wilton, this is Sergeant Gavin Sutherland of the Brooklyn K-9 Unit. Open this door so we can talk," Gavin called through the door.

"You don't get to give me orders," Parker yelled back. He pulled Riley in front of him. "Where's Roarke?"

"I'm here," came Henry's reply. "Are the lieutenant and my sister okay?"

"Henry, we're okay for now," Olivia called to him. "Parker has a detonator in his hand and there's a bomb in here. No explosives at Barclays Center, according to Parker."

"Now who's in control?" Parker yelled. "How do you like it? You made my father go to prison. Now Riley is mine. You took what I love, now I'm taking what you love."

"Listen, buddy," Henry said, his voice calm. "Why don't you open the door and come out. Everyone's going to the concert tonight. Colt Colton. It should be a great time. You could sit with Riley and her friends. There's an extra seat since one of the girls can't make it."

Parker's expression changed, revealing the young soul inside him. "Really?"

Olivia could tell he was excited by the idea. He really was a troubled young man.

Then he scowled, looking at Riley. "You think I'm dumb. The minute I open that door, you're going to arrest me and take Riley away from me. She's mine now. And you better step back, because I'm coming out with her." He pushed Riley toward the door. "But if you do anything at all, I hit the button and everyone goes kaboom."

FIFTEEN

Olivia's heart pounded in her chest, her pulse roared in her ears. She had to stall, do something to keep the troubled young man from imploding and blowing them all sky high. "Parker, why did you try to break into Henry and Riley's condo?"

Parker paused and pointed at the simple gold cross hanging around Riley's neck. "I was hoping I could take that. And then, if she thought she'd lost it and I found it, she'd see I wasn't such a bad guy." His face twisted with rage. "But he stopped me. Him and that dog."

"Why were you following him? You've been doing that for months. Did you recognize him when he brought his vehicle into the Tire Mart?"

"I recognized the name. My dad would write to me. And he'd tell me that an officer named Roarke was the one who put him in jail. That Roarke was the reason we couldn't be together. That Roarke broke up our family."

"You know that's not true." Compassion flooded Olivia. This boy, with his trauma-induced faulty memory, had been brainwashed by an abusive, manipulative father. Parker needed to remember what actually happened so that the truth could release him from this prison of bitterness and his need for revenge. "Your father hurt your mother. He nearly beat her to death, Parker. He would have gone after you, too, if Detective Roarke hadn't intervened."

Parker shook his head again. "No, no, no! I'd remember if my mother had been hurt. Don't say it again. Because I won't believe it." He pounded the fist holding the detonator against the wall.

Olivia's breath froze in her lungs and ice filled her veins. She lifted a fervent prayer to the Lord for some guidance. How could she reach this young man? How could she protect the child growing inside of her?

She wanted to live. She wanted to be a mother and to forge a future for them both. A future she wanted to share with Henry. In a moment of pure clarity, she realized she loved him. He was a man she could count on, a man she could trust with her heart. But there were obstacles in the way.

Their careers. Her investigation.

The baby. He'd already raised one teenager and had said he wasn't interest in parenting again.

The biggest obstacle at the moment, though, was Parker. If she and Riley didn't make it out of here alive, there was no future for either of them.

She had to do something to save them all. Then she could figure out what to do about her feelings for Henry.

As Parker reached for the door handle, Olivia's gaze searched wildly for something, anything, to stop him. There was a baseball sitting on the desk to her right. With two older brothers, she could throw a mean fastball and hit a target.

Parker let go of Riley to grasp the door handle. Seeing her moment, Olivia grabbed the baseball. Parker whipped around as if he sensed her movement. She threw the baseball hard, hitting Parker in the nose. She heard the delicate bones break. The kid screamed and grabbed at his face, the detonator flying from his hand, landing on the rug.

"Now!" Olivia yelled as she threw herself on the detonator.

Parker dove on top of her, clawing at her, trying to get her away from it. She heard the loud splintering of wood as the door was kicked open. The frantic barking of a dog reverberated off the walls.

Snapper latched on to Parker's leg. He screamed and rolled away from Olivia, batting at the dog biting him. "Get it off me!"

Olivia sat up, clutching the detonator to her chest. Blood from Parker's busted nose smeared her clothing.

Cody and Gavin's K-9 both sat in front of the chair, showing their handlers the location of the explosives. From her place on the floor, Olivia had a better view of the small bundle strapped to the bottom of the desk chair with black electrical tape. A shudder worked through her at how close she'd, they'd all, come to being blown to bits.

Gavin and Lani secured Parker, putting him in handcuffs. Snapper backed off, but still growled, making it clear if he resisted the dog would attack him again.

Henry worked on the bomb strapped to the chair. Olivia held her breath, praying he didn't accidently detonate the device. His remarkably steady hands cut wires and pulled the homemade explosive apart, effectively disarming the device and saving them all.

With a shaky hand, Olivia held up the detonator. "Take this. I don't want to hold it anymore."

Gently, Henry pried the device from her fingers and laid it on the desk. He cupped her cheek for a split second before turning his attention to his sister. He undid the tape across her mouth and the zip tie holding her hands together. As soon as she was free, Riley threw her arms around her brother's neck and sobbed into his chest.

Olivia's heart throbbed with love and adrenaline. Watching the two siblings reunite made her so happy.

Then Henry was once again kneeling next to her. "Are you hurt, Olivia?"

"I'm good. It's not my blood." She wanted to hug him tight and not let go. But she had a job to do and it wasn't finished. She needed to end this debacle.

Henry helped her to her feet. Her legs wobbled with the rush of blood thrumming through her veins, though she stayed upright. She leaned on Henry for support for a moment as her equilibrium righted itself.

Before Gavin could lead Parker away, Olivia went to the young man and gripped him by the shoulders. His nose had swelled and blood dripped down his chin.

"Tell me about Davey's injuries from the incident with Detective Roarke in Owl's Head Park," Olivia demanded.

"It was all Davey's idea," Parker said. "It was all his idea. Everything. When I told him about Detective Roarke, he planned it all. He told me what to do. He made the bombs."

"Why would Davey do this?" Olivia pressed.

Parker shrugged. "You'll have to ask him." He turned his focus on Riley. "I wouldn't have hurt you. I love you. Even if you are his sister."

Riley stared at him with anger filling her dark eyes. "You're sick. I hope I never see you again."

Parker hung his head but there were no tears, only anger twisting his face.

More police officers stormed the building. Gavin coordinated the removal of more explosives that were found in the apartment.

"I'll take care of him." Lani took Parker by the biceps. With Snapper at her side, along with several other officers, they escorted him out of the building and into a squad car.

Henry and Cody ushered Olivia and Riley out behind them. The young man would be arrested and put in jail, but Olivia hoped that he would get the help he needed. In fact, she decided she would make sure he was paired with a good psychologist.

But for now, before she could look to the future, there was someone else who needed her help. Henry.

Standing on the sidewalk, she approached Gavin. "I need to speak with Davey Carrell again. Can you have him brought right away to an interrogation room at the K-9 center?"

Gavin nodded. "I'm on it."

"Lieutenant." Henry motioned for her to follow him and led her away from the crowd of officers and residents gathered to watch all the chaos. Riley and Cody were sitting in one of the K-9 unit's vehicles. "There will be time for all that. But right now, I want to make sure you and—" He stopped himself and caressed her cheek. "I want to make sure everything is okay. You mean the world to me."

It wasn't a declaration of love. They weren't free to explore this thing arcing between them. But they would be soon. She would make sure of it. "We need to get out of here. Get your sister home." She started them walking back to the car. "And I have unfinished business with Davey Carrell."

It took a couple hours for officers to bring in Davey Carrell. During that time, Olivia managed to clean up and now sat alone in an interrogation room, writing up her report while she waited. There were just a few things she needed clarified before she could take her report to the review board. She was going to recommend dismissing the charges brought against Henry.

She was confident the board would come to the same conclusion she had. Henry was a good man, full of honor and integrity, who had done his job well. Whatever injuries Davey had sustained during the altercation were not excessive. She believed Henry, not the kid who had helped terrorize the city. Thankfully no one knew of her and Henry's attraction to one another, because if it came to light, the facts of the case wouldn't matter. It would become about them.

There was a knock on the open interrogation room door. She looked up to find Eden Chang standing there. Her long dark hair was pulled back in a braid that hung over her shoulder. She wore a collared navy shirt with the K-9 unit logo and khaki pants. Her gaze was warm as she said, "Lieutenant Vance, I found something on social media I think you'll want to see."

Gathering her papers, Olivia followed Eden back to her office.

Rounding her desk, Eden said, "I told Henry, but we didn't get a chance to connect earlier. Understandable, considering." Eden sat down and fired up her monitors. "So I started trolling all the social media sites that I could find for the night of March twenty-third and decided to keep looking for any mention of the park over the past few months."

She brought up a social media account. "This was posted about two weeks ago. The poster had been visiting the city for the Fourth of July and had no idea he had evidence we needed."

She pushed Play. The skate park came into view. The setting sun cast rays over the skaters gathered around the cement ramps.

"Oh man, this dude's gonna try it," said an unseen male voice, apparently the social media account holder.

Olivia drew closer to the monitor. The "dude" in question stood at the top of what looked like a drained swimming pool, his skateboard poised over the lip of the concrete wall. He had on a helmet but there was no mistaking the face. "That's Davey Carrell."

"Yes," Eden said. "Watch what he does."

Olivia held her breath. Throughout the skate park there were ramps and various other objects for the skaters to roller up and over. But what had Olivia's attention at the bottom of the scooped bowl was a makeshift wooden ramp with large boxes placed in a row.

Davey was going to try to jump over the obstacle,

Evel Knievel–style. Only on a skateboard, not a motorcycle.

Davey tapped his helmet and crouched, with one hand on the tip of his skateboard. Then he pushed off and skated down into the bowl, up over the ramp and across the obstacle. But he lost his board midjump. For a moment, he appeared to float in the air, then he plummeted to the ground, putting out his left hand and landing hard. He let out a scream, "Ow, my wrist!" Clutching his injured limb, he rolled out of view.

"That's how he broke his wrist." Elated by this bit of evidence, Olivia pumped her fist in the air. "Can you make me a copy and send it to my email?"

Eden grinned. "I thought this might be a game changer."

"It certainly is. Did you find anything showing the confrontation between Henry and Davey?"

"As a matter of fact…" Eden's fingers flew over the keyboard again. "Same social media account. It's just the tail end of the confrontation. Like the guy had been watching the skateboarders when he turned around and realized what was happening behind him was more fascinating and started filming."

The video definitely showed Henry securing his weapon by jamming his elbow into the side of Davey's neck, then prying away his service weapon from Davey's right hand.

"Well, that clinches it." Olivia rubbed her hands together. She had the proof necessary to exonerate Henry. "I wish we'd found these sooner."

Eden shrugged. "Like I said, both of these clips were

uploaded recently. Even if I had searched at the time, I wouldn't have found them."

"I'm really glad you did, Eden. You did good work. You are a real asset to the department."

Eden grinned. "Make sure you tell the sarge that."

Olivia grinned back. "Believe me, I will."

By the time she got back to the interrogation room, Davey Carrell, wearing a cast on his left wrist and a neck brace, sat between his lawyer and his parents at the metal table.

"You asked us here," the lawyer said. "What is it?"

She sat down across from the boy and ignored the lawyer. "This is your last chance to come clean, Davey. I need you to tell me the truth about what happened on the night of March twenty-third of this year at Owl's Head Park's skate park."

The boy copped an attitude, his chin jutting out. "I've already told you what happened. That pig cop broke my wrist and injured my neck."

Olivia removed her phone from the pocket of her gray suit jacket, opened her email and found the video of Davey skating. She turned the phone so that all four people on the other side of the table could view the screen.

"What is this?" the lawyer asked.

"Watch." Olivia pushed Play.

When the video ended. Davey was sitting back in his seat, looking a little sick.

"Are you really going to stick with your story?" Olivia asked.

"Objection," the lawyer said. "We were not given that video to review and it doesn't show anything relevant."

Flicking a glance at the well-dressed, no doubt highly paid attorney, Olivia said, "This isn't a court of law, Counselor. And I was just apprised of this video." She found the next email sent by Eden. "As well as this one." She played the video of Henry securing his weapon.

"Davey," Mr. Carrell intoned with disgust. "You lied."

With a mulish expression on his face, Davey's shoulders slumped.

"Parker says you were the mastermind," Olivia stated, gauging the kid's reaction.

"No way!" Davey sat up, outrage making his face red. "It was all him. Parker spotted that cop when he came into the place where Parker works. He concocted the whole thing."

Olivia narrowed her gaze on the young man. "You didn't help him build the bombs?"

"Not even. That's beyond me," Davey said, sitting back. "Parker is wicked smart. And he can be scary at times. You wouldn't want to cross him."

Not sure how to feel about Davey's assessment of Parker, she kept her focus on the matter she needed resolved. "Then you admit that Detective Roarke did not break your wrist and that you tried to relieve him of his sidearm?"

"Don't answer that," the lawyer interjected.

Davey shrugged. "They got the video, man. I never wanted to do this whole thing, but Parker talked me into it."

Beside him his mother made a noise of distress.

Davey glanced at her then turned back to Olivia. "Yes, I broke my wrist on that stupid fall." Davey touched the brace around his neck "But he did hurt my neck when..." He grimaced and slumped again. "He did hurt my neck."

"What about the vandalism to Detective Roarke's vehicle?" Olivia asked. "Were you involved in that?"

Davey shook his head. "I haven't been allowed to leave the house for months."

Satisfied, Olivia gathered her papers and slipped her phone back into her pocket. "Counselor, I assume you'll recant the charges against Detective Roarke."

"In light of this new information, yes, we will ask the DA to drop the charges."

"Good," Olivia said. "I'm sure the DA will be in contact in regard to charging Davey with a felony for attempting to disarm Detective Roarke."

The lawyer rose and faced the family. "You'll need to find new representation. I'll send you my bill." He walked out the door.

As the Carrells left, Olivia shook her head.

Now that the case against Henry would be dismissed, she was free to decide her future. She pressed her hand to her belly.

Something had become clear to her these past few days. Despite her desire to make her family proud by staying in the family tradition of law enforcement and first responders, she wanted something different in life. She wanted to help people in a different way. She was going to resign from the force.

If someone had taken an interest in Parker all those years ago, maybe he would have been mentally stable and lived his life making better choices.

She planned to use her degree in psychology and

criminal justice to offer support and assistance to trauma victims like Parker before it ever became too late.

Henry stood on the grass outside the training center and the K-9 unit building with Cody, the puppies and Brooke, the mama dog. He'd been pacing inside when the vet, Gina, had asked him to make himself useful by taking the dogs out for a break.

Cody and Brooke were keeping the puppies in line while Henry continued his pacing. He'd seen Davey and his entourage leave the headquarters building several minutes ago.

It took all of Henry's willpower not to go find Olivia and ask her what had happened. Was she filing her report now? What was she recommending? Would he resume his duties? Or be charged with excessive force?

He refrained from seeking her out because it wouldn't be appropriate. Though he wanted to know her conclusions, he told himself to exercise some patience. He would find out in due time.

But his career hung in the balance.

His life hung in the balance.

A life he wanted to share with Olivia and her child. He hadn't foreseen falling hard for the beautiful and caring woman. Finding romance while embroiled in an internal affairs investigation had thrown his carefully planned life into chaos. A good kind of chaos. The kind that made his heart pound with joy and terror all at once.

Yet, how could they ever be together while their jobs kept them at odds?

He searched his heart and realized he'd willingly give

up the force if it meant he could spend his life with the woman he'd come to love.

"Are you puppy-sitting?"

He whirled around and found Olivia walking toward him. She was so beautiful, so regal, dressed in a gray suit with a pale purple blouse. Her amber eyes sparkled and the smile on her face caused a ripple of joy to cascade through him. She was warm and alive and glowing.

She held out her hand. Without second-guessing himself, he grasped her smaller hand within his, loving the feel of her soft skin pressed again his palm. Glancing around to make sure no one was watching, he tugged her closer.

She squeezed his hand. "You're in the clear."

"What do you mean?"

"Davey has retracted his accusations. We have proof he was lying. The case will be dismissed. You're free to resume your duties with the K-9 unit."

His knees nearly buckled. But he locked them and stared into her eyes. "That's good news."

Learning he was no longer under investigation lifted a heavy weight off his mind, making him a bit light-headed. He could take a full breath and not feel the pressure of the false accusation.

Olivia squeezed his hand. "And I've decided to leave the force and open my own trauma counseling practice here in Brooklyn."

For a moment the ramifications of her announcement left him speechless. She was resigning from the NYPD. Finding his voice, he said, "Are you sure? I mean, I've already said you made a wonderful counselor, but you're also a really great investigator."

The determination and confidence in her eyes had his heart pounding.

"I am sure. It's what I want to do with my life. How I want to make a difference in the lives of others."

He so admired this remarkable woman. He swallowed, his throat suddenly closing on the words bursting to get out. If he didn't say what was in his heart now, he might never get another chance. "I have to tell you something. And I'll understand if what I'm about to say isn't wanted, but I need you to know. I've fallen in love you, Olivia. You are such a kind and caring woman. You've opened my eyes to viewing the world in different ways. I want you to know I would never purposely hurt or deceive you. I want the best for you and your child."

Olivia's eyes widened and for a fraction of a second he feared she would reject him. Then a soft, beaming smile broke out on her lovely face. "I've fallen for you, too, Henry. I know you are a man of integrity and honor. A man I can trust with my heart."

Relief swept through him. "I'm so glad to hear that."

Then worry clouded her eyes. "Henry, the baby and I come as a package deal."

"I know." He kissed her hand. "I wouldn't have it any other way. I want to be a father. From the beginning. Now that I've had a little practice, I'll be better at it the second time around."

She grinned. "Or a third?"

"Yes." He chuckled. Love and hope and elation filled his chest to overflowing. "Whatever you want. Whenever you want. With God as our rudder, we'll do just fine."

One of the puppies, Maverick, wedged himself between Olivia's legs, his little body quivering with obvious excitement.

Olivia bent down and picked up the puppy, snuggling him close. "Do you think Riley will be okay with us?"

"She's already given us her blessing," he told her. "She told me you would be a great catch."

Olivia laughed. "She told me the same thing about you."

"Then I guess we better not disappoint her." He tugged Olivia close for a kiss.

* * * * *

SPECIAL EXCERPT FROM

LOVE INSPIRED SUSPENSE
INSPIRATIONAL ROMANCE

*Out horseback riding, Dr. Katherine Gilroy
accidentally stumbles into a deadly shoot-out and
comes to US marshal Dominic O'Ryan's aid. Now with
Dominic injured and under her care, she's determined to
help him find the fugitive who killed his partner...before
they both end up dead.*

Read on for a sneak preview of
Mountain Fugitive *by Lynette Eason,*
available October 2021 from Love Inspired Suspense.

Katherine placed a hand on his shoulder. "Don't move," she said.

He blinked and she caught a glimpse of sapphire-blue eyes. He let out another groan.

"Just stay still and let me look at your head."

"I'm fine." He rolled to his side and he squinted up at her. "Who're you?"

"I'm Dr. Katherine Gilroy, so I think I'm the better judge of whether or not you're fine. You have a head wound, which means possible concussion." She reached for him. "What's your name?"

He pushed her hand away. "Dominic O'Ryan. A branch caught me. Knocked me loopy for a few seconds, but not out. We were running from the shooter." His eyes sharpened. "He's still out there." His hand went to his right hip, gripping the empty holster next to the badge on his belt. A star within a circle. "Where's my gun? Where's Carl? My partner, Carl Manning. We need to get out of here."

"I'm sorry," Katherine said, her voice soft. "He didn't make it."

He froze. Then horror sent his eyes wide—and searching. They found the man behind her and Dominic shuddered.

After a few seconds, he let out a low cry, then sucked in another deep breath and composed his features. The intense moment lasted only a few seconds, but Katherine knew he was compartmentalizing, stuffing his emotions into a place he could hold them and deal with them later.

She knew because she'd often done the same thing. Still did on occasion.

In spite of that, his grief was palpable, and Katherine's heart thudded with sympathy for him. She moved back to give him some privacy, her eyes sweeping the hills around them once more. Again, she saw nothing, but the hairs on the back of her neck were standing straight up. "I think we need to find some better cover."

As if to prove her point, another crack sounded. Katherine grabbed the first-aid kit with one hand and pulled Dominic to his feet with the other. "Run!"

Don't miss
Mountain Fugitive *by Lynette Eason,*
available October 2021 wherever
Love Inspired Suspense books and ebooks are sold.

LoveInspired.com

LOVE INSPIRED

INSPIRATIONAL ROMANCE

UPLIFTING STORIES OF FAITH, FORGIVENESS AND HOPE.

Join our social communities to connect with other readers who share your love!

Sign up for the Love Inspired newsletter at **LoveInspired.com** to be the first to find out about upcoming titles, special promotions and exclusive content.

CONNECT WITH US AT:

Facebook.com/LoveInspiredBooks

Twitter.com/LoveInspiredBks

Facebook.com/groups/HarlequinConnection

LISOCIAL2020

Get 4 FREE REWARDS!

We'll send you 2 FREE Books plus 2 FREE Mystery Gifts.

Love Inspired Suspense books showcase how courage and optimism unite in stories of faith and love in the face of danger.

FREE Value Over $20

YES! Please send me 2 FREE Love Inspired Suspense novels and my 2 FREE mystery gifts (gifts are worth about $10 retail). After receiving them, if I don't wish to receive any more books, I can return the shipping statement marked "cancel." If I don't cancel, I will receive 6 brand-new novels every month and be billed just $5.24 each for the regular-print edition or $5.99 each for the larger-print edition in the U.S., or $5.74 each for the regular-print edition or $6.24 each for the larger-print edition in Canada. That's a savings of at least 13% off the cover price. It's quite a bargain! Shipping and handling is just 50¢ per book in the U.S. and $1.25 per book in Canada.* I understand that accepting the 2 free books and gifts places me under no obligation to buy anything. I can always return a shipment and cancel at any time. The free books and gifts are mine to keep no matter what I decide.

Choose one: ☐ **Love Inspired Suspense Regular-Print** (153/353 IDN GNWN)   ☐ **Love Inspired Suspense Larger-Print** (107/307 IDN GNWN)

Name (please print)

Address   Apt. #

City   State/Province   Zip/Postal Code

Email: Please check this box ☐ if you would like to receive newsletters and promotional emails from Harlequin Enterprises ULC and its affiliates. You can unsubscribe anytime.

Mail to the Harlequin Reader Service:
IN U.S.A.: P.O. Box 1341, Buffalo, NY 14240-8531
IN CANADA: P.O. Box 603, Fort Erie, Ontario L2A 5X3

Want to try 2 free books from another series! Call 1-800-873-8635 or visit www.ReaderService.com.

*Terms and prices subject to change without notice. Prices do not include sales taxes, which will be charged (if applicable) based on your state or country of residence. Canadian residents will be charged applicable taxes. Offer not valid in Quebec. This offer is limited to one order per household. Books received may not be as shown. Not valid for current subscribers to Love Inspired Suspense books. All orders subject to approval. Credit or debit balances in a customer's account(s) may be offset by any other outstanding balance owed by or to the customer. Please allow 4 to 6 weeks for delivery. Offer available while quantities last.

Your Privacy—Your information is being collected by Harlequin Enterprises ULC, operating as Harlequin Reader Service. For a complete summary of the information we collect, how we use this information and to whom it is disclosed, please visit our privacy notice located at corporate.harlequin.com/privacy-notice. From time to time we may also exchange your personal information with reputable third parties. If you wish to opt out of this sharing of your personal information, please visit readerservice.com/consumerschoice or call 1-800-873-8635. **Notice to California Residents**—Under California law, you have specific rights to control and access your data. For more information on these rights and how to exercise them, visit corporate.harlequin.com/california-privacy.

LIS21R2